Simply Perfect

Simply Perfect

Mary Balogh

DELACORTE PRESS

SIMPLY PERFECT
A Delacorte Press Book / April 2008

Published by Bantam Dell
A Division of Random House, Inc.
New York, New York

Delacorte Press is a registered trademark of Random House, Inc., and the colophon is a trademark of Random House, Inc.

ISBN-13: 978-0-385-33824-0

Printed in the United States of America
Published simultaneously in Canada

Simply Perfect

Claudia Martin had already had a hard day at school.

First Mademoiselle Pierre, one of the nonresident teachers, had sent a messenger just before breakfast with the news that she was indisposed with a migraine headache and would be unable to come to school, and Claudia, as both owner and headmistress, had been obliged to conduct most of the French and music classes in addition to her own subjects. French was no great problem; music was more of a challenge. Worse, the account books, which she had intended to bring up-to-date during her spare classes today, remained undone, with days fast running out in which to get accomplished all the myriad tasks that needed doing.

Then just before the noonday meal, when classes were over for the morning and discipline was at its slackest, Paula Hern had decided that she objected to the way Molly Wiggins *looked* at her and voiced her displeasure publicly and eloquently. And since Paula's father was a successful businessman and as rich as Croesus and she put on airs accordingly while Molly was the youngest—and most timid—of the charity girls and did not even know who her father was, then *of course* Agnes Ryde had felt obliged to jump into the fray in vigorous defense of the downtrodden, her Cockney accent returning with ear-jarring clarity. Claudia had been forced to deal with the matter and extract more-or-less sincere apologies from all sides and mete out suitable punishments to all except the more-or-less innocent Molly.

Then, an hour later, just when Miss Walton had been about to step outdoors with the junior class en route to Bath Abbey, where she had intended to give an informal lesson in art and architecture, the heavens had opened in a downpour to end downpours and there had been all the fuss of finding the girls somewhere else to go within the school and something else to do. Not that that had been Claudia's problem, but she *had* been made annoyingly aware of the girls' loud disappointment beyond her classroom door as she struggled to teach French irregular verbs. She had finally gone out there to inform them that if they had any complaint about the untimely arrival of the rain, then they must take it up privately with God during their evening prayers, but in the meantime they would be *silent* until Miss Walton had closed a classroom door behind them.

Then, just after classes were finished for the afternoon and the girls had gone upstairs to comb their hair and wash their hands in readiness for tea, something had gone wrong with the doorknob on one of the dormitories and eight of the girls, trapped inside until Mr. Keeble, the elderly school porter, had creaked his way up there to release them before mending the knob, had screeched and giggled and rattled the door. Miss Thompson had dealt with the crisis by reading them a lecture on patience and decorum, though circumstances had forced her to speak in a voice that could be heard from within—and therefore through much of the rest of the school too, including Claudia's office.

It had *not* been the best of days, as Claudia had just been remarking—without contradiction—to Eleanor Thompson and Lila Walton over tea in her private sitting room a short while after the prisoners had been freed. She could do with far fewer such days.

And yet now!

Now, to cap everything off and make an already trying day more so, there was a marquess awaiting her pleasure in the visitors' parlor downstairs.

A *marquess*, for the love of all that was wonderful!

That was what the silver-edged visiting card she held between two fingers said—the *Marquess of Attingsborough*. The porter had just delivered it into her hands, looking sour and disapproving as he did so—a not unusual expression for him, especially when any male who was not a teacher invaded his domain.

"A *marquess*," she said, looking up from the card to frown at her fellow teachers. "Whatever can he want? Did he say, Mr. Keeble?"

"He did not say and I did not ask, miss," the porter replied. "But if you was to ask me, he is up to no good. He *smiled* at me."

"Ha! A cardinal sin indeed," Claudia said dryly while Eleanor laughed.

"Perhaps," Lila suggested, "he has a daughter he wishes to place at the school."

"A *marquess*?" Claudia raised her eyebrows and Lila looked suitably quelled.

"Perhaps, Claudia," Eleanor said, a twinkle in her eye, "he has *two* daughters."

Claudia snorted and then sighed, took one more sip of her tea, and got reluctantly to her feet.

"I suppose I had better go and see what he wants," she said. "It will be more productive than sitting here guessing. But of all things to happen today of all days. A *marquess*."

Eleanor laughed again. "Poor man," she said. "I pity him."

Claudia had never had much use for the aristocracy—idle, arrogant, coldhearted, nasty lot—though the marriage of two of her teachers and closest friends to titled gentlemen had forced her to admit during the past few years that perhaps *some* of them might be agreeable and even worthy individuals. But it did not amuse her to have one of their number, a stranger, intrude into her own world without a by-your-leave, especially at the end of a difficult day.

She did not believe for a single moment that this marquess wished to place any daughter of his at her school.

She preceded Mr. Keeble down the stairs since she did not wish to move at his slow pace. She ought, she supposed, to have gone into her bedchamber first to see that she was looking respectable, which she was quite possibly not doing after a hard day at school. She usually made sure that she presented a neat appearance to visitors. But she scorned to make such an effort for a *marquess* and risk appearing obsequious in her own eyes.

By the time she opened the door into the visitors' parlor, she was bristling with a quite unjustified indignation. How dared he come here to disturb her on her own property, whatever his business might be.

She looked down at the visiting card still in her hand.

"The Marquess of Attingsborough?" she said in a voice not unlike the one she had used on Paula Hern earlier in the day—the one that said she was not going to be at all impressed by any pretension of grandeur.

"At your service, ma'am. Miss Martin, I presume?" He was standing across the room, close to the window. He bowed elegantly.

Claudia's indignation soared. One steady glance at him was not sufficient upon which to make any informed judgment of his character, of course, but *really*, if the man had any imperfection of form or feature or taste in apparel, it was by no means apparent. He was tall and broad of shoulder and chest and slim of waist and hips. His legs were long and well shaped. His hair was dark and thick and shining, his face handsome, his eyes and mouth good-humored. He was dressed with impeccable elegance but without a trace of ostentation. His Hessian boots alone were probably worth a fortune, and Claudia guessed that if she were to stand directly over them and look down, she would see her own face reflected in them—and probably her flat, untidy hair and limp dress collar as well.

She clasped her hands at her waist lest she test her theory by touching the collar points. She held his card pinched between one thumb and forefinger.

"What may I do for you, sir?" she asked, deliberately avoiding calling him *my lord*—a ridiculous affectation, in her opinion.

He smiled at her, and if perfection could be improved upon, it had just happened—he had good teeth. Claudia steeled herself to resist the charm she was sure he possessed in aces.

"I come as a messenger, ma'am," he said, "from Lady Whitleaf."

He reached into an inner pocket of his coat and withdrew a sealed paper.

"From Susanna?" Claudia took one step farther into the room.

Susanna Osbourne had been a teacher at the school until her marriage last year to Viscount Whitleaf. Claudia had always rejoiced at Susanna's good fortune in making both an eligible marriage and a love match and yet she still mourned her own loss of a dear friend and colleague *and* a good teacher. She had lost three such friends—all in the same cause—over the course of four years. Sometimes it was hard not to be selfishly depressed by it all.

"When she knew I was coming to Bath to spend a few days with my mother and my father, who is taking the waters," the marquess said, "she asked me to call here and pay my respects to you. And she gave me this letter, perhaps to convince you that I am no impostor."

His eyes smiled again as he came across the room and placed the letter in her hand. And as if at least his eyes could not have been mud-colored or something equally nondescript, she could see that they were a clear blue, almost like a summer sky.

Susanna had asked him to come and pay his respects? *Why?*

"Whitleaf is the cousin of a cousin of mine," the marquess explained. "Or an *almost* cousin of mine, anyway. It is complicated, as family relationships often are. Lauren Butler, Viscountess Ravensberg, is a cousin by virtue of the fact that her mother married my aunt's brother-in-law. We have been close since childhood. And Whitleaf is Lauren's first cousin. And so in a sense both he and his lady have a strong familial claim on me."

If he was a marquess, Claudia thought with sudden suspicion, and his father was still alive, *what did that make his father?* But he was here at Susanna's behest and it behooved her to be a little better than just icily polite.

"Thank you," she said, "for coming in person to deliver the

letter. I am much obliged to you, sir. May I offer you a cup of tea?" She willed him to say no.

"I will not put you to that trouble, ma'am," he said, smiling again. "I understand you are to leave for London in two days' time?"

Ah. Susanna must have told him that. Mr. Hatchard, her man of business in London, had found employment for two of her senior girls, both charity pupils, but he had been unusually evasive about the identity of the prospective employers, even when she had asked quite specifically in her last letter to him. The paying girls at the school had families to look after their interests, of course. Claudia had appointed herself family to the rest and never released any girl who had no employment to which to go or any about whose expected employment she felt any strong misgiving.

At Eleanor's suggestion, Claudia was going to go to London with Flora Bains and Edna Wood so that she could find out exactly where they were to be placed as governesses and to withdraw her consent if she was not satisfied. There were still a few weeks of the school year left, but Eleanor had assured her that she was perfectly willing and able to take charge of affairs during Claudia's absence, which would surely be no longer than a week or ten days. Claudia had agreed to go, partly because there was another matter too upon which she wished to speak with Mr. Hatchard in person.

"I am," she told the marquess.

"Whitleaf intended to send a carriage for your convenience," the marquess told her, "but I was able to inform him that it would be quite unnecessary to put himself to the trouble."

"Of course it would," Claudia agreed. "I have already hired a carriage."

"I will see about *un*hiring it for you, if I may be permitted, ma'am," he said. "I plan to return to town on the same day and will be pleased to offer you the comfort of my own carriage and my protection for the journey."

Oh, goodness, heaven forbid!

"That will be quite unnecessary, sir," she said firmly. "I have already made the arrangements."

"Hired carriages are notorious for their lack of springs and all other comforts," he said. "I beg you will reconsider."

"Perhaps you do not fully understand, sir," she said. "I am to be accompanied by two schoolgirls on the journey."

"Yes," he said, "so Lady Whitleaf informed me. Do they prattle? Or, worse, do they giggle? Very young ladies have an atrocious tendency to do both."

"My girls are taught how to behave appropriately in company, Lord Attingsborough," she said stiffly. Too late she saw the twinkle in his eyes and understood that he had been joking.

"I do not doubt it, ma'am," he said, "and feel quite confident in trusting your word. Allow me, if you will, to escort all three of you ladies to Lady Whitleaf's door. She will be vastly impressed with my gallantry and will be bound to spread the word among my family and friends."

Now he was talking utter nonsense. But how could she decently refuse? She desperately searched around in her head for some irrefutable argument that would dissuade him. Nothing came to mind, however, that did not seem ungracious, even downright rude. But she would rather travel a thousand miles in a springless carriage than to London in his company.

Why?

Was she overawed by his title and magnificence? She bristled at the very idea.

At his . . . *maleness*, then? She was uncomfortably aware that he possessed that in abundance.

But how ridiculous that would be. He was simply a gentleman offering a courtesy to an aging spinster, who happened to be a friend of his almost-cousin's cousin's wife—goodness, it *was* a tenuous connection. But she held a letter from Susanna in her hand. Susanna obviously trusted him.

An *aging spinster*? When it came to any consideration of age, she thought, there was probably not much difference between the two of them. Now *there* was a thought. Here was this man, obviously at the very pinnacle of his masculine appeal in his middle thirties, and then there was she.

He was looking at her with raised eyebrows and smiling eyes.

"Oh, very well," she said briskly. "But you may live to regret your offer."

His smile broadened and it seemed to an indignant Claudia that there was no end to this man's appeal. As she had suspected, he had charm oozing from every pore and was therefore *not* to be trusted one inch farther than she could see him. She would keep a *very* careful eye upon her two girls during the journey to London.

"I do hope not, ma'am," he said. "Shall we make an early start?"

"It is what I intended," she told him. She added grudgingly, "Thank you, Lord Attingsborough. You are most kind."

"It will be my pleasure, Miss Martin." He bowed deeply again. "May I ask a small favor in return? May I be given a tour of the school? I must confess that the idea of an institution that actually provides an *education* to girls fascinates me. Lady Whitleaf has spoken with enthusiasm about your establishment. She taught here, I understand."

Claudia drew a slow, deep breath through flared nostrils. Whatever reason could this man have for touring a girls' school except idle curiosity—or worse? Her instinct was to say a very firm no. But she had just accepted a favor from him, and it was admittedly a large one—she did not doubt that his carriage would be far more comfortable than the one she had hired or that they would be treated with greater respect at every toll gate they passed and at every inn where they stopped for a change of horses. And he was a friend of Susanna's.

But really!

She had not thought her day could possibly get any worse. She had been wrong.

"Certainly. I will show you around myself," she said curtly, turning to the door. She would have opened it herself, but he reached around her, engulfing her for a startled moment in the scent of some enticing and doubtless indecently expensive male cologne, opened the door, and indicated with a smile that she should precede him into the hall.

At least, she thought, classes were over for the day and all the girls would be safely in the dining hall, having tea.

She was wrong about that, of course, she remembered as soon as she opened the door into the art room. The final assembly of the school year was not far off and all sorts of preparations and rehearsals were in progress, as they had been every day for the past week or so.

A few of the girls were working with Mr. Upton on the stage backdrop. They all turned to see who had come in and then proceeded to gawk at the grand visitor. Claudia was obliged to introduce the two men. They shook hands, and the marquess strolled closer to inspect the artwork and ask a few intelligent questions. Mr. Upton beamed at him when he left the room with her a few minutes later, and all the girls gazed worshipfully after him.

And then in the music room they came upon the madrigal choir, which was practicing in the absence of Mademoiselle Pierre under the supervision of Miss Wilding. They hit an ear-shattering discord at full volume just as Claudia opened the door, and then they dissolved into self-conscious giggles while Miss Wilding blushed and looked dismayed.

Claudia, raising her eyebrows, introduced the teacher to the marquess and explained that the regular choirmistress was indisposed today. Though even as she spoke she was annoyed with herself for feeling that any explanation was necessary.

"Madrigal singing," he said, smiling at the girls, "can be the most satisfying but the most frustrating thing, can it not? There is perhaps one other person out of the group singing the same part as oneself and six or eight others all bellowing out something quite different. If one's lone ally falters one is lost without hope of recovery. I never mastered the art when I was at school, I must confess. During my very first practice someone suggested to me that I try out for the cricket team—which just happened to practice at the same time."

The girls laughed, and all of them visibly relaxed.

"I will wager," he said, "that there is something in your repertoire that you can sing to perfection. May I be honored to hear it?" He turned his smile upon Miss Wilding.

" 'The Cuckoo,' miss," Sylvia Hetheridge suggested to a murmur of approval from the rest of the group.

And they sang in five parts without once faltering or hitting a sour note, a glorious shower of "cuckoos" echoing about the room every time they reached the chorus of the song.

When they were finished, they all turned as one to the Marquess of Attingsborough, just as if he were visiting royalty, and he applauded and smiled.

"Bravo!" he said. "Your skill overwhelms me, not to mention the loveliness of your voices. I am more than ever convinced that I was wise to stick to cricket."

The girls were all laughing and gazing worshipfully after him when he left with Claudia.

Mr. Huckerby was in the dancing hall, putting a group of girls through their paces in a particularly intricate dance that they would perform during the assembly. The marquess shook his hand and smiled at the girls and admired their performance and charmed them until they were all smiling and—of course—*gazing worshipfully at him.*

He asked intelligent and perceptive questions of Claudia as she showed him some of the empty classrooms and the library. He was in no hurry as he looked about each room and read the titles on the spines of many of the books.

"There was a pianoforte in the music room," he said as they made their way to the sewing room, "and other instruments too. I noticed a violin and a flute in particular. Do you offer individual music lessons here, Miss Martin?"

"Indeed we do," she said. "We offer everything necessary to

make accomplished young ladies of our pupils, as well as persons with a sound academic education."

He looked around the sewing room from just inside the door but did not walk farther into it.

"And do you teach other skills here in addition to sewing and embroidery?" he asked. "Knitting, perhaps? Tatting? Crochet?"

"All three," she said as he closed the door and she led the way to the assembly hall. It had been a ballroom once when the building was a private home.

"It is a pleasingly designed room," he said, standing in the middle of the gleaming wood floor and turning all about before looking up at the high, coved ceiling. "Indeed, I like the whole school, Miss Martin. There are windows and light everywhere and a pleasant atmosphere. Thank you for giving me a guided tour."

He turned his most charming smile on her, and Claudia, still holding both his visiting card and Susanna's letter, clasped her free hand about her wrist and looked back with deliberate severity.

"I am delighted you approve," she said.

His smile was arrested for a moment until he chuckled softly.

"I do beg your pardon," he said. "I have taken enough of your time."

He indicated the door with one arm, and Claudia led the way back to the entrance hall, feeling—and resenting the feeling—that she had somehow been unmannerly, for those last words she had spoken had been meant ironically and he had known it.

But before they reached the hall they were forced to pause for a few moments while the junior class filed out of the dining hall in good order, on their way from tea to study hall, where they would catch up on any work not completed during the day or else read or write letters or stitch at some needlework.

They all turned their heads to gaze at the grand visitor, and the Marquess of Attingsborough smiled genially back at them, setting them all to giggling and preening as they hurried along.

All of which went to prove, Claudia thought, that even

eleven- and twelve-year-olds could not resist the charms of a handsome man. It boded ill—or *continued* to bode ill—for the future of the female half of the human race.

Mr. Keeble, frowning ferociously, bless his heart, was holding the marquess's hat and cane and was standing close to the front door as if to dare the visitor to try prolonging his visit further.

"I will see you early two mornings from now, then, Miss Martin?" the marquess said, taking his hat and cane and turning to her as Mr. Keeble opened the door and stood to one side, ready to close it behind him at the earliest opportunity.

"We will be ready," she said, inclining her head to him.

And finally he was gone. He did *not* leave Claudia feeling kindly disposed toward him. Whatever had *that* been all about? She wished fervently that she could go back half an hour and refuse his offer to escort her and the girls to London the day after tomorrow.

But she could not, and that was that.

She stepped into her study and looked into the small mirror that she kept behind the door but rarely consulted.

Oh, goodness gracious! Her hair really *was* flat and lifeless. Several strands had pulled loose from the knot at the back of her neck. There was a faint smudge of ink on one side of her nose left there when she had tried to remove it earlier with her handkerchief. And one point of her collar was indeed slightly curled and the whole thing off center. She adjusted it one-handed, very much too late, of course.

Horrid man! It was no wonder his eyes had laughed at her the whole time.

She remembered Susanna's letter then and broke the seal. Joseph Fawcitt, Marquess of Attingsborough, was the son and heir of the Duke of Anburey, she read in the first paragraph—and winced. He was going to offer to bring Claudia and the girls to London with him on his return from Bath, and Claudia must not hesitate to accept. He was a kind and charming gentleman and entirely to be trusted.

Claudia raised her eyebrows and compressed her lips.

The main reason for Susanna's letter, though, was quickly obvious. Frances and Lucius—the Earl of Edgecombe, her husband—had returned from the Continent, and Susanna and Peter were arranging a concert at their house at which Frances was going to sing. Claudia simply *must* stay long enough to hear her and she simply *must* stay even longer to enjoy a few other entertainments of the Season too. If Eleanor Thompson had expressed a willingness to look after the school for one week, then surely she would be willing to do so for another week or so too, by which time the summer term would be at an end.

The extended invitation was enormously tempting, Claudia had to admit. Frances had been the first of her teachers and friends to marry. With the encouragement of a remarkably enlightened husband, she had since become a singer who was renowned and much sought after all over Europe. She and the earl traveled for several months of each year, going from one European capital to another for various singing engagements. It was a year since Claudia had last seen her. It would be wonderful to see both her and Susanna together within the next week or two and to spend some time in their company. But even so . . .

She had left the study door open. Eleanor poked her head about it after scratching lightly on its outer panel.

"I will take study hall for you tonight, Claudia," she said. "You have had a busy day. Your aristocratic visitor did not eat you alive, then? The school is buzzing with his praises."

"Susanna sent him," Claudia explained. She grimaced. "He has offered to take Edna and Flora and me with him in his carriage when he returns to London the day after tomorrow."

"Oh, my!" Eleanor exclaimed, coming right inside the room. "And I missed seeing him. It is to be hoped that he is tall, dark, and handsome."

"All three," Claudia said. "He is also the son of a duke!"

"Enough said." Eleanor held up both hands, palms out. "He must be the darkest of villains. Though one day I hope to convince you that my brother-in-law, the Duke of Bewcastle, is *not*."

"Hmm," Claudia said.

The Duke of Bewcastle had once been her employer, when for a short time she had been governess to his sister and ward, Lady Freyja Bedwyn. They had *not* parted on the best of terms, to put the matter lightly, and she had strongly disliked him and all who shared his rank ever since. Though if the truth were told, her antipathy to dukes had not started with him...

But she pitied Eleanor's younger sister from the bottom of her heart, married to such a man. The poor duchess was a remarkably amiable lady—and she had once been a teacher herself.

"Frances is back in England," she told Eleanor. "She is going to sing at a concert Susanna and the viscount are organizing. Susanna wants me to stay for it and some other entertainments of the Season. It is a pity it is not all happening after school is over for the year. But by then, of course, the Season will be all but over too. Of course, I have absolutely no aspirations *whatsoever* to move in *ton*nish circles. The very idea gives me the shudders. Only it would have been lovely to see both Susanna and Frances and spend some time in company with them. I can do that some other time, though—preferably in the country."

Eleanor clucked her tongue.

"Of course you must stay in London for longer than a few days, Claudia," she said. "It is what Lady Whitleaf has been urging and I have been encouraging all along. I am perfectly capable of running the school for a few weeks and of giving a suitably stirring and affecting speech on your behalf at the end-of-year assembly. And if you wish to stay even longer than a few weeks, you must do so without suffering any qualms. Lila and I will both be here over the summer to look after the charity girls, and Christine has renewed her invitation for me to take them to Lindsey Hall for a few weeks while she and Wulfric visit some of his other estates. It would give me a chance to spend some time with my mother."

Christine and Wulfric were the Duchess and Duke of Bewcastle. Lindsey Hall was the latter's principal seat in Hampshire. The invitation had astonished Claudia when it had first been made, and she wondered if the duchess had consulted her husband before making it. But then, of course, the charity girls had stayed at Lindsey Hall once before, just a year ago, in fact, on the occasion of Susanna's wedding, and the duke had actually been in residence at the time.

"You must stay," Eleanor said again. "Indeed, you must promise to stay for at least a couple of weeks. I shall be offended if you will not do so. I shall think you do not trust me to take your place here."

"Of *course* I trust you," Claudia said, feeling herself waver. But how could she *not* stay now? "It would be pleasant, I must admit..."

"Of course it would," Eleanor said briskly. "Of course it *will*. That is settled, then. And I must be off to study hall. With the way this day is progressing, the chances are strong that a few desks will be chopped into kindling or some sort of titanic battle will be proceeding if I do not get there soon."

Claudia sat down behind her desk after Eleanor had left, and folded up Susanna's letter. What a very strange day! It seemed to have been at least forty-eight hours long.

What on earth was she going to talk about during all the hours of the journey to London? And how was she to keep Flora from prattling and Edna from giggling? She wished fervently that the Marquess of Attingsborough were at least sixty years old and looked like a toad. Perhaps then she would not feel quite so intimidated by him.

Though the very use of that word in her mind made her bristle all over again.

Intimidated?

She?

By a mere *man?*

By a *marquess?* Heir to a *dukedom?*

She would not give him the satisfaction, she thought indignantly, just as if he had expressed the overt wish of seeing her grovel in servile humility at his feet.

"You will keep in mind what we have spoken of," the Duke of Anburey said as he shook hands with his son, Joseph, Marquess of Attingsborough. It was not a question.

"Of course he will, Webster," the duchess said as she hugged and kissed her son.

They had breakfasted early at the house on the Royal Crescent where the duke and duchess had taken up residence during their stay in Bath. Concern for his father's health—and, admittedly, a direct summons—had brought Joseph here just a week ago in the middle of the spring Season. His father had caught a chill during the winter and had been unable to shake it off completely by the time he should have been returning to town to participate in the business of the House of Lords. He had remained at home instead and then given in to the persuasions of his wife to give the waters a try, even though he had always spoken with contempt of Bath and the people who went there to bathe in the waters and imbibe them for the sake of their health.

Joseph had found his father apparently restored to health. He was certainly quite well enough to grumble about the insipidity of the card games and other entertainments with which he was expected to amuse himself and at the enraptured enthusiasm with which he was greeted wherever he went, especially at the Pump Room. The duchess, on the contrary, was placidly enjoying just the things about which her husband complained. Joseph suspected that she was enjoying herself more than she normally did in London at this time of year.

His father insisted that he was not quite as robust as he would like to be, though. In a private conversation, he had told his son that he suspected his heart had been weakened by the prolonged chill, and his physician in Bath would not contradict him, though he had not actually confirmed his fears either. However it was, the duke had begun to set his affairs in order.

And at the very top of his list was his son and heir.

Joseph was thirty-five years old and unmarried. Worse—and a direct result of the latter fact—he had no sons in his nursery. The succession had not been secured.

The Duke of Anburey had taken steps to supply the lack. Even before summoning his son he had invited Lord Balderston to come down from London, and the two of them had discussed the desirability of encouraging a match between their offspring— the Marquess of Attingsborough and Miss Portia Hunt. They had agreed to share their wishes—really a euphemism for *commands*— with their children and expect a happy outcome before the Season was over.

Hence Joseph's summons from London.

"I will certainly keep it in mind, sir," he said now as he emerged from his mother's embrace. "I cannot think of any lady better suited to be my wife than Miss Hunt."

Which was certainly true when he considered only the fact that his wife was also to be his marchioness and the future Duchess of Anburey—*and* the mother of a future duke. Her lineage was impeccable. So were her looks and manners. He had no great objection to her character either. He had even spent a good deal of time with her a few years ago, just after she had ended her association with Edgecombe and had obviously been trying to prove to the *ton* that she was not brokenhearted. He had admired her spirit and her dignity then. And in the few years since, he had often danced with her at balls or conversed with her at soirees.

Just two or three weeks ago he had taken her driving in Hyde Park at the fashionable hour. Never once, though—before now—had he seriously considered courting her.

Now, of course, he must. He really could not think of anyone he would rather marry. Which was not a powerful argument in favor of marrying Miss Hunt, it was true, but then most men of his rank married more for position than for marked affection.

He hugged his father at the door of the house and hugged and kissed his mother again and promised her that he would not forget a single one of the myriad messages he had memorized for delivery to Wilma, Countess of Sutton, his sister. He looked at his traveling carriage to ascertain that all his baggage had been loaded and that his valet was up on the box beside John. Then he swung up into the saddle of the horse he had hired for the first stage of the journey back to London.

He raised a hand in farewell to his parents, blew another kiss to his mother, and was on his way.

It was always hard to say good-bye to loved ones. It was even harder knowing that his father might well be growing frailer. And yet at the same time his thoughts moved ahead with undeniable eagerness.

At last he was on his way home.

He had not seen Lizzie for over a week and could hardly wait to be with her again. She lived—as she had for more than eleven years—in the house he had purchased thirteen years ago as a swaggering young man about town for the mistresses he would employ down the years. He had only ever employed the one, though. His wild oats had all been sown very soon.

He had gifts for Lizzie in his baggage—a feathered fan and a bottle of perfume, both of which he knew she would adore. He could never resist giving her gifts and watching her face light up with pleasure.

If he had not offered to escort Miss Martin and the two schoolgirls to London, he knew he would have made a push to complete the journey in one long day. But he did not regret his offer. It was the sort of gallantry that would cost him very little except perhaps one extra day on the road. However, he *had* decided that it was in his own best interests to hire a horse. Being inside the carriage with a schoolteacher and two young schoolgirls for the whole journey might be a strain even on his normally even-tempered nerves—not to mention theirs.

He had been given the distinct impression two days ago that Miss Martin did not approve of him, though exactly what her objection to him was he had not fathomed. Women usually liked him, perhaps because he usually liked them. But Miss Martin had been looking rather sourly upon him even before he had asked to see the school, which had genuinely interested him.

Carriage and horse descended the hill to the river and then proceeded along beside it before crossing the Pulteney Bridge and bowling onward in the direction of the school.

Joseph's lips twitched at the memory of his meeting with Miss Martin. She was the quintessential spinster schoolteacher—clad plainly and serviceably in a blue-gray dress that covered her from neck to wrists to ankles even though it was June. Her brown hair was dressed with ruthless severity in a knot at the back of her neck, though it had been looking somewhat disheveled, it was true, as if she had just put in a hard day's work—which no doubt she had. She was neither particularly tall nor particularly thin, but her ramrod-straight posture had given the illusion of both. Her lips had been compressed when she was not speaking, her gray eyes keen with intelligence.

It amused him to realize that this was the woman of whom Susanna had spoken so warmly as one of her dearest friends. The viscountess was small, vivacious, and exquisitely lovely. And yet it was not impossible to imagine her teaching at that school. However dry and severe the headmistress had appeared when she was with him, she must be doing something right. The girls and teachers he had seen had all appeared happy enough, and there was a general atmosphere about the place that he had liked. It had not felt oppressive, as many schools did.

His first impression had been that Miss Martin was surely old enough to be Susanna's mother. But he had revised that thought. She was quite possibly no older than he.

Thirty-five was a rottenly nasty age for a single man who was heir to a dukedom. The necessity of doing his duty and marrying and producing the next heir had been causing him some uneasiness even before his recent interview with his father. Now it was something he could no longer ignore or procrastinate over. For years he had actively resisted all pressures of the matrimonial kind. For all his faults—which were doubtless legion—he did believe in monogamous relationships. And how could he marry when he was so irrevocably bound to a mistress? But it seemed he could resist no longer.

At the far end of Great Pulteney Street carriage and horse executed a series of sharp turns to arrive at the door of the school on Daniel Street. Someone must have been spying at a window, he saw immediately. No sooner had the carriage stopped rocking on its springs than the school door opened to spill girls onto the pavement—a large number of them, all in a state of agitated sensibilities.

Some of them were squealing—perhaps over the sight of the carriage, which was admittedly rather splendid, or perhaps over the sight of his horse, which was *not* but was the best he could do under the circumstances and was at least not lame in any one of its four legs. Or perhaps they squealed over him—arresting thought!—though doubtless he was a few generations too ancient to send them into any grand transports of romantic delight. A few others wept into their handkerchiefs alternately with throwing themselves upon the two who wore cloaks and bonnets and were apparently the travelers. Another girl—or perhaps *young lady* would be a more accurate description since she must be three or four years older than any of the others—ineffectively exhorted the girls to stand in two orderly lines. Joseph guessed that she must be a teacher.

The elderly, sour-faced porter, whose boots creaked just as he recalled they had done two days ago, set two valises out on the step and looked at John as if to say that it was his responsibility to see that they found the rest of their way to the carriage.

One of the travelers was chattering volubly to anyone who cared to listen—and to everyone who did not, for that matter. The other wept.

Joseph looked down upon the chaotic scene with avuncular good humor.

And then Miss Martin stepped out onto the pavement and there was a noticeable hush among the ranks, though the second traveler continued to sob. Another lady came out behind her and addressed them with far more authority than the young teacher had demonstrated.

"Girls," she said, "did you overpower Miss Walton and drag her out here with you? You said your good-byes to Flora and Edna at breakfast, did you not? And should therefore now be in class?"

"We came to say good-bye to Miss Martin, miss," one bold and quick-thinking girl said to the murmured agreement of a few others.

"That was extremely thoughtful of you all," the teacher said, her eyes twinkling. "But Miss Martin would appreciate the gesture far more if you were to stand in two neat lines and conduct yourselves with the proper decorum."

The girls promptly and cheerfully obeyed.

Miss Martin meanwhile was eyeing first the carriage, then Joseph's horse, and then him.

"Good morning, Lord Attingsborough," she said, her voice brisk.

She was dressed neatly and quite unappealingly in a gray cloak and bonnet—probably a sensible choice on a day that was cloudy and dreary despite the fact that it was almost summer. Behind her, the porter was lugging one sizable piece of baggage— no doubt hers—across the pavement and would have attempted to hoist it to the roof if John had not firmly intervened.

"Good morning, Miss Martin," Joseph said, doffing his tall hat and inclining his head to her. "I see I have not arrived too early for you."

"We are a school," she reminded him, "and do not sleep until noon. Are you going to ride all the way to London?"

"Perhaps not *all* the way, ma'am," he said. "But for much of the journey you and your pupils may enjoy having the carriage to yourselves."

It was impossible to know for sure from the severity of her countenance if she was relieved, but he would wager a fortune she was. She turned her head.

"Edna?" she said. "Flora? We must not keep his lordship waiting. Climb into the carriage, please. The coachman is waiting to hand you in."

She looked on without comment as the wailing started up again from the orderly lines of girls and the two travelers moved along them to hug each girl individually. She gazed with pursed lips as, before each scrambled up the steps into the carriage, the teacher who had brought order out of chaos hugged them too and even kissed each girl on the cheek.

"Eleanor," Miss Martin said then as she approached the carriage herself with firm strides, "you will not forget—"

But the other teacher cut her off. "I will not forget a single thing," she said, her eyes still twinkling. "How could I when you had me write out a whole list last evening? There is not a thing for you to worry about, Claudia. Go and enjoy yourself."

Claudia. An eminently suitable name—strong, uncompromising, suggestive of a woman who could look after herself.

Miss Claudia Martin turned to the lines of girls.

"I will expect to hear good things of my senior girls when Miss Thompson writes to me," she said. "At the very least I will expect to hear that you have prevented any of the younger girls from burning the school to the ground or rioting through the streets of Bath."

The girls laughed, though some were teary-eyed.

"We will, miss," one of them said.

"And thank you," Miss Martin said, "for coming out here for the sole purpose of saying good-bye to me. I am deeply touched. You will go inside with Miss Walton and work extra

hard to make up for the minutes you have missed of this class—
after you have waved me on my way. Perhaps at the same time
you would care to wave to Edna and Flora too."

She was capable of humor, then, even if only of a dry sort,
Joseph thought as she set her hand in John's, lifted one side of her
cloak and dress, and followed the two girls inside the carriage.

John climbed up onto the box and Joseph gave him the nod
to proceed.

And so the small cavalcade began its progress to London,
sent on its way by the waving handkerchiefs of a dozen schoolgirls, some of whom were sniveling again while others called
farewells to their fellow pupils who would never return but
would proceed into the harsh world of employment—or so
Susanna had informed Joseph. They were charity girls, among a
sizable group that Miss Martin insisted upon taking in every year.

He was half amused, half affected by what he had seen. It was
like a glimpse into an alien world, one from which his birth and
fortune had firmly insulated him all his life.

Children without the security of a family and fortune behind
them.

By the time they stopped for the night at the Lamb and Flag
Inn in Marlborough, where she had reserved two adjoining
rooms, one for herself and one to be shared by Edna and Flora,
Claudia was wondering if she could possibly have felt stiffer in
the joints or more numb in certain nether parts of her anatomy if
they had come by hired coach, as originally planned.

But she knew from past experience that she could indeed. The
Marquess of Attingsborough's carriage was clean and well
sprung and had luxuriously padded upholstery. It was the sad
condition of the road and the long hours of almost incessant
travel that were responsible for her physical condition.

One blessing at least was that they had had the carriage to
themselves all day, she and her two charges. The marquess had
ridden the whole way, changing mounts when the carriage horses

had been changed. Claudia had seen him only in fleeting glimpses through the window and at the various posting inns where they had made brief stops.

He cut a remarkably fine figure on horseback, of course, she had noticed with annoyance each time it had happened. He was impeccably dressed for riding and looked perfectly at ease in the saddle—even after he had been riding for hours. Doubtless he considered himself God's gift to the human race, particularly the female half—which was a totally unfair judgment, she conceded in the privacy of her own thoughts, though she made no great effort to amend her opinion of him. Of course it had been kind of him to offer his carriage for her convenience, but by his own admission he had done so in order to impress his family and friends.

She was half relieved, half indignant at the prompt, meticulous service they had received everywhere they stopped. She knew it would have been far otherwise had she come in the hired coach. She and the girls were even served refreshments in the carriage instead of having to step inside the various bustling inns to be jostled by other travelers and to wait in line for their purchases.

It had been a long and tedious day nonetheless, and there had been little conversation inside the carriage. The girls had been visibly depressed for the first hour or so and not at all inclined to talk or even look appreciatively at the passing scenery. And even when they had brightened after the first stop and the first round of refreshments, they had both been on their very best behavior in the company of their headmistress with the result that they scarcely spoke at all unless she directed specific questions at them.

Flora had been at the school for almost five years. She had spent all of her childhood at an orphanage in London but had been turned out to fend for herself at the age of thirteen. Edna had been orphaned at the age of eleven, when her parents had been murdered while defending their humble shop from thieves, though as it had turned out there had been precious little to defend. There had been nothing with which to provide for their only daughter. Fortunately, Mr. Hatchard had found her, as he had Flora, and sent her to Bath.

When Claudia stepped inside the Lamb and Flag, she was forced to wait while the landlord finished conducting a leisurely chat with another customer on the fascinating topic of fishing and two other men—*not* to be dignified by the term *gentlemen*—ogled Flora and Edna and desisted with insolent smirks only when Claudia glared at them.

She then looked pointedly at the landlord, who was pretending not to notice her. If another minute passed, she decided, she would certainly speak up.

And then the door from the stable yard opened and closed and everything changed just as if someone had waved a magic wand. The fish conversation ended as if it were of no significance whatsoever and the customer faded away into oblivion. The landlord preened himself with obsequious hand-rubbing and jovial smiles.

It was the Marquess of Attingsborough who had come through the door, Claudia saw when she turned her head to look. And even if the landlord had not yet been informed that he was here—which he no doubt *had* been—there was something written all over the man that proclaimed him an aristocrat, a certain self-confident arrogance that immediately irritated Claudia.

"Welcome to the Lamb and Flag, my lord," the landlord said, "the most hospitable inn in Marlborough. How may I serve you?"

Hospitable indeed! Claudia looked pointedly back at the landlord and opened her mouth to speak.

"I believe," the marquess said, "Miss Martin and her charges came inside before I did."

The landlord did an admirable job of starting with amazement as if the three of them had just materialized out of invisibility.

Claudia fairly quivered with indignation—most of it, quite unfairly perhaps, directed at the Marquess of Attingsborough, who was not at all to blame for the fact that she had been considered a mere nobody until it became clear that a real live *marquess* knew her name. But she certainly had not needed anyone to speak up for her.

"Miss Martin?" the landlord said, smiling jovially at her. She did *not* smile back. "I have your rooms ready for you, ma'am. You may go up immediately."

"Thank—" Claudia got no further.

"I trust," the marquess said, "they are the best rooms in the house?"

"All our rooms are superior, my lord," the landlord assured him. "But the front rooms have been reserved by Mr. Cosman and his cousin."

The marquess had come to stand just behind Claudia's shoulder. She could not see his face, but she could see the landlord's. The marquess did not say another word, but after a moment the landlord cleared his throat.

"But I am quite certain," he said, "the two gentlemen will be only too happy to give up their rooms for the use of such charming ladies and take the two overlooking the stable yard instead."

Where Claudia had stayed each time she had put up at this inn before. She remembered a great deal of noise and light in those small rooms all night long, robbing her of sleep.

"The ladies must certainly have the front rooms," the landlord said, smiling once more at Claudia. "I must insist upon it."

As if she had argued against it. And yet perversely she wanted to argue and she wanted those inferior rooms. She would *not* be beholden to the Marquess of Attingsborough for more comfortable rooms. Good heavens, she was an independent woman. She did not need any man to fight her battles.

"And you have a private dining room?" he asked before she could say a word.

Claudia's nostrils flared. Was she to be humiliated even further?

"Mr. Cosman..." the landlord began. But yet again he paused as he looked at the marquess. "It will be set aside for the ladies as is only right, my lord, the rest of my clients tonight being all gentlemen."

Claudia knew just exactly what had happened. The Marquess of Attingsborough must have raised an aristocratic eyebrow a couple of times. And the landlord had almost fallen all over himself to show how obsequious he could be. It was despicable, to say the least. All because of who the marquess was, or, rather, because of the color of his blood. He was probably nothing more than an idle . . . *rake,* and yet all the world would bow and scrape to him because he had a title and doubtless pots of money to go with it.

Well, *she* would not bow or scrape. She turned to face him. He was smiling that easy, charming smile—and then he winked at her.

He actually *winked!*

And of course he was still looking gorgeous even after a day spent in the saddle. He was tapping his riding whip against the outside of his leather boot. He looked long-limbed and virile and . . . Well, that was quite enough. He even smelled good—of horse and some cologne mingled together into a peculiarly enticing masculine scent.

Claudia looked at him steadily, her lips pressed together in a thin line. But the wink had thrown her off stride for a moment, and then it seemed too late and too petty to declare that she would be quite happy with the small rooms and the public dining room.

Edna and Flora were looking at him too—*gazing worshipfully,* in fact. As if *that* were any surprise.

"Come along, girls," Claudia said briskly. "We will retire to our rooms if the landlord will give us directions."

She strode toward their bags.

"You will have the ladies' baggage taken up immediately?" the marquess said. Clearly he was addressing the landlord.

"Of course, my lord," the landlord said, clicking his fingers as Claudia's nostrils flared. "I was about to give the order."

Two—not one but *two*—menservants came running as if from nowhere, scooped up the bags, and headed in the direction of the staircase with them.

Mary Balogh

Claudia strode after them and the girls came after her.

The rooms, of course, were sizable and comfortable chambers, which overlooked the edge of town and the quiet fields beyond. They were clean and filled with light and were altogether above reproach. The girls squealed with delight and hurried to the window of their room to lean on the windowsill and gaze out at the scenery. Claudia withdrew to her own room and sighed with self-reproach as she admitted to herself that it really was vastly superior to the usual one. She stretched out on the bed to relax for a few minutes.

He had actually *winked* at her. She could not remember the last time any man had done that. Goodness, it probably had not happened since she was a girl.

How dare he!

But oh, the room was quiet and the bed was comfortable and the air coming through the open window was fresh. There was a single bird trilling its heart out. She actually dozed off for a while.

And then she dined with the girls in the comfort and relative quiet of the private dining room on roast beef and potatoes and boiled cabbage followed by suet pudding and custard and tea. She was forced to admit afterward that she felt restored and very relieved that they had not been expected to share the room with the Marquess of Attingsborough. Both girls looked slightly sleepy. She was about to suggest that they all retire for the night even though it was still light outside and really quite early when there was a tap on the door and it opened to reveal the marquess himself.

"Ah," he said, smiling and inclining his head. "Miss Martin? Young ladies? I am delighted that this inn boasts at least one private parlor. I have been regaled throughout dinner with conversation on crops and hunting and boxing mills."

Claudia suspected that he would not even be staying here if he had not committed himself to escorting her. He would probably be putting up at the George and Pelican or the Castle, which were both beyond her means. She hoped he was not expecting to be thanked for the privilege of both this room and their bed-chambers. She still bristled at the memory of how he had wielded power even without the medium of words while she had felt like a helpless, inept woman.

The girls had both scrambled to their feet and were curtsying to him. Claudia too stood but she merely nodded civilly.

"I trust," he said, stepping into the room, "you have passed a reasonably comfortable day. I hope you have not had every bone in your bodies jounced about into a new position."

"Oh, no, my lord," Flora assured him. "I never even dreamed a carriage could be so comfortable. I wish the journey could last a week. Or *two*."

He chuckled, and Edna, looking rather like a frightened rabbit, giggled.

"I suppose," he said, "you are both desperately unhappy at having to leave your school and your friends behind and impossibly excited at the prospect of beginning new lives as adults."

Edna bobbed a curtsy again.

"Some of those girls are like sisters, though," Flora told him. "And it hurts *here* to know we may never see them again." She smote her fist against her bosom. "But I *am* ready to work for my living, my lord. We cannot stay at school forever, can we?"

Claudia looked steadily at the marquess, expecting to see him astonished that either girl would have the effrontery to answer him in more than a monosyllable. Instead, he continued to smile.

"And to what employment do you go, Miss . . . ?"

"Bains, my lord," she told him.

"Miss Bains," he said.

"I am going to be a governess," she said. "I have always wanted to be one ever since I learned to read and write when I was thirteen. I think being able to teach those things to other people is the most wonderful thing anyone could possibly do in life. Would you not agree, my lord?"

Claudia was very afraid that Flora might talk too much. However, she was pleased to hear that even in the excitement of the moment the girl spoke with a decent accent and correct grammar—far differently from the way she had spoken when she arrived at the school five years earlier.

"I do indeed," he said, "though I cannot say that I regarded my first tutor as a saint when he taught me to read. He used the rod far too often for my liking!"

Edna giggled.

"Well, that was silly," Flora said. "How could you learn properly when you were being beaten? And even worse, how could you *enjoy* learning? It reminds me of the orphanage when we were taught to sew. I never did learn properly, and I still hate sewing. We never *ever* got beaten at school, and I will never *ever* beat my pupils no matter how badly behaved they are or slow to learn. Or my children—if I ever have any."

Claudia pursed her lips. Flora *was* running on rather. However, her passion was to be commended.

"I can see," the marquess said, "that you will be a superior governess, Miss Bains. Your pupils will be fortunate children. And you, Miss . . . ?"

He looked with raised eyebrows at Edna, who blushed and giggled and looked as if she wanted nothing more than for a black hole to appear at her feet to swallow her up.

"Wood, your grace," she said. "I mean, my lord."

"Miss Wood," he said. "Are you to be a governess too?"

"Yes, my lord," she said. "I-I mean your grace."

"I believe," he said, "that titles must have been invented to confuse us all horribly. As if the fact that most of us are blessed with at least two names is not challenge enough for those who meet us in the course of our lives! And so you are to be a governess, Miss Wood. And doubtless a superior one too, well educated and well trained at Miss Martin's School."

He looked immediately at Claudia in such a way as to signal to Edna that she need not feel the necessity of composing a reply to his observation. It was, Claudia admitted grudgingly, thoughtful of him.

"Miss Martin," he said, "I came to see if the three of you are ready to retire for the night. If you are, I shall escort you through the crowded dining room and up to your rooms and see that no one accosts you on the way."

"Thank you," Claudia said. "Yes, it has been a long day, and there is another facing us tomorrow."

And yet after escorting them upstairs past several groups of loudly talking men and seeing Flora and Edna safely inside their room with the door shut, he did not immediately hurry off back downstairs.

"Of course," he said, "it is still rather early, Miss Martin. And weary as I am after such a long ride, I feel the need to stretch my legs before I lie down. You may feel a similar need and an additional one to draw fresh air into your lungs. Would you care to accompany me on a short walk?"

She would like no such thing.

But her dinner was still sitting heavy in her stomach even though she had not taken large helpings of anything. And she was still feeling cramped from the journey with as much distance again to travel tomorrow. She craved fresh air and exercise.

She could not go walking alone in a strange town when it was already dusk.

The Marquess of Attingsborough was Susanna's friend, she reminded herself. Susanna had spoken highly of him. The only reason she could possibly have for *not* going with him was that she did not like him, though really she did not know him, did she? And that he was a man—but that was patently ridiculous. She might be an aging spinster, but she was not going to dwindle into the type of old maid who simpered and blushed and generally went all to pieces as soon as a male hove into sight.

"Thank you," she said. "I will fetch my cloak and bonnet."

"Good," he said, "I will wait for you at the head of the stairs."

Miss Claudia Martin, Joseph noticed, wore the same gray
cloak and bonnet she had worn all day. Once they were outside
the inn, they walked along the street beyond the stable yard until
they turned onto a narrower lane that would take them out into
the country. She strode along at his side, making it unnecessary
for him to reduce his stride. He did not offer his arm. He sensed
that it would be the wrong thing to do.

It was already dusk, but it would not be a dark night, he
judged. Now that it was too late for the sun to shine, the clouds
had moved off and the moon was already up.

"Perhaps," he said, "tomorrow will be a brighter day."

"It is to be hoped so," she agreed. "Sunshine is always preferable to clouds."

He did not know quite why he had invited her to walk with
him—except that her school interested him. She had never shown
one sign of liking him.

"I trust your rooms meet with your approval," he said.

"They do," she said. "But so would the other rooms have
done, the ones I reserved, the ones overlooking the stable yard."

"They might have been noisy," he said.

"They *are* noisy," she told him. "I have stayed in one or other
of them before."

"You *like* noise?" He turned his head to look at her. She was
gazing straight ahead, her chin up, her nose in the air. Good

Lord, she was annoyed. With *him*? For insisting that she be treated with courtesy and respect at that inn?

"I do not," she said. "Neither do I like the light of a dozen lanterns shining into my room or the smell of the stables. But they are only rooms and only for one night. And they *are* what I reserved."

"Are you *quarreling* with me, Miss Martin?" he asked her.

That brought her head around. She looked at him with steady eyes and raised eyebrows, and her pace slowed somewhat.

"Your carriage is very much more comfortable than the hired one would have been," she said. "The rooms in which the girls and I have been placed are vastly superior to the ones that had been assigned to us. The private dining room was a great improvement upon the public room. But these are all details of life that are not strictly necessary. They are what you and your class take for granted, no doubt. I am not of your class, Lord Attingsborough, and have no wish to be. Moreover, I am a woman who has made her own way in life. I do not need a man to protect me or an aristocrat to procure special favors for me."

Well! He had not been so roundly scolded since he was a boy. He looked at her with renewed interest.

"I must apologize, then," he said, "for wishing to see you comfortable?"

"You must do no such thing," she said. "If you do, I shall be forced to admit how very ungracious my own behavior has been. I ought to be grateful to you. And I am."

"No, you are not," he said, grinning.

"No, I am not."

She almost smiled. Something caught at the corners of her mouth. But clearly she did not wish to show any such sign of weakness. She pressed her lips into a thin line instead, faced front once more, and lengthened her stride.

He had better change the subject, he decided. And he must be very careful to do Miss Martin no favors in the future.

"All the girls in the class I saw this morning seemed sad to see

Miss Bains and Miss Wood leave," he said. "Is there never con-
flict between the paying pupils and the charity girls?"

"Oh, frequently," she said, her voice brisk, "especially when
the charity girls first arrive, often with poor diction and unpol-
ished manners and very frequently with a grudge against the
world. And of course there will almost always be an unbridge-
able social gap between the two groups once they have left the
school and taken their divergent paths into the future. But it is an
interesting lesson in life, and one I and my teachers are at great
pains to teach, that we are all human and not so very unlike one
another when the accidents of birth and circumstance are
stripped away. We hope to instill in our girls a respect for all
classes of humanity that they will retain for the rest of their
lives."

He liked her answer. It was sensible yet realistic.

"What gave you the idea of taking in charity pupils?" he
asked.

"My lack of fortune," she told him. "My father's property
was entailed and went to a cousin on his death when I was
twenty. My portion was modest, to say the least. I could not dis-
tribute largesse as I might have done if I had had limitless funds.
And so I had to find a way of giving to others that involved service rather than money."

Or she could have chosen not to give at all.

"And yet," he said, "it must cost you dearly to educate these
girls. You have to house and clothe and feed them. And their
presence at the school presumably precludes that of other girls
whose parents might pay."

"The school fees are high," she told him. "I make no apology
for that fact. We give good value, I firmly believe, and any parents
who think otherwise are perfectly at liberty to send their daughters elsewhere. And the school does have a very generous benefactor, who is unfortunately anonymous. It has always weighed
heavily upon me that I have never been able to thank him in
person."

They had left the town behind them and were on a dirt path

that wound its way between low hedgerows with fields and meadows beyond. A slight breeze blew in their faces and lifted the brim of her bonnet.

"And so," he said, "you have paying pupils and charity pupils. Have you ever aimed at further diversification? Have you ever had any pupils with handicaps, for example?"

"Lameness, do you mean?" she said. "Or deafness? Or mental slowness? I confess I have not considered it. There would be all sorts of challenges to face, would there not?"

"And you are not up to them?" he asked.

She considered her answer as they walked onward.

"I do not know," she said. "I have never been confronted with such a possibility. I suppose most parents with handicapped children—especially if they are girls—consider them incapable of learning in any normal way and so do not even try to enroll them in a school. If any *did* try and came to me, I...well, I do not know *how* I would respond. I suppose it would depend upon the handicap. A lame child might be easily educable though she might not be able to dance or participate in any vigorous games. A deaf or a mentally slow child might not. It is an interesting question, though."

She turned her head to look at him with grave but perhaps approving eyes.

"It is one I must ponder more deeply," she said.

"I must be sure to ask you again if I see you after we arrive in London, then," he said, smiling at her. "Did you always want to be a teacher?"

She considered her answer again. She was not, he concluded, a woman given to frivolous conversation.

"No," she said eventually, "not always. I had other dreams as a girl. But when it became obvious that they were not to be realized, I had a choice. As a lady and the daughter of a gentleman of property, I could have remained at home to be supported by my father. And I suppose after his early death my cousin would have felt obliged to continue to support me. Or I could make a life for myself. I chose the latter course. And then there was a further choice—to be a companion or a teacher. For me it was really no choice at all. I could not *bear* to be at the beck and call of a silly, crotchety old lady for twenty-four hours of every day. I took a position as a governess."

A dog barked in the distance. The dusk deepened around them.

She had dreamed, then. She had not always been as prosaic as she seemed now. She had dreamed presumably of marriage, perhaps of love too. Why had she abandoned that dream even before the age of twenty? She would not be bad-looking even now if she would just allow herself to relax and smile now and then. She might have been pretty as a girl. And she had admitted to a modest portion. There must have been men who would have responded to a little encouragement. Or perhaps there had been a specific dream, a specific man . . .

It really was none of his business, was it?

"A governess?" he said when it seemed that she would not continue unless prompted.

"To a family of three energetic young children at first," she said. "I adored them. Unfortunately their father was posted to India only four months after I had joined them, and they went with him. Then I worked with an atrociously badly behaved girl who believed that her elevated rank gave her license to treat the rest of humanity exactly as she pleased."

"Which was not very well at all?" He grinned down at her.

"That would be an understatement," she said. "And when I reported honestly to her brother on the difficulties she presented to the effective accomplishment of my duties—I was *not* complaining, merely giving the weekly report he had demanded—but *when* I did, he informed me that he paid me very well indeed to educate his sister and that if I did not enjoy being treated like a worm then I must simply do something about it."

"And did you?" He continued to grin. She was fairly bristling with indignation at the remembered scene. Her stride had lengthened. He doubted she even saw any of the darkening scenery around them.

"I walked out in the middle of one afternoon," she said. "I refused to accept a carriage ride or a letter of recommendation or even the week's salary to which I was entitled. And a month later I opened my school in Bath."

"I daresay," he said, "that showed them you were no worm, Miss Martin. Well done."

She laughed suddenly and unexpectedly and her steps slowed.

"I suppose," she said, "they spared me not a moment's thought once I had disappeared down the driveway—or even before I had disappeared, for that matter."

"It sounds to me, though," he said, "as if they did you a favor without ever intending it."

"That is what I have always believed," she said. "I believe that life is very generous with us once we have shown the will to take a positive course. It is very ready to keep on opening doors for us. It is just that sometimes we lose our willpower and courage and prefer to stay on the familiar, safe side of each door. I might have cowered in that employment for a long time and been miserable every moment and then perhaps have moved on to another similar one, all confidence in myself and all joy in my chosen career lost forever."

"And *does* it give you joy, then?" he asked her. "Teaching, I mean, and running your school?"

They had reached a sharp bend in the lane. Ahead of them a wooden stile separated the path from a darkened meadow beyond. They stopped walking by unspoken consent, and he set one elbow on the top bar of the stile and one booted foot on the bottom rung.

"Yes, it does," she said briskly after giving the question some consideration. "I am happy. One of my reasons for going to London is to inform my man of business that I no longer need the assistance of my benefactor. The school is paying for itself and providing me a little profit besides to put by for my old age. I am contented."

"I envy you," he surprised himself by saying.

"I think that hardly likely, Lord Attingsborough," she said

rather sharply as if she believed he mocked her. In the growing darkness it was impossible to see her face clearly.

He laughed and pointed to the west.

"We have not seen the sun all day," he said, "but at least we have been granted the remnants of a sunset to admire."

She turned her head away to look at the thin, fiery line of red and purple stretched across the horizon and then up at the dark sky, which was filled with stars and a moon almost at the full.

"How absolutely beautiful," she said, her voice somehow different, warm and feminine and filled with a nameless longing. "And I have been talking all the time and missing it. How much beauty we allow to pass us by unheeded."

"Indeed," he said, looking down at her.

There was something unexpectedly appealing about a woman who had stridden out to meet life head on and believed passionately in the tasks she had set herself. Not *physically* appealing, perhaps, though she was not exactly an antidote, but...

Well, he was not sorry after all that he had invited her out for this walk. Apart from the scolding, he liked what he had heard from her. Which gave him some faint hope...

She sighed, her face still lifted to the sky.

"I did not even realize," she said, "how much I needed this walk. It is far more restoring to the spirit than an early retirement to bed."

Was she *really* happy? he wondered. Did she ever feel nostalgia for any of her girlhood dreams? But life was made up of a succession of dreams, some few to be realized, most to be set aside as time went on, one or two to persist for a lifetime. It was knowing when to abandon a dream, perhaps, that mattered and distinguished the successful people in life from the sad, embittered persons who never moved on from the first of life's great disappointments. Or from the airy dreamers who never really lived life at all.

"I *do* envy you," he said again. "You did not stroll passively along the highway life appeared to have set before you but have stridden purposefully along a path of your own making instead. That is admirable."

She set a gloved hand on the top bar of the stile, not far from his elbow, and turned her head to look into his face, though he doubted she could see much of it in the darkness.

"And you have not done so?" she asked him. She sounded like a stern schoolteacher calling a pupil to account.

He chuckled softly.

"When one is endowed with the courtesy title of marquess at birth and knows that one day one will be a duke with all the wealth and privilege and responsibility that come with the title," he said, "one does not think often about escaping onto a new path. One *could* not. There is such a thing as duty."

Though he *had* dreamed of escape...

"But there is always choice," she said. "Life need never be bland. Duties can be shirked, or they can be performed with a minimum of effort and enthusiasm, or they can be embraced with firmness of purpose and a determination to excel."

"I hope there is no question pending," he said, laughing. "You are not about to ask me into which of the three categories I fit, Miss Martin, are you?"

"No," she said. "I beg your pardon. I have grown too accustomed to haranguing my girls. Enthusiasm and a sense of purpose atone for any number of sins, I believe, and surmount any number of hurdles. Passivity is what I find hard to tolerate. It is such a *wasteful* attitude to life."

He doubted she would fully approve of him, then. He had done well at school, it was true, and had always striven for excellence. He had been a voracious reader ever since. He had spent a great deal of time with his father's steward as a boy and very young man, learning the business and duties of being a large landowner, and he had always kept himself informed of what went on in both the upper and lower Houses of Parliament since one day—if he survived his father—he would be a member of the latter. But his father appeared to have resented his efforts—*as if*

you are waiting with bated breath for my demise, he had said irritably once when Joseph returned, wet and muddy and happy
from an inspection of a new drainage ditch at Anburey with the
steward.

And so Joseph's adult life had been an essentially idle one—as
was that of most of his peers, it was true. He kept an eye on proceedings at Willowgreen, the home and modest estate his father
had granted him on his twenty-first birthday, though his desire to
remain close to Lizzie in London stopped him from going there as
often as he would like. His life had not been characterized by any
particular vice or excessive extravagance—unlike that of most of
those same peers. He paid his servants and all his bills promptly
and gave generously to various charities. He did not gamble to
excess. He was not a womanizer. There had been the usual
succession of brief sexual encounters when he was a very
young man, it was true, but then there had been Sonia, and then
Lizzie—and just before Lizzie there had been Barbara. All well
before he was even twenty-five.

He clenched his hand on the bar of the stile and unclenched it
again, gazing off at the fading line of the sunset as he did so. For
a number of years now his life had felt essentially empty, as if
much of the color had been drawn from it, leaving behind far too
many shades of gray. An essentially passive life.

But now at last he was being nudged into taking a giant step
that he had determinedly avoided for years. He would marry
Portia Hunt before the year was out. Would marriage improve
the quality of his life, restore the color to it? After the nuptials he
would proceed with the immediate duty of putting a child in his
nursery. That might help—though the very thought of fathering a
child caused a tightening in his chest that felt like grief.

For still and always there would be Lizzie.

He became aware suddenly that they had not talked for a
while and that he was still opening and closing his hand, only
inches from Miss Martin's.

"I suppose," he said, lowering his foot to the ground, "we
ought to make our way back. The breeze is starting to feel chilly."

She fell into step beside him again but made no attempt to revive the conversation. He found her company curiously restful. If he had been walking with Miss Hunt or almost any other lady of his acquaintance, he would have felt obliged to keep some light chatter going, even if it were about nothing at all of any significance to either of them.

Miss Claudia Martin, he thought, was a woman to be respected. She had character in abundance. He even thought that he would probably like her if he ever got to know her better.

It no longer puzzled him that she was Susanna's friend.

"Shall we make a start at the same time tomorrow morning?" he suggested when they had arrived back at the inn and he had escorted her to the top of the stairs.

"The girls and I will be ready," she said briskly as she removed her gloves. "Thank you for the walk, Lord Attingsborough. I needed it, but I would not have dared venture out alone. There *are* severe disadvantages to being a woman, alas."

He smiled at her as she extended a hand to him, and he took it in his. But instead of shaking it and releasing it as she had surely intended, he raised it to his lips.

She withdrew it firmly, turned without another word, and had soon disappeared inside her room. The door closed with an audible click.

That was a mistake, he thought, frowning at the closed door. She was certainly not the kind of woman whose hand one kissed. Her fingers had clasped his firmly, not lain limp there waiting for him to play the gallant.

Dash it, that had been gauche of him.

He descended the stairs and went in search of company. From the sounds that proceeded from behind the taproom door, he guessed that not many of the other guests had yet retired for the night.

He was glad about it. He felt suddenly and unaccustomedly lonely.

Flora had fallen into a doze, her head flopped over to one side, her mouth open. Edna was gazing pensively out the carriage window. So was Claudia.

Whenever she could see him, she gazed with a frown at the Marquess of Attingsborough, mounted on another hired horse and looking as smart and as fresh as he had yesterday morning when they set out from Bath. He was remarkably handsome and charming. He was also—she hated to admit it—surprisingly good company. She had thoroughly enjoyed their walk and most of their conversation last evening. There had been a certain novelty about walking outdoors during the evening with a gentleman.

And then he had spoiled a memorable evening—and restored her initial impression of him—by kissing her hand when bidding her good night. She had been extremely annoyed with him. They had enjoyed a sensible conversation of equals—or so it had seemed. She had not needed to be dropped a crumb of his gallantry just as if she were any silly flirt.

She could see that it was raining again—it had been drizzling on and off all morning. But this time it was more than drizzle. And within moments it was more than just a gentle rain.

The carriage stopped, the coachman descended from his box, there was the sound of voices, and then the door opened and the marquess climbed into the carriage without benefit of the steps. Claudia moved to the far side of the seat as he sat beside her. But carriage seats were not really very wide. Nor was a carriage interior very large. He instantly seemed to fill both. Flora awoke with a start.

"Ladies," he said, smiling and dripping water all over the floor—and doubtless over the upholstery as well, "pardon me if you will while I travel with you until the rain stops."

"It is your own carriage," Claudia said.

He turned his smile on her and she had an unwilling memory of the warmth of those smiling lips against the back of her hand.

"And I hope it is not too uncomfortable," he said, "or the journey too tedious. Though that is a forlorn hope, I daresay. Journeys are almost always tedious."

He smiled about at each of them.

Claudia felt somehow suffocated by his presence—a remarkably silly feeling. But why could the rain not have held off? She could smell the damp fabric of his coat and his cologne. She could also smell horse, as she had yesterday. Try as she would, she could not keep her shoulder from touching his while the carriage bounced and swayed as it bowled along the highway.

What nonsense to be suddenly so discomposed—just like a green girl, or a silly spinster. What utter nonsense!

He asked the girls questions about school—skilled questions that had even Edna responding with more than just blushes and giggles. Soon they seemed quite at ease with him. And he, of course, looked perfectly comfortable as if it were an everyday occurrence with him to be sharing his carriage with two exschoolgirls and their headmistress.

"You told me last evening," he said eventually, settling his shoulders against the corner of the seat and rearranging his long legs in their mud-spattered leather riding boots so that he did not crowd any of them—though Claudia was *so* aware of those legs, "about your planned employment and hopes for success. What about your dreams, though? We all dream. What would your lives be if you could have any wish come true?"

Flora did not hesitate.

"I would marry a prince," she said, "and live in a palace and sit on a golden throne and wear diamonds and furs all day long and sleep on a feather bed."

They all smiled.

"You would not sit on a throne, though, Flo," Edna pointed out, ever the realist, "unless you were married to a king."

"Which can be easily arranged," Flora said, undaunted. "His father would die tragically the day after our wedding. Oh, and my prince would have twenty younger brothers and sisters and I would have a dozen children and we would all live together in the palace as one big, jolly family."

She sighed soulfully and then laughed.

Claudia was touched by those last details. In reality Flora was so alone in life.

"A worthy dream," the marquess said. "And you, Miss Wood?"

"My dream," Edna said, "is to have a little shop as my mama and papa did. But a *book*shop. I would live among the books all day long and sell them to people who loved them as much as I and..." She blushed and stopped.

She had strung more words together in that one speech than Claudia had heard her utter during the whole journey.

"And one of those customers would be a handsome prince," Flora added. "But not *my* prince, if you please, Ed."

"Perhaps Edna dreams of someone more humble," Claudia said. "Someone who would love books and help her run the bookshop."

"That would be foolish," Flora said. "Why not reach for the stars if one is dreaming? And what about you, my lord? What is *your* dream?"

"Yes," Edna added, looking at him with eager eyes. "But don't you already have everything?" And then she blushed and bit her lip.

Claudia raised her eyebrows but said nothing.

"No one ever has everything," he said, "even those who have so much money that they do not know what to spend it on. There are other things of value than just possessions that money can buy. Let me see. What is my greatest dream?"

He folded his arms and thought. And then Claudia, glancing at him, saw his eyes smile.

"Ah," he said. "Love. I dream of love, of a family—wife and children—which is as close and as dear to me as the beating of my own heart."

The girls were charmed. Edna sighed soulfully and Flora clasped her hands to her bosom. Claudia looked on with skepticism. His answer had very obviously been crafted for their benefit. It was, in fact, utter drivel and not a genuine dream at all.

"And you, Miss Martin?" he asked, turning his laughing eyes on her and making her wonder for an unguarded moment what it might feel like to be nearer and dearer to his heart than its own beating.

"*Me?*" she said, touching a hand to her bosom. "Oh, I have no dreams. And any I did have are already fulfilled. I have my school and my pupils and my teachers. They are a dream come true."

"Ah, but a fulfilled dream is not allowed," he said. "Is it, young ladies?"

"No," Flora said.

"No, miss. Come on," Edna said at the same moment.

"This game must be played by the rules," the Marquess of Attingsborough added, resetting his shoulders so that he could look more directly at her. His eyes looked very blue indeed from this distance.

What game? *What* rules? But she had been undeniably interested in hearing from the other three, Claudia conceded. Now it was time to be a good sport.

She felt very resentful, though.

"Oh, let me see," she said, and willed herself not to flush or otherwise get flustered. This was remarkably embarrassing before two of her pupils and an aristocratic gentleman.

"We will wait," the marquess said. "Will we not, young ladies?"

"Yes," Edna and Flora said together.

"We have all the time in the world," he added.

"Oh," Claudia said at last, "my dream. Yes, it is to live in the country again in a small cottage. With a thatched roof and hollyhocks and daffodils and roses in the garden. Each in their season, of course."

"*Alone,* Miss Martin?"

She looked unwillingly into his eyes and could see that he was enjoying himself immensely at her expense. He was even smiling fully and showing his white, perfectly shaped teeth. If there was a more annoying gentleman in existence, she certainly did not wish to meet him.

"Well, perhaps," she added, "I would have a little *dog*." And she raised her eyebrows and allowed her eyes to laugh back into his for a moment while mentally daring him to press her further on the subject.

He held her glance and chuckled softly while Edna clapped her hands.

"We used to have a dog," she cried. "I loved him of all things. I think I must have one in my bookshop."

"I want horses," Flora said. "A whole stableful of them. One for each day of the week. With red, jingling bridles."

"Ah," the marquess said, finally shifting the focus of his eyes so that he was looking out through the window on Claudia's side, "I see that the rain has stopped. There is even a patch of blue sky over there, but you had better look quickly or you may miss it."

He half stood and leaned forward to rap on the front panel, and the carriage drew to a halt.

"I shall return to my horse," he said, "and allow you ladies some privacy again."

"Ah," Edna said with obvious regret and then blushed and looked self-conscious.

"My sentiments exactly," he said. "This has been a pleasant hour indeed."

After he had got out and closed the door behind him, the smell of his cologne lingered but the animation that had buoyed them all while he was there drained away and left the carriage feeling damp and half empty. Was it always thus when one was in male company, Claudia wondered crossly—did one come almost to *need* men, to *miss* them when they were not around?

But fortunately she remembered Mr. Upton and Mr. Huckerby, two of her teachers. She did not wilt—or notice anyone else wilting—when they went home every evening. She did not need Mr. Keeble, except to be the porter at her school.

She watched resentfully as the Marquess of Attingsborough swung with ease into his saddle, looking impossibly handsome as he did so. She was really coming to dislike him quite intensely.

Gentlemen had no business trying to charm ladies who had no wish whatsoever to be charmed.

"What a lovely gentleman he is," Flora said with a sigh, looking after him too. "If he were only ten years or so younger!"

Edna sighed too.

"We will be in London soon," Claudia said cheerfully, "and we will see Viscountess Whitleaf again."

Susanna and Peter had insisted that the girls stay at their house on Grosvenor Square as well as Claudia until they began their teaching duties.

"And the baby," Edna said, brightening. "Do you suppose she will allow us to see him, miss?"

"She will probably be delighted to show him off," Claudia said with a pang of something that felt uncomfortably like envy. Susanna had given birth to Baby Harry just a month ago.

"I hope she lets us hold him," Flora said. "I used to get to hold the babies in the orphanage. It was my *favorite* thing."

The carriage moved onward and for a short while the Marquess of Attingsborough rode alongside it. He dipped his head to look in and his eyes met Claudia's. He smiled and touched the brim of his hat.

She wished—she really, *really* wished that he were not so very male. Not all men were. Not that the others were necessarily effeminate. But this man possessed maleness in an unfair abundance. *And* he knew it. She hoped fervently she would not see him again after her arrival in London. Her life was peaceful. It had taken her many years to achieve that state of tranquillity. She had no desire whatsoever to feel again all the turmoil and all the needs she had fought so hard through her twenties before finally suppressing them.

She truly resented the Marquess of Attingsborough.

He made her feel uncomfortable.

He somehow reminded her that apart from everything she had achieved during the past fifteen years, she was also a woman.

The Marquess of Attingsborough's carriage delivered Claudia and the girls directly to the door of Viscount Whitleaf's mansion on Grosvenor Square in Mayfair late in the afternoon, and Susanna and Peter were in the open doorway smiling their welcome even before the coachman had let down the steps.

It was a very splendid home indeed, but Claudia only half noticed in all the bustle and warmth of the greetings that awaited them all. Susanna hugged her, looking radiantly healthy for a woman who had given birth only one month previously. Then she hugged Edna, who squealed and giggled at seeing her old teacher again, and Flora, who squealed also and talked at double speed while Peter greeted Claudia with a warm smile and handshake and then welcomed the girls.

The marquess did not stay but rode off on his hired horse after exchanging pleasantries with Susanna and Peter, bidding Claudia farewell, and wishing Flora and Edna well in their future employment.

Claudia was not sorry to see him go.

Flora and Edna were given rooms on the nursery floor, a fact that delighted both of them after they had seen the dark-haired little Harry and had been assured that they would have other chances to peep in on him before they left. They were to take their meals with the housekeeper, who was apparently anticipating their company with considerable pleasure.

Claudia was simply to enjoy herself.

"And that is an order," Peter said, his eyes twinkling, after Susanna had told her so. "I have learned not to argue with my wife when she uses that tone of voice, Claudia. There are dangers in marrying a schoolteacher, as I have found to my cost."

"You look like a man who is hard done by," Claudia said. He was another handsome, charming man with merry eyes that were more violet than blue.

Susanna laughed. But she already had an array of activities lined up for her friend's entertainment, and since there was a letter from Mr. Hatchard's office awaiting Claudia conveying the unfortunate news that he had been called away from town for several days on business and would, with regret, be unable to see Miss Martin until after his return, she relaxed and allowed herself to be taken on visits to the shops and galleries and on walks in Hyde Park.

Of course, the delay did mean that she might have stayed at school for another week, but she did not allow herself to fret over that unforeseeable circumstance. She knew Eleanor was delighted to be in charge for once. Eleanor Thompson had come to teaching late in life, but she had discovered in it the love of her life—her own assertion.

They did not see Frances until the day of the concert. She and Lucius had gone to visit Frances's elderly aunts in Gloucestershire before coming to London. But Claudia enjoined patience on herself. At least she was to be here for the entertainment, and then she would be together with two of her dearest friends again. If only Anne could be here too, her happiness would be complete, but Anne—the former Anne Jewell, another ex-teacher at the school—was in Wales with Mr. Butler and their two children.

Claudia dressed early and with care on the appointed day, half excited at the prospect of seeing Frances again—she and Lucius were coming for dinner—and half alarmed at the realization that the concert was to be a much larger affair than she had expected. A large portion of the *ton* was to be in attendance, it seemed. It did not really help to tell herself that she despised

grandeur and did not need to feel at all intimidated. The truth
was that she was nervous. She had neither the wardrobe nor the
conversation for such company. Besides, she would know no one
except her very small group of four friends.

She did think of creeping into the back of the room at the last
minute to listen to Frances as Edna and Flora had been told they
might do. But unfortunately she expressed the thought aloud,
and Susanna had firmly forbidden it, while Peter had shaken his
head.

"It cannot be allowed, I am afraid, Claudia," he had said. "If
you try it, I shall be compelled to escort you in person to the
front row."

Susanna's personal maid had just finished styling Claudia's
hair—despite Claudia's protest that she was quite capable of seeing to it herself—when Susanna herself arrived at her dressing
room door. The maid opened it to admit her.

"Are you ready, Claudia?" Susanna asked. "Oh, you *are*.
And you do look smart."

"It is not Maria's fault that I have no curls or ringlets,"
Claudia was quick to assure Susanna as she got to her feet. "She
coaxed and wheedled, but I absolutely refused to risk looking
like mutton dressed as lamb."

Her hair consequently was dressed in its usual smooth style
with a knot at the back of the neck. Except that it looked noticeably different from usual. It somehow looked shinier, thicker,
more becoming. How the maid had accomplished the transfor-
mation Claudia did not know.

Susanna laughed. "Maria would not have made you look any
such thing," she said. "She has impeccable good taste. But she
has made your hair look extremely elegant. And I do like your
gown."

It was a plain dark green dress of fine muslin with a high
waistline, a modest neckline, and short sleeves, and Claudia had
liked it the moment she set eyes on it in a dressmaker's shop on
Milsom Street in Bath. She had bought three new dresses to come

to London, a major extravagance but one she had deemed necessary for the occasion.

"And you, of course," Claudia said, "are looking as beautiful as ever, Susanna."

Her friend was dressed in pale blue, a lovely color with her vibrant auburn curls. She was also as slender as a girl with no visible sign at all of her recent confinement except perhaps an extra glow in her cheeks.

"We had better go downstairs," Susanna said. "Come and see the ballroom before Frances and Lucius arrive."

Claudia draped her paisley shawl about her shoulders and Susanna linked an arm through hers and drew her out of the room in the direction of the staircase.

"Poor Frances!" Susanna said. "Do you suppose she is horribly nervous?"

"I daresay she is," Claudia said. "I suppose she always is before a performance. I can remember her telling the girls in her choirs when she taught at the school that if they were not nervous before a performance they were sure to sing poorly."

The ballroom was a magnificently proportioned room, with a high, gilded ceiling and a hanging chandelier fitted with dozens of candles. One wall was mirrored, giving the illusion of an even greater size and of a twin chandelier and twice the number of flowers, which were displayed everywhere in large urns. The wooden floor gleamed beneath the rows of red-cushioned chairs that had been set up for the evening.

It was a daunting sight.

But then, Claudia thought, she had never bowed to nervousness. And why should she now? She despised the *ton,* did she not? The portion of it that she did not know personally, anyway. She squared her shoulders.

And then Peter appeared in the doorway, looking all handsome elegance in his dark evening clothes, and behind him came Frances and Lucius. Susanna hurried toward them, Claudia close behind her.

"Susanna!" Frances exclaimed, catching her up in a hug. "You are as pretty as ever. And Claudia! Oh, how very dear and how very fine you look."

"And you," Claudia said, "look more distinguished than ever and . . . beautiful." And glowing, she thought, with her vivid dark coloring and fine-boned, narrow face. Success certainly agreed with her friend.

"Claudia," Lucius said, bowing to her after the first rush of greetings had been spoken, "we were both delighted when we heard that you were to be here this evening, especially as this will be Frances's last concert for a while."

"Your *last*, Frances?" Susanna cried.

"And very wise too. You have had a busy time of it," Claudia said, squeezing Frances's hands. "Paris, Vienna, Rome, Berlin, Brussels . . . and the list goes on. I hope you will take a good long break this time."

"Good *and* long," Frances agreed, looking from Claudia to Susanna with that new glow in her eyes. "Perhaps forever. Sometimes there are better things to do in life than singing."

"*Frances?*" Susanna clasped her hands to her bosom, her eyes widening.

But Frances held up a staying hand. "No more for now," she said, "or we will have Lucius blushing."

She did not need to say any more, of course. At last, after several years of marriage, Frances was going to be a mother. Susanna set her clasped hands to her smiling lips while Claudia squeezed Frances's hands more tightly before releasing them.

"Come to the drawing room for a drink before dinner," Peter said, offering his right arm to Frances and his left to Claudia. Susanna took Lucius's arm and followed along behind them.

Claudia was suddenly very glad to be where she was—even if there *was* something of an ordeal to be faced this evening. She felt a welling of happiness for the way life had dealt with her friends over the past few years. She shrugged off a feeling of slight envy and loneliness.

She wondered fleetingly if the Marquess of Attingsborough

would be in attendance this evening. She had not seen him since her arrival in town and consequently she had been her usual placid, nearly contented self again.

When Joseph wandered into White's Club the morning after his return from Bath, he found Neville, Earl of Kilbourne, already there, reading one of the morning papers. He set it aside as Joseph took a chair close to his.

"You are back, Joe?" he asked rhetorically. "How did you find Uncle Webster?"

"Thriving and irritated by the insipidity of Bath society," Joseph said. "And imagining that his heart has been weakened by his illness."

"And has it?" Neville asked.

Joseph shrugged. "All he would say was that the physician he consulted there did not deny it. He would not let me talk to the man myself. How is Lily?"

"Very well," Neville said.

"And the children?"

"Busy as ever." Neville grinned and then sobered again. "And so your father believed that his health was deteriorating and summoned you to Bath. It sounds ominous. Am I guessing his reason correctly?"

"Probably," Joseph said. "It would not take a genius, would it? I *am* thirty-five years old, after all, and heir to a dukedom. Sometimes I wish I had been born a peasant."

"No, you don't, Joe," Neville said, grinning again. "And I suppose even peasants desire descendants. So it is to be parson's mousetrap for you, is it? Does Uncle Webster have any particular bride in mind?"

"Miss Hunt," Joseph said, raising a hand in greeting to a couple of acquaintances who had entered the reading room together and were about to join another group. "Her father and mine have already agreed in principle on a match—Balderston was called to Bath before I was."

"Portia Hunt." Neville whistled but made no other comment. He merely looked at his cousin with deep sympathy.

"You disapprove?"

But Neville threw up his hands in a defensive gesture.

"Not my business," he said. "She is dashed lovely—even a happily married man cannot fail to notice *that*. And she never puts a foot wrong, does she?"

But Nev did not like her. Joseph frowned.

"And so you have been sent back to make your offer, have you?" Neville asked.

"I have," Joseph said. "I don't dislike her, you know. And I have to marry *someone*. I have been more and more aware lately that I cannot delay much longer. It might as well be Miss Hunt."

"Not a very ringing endorsement, Joe," Neville said.

"We cannot all be as fortunate as you," Joseph told him.

"Why not?" Neville raised his eyebrows. "And what will happen with Lizzie when you marry?"

"Nothing will change," Joseph said firmly. "I spent last evening with her and stayed the night, and I have promised to go back this afternoon before going to the theater this evening with Brody's party. I'll be escorting Miss Hunt there—the campaign begins without delay. But I am not going to neglect Lizzie, Nev. Not if I marry and have a dozen children."

"No," Neville said, "I cannot imagine you will. But I do wonder if Miss Hunt will object to spending most of her life in London while Willowgreen sits empty for much of the year."

"I may make other plans," Joseph said.

But before he could elaborate on them, they were interrupted by the approach of Ralph Milne, Viscount Sterne, another cousin, who was eager to talk about a pair of matched bays that were going up for auction at Tattersall's.

Joseph had accepted his invitation to attend the concert on Grosvenor Square by the time he escorted Miss Hunt to the theater that evening. He was related to neither Whitleaf nor his wife, but he had long ago accepted them as cousins of a family that embraced more members than just his blood relatives. Certainly he felt that he ought to attend any entertainment to which they had been obliging enough to invite him. He wanted to attend also because he had heard good things about the singing voice of the Countess of Edgecombe and welcomed the opportunity to hear it for himself. He wanted to attend because Lauren—Viscountess Ravensberg, his cousin of sorts—upon whom he had called after leaving White's, had told him that she and Kit would be there as well as the Duke and Duchess of Portfrey. Elizabeth, the duchess, was another almost-relative of his. He had always thought of her as an aunt though she was in fact the sister of his uncle by marriage. He wanted to attend because Neville's wife, Lily, who had also been visiting Lauren, had invited him to dinner before the concert.

And he was to attend, he discovered during the course of the evening, despite the fact that Portia Hunt was *not*. It was regrettable, he supposed, but unavoidable under the circumstances.

During one of the intervals between acts of the play, Miss Hunt asked him if he was going to Lady Fleming's soiree a few evenings hence. There was something quite new in her manner toward him, he had realized all evening—something rather proprietary. Clearly her father had spoken with her. He was about to reply in the affirmative when Laurence Brody interjected with a question of his own.

"You are not going to the Whitleaf concert on that evening, then, Miss Hunt?" he asked. "I have heard that everyone is going there. Lady Edgecombe is to sing and the whole world is eager to hear her."

"Not the *whole* world, Mr. Brody," Portia said with controlled dignity. "*I* am not eager to go, and neither is my mother or any number of other people of good taste whom I could name. We have already accepted Lady Fleming's invitation. I expect to find superior company and conversation at her soiree." She smiled at Joseph.

He could have kicked himself then. *Of course* she would not be going to the concert. The Countess of Edgecombe was married to the man Portia had firmly believed for most of her life *she* was going to marry. It was during the days and weeks following the ending of that relationship that he, Joseph, had first befriended her.

"I regret that I must miss the soiree, Miss Hunt," he said. "I have already accepted my invitation to Lady Whitleaf's concert."

He would have refused his invitation if he had remembered—as he ought to have done—that connection between the Edgecombes and Miss Hunt. And she was clearly not pleased with him. She was very quiet for the rest of the evening, and when she *did* speak, it was almost exclusively to other members of the party.

He arrived on the appointed evening with Lily and Neville and paid his respects to Whitleaf and Susanna. The ballroom, he could see, was already filling nicely. The first person he saw when they stepped inside was Lauren, who had a smile on her face and an arm raised to attract their attention from the other side of the room. Kit was with her as were Elizabeth and Portfrey.

And Miss Martin.

He had thought of the schoolteacher a number of times since his return to town. He had liked her more than he had expected to during the journey to London. She was prim and straightlaced and severe, it was true, and independent to a fault. But she was also intelligent and capable of dry humor.

But he had thought of her mainly for other reasons. He intended to have another talk with her before she returned to Bath, though tonight was probably not the right time for that. She was smartly dressed in green muslin, he noticed. Her hair was styled a little more becomingly than it had been at the school or on the journey to London. Even so, anyone looking at her this evening could surely not mistake her for anything other than what she was—a schoolteacher. It was something to do with the discipline of her posture, the sternness of her expression, the total absence of frills or curls or jewels about her person.

As he approached with Lily and Neville, she turned to see them come.

"Lily, Neville, Joseph," Lauren said as they joined the group, and there followed a flurry of greetings and handshakes and kisses on the cheek. "Have you met Miss Martin? These are the Countess of Kilbourne, Miss Martin, and my cousins, the Marquess of Attingsborough and the earl."

"Miss Martin?" Neville smiled and bowed.

"I am delighted to meet you, Miss Martin," Lily said with her customary warm smile as Miss Martin inclined her head and bade them all a good evening.

"We have already met," Joseph said, extending a hand for hers and remembering that the last time he did so he had committed the faux pas of kissing it. "I had the pleasure of escorting Miss Martin up from Bath a week ago."

"But yes, of course," Lauren said.

"I have not set eyes on you since then, Joseph," Elizabeth said. "How is your father?"

"Considerably better, thank you," he said, "though he chooses to believe otherwise. He is certainly fit enough to grumble about everyone and everything. My mother, meanwhile, appears to be enjoying Bath society."

"I am delighted to hear it," Elizabeth said. "I know she was disappointed not to be coming up to town this year."

"Miss Martin," Portfrey said, "both the Countess of Edgecombe and Lady Whitleaf were once teachers at your school, I understand?"

"They were," she said. "I still mourn their loss. However, I am exceedingly proud of my present staff of teachers."

"Christine tells us," Kit said, speaking of the Duchess of Bewcastle, "that Miss Thompson is very happy there."

"I believe she is," Miss Martin told him. "She was clearly born to teach. My girls love her and learn from her and obey her without question."

"I am fascinated by the idea of a girls' school," Lily said. "I must talk with you about it sometime, Miss Martin. I have a hundred questions to ask."

"All of which must wait, my love," Neville said. "I believe the concert is about to begin."

"We should take our seats, then," Elizabeth said.

"Would you care to sit beside me, Miss Martin?" Joseph asked.

But she was looking suddenly prim and severe again, he could see.

"Thank you," she said, "but there is something I must go and attend to."

He took a seat beside Lauren and prepared to be entertained. The Countess of Edgecombe was not the only performer, he had learned, though she was certainly the main attraction. He was about to make some remark to Lauren when he became aware that Miss Martin had taken only a few steps away into the center aisle and was now standing rooted to the spot, looking as if she might have seen a ghost. He got hastily to his feet again.

"Miss Martin?" he said. "Do you feel unwell? May I—"

"No," she said. "Thank you. I *will* sit beside you after all, though, if I may. Thank you."

And she sat hastily on the empty chair beside his and bowed her head. She clasped her hands in her lap, and he noticed that they were shaking slightly. Now this was strange, he thought, coming from a woman who did not seem to be the vaporish sort. But it was impossible to know what had happened to discompose her, and she offered no explanation.

"Have Miss Wood and Miss Bains been safely delivered to their new employers?" he asked her, hoping to distract her mind from whatever it was that had upset her.

She looked blankly at him for a moment.

"Oh. No," she said. "Not yet. Mr. Hatchard, my man of business, has been out of town. He returned today, though, and sent word to inform me that I may call upon him tomorrow."

Some color was returning to her cheeks. She straightened her shoulders.

"And have you been well entertained in the meantime?" he asked.

"Oh, yes, indeed," she said without elaborating.

But the concert was about to begin. Whitleaf had moved to the front of the room and was standing on the low dais that had been set up for the performers so that they would be visible to everyone in the ballroom. There were some shushing sounds from the audience and then silence.

The concert began.

Joseph was impressed by the high caliber of the performances. There was a recital by a string quartet, a series of offerings by a young baritone who was engaged to sing in the opera house in Vienna during the autumn, and a pianoforte recital by the lame, dark-haired Countess of Raymore, who was a celebrity in her own right and whom Joseph had heard with enjoyment on other occasions. She also sang a melancholy folk song to her own accompaniment in her lovely contralto voice. And then, of course, there was the Countess of Edgecombe, whose soprano voice was rich and full, though she soon proved that she could hit some incredibly high notes.

He could easily understand what all the fuss was about.

Getting to his feet with the rest of the audience to coax an encore out of her with the volume of their applause after she had finished, Joseph realized that he would have been deprived of one of life's great aesthetic experiences if he had gone to the soiree instead of coming here. Also, of course, he was interested to see in action the woman who had supplanted Portia Hunt in Edgecombe's affections. He had set eyes on her before, it was true, but he had not appreciated her exquisite beauty until tonight, when her narrow, expressive face was lit from within and her very dark hair gleamed in the candlelight.

By the time the countess had finished her encore, Miss Martin had her hands clasped very tightly together and was holding them beneath her chin. Her eyes glowed with pride and affection. The teachers at her school really had done rather well for themselves in the matrimonial market, he thought. It must be a very good school indeed to attract such charm and talent onto its staff.

Miss Martin's eyes were brimming with unshed tears when she turned to look behind her, perhaps to share her joy with Susanna. Joseph turned toward her, intending to invite her to join his family group for the refreshments that were to be served in the supper room.

But she grasped his arm suddenly before he could make the offer and spoke urgently to him.

"There is someone coming this way with whom I do *not* wish to speak," she said.

He raised his eyebrows. Most of the audience was dispersing in the direction of the supper room. But there was indeed one man making his way against the flow, obviously heading in their direction. Joseph knew him vaguely. He had met him at White's. The man had arrived recently from Scotland. McLeith—that was the name. He held a Scottish dukedom.

And Miss Martin knew him—but did not wish to speak with him?

This was interesting. Did this have anything to do with her earlier perturbation? he wondered.

He set a hand reassuringly over hers on his arm. It was too late to whisk her out of the man's way.

Claudia had met Viscount Ravensberg and his wife before—at two weddings, in fact. Anne Jewell had married the viscount's brother, and Susanna had married the viscountess's cousin.

It had been something of a relief to see familiar faces, especially as they had recognized her and come to speak with her in the ballroom. Frances and Lucius had gone to the music room to be quiet for a while and prepare for the performance, and Susanna and Peter were busy greeting guests at the ballroom doors. It was *not* a comfortable thing to be alone in a crowd, knowing no one and trying to pretend that one was actually enjoying one's lone state.

She took an instant liking to Viscountess Ravensberg's aunt and uncle, who were with them, despite their elevated rank. They were courteous, amiable people and made an effort to include her in the conversation. The same could be said of the Earl and Countess of Kilbourne after they had arrived and joined the group. It was not even entirely disagreeable to see the Marquess of Attingsborough again. His was, after all, another familiar face when she had convinced herself that she would know no one at all. Of course, he was looking more gorgeous than ever in evening clothes of dark blue and silver with white linen.

She did spare herself a moment of private amusement as she stood with the group. Not a single one of them was without a title—and there was she in their midst and even rather enjoying their company. She would make much of this particular part of the evening when she was telling Eleanor about it after her return home. She would even laugh merrily at her own expense.

But amusement turned to sudden embarrassment when the Duchess of Portfrey suggested that they take their seats and the marquess asked her if she wished to sit beside him. Really he had no choice but to make the offer since she had stood there within their family group instead of moving off elsewhere after the initial pleasantries had been exchanged as she ought to have done.

Goodness, they would think her gauche and ill-mannered in the extreme.

And so she made that hasty excuse about having to go and attend to something. She would make it the truth, of course. She would find Edna and Flora and make sure that they found space at the back of the ballroom once all the invited guests had been seated. And she would remain with them after all despite the dire consequences Peter had promised. Edna had once sung in the junior choir that Frances had conducted and had been beside herself with excitement all day at the prospect of hearing her old, revered teacher sing in a real concert. Flora had been more animated at the prospect of seeing so many rich and important people gathered in one place and all dressed up in their best evening finery.

But Claudia did not get far on her self-appointed mission. Because it was not in her nature to cower even when she felt self-conscious, she deliberately looked about at the audience as she moved away from where she had been standing, almost at the front of the ballroom, wondering idly if she would recognize anyone else.

She very much doubted she would.

But then she did.

There, halfway back and to the left of the center aisle in which Claudia stood, sat Lady Freyja Bedwyn, now the Marchioness of Hallmere, in animated conversation with Lord Aidan Bedwyn, her brother, beside her and Lady Aidan beyond him—Claudia had met *them* too at Anne's wedding breakfast in Bath. The Marquess of Hallmere sat on the other side of his wife.

Claudia bristled with instant animosity. She had seen Lady Hallmere a number of times since walking out of the schoolroom at Lindsey Hall itself on that memorable afternoon long ago—most notably when, still as Lady Freyja Bedwyn, she had turned up at the school one morning, quite out of the blue, looking haughty and condescending and asking if there was anything Claudia needed that she might supply.

Claudia's temperature could still soar at the memory.

Seeing the woman again now, though, would not in itself have caused her to retrace the few steps she had taken and drop hastily into the empty seat beside Lord Attingsborough. After all, if she had thought about it, she would have expected that at least some of the Bedwyns would be in town for the Season and that any who were here might very well put in an appearance at tonight's concert.

No, if they had been the only faces she had recognized, she would merely have stiffened her backbone, pressed her lips more tightly together, lifted her chin, and proceeded on her way undaunted.

But a mere second after Claudia noticed Lady Hallmere, her eyes were drawn to the gentleman sitting directly in front of her—the one who was looking very intently at *her*.

Her knees threatened to turn to jelly, and her heart jumped right up into her throat—or so it seemed from the uncomfortable beating there. How she recognized him when she had not set eyes upon him for half her lifetime she did not know, but she did—instantly.

Charlie!

There was no thought—there was no *time* for thought. She acted purely from craven instinct, aided by the fact that Lord Attingsborough got to his feet and asked her if she was unwell. She ducked into the seat beside him with ungainly haste and was scarcely aware of what he said to her as she clasped her hands in her lap and tried to impose calm on herself.

Fortunately, the concert began shortly after that and she was able gradually to still the erratic beating of her heart and to feel somewhat embarrassed that after all she was imposing on the company of this aristocratic family group. She willed herself to listen to the music.

So Charlie was here in London and here tonight.

So what?

Doubtless he would disappear as soon as the concert was over. He must be as reluctant as she that they come face-to-face. Or else he would remain and ignore her out of sheer indifference. Eighteen years was a long time, after all. She had been seventeen the last time she saw him, he one year older.

Goodness, they had been little more than children!

Quite possibly he had not even recognized her but had merely been resting his eyes idly upon her because she was one of the last persons standing.

She schooled herself to concentrate when Frances was announced and took her place on the low dais. This was what she had looked forward to most even before leaving Bath, and she was *not* going to allow Charlie of all people to deprive her of appreciating the performance to the full. After a few moments, of course, she no longer had to use willpower in order to concentrate. Frances was purely magnificent.

Claudia rose with everyone else at the end of the recital to applaud. By the time the encore was over, she was aware of nothing else but a glow of pleasure in the entertainment and of pride in Frances and happiness for herself that she was here tonight for what might well be her friend's final public appearance for a long while, maybe forever.

She turned again as the applause finally died down and Peter announced that refreshments would be served in the supper room. She blinked away the tears that had filled her eyes. She wanted to find Susanna, and she wanted to see that Edna and Flora had indeed been able to come inside to listen. She wanted to move away before Lord Attingsborough or Lady Ravensberg or someone else in the group felt obliged to invite her to join them for refreshments. How mortifying that would be!

And she wanted to assure herself that Charlie really had gone away.

He had not.

He was walking purposefully down the center aisle toward her though everyone else was moving in the opposite direction. His eyes were fixed on her, and he was smiling.

Claudia was no more ready to deal with the shock of this unexpected encounter now than she had been when she first spotted him earlier. She grabbed the marquess's arm without thinking and gabbled something to him.

His hand covered hers on his arm—a large, warm hand that felt enormously comforting. She felt almost safe.

It was a measure of the confusion of her mind that she did not even question the uncharacteristic abjectness of her reactions.

And then Charlie was there, standing a mere foot or two in front of her, still smiling, his brown eyes alight with pleasure.

He definitely looked older. His fair hair had thinned and receded though he was not yet bald. His face was still round and pleasant rather than handsome, but there were lines at the corners of his eyes and beside his mouth that had not been there when he was a boy. He was more solid in build now though he was not by any means fat. He had not grown taller after the age of eighteen. His eyes were still on a level with her own. He was dressed with quiet elegance, unlike the careless way he had used to dress.

"Claudia! It *is* you!" he said, stretching out both hands toward her.

"Charlie." She could scarcely persuade her lips to move. They felt stiff and beyond her control.

"But what a delightful surprise!" he said. "I could hardly believe my—"

"Good evening to you, McLeith," the Marquess of Attingsborough said, his voice firm and pleasant. "A fine concert, was it not?"

Charlie looked at him as if he had only just noticed him

standing there beside her, holding her hand on his arm. His own arms fell to his sides.

"Ah, Attingsborough," he said. "Good evening. Yes, indeed, we have been royally entertained."

The marquess inclined his head courteously. "You will excuse us?" he said. "Our group is already halfway to the supper room. We would not wish to lose our places with them."

And he drew Claudia's hand right through his arm and kept his hand over hers.

"But where are you living, Claudia?" Charlie asked, returning his attention to her. "Where may I call on you?"

"Your shawl has slipped from your shoulder," the marquess said almost simultaneously, his voice full of solicitous concern as he replaced it with his free hand, half turning in front of her as he did so. "Good night, McLeith. Good to see you."

And they were on their way up the aisle with a crowd of other guests, leaving Charlie behind.

"He is trouble?" the marquess asked when they were out of earshot, bending his head closer to hers.

"*Was,*" she said. "A long time ago. A lifetime ago."

Her heart was beating up into her throat again, almost deafening her. She was also returning to herself and an embarrassing realization that she had been behaving without any of her usual firmness of character. Goodness, she had even grabbed the marquess's arm and begged for his help and protection—*after what she had said to him in Marlborough about independence.* How very humiliating! Suddenly her nostrils were assailed by the smell of his cologne—the same one she had noticed at the school and in the carriage. Why did masculine colognes always smell more enticing than female perfumes?

"I do beg your pardon," she said. "That was very foolish of me. It would have been much better—and far more like me—to have conversed civilly with him for a few minutes."

He had actually been delighted to see her. He had wanted to take both her hands in his. He had wanted to know where she was living so that he could call on her. Distress turned to anger.

She straightened her spine, which was in no way slouching to start with.

"You really do not need to take me any farther," she said, slipping her hand free of the marquess's arm. "I have imposed enough upon your time and good nature, and for that I apologize. Do go and join your family before it is too late."

"And leave you alone?" he said, smiling down at her. "I could not be so unmannerly. Allow me to distract your mind by introducing you to a few more people."

And he cupped her elbow and turned her, and there, almost face-to-face with her, were Lord and Lady Aidan Bedwyn, the Marquess and Marchioness of Hallmere, and—*gracious heaven!*—the Duke and Duchess of Bewcastle.

"Joseph," the duchess said, all warm smiles. "We could see you sitting with Lauren and Kit. Was this evening not perfectly delightful? And—yes, it is! Oh, do pardon my manners, Miss Martin. How are you?"

Claudia—another measure of her distraction—dipped into a curtsy and the gentlemen bowed, the duke with a mere half tilt of his head. Lady Aidan and Lord Hallmere smiled and Lady Hallmere looked haughty.

"Miss Martin," Lord Aidan said. "The owner of the school in Bath where Sydnam Butler's wife once taught, I believe? We met at their wedding breakfast. How do you do, ma'am?"

"I see that introductions are not needed after all," Lord Attingsborough said. "I had the pleasure of escorting Miss Martin and two of her pupils up from Bath last week."

"I trust you left the school in good hands, Miss Martin," Lady Hallmere said, looking along the length of her rather prominent nose.

Claudia bristled.

"Of course I did," she retorted. "It is hardly likely I would leave it in *poor* hands, is it?"

Too late she realized that she had spoken sharply and without any forethought and had been remarkably rude as a result. If one of her girls had done such a thing in her hearing, she would have taken the girl aside and lectured her for five minutes without stopping to draw breath.

Lady Hallmere's eyebrows arched upward.

The duke's right hand curled about the handle of his jeweled quizzing glass.

Lord Hallmere grinned.

The duchess laughed.

"You will offend me if you quiz Miss Martin on that score any further, Freyja," she said. "She has left *Eleanor* in charge, and I am quite confident that my sister is very competent indeed. She is also delighted, I might add, Miss Martin, that you have shown such trust in her."

And there spoke the genuine lady, Claudia thought ruefully, smoothing over a potentially awkward moment with charm and grace.

The Marquess of Attingsborough cupped Claudia's elbow again.

"Lauren and Kit and the Portfreys and Kilbournes will be keeping places at their table for us," he said. "We must go and join them."

"I do beg your pardon—yet again," Claudia said as they made their way toward the door. "I teach my girls that courtesy must take precedence over almost any personal feeling at all times, yet I have just ignored my own teachings in rather spectacular fashion."

"I believe," he said, and she could see that he was actually amused, "Lady Hallmere intended her question as a mere polite conversational overture."

"Oh, not *that* woman," she said, forgetting her contrition. "Not Lady Freyja Bedwyn."

"You knew her before her marriage?" he asked.

"*She* was the pupil I told you about," she said.

"*No!*" His hand closed more tightly about her elbow, drawing her to a halt beyond the ballroom doors but just outside the supper room. He was grinning openly now. "And Bewcastle was the one who so ruthlessly directed you to fend for yourself? You thumbed your nose at *Bewcastle*? And strode off down the drive-way of *Lindsey Hall*?"

"It was not funny," she said, frowning. "There was nothing remotely amusing about it."

"And so," he said, his eyes alight with merriment, "I took you from the frying pan into the fire when I led you straight from McLeith to the Bedwyns, did I not?"

She regarded him with a deepening frown.

"I believe, Miss Martin," he said, "you must have led a very interesting life."

Her spine stiffened and she pressed her lips tightly together before replying.

"I have not—" she began.

And then saw the last ten minutes or so as they must have appeared through his eyes.

Her lips twitched.

"Well," she conceded, "in a way I suppose I have."

And for some inexplicable reason they both found her admission enormously tickling and dissolved into laughter.

"I do beg your pardon," he said when he could.

"And I yours," she replied.

"And to think," he said, taking her elbow again and leading her into the supper room, "that I might have gone to Lady Fleming's soiree this evening instead of coming here."

The Duchess of Portfrey was smiling and beckoning from one of the tables and the Earl of Kilbourne was standing to draw out a chair for Claudia.

It was unclear to Claudia if the marquess regretted the choice he had made. But she was very glad he had come. He had somehow restored her disordered spirits—even if he *had* been the un-witting cause of some of them. She could not remember when she had last laughed so hard.

She was in grave danger, she thought severely as she took her seat, of revising her opinion of him and actually *liking* him.

And here she was in the midst of a family group she ought to have left a few hours ago. And she had no one to blame for her renewed discomfort but herself. When had she *ever* before clung to a man for support and protection?

It was really quite lowering.

Claudia fell asleep—admittedly after a long spell of wakefulness—thinking about the Marquess of Attingsborough and awoke thinking about Charlie—*the Duke of McLeith.*

Oh, yes, indeed, she had come honestly by her antipathy toward the aristocracy, particularly toward dukes. It had not started with the odious and arrogant Duke of Bewcastle. Another duke had destroyed her life well before she met him.

She had lived and breathed Charlie Gunning during her childhood and girlhood, or so it seemed in retrospect. They had been virtually inseparable from the moment he had arrived at her father's house, a bewildered and unhappy five-year-old orphan, until he had gone away to school at the age of twelve, and even after that they had spent every waking moment of his holidays together.

But then, when he was eighteen and she seventeen, he had gone away never to return. She had not seen him since—until last evening. She had not *heard* from him for almost seventeen years.

Yet last evening he had spoken to her as if there had been no abrupt and ruthless ending to their relationship. He had spoken as if there were nothing in the world for him to feel guilty about.

But what a delightful surprise!

But where are you living?

Where may I call on you?

Had he really believed he had the right to be *delighted*? And to *call* on her? How dared he! Seventeen years might be a long time—almost half her life—but it was not *that* long. There was nothing wrong with her memory.

But she firmly cast aside memory as she dressed for breakfast and her visit to Mr. Hatchard's office later in the morning. She had decided to go alone, without Edna and Flora. Frances was coming to the house, and she and Susanna were going to take the girls shopping for new clothes and accessories.

And since Frances came in a carriage and bore the other three off in it not long after a prolonged breakfast, Claudia found herself riding to her appointment in Peter's town carriage. He had refused even to listen to her protests that she would enjoy the walk on such a sunny day.

"Susanna would never forgive me," he had said with a twinkle in his eye. "And I would hate that. Have pity on me, Claudia."

She was buoyed by high spirits as she rode through the streets of London, despite a niggling worry that the employment Mr. Hatchard had found for the two girls might not be suitable after all. Now that the time had come, she was fairly bubbling with excitement over the fact that she was about to put the final touch to her independence, to her success as a single woman.

There was no longer any need of assistance from the benefactor who had so generously supported the school almost from the start. She had a letter for him tucked into her reticule—Mr. Hatchard would deliver it for her. It was regrettable that she would never know who the man was, but she respected his desire for anonymity.

The school was flourishing. Within the last year she had been able to extend it into the house next door and add two more teachers to the staff. Even more gratifying, she was now able to increase the number of charity pupils she took in from twelve to fourteen. And the school was even turning a modest profit.

She was looking forward to the next hour or so, she thought as Peter's coachman handed her down from the carriage and she stepped inside Mr. Hatchard's office.

Less than an hour later Claudia hurried back outside onto the pavement. Viscount Whitleaf's coachman jumped down from the box and opened the carriage door for her. She drew breath to tell him that she would walk home. She was far too agitated to ride. But before she could speak, she heard her name being called.

The Marquess of Attingsborough was riding along the street

with the Earl of Kilbourne and another gentleman. It was the
marquess who had hailed her.

"Good morning, Miss Martin," he said, riding closer. "And
how are you this morning?"

"If I were any angrier, Lord Attingsborough," she said, "the
top might well blow off my head."

He raised his eyebrows.

"I am going to walk home," she told the coachman. "Thank
you for waiting for me, but you may return without me."

"You must permit me to escort you, ma'am," the marquess said.

"I hardly need a chaperone," she told him sharply. "And I
would *not* be good company this morning."

"Allow me to accompany you as a friend, then," he said, and
he swung down from his saddle and turned to the earl. "You will
take my horse back to the stable, Nev?"

The earl smiled and doffed his hat to Claudia, and it was too
late to say a firm no. Besides, it was something of a relief to see
a familiar face. She had thought she would have to wait for
Susanna to return from her shopping expedition before she
would have anyone with whom to talk. She might well burst before then.

And so just a minute later they were walking along the pavement together, she and the Marquess of Attingsborough. He offered his arm, and she took it.

"I am *not* much given to distress," she assured him, "despite
last evening and now this morning. But this morning it is anger—
fury—rather than distress."

"Someone upset you in there?" he asked, nodding toward the
building from which she had just emerged.

"That is Mr. Hatchard's office," she explained to him. "My
man of business."

"Ah," he said. "The employment. It did not meet with your
approval?"

"Edna and Flora will return to Bath with me tomorrow,"
she said.

"That bad?" He patted her hand on his arm.

"Worse," she assured him. "*Far* worse."

"Am I permitted to know what happened?" he asked.

"The Bedwyns," she said, sawing at the air with her free hand as they crossed a street, avoiding a pile of fresh manure. "*That* is what happened. The *Bedwyns*! They will be the death of me yet. I swear they will."

"I do hope not," he said.

"Flora was to be employed by Lady Aidan Bedwyn," Claudia said, "and Edna by none other than *the Marchioness of Hallmere*!"

"Ah," he said.

"It is *insufferable*," she told him. "I do not know how that woman has the nerve."

"Perhaps," he suggested, "she remembers you as a superior teacher who will not compromise her principles and high standards even for money or position."

Claudia snorted.

"And perhaps," he said, "she has grown up."

"Women like her," Claudia said, "do not grow up. They just grow nastier."

Which was ridiculous and unfair, of course. But her antipathy toward the former Lady Freyja Bedwyn ran so deep that she was incapable of being reasonable where the woman was concerned.

"You have an objection to Lady Aidan Bedwyn too?" he asked, touching the brim of his hat to a couple of ladies who were walking in the opposite direction.

"She married a Bedwyn," Claudia said.

"She has always struck me as being particularly amiable," he said. "Her father was apparently a Welsh coal miner before making his fortune. She has a reputation for helping people less fortunate than herself. Two of her three children are adopted. Is it for them she needs a governess?"

"For the girl," Claudia said, "and eventually for her younger daughter."

"And so you are to return to Bath with Miss Bains and Miss Wood," he said. "Are they to be given any choice in the matter?"

"I would not send them into servitude to be miserable," she said.

"Perhaps," he suggested, "they might not see it that way, Miss Martin. Perhaps they would be excited at the prospect of being governesses in the houses of such distinguished families."

A young child with a harried-looking nurse in hot pursuit was bowling his hoop along the pavement. The marquess drew Claudia to one side until they were all past.

"Little whippersnapper," he commented. "I would wager he promised most faithfully that he would carry the thing except when he was in the park with plenty of open space."

Claudia drew a slow breath.

"Are you suggesting, Lord Attingsborough," she said, "that I reacted overhastily and unreasonably at Mr. Hatchard's office?"

"Not at all," he said. "Your anger is admirable as is your determination to burden yourself with the girls again by taking them back to Bath rather than placing them in employment that might bring them unhappiness."

She sighed.

"You are quite right," she said. "I *did* react too hastily."

He grinned at her.

"Did you give Hatchard a definite no?" he asked.

"Oh, I did," she said, "but he insisted that he would do nothing until tomorrow. He wants the girls to attend interviews with their prospective employers."

"Ah," he said.

"I suppose," she said, "I ought to give them the choice, ought I not?"

"If you trust their judgment," he said.

She sighed again. "It is one thing we are at pains to teach," she said. "Good judgment, reason, thinking for oneself, making one's own decisions based upon sense as well as inclination. That is more than one thing. We try to teach our girls to be informed, thinking adults—especially the charity girls who will not simply marry as soon as they are out of the schoolroom and allow their husbands to do all the thinking for them for the rest of their lives."

"That is not a very rosy picture of marriage," he said.

"But a very accurate one," she retorted.

They were walking beneath an avenue of trees that lined the pavement. Briefly Claudia raised her face to the branches and leaves overhead and to the blue sky and sunshine above.

"I will warn them," she said. "I will explain that the Bedwyns, led by the Duke of Bewcastle, are a family that has enjoyed wealth and privilege for generations, that they are arrogant and contemptuous of all who are below them on the social scale—and that includes almost every other mortal in existence. I shall explain that Lady Hallmere is the worst of the lot. I shall advise them not even to attend an interview but to pack their bags and return to Bath with me. And then I shall allow them to decide for themselves what they wish to do."

She remembered suddenly that both girls had actually stayed at Lindsey Hall with the other charity girls last summer for the occasion of Susanna's wedding. They had actually met the Duke and Duchess of Bewcastle.

The Marquess of Attingsborough was laughing softly. Claudia looked sharply at him. And then she laughed too.

"I am a tyrant only when I am wrathful," she said. "Not simply annoyed, but *wrathful*. It does not happen often."

"And I suspect that when it does," he said, "it is because someone has threatened one of your precious girls."

"They *are* precious," she told him. "Especially those who have no one to speak up for them but me."

He patted her hand again, and she suddenly realized that she had been walking with him for several minutes without paying any attention whatsoever to the direction they took.

"Where are we?" she asked. "Is this the way back to Susanna's?"

"It is the long and the best way home," he told her. "It passes Gunter's. Have you tasted their ices?"

"No, I have not," Claudia said. "But this is the *morning*."

"And there is some law that states one can indulge in an ice only in the afternoon?" he said. "There will be no time this afternoon. I will be at Mrs. Corbette-Hythe's garden party. Will you?"

Claudia winced inwardly. She had completely forgotten about that. She would far rather stay at home, but of course she must go. Susanna and Frances expected it of her, and she expected it of herself. She did not enjoy moving in *ton*nish circles, but she would not absent herself from any entertainment just because she was self-conscious and felt she did not belong.

Those things were all the more reason to go.

"Yes," she said.

"Then we will stop for an ice at Gunter's this morning," he said, patting her hand once more.

And for no reason at all, Claudia laughed again.

Where had her anger gone? Had she by any chance been *manipulated*? Or had she just been given the benefit of the wisdom of a cooler head?

Wisdom?

The Marquess of Attingsborough?

She remembered something suddenly, and it put to flight the remnants of her anger.

"I am *free,*" she told the marquess. "I have just informed Mr. Hatchard that I do not need my benefactor any longer. I have just handed him a letter of thanks for the man."

"A cause for celebration indeed," he said. "And what better way to celebrate than with one of Gunter's ices?"

"If there is one, I cannot think what it might be," she agreed.

6

The garden at Mrs. Corbette-Hythe's home in Richmond was spacious and beautifully landscaped. It stretched down to the bank of the River Thames and was an ideal setting for a large garden party—and this particular one was large.

Joseph knew almost everyone, as he usually did at such events. He wandered from group to group, a glass of wine in one hand, conversing with acquaintances and generally making himself agreeable before moving on.

The weather was ideal. There was scarcely a cloud in the sky. The sun was hot and yet the air remained fresh, perfumed with the scents of the thousands of flowers that filled beds and borders in the formal parterre gardens below the terrace and offered a feast of color to the beholder besides. There was a rose arbor to one side of the house. A string quintet close to its arched entry-way played soft music to mingle pleasingly with birdsong and laughter and the sound of voices in conversation with one another.

When Joseph arrived at the group that included Lauren and Kit, it was to find his cousin brimming with news.

"Have you spoken with Neville and Lily yet?" she asked. But she did not wait for his answer. "Gwen and Aunt Clara will be coming to Alvesley for the summer."

"Ah, great news!" he said. Kit's parents, the Earl and Countess of Redfield, were to celebrate their fortieth wedding anniversary during the summer. Alvesley Park, their home and Kit and Lauren's, was to be filled with guests, himself included. Gwen was Neville's sister, Aunt Clara his mother.

"Anne and Sydnam are going to be there too," Lauren added.

"I shall look forward to seeing them," Joseph assured her. "There is nothing quite like a family gathering in the country to lift the spirits, is there?"

Miss Hunt was punishing him for last evening, Joseph had been made aware almost from the moment of his arrival. He had joined her group as soon as he finished greeting his hostess, quite prepared to spend the whole afternoon in her company. She had smiled graciously at him and then turned her attention back to the conversation she was holding with Mrs. Dillinger. And when that topic exhausted itself shortly after, she introduced one of her own—the latest style in bonnets. Since he was the only man in the group, he had felt quite pointedly excluded and soon wandered away to find more congenial company.

She had given him the cut direct, by Jove.

She looked even more than usually beautiful this afternoon. While other ladies had donned brightly colored dresses for the occasion, Miss Hunt must have realized that she could not hope to vie with the flowers or the sunshine in splendor and so had worn unadorned white muslin. Her blond hair was artfully styled beneath a white lacy hat decorated with white rosebuds and just a touch of greenery.

He mingled with a few other groups before eventually strolling alone down to the water's edge. The garden had been artfully designed to display flowers and a riot of color close to the house while nearer to the water there were more trees, and every-thing was varying shades of green. The upper garden was not even visible from down here, and only part of the roof and chim-neys of the house. He could still hear faint strains of music, but the sounds of voices and laughter were muted.

Most of the guests had remained close to the house and the company and the food. A few people, though, were out on the water, having taken the small rowing boats from the jetty. A young couple awaited their turn. One lady walked alone a short distance away, in the shade of some willow trees.

She was wise to have escaped from the direct heat of the sun for a while, Joseph thought, but surely she did not need to be alone—not at a party, at least, where the idea was to mingle. But then, of course, *he* was alone. Sometimes a brief respite from the demand of the crowds was as good as a breath of fresh air.

She was Miss Martin, he realized suddenly as she stopped walking and turned to gaze out across the water. He hesitated. Perhaps she would prefer to remain alone—after all, he had taken a good deal of her time this morning. Or perhaps she was feeling lonely. There must not be many people here that she knew, after all.

He remembered the laughter they had shared outside the supper room last evening and smiled at the memory. Laughter somehow transformed her and stripped years off her age. And he remembered her at Gunter's this morning, eating her ice slowly in small spoonfuls, savoring each mouthful and then going on the defensive when she realized he was amused.

"You must understand," she had explained, "that this is not something I do every day—or even every year. Or every *decade*."

He turned his steps in her direction.

"I see you have found some shade," he said, raising his voice as he approached, lest he startle her. "May I be permitted to share it?"

She looked startled anyway.

"Of course," she said. "I believe the outdoors belongs equally to everyone."

"Doubtless that is the creed of all trespassers and poachers," he said, grinning at her. "Are you enjoying yourself?"

Any normal woman would have smiled politely and assured him that indeed she was, and the conversation would have moved on to predictable insipidities. Miss Martin hesitated and then spoke what was obviously the truth.

"Not really," she said. "Well, actually, not at all."

She offered no explanation but regarded him almost ferociously. With her neat cotton dress and hair dressed severely beneath her hat, she could easily be mistaken for the housekeeper—or
for the headmistress of a girls' school.

Honesty in polite conversation was rare in ladies—or gentlemen, for that matter. No one could admit to being discontented
without seeming ill-mannered.

"I suppose," he said, "that when you are in your usual milieu
at your school no one ever imposes social obligations upon you
or bullies you into enjoying yourself. I suppose you usually have
a great deal of freedom and independence."

"And you do not?" she asked him, raising her eyebrows.

"Quite the contrary," he told her. "When one is in possession
of a title, even if it *is* only a courtesy title, one is under an obligation to be available to help fill every ballroom or drawing room
or garden to which one is invited during the Season so that the
hostess will be able to claim that it was a veritable squeeze and
thus be the envy of all her acquaintances. And one is obliged to
be courteous and sociable to all and sundry."

"Am I *all*?" she asked him. "Or am I *sundry*?"

He chuckled. He had seen flashes of her dry humor before
and rather liked it.

She was looking steadily at him, the light from the water
dancing in patterns across one side of her face.

"And that is *all* you do?" she asked him without waiting for
a reply. "Attend parties and make yourself agreeable because
your rank and society demand it of you?"

He thought of the time he spent with Lizzie, more than ever
since Christmas, and felt the now-familiar heaviness of heart. He
would have introduced a new topic of conversation then, one he
certainly *meant* to raise with her before she returned to Bath, but
she spoke again before he had found the right words.

"You do not sit in the House of Lords?" she asked. "But no,
of course you do not. Yours is a courtesy title."

"I am a duke in waiting," he told her, smiling. "And I would prefer to keep it that way, given the alternative."

"Yes," she said, "it is not a happy thing to lose a parent. It leaves a great yawning, empty hole in one's life."

Her father's death had disinherited her, he realized, whereas the opposite would happen in his case. But when all was said and done, a human life mattered more than any fortune. Especially when it was the life of a loved one.

"Family always matters more than anything else," he told her.

"I thought I would enjoy a couple of weeks here with Susanna and Frances," Miss Martin said with a sigh as she turned her face to look across the water. "And indeed it has been lovely to see them. But being with them means also being at events like this. Now I think I would like to return to Bath as soon as I may. My life is lived in a very different world than this."

"And you would prefer your own," he said. "I cannot blame you. But in the meanwhile, Miss Martin, allow me to do what I do best. Allow me to entertain you. I see that there is no one in line for the boats at the moment. And it appears that Crawford and Miss Meeghan are on their way in. Shall we take their boat?"

"On the *water*?" she asked, her eyes widening.

"The boat is small," he said. "I suppose we *could* hoist it up over our heads and run about the garden with it. But our fellow guests might think us eccentric, and I for one have to associate with them in the future."

She dissolved into mirth, and he regarded her with a smile. How often did she laugh? He guessed that it was not often enough. But it certainly ought to be. It was as if a whole suit of armor was shed from her person when she did so.

"It *was* a foolish question to ask," she admitted. "I should love a boat ride of all things. Thank you."

He offered her his arm and she took it.

She sat with rigidly straight back and severe demeanor after he had handed her into the boat as if she felt she had to atone for her earlier laughter and ardor. She did not move a muscle while he rowed out into the center of the river and then along it, passing by other grand mansions with lavish gardens and willow trees draping their greenery over the water. She kept her hands in her lap, cupped one on top of the other. She did not have a parasol as most of the other ladies did. But her straw hat was wide-brimmed and shaded her face and neck from too much exposure to the sun. The hat had seen better days, but it was not unbecoming.

"Do you go boating in Bath?" he asked her.

"Never," she said. "We used to go boating when I was a girl, but that was a long, long time ago."

He smiled at her. Not many ladies would have added that extra *long* to imply an advanced age. But she seemed to be a woman without vanity.

"This is heavenly," she said after a minute or two of silence—though she still looked like a teacher keeping a watchful eye upon her students as they worked. "Absolutely heavenly."

He remembered something she had said last evening—*A long time ago. A lifetime ago.* She had been speaking of her acquaintance with McLeith.

"Did you grow up in Scotland?" he asked her.

"No, in Nottinghamshire," she said. "Why do you ask?"

"I thought perhaps you grew up in the same neighborhood as McLeith," he said.

"I did," she told him. "In the same house actually. He was my father's ward after losing his parents when he was five. I was very fond of him. He lived with us until he was eighteen, when he inherited his title quite unexpectedly from a relative he hardly even knew of."

She had been fond of him and yet had avoided his company last evening?

"That must have been a pleasant surprise for him," he said.

"Yes," she agreed. "Very."

Pleasant for McLeith, he guessed. Not necessarily for her. She had lost a lifelong friend. Or had she had tender feelings for the man? He was at the garden party. He had arrived late, but Joseph had seen him just before he strolled down to the river. McLeith had been talking with the Whitleafs. He wondered if he ought to tell her but decided against it. He did not want to spoil her enjoyment of the boat ride. And she must be enjoying it. She had called it heavenly.

What a disciplined, restrained woman she was. And yet again he thought of the image of armor. Was there a woman behind the armor? A woman of warmth and tenderness and perhaps even passion? Yet he already knew that she possessed at least the first two.

But *passion*?

It was an intriguing possibility.

She lifted one hand away from the other after a while, slipped off her glove, and touched her fingers to the water. Then she trailed them through it, her head turned to the side, all her concentration upon what she did.

He found the picture she presented curiously touching. She looked lost in her own world. She looked somehow lonely. And even though she lived at a school surrounded by schoolgirls and other teachers, he supposed it was altogether possible that she *was* lonely. The Countess of Edgecombe and Viscountess Whitleaf were her friends, but they had married and left both her staff and Bath.

"I suppose," he said at last, surprised by the reluctance he felt, "we had better turn back. Unless, that is, you would like to row past the city down to Greenwich and on out to sea."

"And away to the Orient," she said, looking up at him as she brought her hand back inside the boat, "or to America. Or simply to Denmark or France. To have an *adventure*. Have you ever had an adventure, Lord Attingsborough?"

He laughed and so did she.

"I suppose," she said, "the adventure would not seem such a magical thing when night came on and I remembered that I do not have my shawl with me and you developed blisters on your hands."

"How very unromantic of you," he said. "We will have to save the adventure for another time, then, when we can make more sensible plans. Though romance does not always have to be sensible."

The sun shaded her face less efficiently as he turned the boat in the middle of the river. Somehow their eyes met and locked and held before she looked away rather jerkily and *he* looked away just a moment later.

There was a curiously charged feeling to the air around them.

He was almost certain she had been blushing as she looked away.

Good Lord, what had *that* been all about?

But it was a redundant question. It had been a moment of pure sexual awareness—on both their parts.

He could not have been more astonished if she had stood up and executed a swallow dive into the river.

Good Lord!

By the time he looked back at her, she had donned full armor again. She was stiff and stern and tight-lipped.

He rowed the rest of the way back to the jetty in a silence she did not attempt to break and he could not think of a way of breaking. Strange, that—he was normally quite adept at making small talk. He tried to persuade himself that nothing untoward had happened after all—as indeed nothing had. He hoped fervently that she was not feeling as uncomfortable as he.

But, good Lord, they had merely been sharing a joke.

. . . *romance does not always have to be sensible.*

His sister was standing on the riverbank close to the jetty, he could see as the boat drew closer. So were Sutton and Portia Hunt. He had never been more glad to see them. They gave him a way of breaking the silence without awkwardness.

"You have discovered the best part of the garden, have you?" he called cheerfully as he tied up the boat, stepped out onto the jetty, and handed Miss Martin out.

"The river is picturesque," Wilma said. "But both Miss Hunt and I are agreed that Mrs. Corbette-Hythe's gardener has been remiss in not having planted some flower beds here."

"May I present Miss Martin?" he said. "She is owner and

headmistress of a girls' school in Bath and is staying with Viscount Whitleaf and his wife for a short while. My sister, the Countess of Sutton, Miss Martin, and Miss Hunt and the earl."

Miss Martin curtsied. Wilma and Miss Hunt favored her with identical gracious nods, while Sutton, not to be outdone in cold civility, inclined his head just sufficiently to indicate that he did not choose to insult his brother-in-law.

The temperature must have dropped at least five degrees within the minute.

Wilma and Sutton would not enjoy being introduced to a mere schoolteacher, Joseph thought with what would have been wry amusement if he had not been concerned for the lady's feelings. She could hardly fail to notice the frostiness of her reception.

But she took matters into her own hands, as he might have expected she would.

"Thank you, Lord Attingsborough," she said briskly, "for rowing me on the river. It was very obliging of you. I will go and join my friends now if you will excuse me."

And she strode off in the direction of the house without a backward glance.

"*Really!*" Wilma said when she was scarcely out of earshot. "A schoolteacher, Joseph! I suppose she hinted that she would like to go out on the river, and you could not bring yourself to deny her the treat. But you really ought to have done so, you know. Sometimes you are just too good-natured. You are easily imposed upon."

It often amazed Joseph that he and Wilma could have been born of the same parents and raised in the same home.

"I escorted Miss Martin up from Bath last week when I came back to town," he said. "I did it as a favor to Lady Whitleaf, who used to teach at her school."

"Yes, well," she said, "we all know that Viscount Whitleaf married beneath him."

He was not about to wrangle with his sister at a garden party. He turned to Portia Hunt instead.

"Would you care for a turn on the river, Miss Hunt?" he asked her.

"Yes, I would, Lord Attingsborough," she said, smiling and allowing him to hand her into the boat. She raised a white lacy parasol above her head, angled just so to shield her complexion from the sun.

"It was extremely kind of you," she said after he had pushed off, "to bring that teacher out here. It is to be hoped that she is properly grateful, though to her credit she *did* thank you."

"I enjoyed Miss Martin's company," he said. "She is an intelligent woman. And a very successful one."

"Poor lady," she said as if he had just told her that Miss Martin was dying of some incurable disease. "Lady Sutton and I were speculating about her age. Lady Sutton declares that she must be on the wrong side of forty, but I could not be so cruel. I believe she must be a year or two under that age."

"I think you are probably right," he said, "though one can hardly be blamed for one's age whatever it is, can one? And Miss Martin has much to show for the years she has lived, however many they are."

"Oh, absolutely," she said, "though having to *work* for a living must be unpleasantly demeaning, would you not agree?"

"Demeaning, no," he said. "Never. Tedious, possibly, especially if one has to take employment at something one does not enjoy. Miss Martin enjoys teaching."

"Is this not a delightful garden party?" she said, twirling her parasol.

"Indeed it is," he agreed, smiling at her. "Was the soiree enjoyable last evening? I am sorry I had to miss it."

"The conversation was very agreeable," she said.

He tipped his head to one side as he rowed. "Am I forgiven, then?" he asked.

"Forgiven?" Her eyes widened and she twirled her parasol once more. "Whatever for, Lord Attingsborough?"

"For going to the Whitleafs' concert instead of the soiree," he said.

"You may do whatever you wish in life and go wherever you please," she told him. "I would not presume to question your decisions even if I had some right to do so."

"That is kind of you," he said. "But I assure you I would never demand so compliant a companion. Two people, however close they are, ought to be able to express displeasure openly with each other when provoked."

"And I assure *you,* my lord," she said, "that I would never dream of expressing displeasure with anything a gentleman chose to do—if that gentleman had some claim to my loyalty and obedience."

Of course, there was more than one way of expressing displeasure. There was open, forthright speech, or there was something altogether more subtle—like introducing the topic of bonnets into the conversation when the only man present was the one to whom one owed loyalty and obedience. Not that Miss Hunt owed him anything yet.

"The weather is almost perfect for a garden party," she said, "though it is perhaps a little on the hot side."

"But heat is preferable to rain," he said, his eyes twinkling.

"Oh, absolutely," she agreed. "But I do think some clouds and some sunshine in equal measure make for the perfect summer day."

They fell into an easy conversation in which there was not a moment's silence though nothing of any significance was said. That last fact did not particularly concern him. It was no different from a dozen conversations he held with various people every day. Not all persons could be Miss Martin, after all.

Miss Hunt looked even more lovely out here on the river, the white of her apparel and the delicacy of her complexion in marked contrast with the deep green of the water. He found himself wondering—as he had with Miss Martin—if there was any passion underlying the inbred elegance and refinement of her manner.

He certainly hoped so.

Claudia strode up the sloping lower lawn until the flower gardens and the terrace came into view again. Then she changed direction and headed toward the orchestra. She needed to calm herself before joining her friends. Her body and mind were seething with unfamiliar, and quite unwelcome, emotions and sensations. She felt like a girl again, totally out of control of her own normally tranquil center.

She ought not to have agreed to the boat ride. She actually enjoyed conversing with the Marquess of Attingsborough. He seemed to be an intelligent man, even if he *did* live an essentially idle existence. But he also happened to be easily the most attractive man she had ever encountered—not to mention handsome— and from the start she had been aware of the dangers of his practiced charm. Except that she had been aware of them on Flora and Edna's behalf during the journey, assuming herself to be immune.

Oh, but she *had* enjoyed the boat ride—both the exhilaration of being on the water and actually running her fingers through it and the pleasure of being rowed by a personable man. She had even indulged in a little romantic daydreaming if the truth were known. There she was on a warm summer afternoon boating on the River Thames with a gentleman with whom she had shared laughter both last evening and this morning. She had consciously liked him.

Until he had spoken those words.

. . . *romance does not always have to be sensible.*

She *knew* he had meant nothing by them. She *knew* he had not been flirting with her. But suddenly fantasy had not remained buried deep in her thoughts but had obviously shown openly on her face for a fraction of a moment—but quite long enough for him to notice.

How horribly, utterly humiliating!

She looked around for a seat on which to relax while listening to the music but, seeing none, she stood on the lawn close to the rose arbor instead.

And if she had not been feeling raw enough with embarrassment—for his silence during the return to shore had clearly indicated that he *had* noticed—there had been that introduction to the Earl and Countess of Sutton and Miss Hunt.

She bristled at the memory. They had behaved just *exactly* the way she always expected the aristocracy to behave. Nasty, superior lot! Yet all three of them probably had nothing but fluff between their ears. And money to burn. She despised herself more than she did them for allowing herself to be upset by them.

She applauded politely with a few other guests as the orchestra finished playing one piece and arranged its music for the next.

And then Claudia smiled despite herself. The very ferocity of her indignation amused her. All three of them had appeared to be sniffing the air as if they smelled something nasty. But really they had done her no harm at all. They had done her a favor if anything. They had given her an excuse for getting away from the Marquess of Attingsborough. She had certainly been in need of one. Indeed, she would still be quite happy to dig a hole in the lawn at her feet and stick her head in if someone would just offer her a shovel. Instead, she headed for the rose arbor.

She fervently hoped she would never see the Marquess of Attingsborough ever again.

Some holiday *this* was turning into!

7

"Claudia!"

Even before she reached the rose arbor Claudia heard the sound of her name being called and turned her head to see Susanna hurrying toward her from the direction of the terrace. Peter was some distance behind with Viscount and Viscountess Ravensberg—and Charlie.

"Wherever have you been?" Susanna asked as she came closer. "We have been looking for you. Frances was feeling tired and Lucius has taken her home."

"Ah. I am sorry to have missed saying farewell to them," Claudia said. "I have been down by the river."

"Have you been having a good time?" Susanna asked.

"It is beautiful down there," Claudia replied. She hesitated. "I have actually been *on* the river. The Marquess of Attingsborough was obliging enough to take me out in one of the boats."

"How good of him," Susanna said. "He is an amiable and charming gentleman, is he not? He deserves the very best out of life. I am not sure he will have it with Miss Hunt."

"Miss Hunt?" Claudia asked, remembering the haughty, beautiful lady dressed all in white who had treated her with such icy civility a short while ago.

Susanna pulled a face.

"She is *the* Miss Hunt," she said, and when Claudia looked blankly at her she explained. "Miss *Portia* Hunt. The one Lucius almost married instead of Frances. And now Lauren tells me that Joseph is to marry her. Of course, they *do* make a handsome couple."

They did, Claudia agreed. Oh, goodness, indeed they did. She felt somehow foolish as if everyone within sight of her would realize what silly daydreams she had indulged in while out on the river. Miss Claudia Martin was not usually given to daydreams, especially silly ones—and more especially *romantic* ones.

"But Claudia," Susanna continued, smiling warmly as the rest of her group came up to them, "we have been having a long talk with the Duke of McLeith, and he has been telling us that you grew up together almost like brother and sister."

They were all smiling, obviously happy for her. Charlie was beaming.

"Claudia," he said, "we meet again."

"Good afternoon, Charlie," she said. *Brother and sister,* indeed!

"How wonderful that you should meet again now," Lady Ravensberg said, "when you have not been in England for years, your grace, and Miss Martin has come to town for just a week or two."

"I can scarcely believe my good fortune," Charlie said.

"Kit and I are organizing a party to Vauxhall Gardens the evening after tomorrow," the viscountess continued. "We would be delighted if the two of you could join us. Susanna and Peter have already said yes. Will you come too, Miss Martin?"

Vauxhall Gardens! It was one place Claudia had always wanted to see. It was famous for its outdoor evening entertainments, with concerts and dancing and fireworks and fine food and lantern-lit pathways and alleys to stroll along. It was said to be a magical and unforgettable experience.

"I would love to," she said. "Thank you."

"And your grace?"

"You are most kind," he said. "I shall be delighted."

Claudia felt less shock at seeing him today. It was almost inevitable that they meet again, she had realized this morning when she woke up. And perhaps it was just as well it had happened. The long-ago past had never been quite exorcised. Perhaps now it would be and she could let go of the memories at last.

"Oh, lovely!" Lady Ravensberg said. "Our party is complete, then, Kit. Elizabeth and Lyndon will be coming and Joseph and Miss Hunt and Lily and Neville. Oh, and Wilma and George too."

Lovely indeed, Claudia thought with heavy irony. And so she would see him again after all—*him* being the Marquess of Attingsborough. Well, she would just have to frown and look stern and make him believe that he must have been mistaken out there on the river. And those last two people the viscountess had named must be the Earl and Countess of Sutton. She really had walked into the fire with her enthusiastic acceptance of her invitation, but it was too late now to withdraw it.

Besides, she wanted very much to see Vauxhall Gardens, and why should she *not* go? She would have friends there.

"Claudia," Charlie said, "would you care to take a stroll with me?"

Everyone else beamed happily at them as they moved away from the group, weaved their way among other guests, a few of whom greeted him as they passed, and headed in the general direction of the river.

"You live in Bath, Claudia?" he asked, offering his arm, though she did not take it.

He knew nothing about her, then? But she knew nothing about him either, did she? Not anything that had happened to him since her father's death, anyway.

"Yes," she said. "I own and run a girls' school there. It is quite successful. All my dreams have come true, in fact. I am very happy."

And how was *that* for a defensive answer to his question?

"A school!" he said. "Well done, Claudia. I thought you were a governess."

"I was for a short while," she said. "But then I took a chance on opening my own establishment so that I could enjoy more independence."

"I was surprised when I heard that you had taken employment at all," he said. "I thought you would marry. You had any number of admirers and would-be suitors, as I remember."

She felt a flash of anger as they started down the long slope. But there was some truth in his words. Even apart from her modest dowry, she had been a pretty enough girl, and there had been something in her nature that had attracted attention from the young men of the neighborhood. But she had had eyes for none of them, and after Charlie left—or at least after the last letter he wrote her less than a year later—she had renounced the very thought of marrying. Her decision had caused her father some pain—she knew that. He would have liked grandchildren.

"Did you know that Mona had died?" Charlie asked.

"Mona?" she said a fraction of a second before she realized that he was speaking of his wife.

"The duchess," he said. "She died more than two years ago."

"I am sorry," she said. At one time that name had been written on her heart as if with a sharp instrument—Lady Mona Chesterton. He had married her just before Claudia's father died.

"You need not be," he said. "It was not a particularly happy marriage."

Claudia felt a renewed flash of anger on behalf of the dead duchess.

"Charles is at school in Edinburgh," he told her. "My son," he added when she turned her head to look at him. "He is fifteen."

Oh, goodness, only three years younger than Charlie had been when he left home. How time went by!

The Marquess of Attingsborough and Miss Hunt, she could see, were walking up the slope from the river. They would meet soon.

She wished suddenly that she had never left the tranquillity of her school. Though she half smiled at the thought. *Tranquillity?*

School life hardly offered that. But at least there she always felt more or less in control.

"I am sorry, Claudia," Charlie said. "You really do not know anything about my life, do you? Just as I know nothing of yours. How could we have grown so far apart? We were once as close as any brother and sister, were we not?"

She pressed her lips together. They *had* been like siblings once upon a very long time ago, it was true. But not toward the end.

"It was not your fault, though, that I left home never to return, was it?" he said. "Or mine either for that matter. It was the fault of circumstances. Who could have predicted that two men and one boy, none of whom I knew, would all die within four months of one another, leaving me with the title of McLeith and properties that went with it?"

He had been planning a career in law. She could remember how stunned he had been when the Scottish solicitor had arrived on her father's doorstep one afternoon—and then how consumed with excitement and happiness.

She had tried to be happy for and with him, but there had been a chill of apprehension too—one that had been fully justified as later developments had proved.

It was the fault of circumstances.

Perhaps he was right. He had been just a boy thrust into a world so different from the one in which he had grown up that it might have been a different universe. But there was no real excuse for cruelty no matter what the age of the perpetrator.

And he had certainly been cruel.

"We ought to have continued to write to each other after your father's passing," he said. "I have missed you, Claudia. I did not realize how much until I saw you again last evening."

Had he really forgotten? It was astounding—*we ought to have continued to write to each other* . . .

Miss Hunt was all gracious smiles as she approached on the marquess's arm, her eyes on Charlie. Claudia might have been invisible.

"Your grace," she called, "is this not a lovely party?"

"It has just," he said, smiling and bowing, "turned even love-lier, Miss Hunt."

Joseph found himself facing a dilemma. Miss Martin was walking with McLeith. Did she need rescuing again, as she had last evening? But why should he feel responsible for her today? She was no wilting violet of a woman. She was quite capable of extricating herself from McLeith's company if she wished.

Besides, he had been rather hoping not to encounter her again today. He had embarrassed himself earlier. He did not know quite what had come over him. She was looking severe and unap-proachable, the quintessential spinster schoolmistress again— certainly not the type of woman with whom he would expect to share a spark of sexual awareness.

Should he stop now to see if she showed any sign of distress about her companion? Or should he merely nod genially and pass by? But the matter was taken out of his hands. Portia, it seemed, had an acquaintance with the duke and hailed him as soon as they were close enough to be heard clearly.

"You flatter me, your grace," she said in reply to his lavish compliment. "The Marquess of Attingsborough and I have been on the river. It was very pleasant, though the breeze is a little too cool out there and the sun is glaring enough to damage the complexion."

"But not yours, Miss Hunt," the duke said. "Not even the sun has that much power."

Joseph meanwhile had caught Miss Martin's eye. He half raised his eyebrows and inclined his head slightly in the direction of McLeith—*do you need help?* Her eyes widened a fraction in return and she shook her head almost imperceptibly—*no, thank you.*

"You are too kind, your grace," Portia said. "We are on our way up to the terrace for tea. Have you eaten?"

"An hour or more ago," he said, "but I suddenly find myself ravenous again. Are you hungry, Claudia? And have you been introduced to Miss Hunt?"

"I have," she said. "And I have not eaten yet this afternoon though I am not hungry."

"You must come and eat now, then," Miss Hunt said, addressing herself to McLeith. "Are you enjoying being in England again, your grace?"

And then all four of them were walking in the direction of the house, though they had somehow changed partners. Miss Hunt was slightly ahead with McLeith while Joseph fell behind with Miss Martin.

He clasped his hands behind his back and cleared his throat. He was *not* going to allow an uncomfortable silence to descend upon them again.

"I forgot to ask when I spoke with you earlier," he said, "if you had spoken with Miss Bains and Miss Wood yet."

"I have," she said, "and, as you suspected, they were ecstatic. They can scarcely wait for tomorrow to come so that they can present themselves for interviews. They paid not the slightest attention to my warnings. They showed me, in fact, that my teachings have been altogether successful. They can think for themselves and make their own decisions. I should be ecstatic too."

He chuckled even as Miss Hunt tittered lightly at something McLeith had said. The two of them were walking faster than he and Miss Martin.

"You will go with them to the interviews?" he asked.

"No." She sighed. "No, Lord Attingsborough. A teacher— just like a mother—must learn when to let her charges go to make their own way in the world. I would never abandon any of my charity girls, but neither would I keep them in leading strings all their lives. Though I was prepared to do just that this morning, was I not?"

The other two had moved far enough ahead by now that he could speak without fear of being overheard.

"*Did* you need rescuing just now?" he asked.

"Oh, not really," she said. "I did not last evening either, but then there was the shock of seeing him so suddenly after so many years."

"You parted on bad terms?" he asked.

"We parted on the best of terms." They had stepped onto one of the paved paths through the parterre gardens and slowed their steps by unspoken consent until they stopped walking altogether. "We were betrothed. Oh, unofficially, it is true—he was eighteen and I was seventeen. But we were in love, as perhaps only the very young can be. He was going to come back for me."

"But he never did." He looked down at her, trying to see the romantic girl she must have been and imagining by what slow stages she had grown into the severe, disciplined woman she was today—most of the time anyway.

"No," she said. "He never came. But that is all very ancient history. We were children. And how we can exaggerate or even distort events in memory! He remembers only that we grew up with the closeness of brother and sister, and he is quite right. We were friends and playmates for years before we imagined ourselves in love. Perhaps I have exaggerated those events and emotions in my memory. However it is, I have no reason to avoid him now."

And yet, he thought, McLeith had ruined her life. She had never married. Though who was he to make that judgment? She had done good things with her life instead. And perhaps a marriage to McLeith would not have turned out half so well for her.

"Have *you* ever been in love, Lord Attingsborough?" she asked.

"Yes," he said. "Once. A long time ago."

She looked steadily at him.

"But it did not work out?" she asked. "*She* did not love *you*?"

"I believe she did," he said. "Indeed, I know she did. But I would not marry her. I had other commitments. Finally she must have understood. She married someone else and now has three children and is—I hope—living happily ever after."

Beautiful, sweet-natured Barbara. He no longer loved her, though he felt a residual tenderness whenever he set eyes upon her, which was often enough since they moved in much the same circles. And sometimes, even now, he thought he caught a look of wounded puzzlement in her eyes when she looked at him. He had never given her a reason for his apparently cooled ardor. He still did not know if he ought to have. But how could he have explained the advent of Lizzie in his life?

"Other commitments?" Miss Martin asked. "More important than love?"

"*Nothing* is more important than love," he said. "But there are different kinds and degrees of love, and sometimes there are conflicts and one has to choose the greater love—or the greater obligation. If one is fortunate, they are one and the same."

"And were they in your case?" she asked, frowning.

"Oh, yes," he said.

She looked around suddenly at the gardens and the milling guests as if she had forgotten where she was.

"I do beg your pardon," she said. "I am keeping you from tea. I really am not hungry. I believe I will go to the rose arbor. I have not seen it yet."

It was his chance for escape. But he found he no longer wished to get away from her.

"I will come with you if I may," he said.

"But is your place not with Miss Hunt?" she asked him.

"Should it be?" He raised his eyebrows and leaned a little closer to her.

"Are you not to marry her?" she asked.

"Ah," he said, "news travels on the wind. But we do not need to live in each other's shadow, Miss Martin. That is not the way polite society works."

She looked across the formal gardens and up to the terrace, where McLeith and Portia Hunt were standing at one of the food tables, plates in hand.

"Polite society is often a mystery to me," she said. "Why would one choose not to spend as much time as one can with a loved one? But please do not answer." She looked back into his eyes and held up one hand, palm out. "I do not believe I wish to hear that you gave up on love years ago and are now prepared to marry without it."

She was startlingly forthright. He ought to have been angry with her. He was amused instead.

"Marriage," he said, "is another of those obligations of rank. One dreams as a very young man of having both—love and marriage. As one grows older one becomes more practical. It is wise to marry a woman of one's own rank, of one's own world. It makes life so much easier."

"That," she said, "is exactly what Charlie did." She shook her head as if astonished that she had made such an admission aloud. "I am going to the rose arbor. You may come with me if you wish. Or you may rejoin Miss Hunt. You must not feel in any way responsible for keeping me company."

"No, Miss Martin." He set his head to one side as he regarded her with eyes squinted against the sun. "I know you are perfectly capable of looking after yourself. But I have not yet seen the rose arbor, and I believe I have more of an appetite for roses than for food. *May* I accompany you?"

Her lips quirked at the corners, and then she smiled outright before turning and walking diagonally across the parterres in the direction of the rose arbor.

That was where they spent the remaining half hour of the garden party, looking at the roses, a bloom at a time, dipping their heads to smell some of them, exchanging greetings with acquaintances—at least, *he* did—and finally sitting on a wrought-iron seat beneath an arch of roses, gazing about at all the beauty and breathing in the fragrant air and listening to the music and speaking very little.

It was possible to sit silently with Miss Martin now that the discomfort he had felt out on the river had disappeared. With almost anyone else he would have felt obliged to keep a conversation going. Even with Miss Hunt. He wondered if it would always be so or if marriage would bring them enough contentment in each other's company that they could be satisfied with a shared silence.

"Silence," he said at last, "is not the absence of everything, is it? It is something very definite in its own right."

"If it were *not* a very definite something," she said, "we would not so assiduously avoid it through much of our lives. We tell ourselves that we are afraid of darkness, of the void, of silence, but it is of ourselves that we are afraid."

He turned his head to look at her. She was sitting with straight spine, not quite touching the back of the seat, her feet side by side on the ground, her hands resting palm up, one on top of the other, in her lap—a growingly familiar pose. The slightly floppy brim of her hat did not quite hide the rather severe lines of her face in profile.

"That sounds bad," he said. "Are we such nasty creatures at heart, then?"

"Not at all," she said. "Quite the contrary, in fact. If we were to see the grandeur of our real selves, I suspect we would also see the necessity of living up to who we really are. And most of us are too lazy for that. Or else we are having too good a time enjoying our less than perfect lives to be bothered."

She turned her face to his when he did not answer.

"You believe in the essential goodness of human nature, then," he said. "You are an optimist."

"Oh, always," she agreed. "How could life be supported if one were not? There is a great deal to feel gloomy about— enough to fill a lifetime to the brim. But what a waste of a lifetime! There is at least as much to be happy about, and there is so much joy to be experienced in working toward happiness."

"And so silence and . . . darkness hold happiness and joy?" he said softly.

"Assuredly," she said, "provided one really listens to the silence and gazes deeply into the darkness. Everything is there. *Everything.*"

He made a sudden decision. Ever since deciding to call upon

her in Bath, and especially since being shown around her school and talking with her on the road to London, he had been meaning to take matters further with her. Now was as good a time as any.

"Miss Martin," he said, "do you have any plans for tomorrow? In the afternoon?"

Her eyes widened as she continued to look at him.

"I do not know what Susanna has planned," she said. "Why do you ask?"

"I would like to take you somewhere," he said.

She looked at him inquiringly.

"I own a house in town," he said. "It is not my place of residence, though it is on a quiet, respectable street. It is where—"

"*Lord Attingsborough,*" she said in a voice that must surely have even the most intrepid of her pupils quaking in her shoes whenever she used it in school, "where *exactly* are you suggesting that you take me?"

Oh, Lord! As if...

"I am not—" he began.

She had inhaled sharply while he spoke the three words, and her bosom had swelled. She looked forbidding to say the least.

"Do I understand, sir," she said, "that this *house* is where you keep your *mistresses*?"

Plural. Like a harem.

He leaned back in the seat, resisting the sudden urge to bellow with laughter. How could he possibly have been so gauche as to give rise to such a misunderstanding? His choice of words today was proving quite disastrous.

"I must confess," he said, "that the house was bought for just that purpose, Miss Martin. It was years ago. I was a swaggering young sprout at the time."

"And *this,*" she said, "is where you wish to take *me*?"

"It is not unoccupied," he told her. "I want you to meet the person who lives there."

"Your *mistress*?"

She was the very picture of quivering outrage. And part of him was still amused at the misunderstanding. But really this was no joke.

Ah, this was not funny at all.

"Not my mistress, Miss Martin," he said softly, his smile fading. "Lizzie is my *daughter*. She is eleven years old. I would like you to meet her. Will you? Please?"

8

Claudia gave herself one more look-over in the pier glass in her dressing room and drew on her gloves as she turned toward the door. She felt rather self-conscious because Susanna was standing there.

"I am sorry," she said briskly, not for the first time, "that I will be unable to come visiting with you this afternoon, Susanna."

"No, you are not." Her friend was smiling impishly. "You would much rather go driving in the park with Joseph. I would in your place. And today is as sunny and warm as yesterday."

"It was very kind of him to offer," Claudia said.

"*Kind.*" Susanna tilted her head to one side and regarded her closely. "It is what you said at breakfast, and I objected to it then, as I do now. Why should he *not* take you for a drive? He must be close to you in age and he enjoys your company. He proved that the evening before last when he sat beside you at the concert and took you in for supper before Peter could find you to bring you to our table. And yesterday he walked you home from Mr. Hatchard's and then took you out on the river during the garden party and was sitting in the rose arbor with you when we came looking for you to bring you home. You must not talk of his interest as mere kindness, Claudia. It belittles you."

"Oh, very well, then," Claudia said. "I daresay he has conceived a violent passion for me and is about to beg me to become his marchioness. I might end up a duchess yet, Susanna. Now *there* is a thought."

Susanna laughed.

"I would rather see him marry you than Miss Hunt," she said. "His engagement has not yet been announced, and there is something about her I do not like though I cannot explain quite what it is. But I hear sounds downstairs. Joseph must have arrived."

He had indeed. He was standing in the hall when Claudia went down with Susanna, talking with Peter. He smiled up at them in greeting.

He was, of course, looking as handsome as ever and alarmingly virile in a dark green coat with buff pantaloons and white-topped Hessian boots. At least his colors coordinated with hers, Claudia thought wryly. She was wearing the third and last of her new dresses—a sage green walking dress that she had thought very smart when she bought it. And really, what did it matter that she looked far less grand than anyone else she had met socially in the last few days? She did not *want* to look grand, only presentable.

He had brought a curricle instead of a closed carriage, she saw as soon as they stepped outside the door a couple of minutes later, Susanna and Peter coming too to see them on their way. He handed her up to the passenger seat and climbed up to sit beside her before taking the ribbons from his young tiger, who then proceeded to jump up behind them.

Despite herself Claudia felt a rush of exhilaration. Here she was in London, staying at a grand house in Mayfair, and riding in a gentleman's curricle with the gentleman up beside her. Their shoulders were, in fact, all but touching. And she could smell his cologne again. She did not need to remind herself, of course, that this was no mere pleasure trip but that he was, in fact, taking her to meet his daughter—his *illegitimate* daughter, the offspring, no doubt, of one of his mistresses. Lila Walton must have been right on that visit of his to the school. He had a daughter he wished to place there.

And the nature of his interest in her was now quite apparent. So much for romantic daydreams.

She was not really shocked at the revelation he had made yesterday. She was well aware that gentlemen had their mistresses and that sometimes those mistresses, as was nature's way, bore them children. If the mistresses and their children were fortunate, the gentlemen also supported them. The Marquess of Attingsborough must be of that number, she was happy to know. His mistress and daughter were living comfortably in a house he had bought years ago. And if he chose to send the girl to her school, well . . . She did not doubt he could afford her fees.

Yet despite the existence of a longtime mistress and mother of his child, he was courting Miss Hunt. It was the way of the world, Claudia knew, at least of his world. He needed a wife and legitimate heirs, and a man did not marry his mistress.

She was *very* glad she did not move in his world. She far preferred her own.

She wondered how Miss Hunt would feel about the existence of the woman and child if she knew about them. But then it was altogether possible that she did.

Claudia waved to Susanna and Peter as the curricle rocked into motion, and then folded her hands in her lap as it made its way out of the square. She disdained clinging to the rail beside her. She was no coward, and she was determined to enjoy every moment of the novelty of bowling along through the streets of London in a smart open vehicle, looking down on the world from her high perch.

"You are very quiet today, Miss Martin," the marquess said after a few minutes had passed. "Have Miss Bains and Miss Wood been interviewed yet?"

"Yes," she said. "Both of them went this morning. And both were successful—in their own eyes anyway. Flora said that Lady Aidan was extremely kind to her and asked only a few questions before telling her all about Ringwood Manor in Oxfordshire and the people who live there and assuring her that she is bound to be happy there as she will be just like a member of the family. The last governess has recently married—as did the governess before her. Then Flora was taken to meet the children, whom she liked exceedingly well. She will be leaving for her new life tomorrow."

"And was Lady Hallmere as amiable to Miss Wood?" the marquess asked, turning his head to grin at her—goodness, but he was close.

He was turning the curricle into Hyde Park. Claudia had thought she was lying when she told Susanna that this was to be their destination. Perhaps it would turn out to be only a white lie.

"She asked Edna many questions," she told him, "both about herself and about the school. Poor Edna! She does not do well when she is being questioned, as you may remember. But Lady Hallmere surprised her by telling her that she remembered hearing about the burglary that killed Edna's parents and made an orphan of her. And although Edna said she was very haughty and intimidating, it was obvious that she admired the woman greatly. And Lord Hallmere was also present and was kind to her. She loved the children when she met them. And so Edna too will be leaving us tomorrow." She sighed audibly.

"They will be fine," the marquess assured her, turning his curricle onto an avenue that stretched ahead between rolling green lawns and ancient, shady trees. "You have given them a good home and a sound education, and now you have found them decent employment. It is up to them how they conduct the rest of their lives. I liked them both. They will be fine."

And he startled her by freeing one of his hands from the ribbons and reaching across to squeeze both her hands in her lap. She did not know whether to jump with alarm or bristle with indignation. She did neither. She carefully remembered the purpose of this drive.

"Is your mis— Is your daughter's mother expecting us?" she asked.

There had been no time yesterday for any real explanations. Even as he had told her that the person he wished her to visit— Lizzie—was his daughter, Susanna and Peter had been stepping into the rose arbor, looking for her.

"Sonia?" he said. "She died just before Christmas last year."

"Oh," Claudia said, "I am sorry."

"Thank you," he said. "It was a very sad and difficult time."

And so now he was left with the problem of an illegitimate daughter to provide for. His decision to send her to school, even though she was only eleven years old, was even more understandable. For the rest of her girlhood he would not have to worry about anything more than paying the school fees. And then he would probably find her a husband capable of supporting her for the rest of her life.

What had he said yesterday? She frowned slightly, trying to remember. And then she did.

Nothing *is more important than love.*

He had put emphasis on the first word. But she wondered if there had been any real conviction behind those words. Had his own daughter become an encumbrance, a nuisance, to him?

They did not linger in the park. Soon they were back out on the crowded streets of London again, and the sun began to feel uncomfortably hot. But finally they turned into quieter residential streets, clean and respectable though obviously not inhabited by the most fashionable set. They drew to a halt outside one particular house, and the tiger jumped down from behind and held the horses' heads while the marquess descended to the pavement, came around the curricle, and held up a hand to help Claudia alight.

"I hope," he said as he rapped on the door, "you will like her."

He sounded almost anxious.

He handed his hat and whip to the elderly and very respectable-looking manservant who answered the door.

"Take Miss Martin's things too, Smart," he said, "and let Miss Edwards know that I am here. How is Mrs. Smart's rheumatism today?"

"Better, thank you, my lord," the man said as he waited for Claudia to remove her gloves and bonnet. "But it always is in the dry weather."

He took their outdoor things away and came back a few minutes later to inform them that Miss Edwards was in the parlor with Miss Pickford. He turned and led the way upstairs.

Miss Edwards turned out to be a small, pretty, petulant-looking young lady, who was obviously too old to be Lizzie. She met them at the parlor door.

"She is not having a very good day today, I am afraid, my lord," she said, curtsying to the marquess and glancing sidelong at Claudia.

The room behind her was in semidarkness, all the heavy curtains being drawn across the windows. In the hearth a fire burned.

"Is she not?" the marquess said, but it seemed to Claudia that he sounded more impatient than concerned.

"Papa?" a voice said from inside the room. And then more gladly, filled with excitement, *"Papa?"*

Miss Edwards stood aside, her hands clasped at her waist.

"Stand and curtsy to the Marquess of Attingsborough, Lizzie," she said.

But the child was already on her feet, her arms held out toward the door. She was small and thin and pale, with dark hair waving loose down her back to her waist. Her face was alight with joy.

"Yes, I am here," the marquess said, and strode across the room to fold the child in his arms. She wrapped her own tightly about his neck.

"I *knew* you would come," she cried. "Miss Edwards said you would not because it is a sunny day and you would have a thousand things more important to do than coming to see me. But she always says that, and you always come when you say you will. Papa, you smell good. You *always* smell good."

"Especially for you," he said, untwining her arms from about his neck and kissing both her hands before releasing them. "Miss Edwards, why on earth is there a fire burning?"

"I was afraid that Lizzie would catch a chill after you took her out in the garden last evening, my lord," she said.

"And why the darkness?" he asked. "Is there not enough darkness in Lizzie's life?"

Even as he spoke he was striding over to the windows and throwing back the curtains to flood the room with light. He opened the windows wide.

"The sun was shining directly in, my lord," Miss Edwards said. "I wanted to protect the furniture from fading."

He looked at Claudia as he moved back to his daughter's side and set one arm about her shoulders.

"Lizzie," he said, "I have brought someone to meet you. She is Miss Martin, a friend of mine. Miss Martin, may I present my daughter, Lizzie Pickford?"

There was something strange about the child's eyes, Claudia had seen as soon as the curtains were drawn back. One was almost closed. The other was more open, though the eyelid fluttered, and the eye wandered beneath the lid.

Lizzie Pickford was *blind*. And if Claudia's guess was correct, she had been blind from birth.

"Lizzie," Miss Edwards said, "make your curtsy to Miss Martin."

"Thank you, Miss Edwards," Lord Attingsborough said. "You may take a break. You will not be needed for the next hour or so."

"Lizzie Pickford," Claudia said, walking closer to the child, taking her hot, thin little hand in her own and squeezing it before letting it go, "I am pleased to make your acquaintance."

"Miss Martin?" the girl said, turning her face to her father.

"I had the pleasure of visiting her last week when I was away from you for a while," he said, "and then of escorting her to London. She has a school in Bath. Would you like to offer Miss Martin a seat and me too since we are visiting you? My legs are aching from all the standing."

The girl chuckled, a light, childish sound.

"Oh, *silly* Papa," she said. "You did not walk here. You rode. In your curricle—there was more than one horse. I heard them. I told Miss Edwards that you had come, but she said she had heard

nothing and that I must not get my hopes up and become fever-
ish. You are *not* tired of standing. Or Miss Martin either. But I
am pleased you have come, and I hope you will stay forever and
ever until bedtime. Miss Martin, will you please sit? Papa, will
you? I will sit beside you."

She seated herself very close to him on a sofa while Claudia
sat as far from the dying fire as she was able. The child took his
hand in hers and laced their fingers. She rubbed her cheek against
his sleeve, just below his shoulder.

He smiled down at her with such tenderness that Claudia was
ashamed of what she had thought of him on the way here. He
very obviously *did* know a great deal about love.

"Miss Martin's school is just for girls," he told his daughter.
"It is a delightful place. They learn lots of things, like history and
mathematics and French. There is a music room full of instruments, and the girls have individual instruction. They sing and
have choirs. They knit."

And not a single one of them, Claudia thought, had ever been
blind. She remembered his asking if she had ever thought of taking in girls with handicaps. However did one teach a blind child?

"When I heard the violin that one time with you, Papa," the
child said, "Mother said there must never be one in this house as
the sound of it would give her the headache. And when I sing the
songs Mrs. Smart taught me, Miss Edwards says I give *her* the
headache."

"I think," he said, "Miss Edwards is beginning to give *me* the
migraines, Lizzie."

She laughed with glee.

"Shall I send her to work for someone else?" he asked.

"Yes," she said without hesitation. "Oh, yes, if you please,
Papa. Will *you* come to live with me instead this time?"

His eyes met Claudia's, and they looked suddenly bleak.

"I wish it were possible," he said, "but it is not. I come to see
you every day, though, when I am in London. How could I not
when you are my favorite person in the whole wide world? Shall

we be polite and include Miss Martin in this conversation since I have brought her just to meet you?"

The girl turned her face in Claudia's direction. She looked in dire need of air and sunshine and exercise.

"Do you read stories at your school, Miss Martin?" she asked politely.

"We do indeed," Claudia told her. "My girls learn to read as soon as they come there if they have not learned before, and they read many books during their years with me. They may choose among the numerous volumes we have in the library. A library is a place where there are shelves and shelves of books."

"So many stories all in one place," the child said. "Mother could not read me stories because she could not read though Papa told her many times that he would teach her if she wished. And Mrs. Smart does not read. Mr. Smart does, but he does not read to *me*. Miss Edwards does because it is one thing Papa told her she must do when she came here as my companion, but she does not choose interesting stories and she does not find them interesting. I can tell from the way she reads them. She has a flat voice. She makes me yawn."

"*I* read you stories, Lizzie," the marquess said.

"You do, Papa," she agreed, lifting her free hand and touching his face before patting it with her fingertips. "But sometimes you pretend to read when really you are making up your own stories. I can tell. But I don't mind. Indeed, I like those stories best. I tell stories too but only to my doll."

"If you told them to someone who could write," Claudia said, "then that someone could write them down for you and read them to you whenever you wished to hear your own story again."

The child laughed. "That would be funny," she said.

A plump, elderly woman entered the room then, carrying a large tray of tea and cakes.

"Mrs. Smart," Lizzie said, "I know it is you. This is Miss Martin. She is Papa's friend. She has a school and it has a library. Do you know what a library is?"

"You tell me, dearie," the servant said, smiling fondly at her after nodding politely to Claudia.

"It is a room full of books," Lizzie said. "Can you imagine?"

"They would not be much good to me, dearie," Mrs. Smart said, pouring the tea and handing around the cups. "Or you either."

She left the room.

"Lizzie," the marquess said after they had eaten some cakes, "do you think you would ever like to go to a school?"

"But who would take me, Papa?" she asked. "And who would bring me home?"

"It would be a school where you could stay," he said, "and be with other girls, though there would be holidays when you would come home and I would have you all to myself again."

She was silent for some time. Her lips moved, Claudia could see, though whether it was with trembling or silent words it was impossible to tell. And then she cast aside her empty plate and climbed hastily onto her father's lap and burrowed close to him, her face hidden against his shoulder.

He stared bleakly at Claudia.

"Miss Edwards said I was not to do this ever again," Lizzie said after a short while. "She said I was too old. She said it was unseemly. *Is* it, Papa? Am I too old to sit on your lap?"

But the child had no eyes, Claudia thought. The sense of touch must be far more important to her than it was to other children of her age.

"How could I bear it," he said, resting his cheek against her hair, "if you were ever too old to want my arms around you, Lizzie? As for sitting on my lap—I think it is quite unexceptionable until you turn twelve. That gives us five whole months longer. What does Miss Martin have to say on the subject?"

"Your father is absolutely right, Lizzie," Claudia said. "And I have a rule at my school. It is that no girl is ever forced to go there against her will. No matter how much her parents may wish for her to come and learn from me and my teachers and make friends with other girls, I will not allow her to set foot over the doorstep unless she has told me that yes, it is what she wants. Is that clear to you?"

Lizzie had half turned her head though she was still burrowed safely against her father like a much younger child.

"You have a nice voice," she said. "I can believe your voice. Sometimes I do not believe voices. I can always tell which ones to believe."

"Sweetheart," the marquess said, "I am going to take Miss Martin home now. Later, I am going to come back on my horse. I will take you out for a ride on him. Would you like that?"

"*Yes!*" She sat up, her face alight with joy again. "But Miss Edwards says—"

"Don't worry about what Miss Edwards says," he told her. "You have ridden up with me before and always been perfectly safe, have you not? I will have a word with her after I bring you home, and she will be gone by tomorrow, I daresay. Just be polite to her until then. Will you?"

"I will, Papa," she promised.

Claudia took her hand again before leaving. Despite the strange eyes, she could grow into something of a beauty if there was enough stimulation in her life to bring animation into her face even when her father was not with her—and if she was exposed to more fresh air and sunshine.

"I take it," Claudia said after she had been helped up to the seat of the curricle again and they were on their way back to Grosvenor Square, the tiger up behind, "that you wish to send Lizzie to my school."

"Is it possible?" he asked, his voice without any of its customary pleasant good humor. "Is *anything* possible for a blind child, Miss Martin? Help me, please. I love her so much it hurts."

Joseph felt more than a little foolish.
Help me, please. I love her so much it hurts.
By the time he turned his curricle back into Hyde Park, Miss Martin had still said nothing in response. They were the last

words that had been spoken between them. He felt the urge to spring his horses, to return her to Whitleaf's house as soon as he possibly could, and to be very careful not to run into her again while she was still in London.

He was unaccustomed to baring his soul to others, even to his closest friends—except perhaps Neville.

She broke the silence once they had left the busy streets behind.

"I have been wishing," she said, "that Anne Butler were still on my staff. She was always exceptionally good with girls who were in any way different from the norm. But I have just realized that *all* girls are different from the norm. In other words, the norm does not exist except in the minds of those who like tidy statistics."

He did not know how to answer her. He did not know if she expected an answer.

"I am not sure I can help you, Lord Attingsborough," she said.

"You will not take Lizzie, then?" he asked, his heart sinking with disappointment. "A blind child is uneducable?"

"I am quite sure Lizzie is capable of a great deal," she said. "And the challenge would certainly be interesting from my point of view. I am just not sure school would be best for *her*, though. She appears to be very dependent."

"Is that not all the more reason for her to go to school?" he asked.

And yet even as he argued the point his heart was breaking. How would Lizzie cope in a school setting, where she would have to fend for herself much of the time, where other girls might be unkind to her, where by the very nature of her handicap she would be excluded from all sorts of activities?

And how could he bear to let her go? She was just a *child*.

"She must be missing her mother terribly," Miss Martin said. "Are you sure she should go away to school so soon after losing her? I take in abandoned children, Lord Attingsborough. They are often much damaged—perhaps always, in fact."

Abandoned. Lizzie? Is that what he would be doing to her if he sent her to school? He sighed and drew the curricle to a halt. This particular part of the park was quiet and secluded.

"Shall we walk awhile?" he suggested.

He left the curricle and horses in the care of his tiger, who did not even try to hide his delight, and he walked beside Miss Martin along a narrow footpath, which wound its way through a copse of trees.

"Sonia was very young when I first employed her," he told her. "So was I, of course. She was a dancer—very lovely, very much in demand, very ambitious. She expected a life of glamour and wealth. She expected to bask in the admiration of a series of titled, powerful, wealthy men. She was a courtesan by choice, not necessity. She did not love me; I did not love her. Our arrangement had nothing to do with love."

"No," she said dryly, "I suppose it did not."

"I would not even have kept her longer than two or three months, I suppose," he said. "I was intent upon sowing some wild oats. But then along came Lizzie."

"I daresay," she said, "neither of you had even considered the possibility."

"The young," he said, "are often very ignorant and very foolish, Miss Martin, especially upon sexual matters."

He looked down at her, supposing he was shocking her. This was not, after all, the sort of conversation with which he usually regaled the ears of ladies. But he felt he owed her an honest explanation.

"Yes," she agreed, "they are."

"Sonia did not particularly enjoy motherhood," he said. "She hated having a blind child. At first she wanted to put her into an asylum. But I would not allow it. And if I was to insist that she be a mother, then I had to take on the responsibility of being a father—not difficult right from the first moment. Never difficult. And so we remained together until her death, Sonia and I. She found her life irksome though I gave her almost everything money could buy—and my loyalty too. I hired the Smarts, who took some of the burdens of being a parent off her shoulders when I could not be at the house and have been like kindly grandparents to Lizzie. Sonia did not have much idea how to entertain or educate or train a blind girl, though she was never actively cruel. Of course Lizzie was inconsolable when she died. And of course she misses her. I do myself."

"Lizzie needs a home more than a school," Miss Martin said.

"She *has* a home," he said sharply. But he knew what she meant. "It is not enough, though, is it? After Sonia's death I hired a companion for her. There have been three others since then. Miss Edwards is the latest. And this time I chose someone young and apparently sweet and eager to please. I thought her very youth would be good for Lizzie. But she is obviously not up to the task at all. Neither were the other three. Where can I find someone to be with my daughter at home and give her all she needs? The Smarts are too elderly to do it alone, and they are talking of retirement. Would one of your pupils do it, Miss Martin? It crossed my mind, I must confess, to offer the position to Miss Bains or Miss Wood if the employment for which they came here proved unsuitable."

They were about to step free of the copse of trees onto an open stretch of grass, where a number of people were strolling or sitting, enjoying the warm summer afternoon. They both stopped walking instead and stayed in the shade of an old oak tree, looking out into the bright sunshine.

"I do not know if any very young person would be up to the task," Miss Martin said. "And in London of all places. That child needs air and exercise, Lord Attingsborough. She needs the countryside. She needs a mother."

"Which is the one thing I can never give her," he said, and he could see from the look in her eye that she understood that even his marriage could not provide Lizzie with a mother. His daughter was illegitimate and must forever be kept apart from—and secret from—any legitimate family he might have in future.

Everything had been reasonably simple as long as Sonia was alive. He had known, of course, that his daughter was living a less than ideal existence, but her basic needs had always been provided and she had always had a home and security and affection from the Smarts—oh, and from Sonia too—and love in abundance from him.

"Anxiety has become my constant companion since Sonia's death, Miss Martin," he said. "I suppose it was there before that, but it is only since that I have faced the fact that Lizzie is growing up. A handicapped child can be pampered and protected and held on one's lap and within the circle of one's arms when she is very young. But what is to become of her as an adult? Will I be able to find her a husband who will be kind to her? I can shower her with wealth, of course, but what of her inner being? What will there be to sustain her or give her any happiness? What will happen to her when I die?"

Miss Martin set a hand on his arm, and he turned his head to look down at her, strangely comforted. Her intelligent gray eyes gazed steadily into his and without thinking he covered her hand with his own.

"Let me get to know Lizzie better, Lord Attingsborough," she said. "And let me think about the possibility of her attending my school. *May* I see her again?"

He realized suddenly and in some embarrassment that his eyes had filled with tears. He blinked them away.

"Tomorrow?" he said. "At the same time?"

"If the weather is still fine, perhaps we can take her out," she said, sliding her hand free of his arm. "Or are you reluctant to be seen with her?"

"We could take her for a picnic," he suggested, "to Richmond Park or Kew Gardens."

"I will leave that for you to decide," she said. "Does anyone know about your daughter?"

"Neville," he said. "The Earl of Kilbourne. He has met her and sometimes looks in on her when I am away, as I was in Bath recently. But basically a gentleman takes care of such matters himself. It is not something he talks about with his peers."

"And does Miss Hunt know?" she asked.

"Good Lord, no!"

"And yet," she said, "you are to marry her."

"That," he said, "is a recent development, Miss Martin. My father has been ill and now fancies—perhaps correctly—that his heart has been affected. Before summoning me to Bath he had Lord Balderston, Miss Hunt's father, as his guest, and the two of them concocted the marriage scheme. It makes sense. Miss Hunt and I are both single and of the same world. We have known each other for a few years and have always dealt well enough together. But until very recently I did not think actually of *courting* her. I was unable to think of courting anyone as long as Sonia lived. I believe in monogamous relationships even if the woman is but a mistress. Unfortunately, we grew apart over the years even though I believe we always remained fond of each other. Indeed, for the last two or three years of her life we did not even . . . Well, never mind."

He had discovered with some surprise that Sonia was unfaithful to him. And while he had felt unable to turn her out because of Lizzie, he had never again slept with her.

Miss Martin was no simpering miss.

"You have been celibate for more than two years, then?" she asked.

He chuckled despite himself.

"A lowering thing for a gentleman to admit, is it not?" he said.

"Not at all," she retorted. "I have been celibate far longer than that, Lord Attingsborough."

"Not all your life?" he asked, feeling somewhat as if he were in the middle of a bizarre dream. Was he really having this very improper conversation with Miss Claudia Martin of all people?

"No," she said softly after a short silence. "Not *all* my life."

Good Lord!

And of course his mind immediately framed the question—*who?*

And just as immediately came up with an answer.

McLeith?

Damn the man!

If it was true, he deserved to be hanged, drawn, and quartered. At the very least!

"Oh," she said suddenly, her eyes focusing upon something out in the sunshine while she turned instantly into the prim, outraged schoolteacher. "Oh, just look at that!"

And she strode out onto the wide expanse of grass and began to remonstrate with a working man who was at least three times her size because he had been beating a scrawny black and white dog, which was whining in fright and pain.

Joseph did not immediately go after her.

"You cowardly bully!" she said. It was interesting to hear that she did not yell, though her voice acquired power enough to be heard for some distance. "*Stop* that immediately."

"And 'o is going to stop me?" the man asked insolently as a few passersby paused to watch and listen.

Joseph took one step forward as the man raised his stick and brought it down on the dog's cringing back again—except that it stopped in midair, Miss Martin's hand beneath it.

"Your own conscience, it is to be hoped," she said. "Animals must be loved and fed if they are to give loyal service. They are not to be beaten and starved by brutish louts."

There was a faint cheer from the bystanders. Joseph grinned.

" 'Ere," the man said, "watch 'o you are calling brutish or I'll give you good reason. And p'raps *you* want to love and feed the good-for-nothing 'ound if you are so 'igh and mighty about it. 'E's useless to me."

"Ah," Miss Martin said. "So now you would add abandonment to your other sins, would you?"

He looked at her as if he would love nothing better than to plant her a facer—Joseph hurried closer—and then leered, displaying a fine mouthful of rotten teeth.

"Yeh," he said, stooping down suddenly to scoop the whimpering dog up in one hand and push him against her until her arms came beneath him to hold him. "Yeh, that's exactly wot I'm doing. Make sure you love and feed 'im, ma'am. And don't ha-bandon 'im and add to your sins."

He grinned in appreciation of his own wit and he went strid-ing off across the park to the mingled cheers of a few young blades and the murmured disapproval of other, more genteel by-standers.

"Well," Miss Martin said, turning toward Joseph, her hat slightly askew on her head, giving her a rakish air, "I seem to have acquired a dog. Whatever am I to do with him?"

"Take him home and bathe and feed him?" Joseph grinned. "He is a border collie but a very poor specimen of his breed, poor thing."

He also smelled.

"But I have no home to take him *to*," she said while the dog looked up at her and whined. "And even if I were in Bath I could not have a dog at the school. Oh, dear me. Is he not adorable?"

Joseph laughed aloud. The dog was anything but.

"I will house him in my stables if you wish," he said, "and look around for a permanent home for him."

"In a stable?" she said. "Oh, but he has been dreadfully mis-treated. One only has to look into his eyes to know that—even if one had not witnessed that shocking display of brutality. He needs company and he needs *love*. I will have to take him to Susanna's and hope that Peter will not toss both him and me out."

She laughed.

Ah, yes, he thought, she was capable of passion right enough—even if only passion for justice toward the downtrod-den.

They walked side by side back along the path to his curricle, and he felt suddenly cheerful again. She was not the sort of woman who would abandon even a dog in need or delegate the giving of tender care to someone else. Surely she would help Lizzie too—though she was under no obligation to do so, of course.

He took the dog from her arms and placed him in the hands of his astonished tiger while he helped her up onto the seat of his curricle again. Then he placed the dog in her lap and she cradled him safely with her skirt and her arms.

"Part of your dream has come true, I believe, ma'am," he said.

She looked at him with uncomprehending eyes for a moment and then laughed.

"Now all I need is the rustic cottage and the hollyhocks," she said.

He liked her laughter. It made him feel cheerful and hopeful.

"He was not a weakling, that brute," she said as Joseph took his place beside her and gathered the ribbons in his hands. "I will probably bear the welt of that stick across my palm for a good day or two. I would have screamed if I had been willing to give him the satisfaction."

"The devil!" Joseph exclaimed. "*Did* he hurt you? I ought to have blackened both his eyes."

"Oh, no, no," she said. "Violence is no answer to violence. It just breeds more."

"Miss Martin," he said, turning his head to grin at her yet again, "you are remarkable."

And really quite good-looking, he thought, with her cheeks flushed, her hat off-center, and her eyes glowing.

She laughed again.

"And sometimes," she said, "an impulsive fool. Though, goodness, I have not been that for years and years. Doggie, what is your name? I suppose I will have to give you a new one."

Joseph continued to grin at his horses' heads.

He was really quite charmed by her. There was certainly a great deal more to her than just the prim, stern schoolteacher.

Claudia had scarcely a moment for reflection from the minute of her return from the visit to Lizzie Pickford until the time came to go on a picnic the following afternoon.

She was busy for an hour or two bathing and grooming and feeding the collie, which was little more than a pup, reassuring him when he seemed frightened, and taking him out into the garden a few times to relieve himself. She left him with Edna and Flora while she and Susanna and Peter went to dine and spend the evening at Marshall House with Frances and Lucius, but he slept the night in her room—actually on her bed much of the time—and got her up early to go outside again. At least, she had discovered with some relief, he was house-trained. Susanna and Peter had been remarkably tolerant about the sudden invasion of their home by a scruffy dog, but they might have been less so of puddles on their carpets.

And this was the very morning Edna and Flora were to leave the house on Grosvenor Square to take up their new appointments. Bidding them farewell and waving them on their way in Peter's carriage, Edna tearful, Flora unusually quiet, was as emotionally wrenching as such occasions always were. This was Claudia's least favorite part of her job.

Then, just as she and Susanna were consoling themselves with a cup of tea, there was an unexpected visit from Frances, who came to tell them that she and Lucius had decided to leave for Barclay Court, their home in Somersetshire, the following morning so that she could get the rest she needed for the remainder of her confinement.

"But you *must* come to visit us afterward," she said. "Both of you must come for Easter—and Peter too, of course. We will entertain the three of you together."

"Why only three?" Susanna asked, her eyes dancing with mischief. "Why not four? Claudia is going out for a drive with Joseph, Marquess of Attingsborough, this afternoon, Frances, *for the second day in a row*. And they are both to be at Vauxhall Gardens this evening with Lauren and Kit's party. And did you know that the reason we could not find her at the garden party the day before yesterday was that she was out on the river with him?"

"Oh, famous!" Frances said, clapping her hands. "I have always thought the marquess a handsome and charming gentleman. I must confess I find it hard to understand his interest in Miss Hunt—a personal bias, I daresay. But Claudia, you simply *must* supplant her in his affections."

"But she cannot, Frances," Susanna said, her eyes wide. "It is out of the question. He will be a *duke* one day, and you know how Claudia feels about dukes."

Both of them laughed merrily while Claudia raised her eyebrows and stroked her hand over the back of the dog, who was curled up beside her, his head in her lap.

"I see you are having a great deal of enjoyment at my expense," she said, desperately hoping she could keep herself from blushing. "I hate to ruin your pleasure, but there is absolutely no romantic motive whatsoever behind Lord Attingsborough's taking me driving and boating. He is simply interested in the school and in education... for girls."

The explanation sounded ridiculously lame, but how could she tell the truth even to her closest friends? She would thereby divulge a secret that was not hers to tell.

They looked at her with identical sober expressions before looking at each other.

"In the *school*, Susanna," Frances said.

"In *education*, Frances," Susanna said.

"For *girls*."

"It makes all the sense in the world. Why did we not guess for ourselves?"

They went off into peals of merry laughter.

"But let us not forget about the Duke of McLeith," Susanna said. "*Another* duke. He insists that he and Claudia were like brother and sister when they were growing up, but they are adults now. He is very personable, did you not think, Frances?"

"*And* a widower," Frances added. "And he was *very* eager to see Claudia again when Lucius and I were still at the garden party."

"If I were the two of you," Claudia said, "I would not buy new gowns for my wedding just yet."

"Your cheeks are pink," Frances said, getting to her feet. "We have embarrassed you, Claudia. But really, I *do* wish . . . Oh, well, never mind. I daresay you have no love to spare from that little dog at the moment. He is dreadfully thin, is he not?"

She bent to tickle him beneath his chin.

"You should have seen him yesterday," Susanna said. "He was scruffy and dirty and looked rather like an abandoned sewer rat—or so Peter claimed. But we have all fallen in love with him."

The dog raised his eyes to Claudia without lifting his head and sighed deeply.

"That is the trouble," Claudia said. "Love is not always a comfortable or convenient thing. Whatever am I to do with him? Take him back to school with me? The girls would riot."

"Apparently Edna and Flora almost quarreled last evening while we were out," Susanna said. "They both wanted to hold him at the same time and pet him and play with him."

Frances laughed. "I must be on my way," she said. "I promised Lucius I would be home for luncheon."

And then there were all the hugs and good-byes to go through again, just as painful as the ones earlier. It might be a long time before either Claudia or Susanna saw Frances again. And she had all the dangers of a confinement to go through before then.

Claudia felt quite in need of a rest by the time the morning came to an end. But she had to take the dog for a walk before leaving him in the care of the kitchen staff for the afternoon— a charge they undertook cheerfully. Indeed, the little collie would soon be fat if left for long to the tender ministrations of Susanna's cook.

But despite a certain weariness, most of it emotional, Claudia was looking forward to the picnic in Richmond Park or Kew Gardens with the Marquess of Attingsborough and his daughter. She knew she must keep reminding herself that in a sense it was just work—looking over a prospective pupil. And it was not an easy task she had been set. She liked Lizzie Pickford. She also felt desperately sorry for her. But that was an emotion to be quelled. Nothing could be gained from pity alone. The real question was, could she do anything for the child? Could her school offer anything of value to a blind girl?

She was looking forward to the afternoon nevertheless, and not entirely because of Lizzie. Despite all the distractions of last evening and this morning, she had been unable to keep her mind entirely off that conversation she had had with the Marques of Attingsborough in Hyde Park. He had made some startling revelations.

So had she.

He had actually told her in so many words that he had been celibate for more than two years!

And she had told him...Well, it was better not even to *think* about that. Maybe, if she was very fortunate indeed, he had forgotten.

They went to Richmond Park. They drove there in a closed carriage, Lizzie sitting close to Joseph's side while Miss Martin sat facing them. Lizzie said nothing, but she clung to his hand and sometimes patted it or his knee with her free hand. He knew she was both excited and nervous.

"Lizzie has never ventured far from home," he explained to

Miss Martin. "Her mother thought it best that she remain in familiar surroundings, where she feels safe."

Miss Martin nodded, her eyes upon his daughter.

"We all do that most of our lives," she said, "though our familiar surroundings usually consist of a broader compass than just a house and garden. It is good to feel safe. It is also good to step out into the unknown on occasion. How else can we grow and acquire knowledge and experience and wisdom? And the unknown is not always or even often unsafe."

He squeezed Lizzie's hand and she pressed the side of her head against his arm.

When they arrived at the park he led her inside. The footman who had accompanied the carriage spread a large blanket on the grass in the shade of an ancient oak tree and then fetched the picnic basket before returning to the carriage.

"Shall we sit?" Joseph suggested. "Is anyone ready for tea yet? Or shall we wait until later?"

Lizzie let go of his hand in order to drop to her knees and feel the blanket around her. She was still very quiet. And yet he knew that she would talk about this afternoon for days to come. He had never taken her for a picnic before. He had allowed Sonia to set the rules and had unconsciously concurred with them—his beloved blind child was to be protected at all costs. But why had he never given her a treat like this before?

"Oh, let us wait until later," Miss Martin said. "Should we not go for a walk first and get some exercise? It is such a lovely day and such a lovely park."

Joseph frowned at her. Lizzie turned a panicked face up to him and clutched the blanket with both hands.

"But I do not know where we *are*," she said. "I do not know where to go. *Papa?*" She lifted one hand and searched the air with it.

"I am here," he said, stooping down and taking her hand in his, while Miss Martin stood there, very straight and very still, her hands clasped at her waist. For an irrational moment he resented her. "A walk is probably a good idea. We might as well have had a picnic in the garden if we are not to make the most of all this space. We will go just a little way, sweetheart. I'll draw your hand snugly through my arm like this, and you will be as safe as you can possibly be."

He raised her to her feet as he spoke. She was so small and thin, he thought. Surely she was small for her age.

They moved slowly and haltingly forward, Lizzie's arm tense within his. He could almost read Miss Martin's thoughts as she moved beside them. How could this child possibly be ready for school?

And indeed, how *could* she? He was wasting Miss Martin's time. But then she spoke up, her voice firm but not ungentle.

"Lizzie," she said, "we are walking along a straight and lengthy avenue of smooth green grass with great old trees on either side. There are no obstacles to cause you harm. You can step forward with absolute confidence that you will not collide with anything or step into any holes, especially as your father has hold of your arm. If you were to take mine too, I daresay we could stride along at a spanking pace and maybe even break into a run. Shall we try it?"

Joseph looked over his daughter's head at her. He found himself smiling. She was very obviously a woman accustomed to managing girls.

But Lizzie looked up, pale and frightened.

"Mother said I was never to leave the house and garden and that I must never walk fast," she said. "And Miss Edwards said . . ."

But she paused in the middle of the sentence, and before Joseph could speak, she grinned—an expression he saw far too rarely on her face. It made her look downright mischievous.

"But Miss Edwards is gone. Papa sent her away this morning and gave her money for six months."

"Your mother was a wise lady," Miss Martin told her. "You should indeed remain at home unless you are accompanied by someone you trust. And you should always walk with caution when you are alone. But today you are with your papa, whom

you trust more than anyone else you have known, I daresay, and
you are certainly not alone. If you hold your papa's arm and take
mine too, we will be cautious *for* you and see that you come to no
harm. I believe your papa trusts me."

"Certainly I do," he said, still smiling at her over Lizzie's
head.

"Shall we try it?" she asked.

Lizzie reached out a hand, and Miss Martin drew it through
her arm. And they walked sedately onward in a tight line until
Joseph realized Miss Martin was increasing the pace. He grinned
and increased it even more. Lizzie, clinging tight, chuckled suddenly and then shrieked with laughter.

"We really are *walking*," she cried.

He felt the ache of unshed tears in his throat.

"And so we are," he said. "Perhaps we should run?"

They did so for a very short distance before slowing to a walk
again and then stopping altogether. They were all laughing by
then, and Lizzie was panting too.

He met Miss Martin's eyes over the top of Lizzie's head again.
She was flushed and bright-eyed. Her slightly faded cotton dress
was creased and the brim of her straw hat—the same one she had
worn to the garden party—had blown out of shape. One errant
lock of her hair hung loose about her shoulders. Her face was
glistening with moisture.

Suddenly she looked very pretty indeed.

"Oh, listen!" Lizzie said suddenly, her head bent forward, her
body very still. "Listen to the birds."

They all listened intently, and indeed, there must have been a
vast choir of them hidden among the leaves and branches of the
trees, all singing their hearts out. It was a lovely summer sound,
so easily missed when there was so much else to occupy the eyes
or the mind.

Miss Martin was the first to move. She released Lizzie's arm
and stepped in front of her.

"Lizzie," she said, "lift your face to the sun. Here, let me fold
back this wide brim on your bonnet so that you can feel the

lovely heat on your cheeks and eyelids. Breathe it in as you listen to the birds."

"But Mother said—" Lizzie began.

"And she was very wise," Miss Martin told her, folding back the soft brim to expose his daughter's pale, thin face and her blind eyes. "No lady exposes her complexion to the sun long enough to bronze or burn her skin. But it is actually good to do so for a few minutes at a time. The warmth of the sun on the face is very good for the spirits."

Ah, why had he never thought of that for himself?

Thus permitted, Lizzie tipped back her head so that the light and heat were full on her face. Her lips parted after a few moments and she slid her hand free of Joseph's arm and held up her hands to the sun, palms out.

"Oh," she said on a long sigh while Joseph felt that ache in his throat again.

She stood like that for some time until with sudden fright she pawed at the air with one hand.

"Papa?"

"I am right here, sweetheart," he said, but he did not reach for her as he would normally have done. "I am not going to leave you. Neither is Miss Martin."

"The sun *does* feel good," she said, and, still holding up her hands, she turned to her right and then kept turning very slowly until she was facing almost in the direction from which she had started. The sun's warm rays must have been her guide.

She laughed with the sheer carefree happiness of any child.

"Perhaps now," Miss Martin said, "we should return to the blanket and have some tea. It is never good to overdo any exercise—and I am hungry."

They turned and linked arms again and set off in the direction from which they had come. But Lizzie was not the only one bubbling with exuberance.

"Walking and running," Joseph said. "They are tame stuff. I propose that we skip the rest of the way to the blanket."

"Skip?" Lizzie asked as Miss Martin raised her eyebrows.

"You hop first on one foot and then on the other, all the while moving forward," he said. "Like this."

And he skipped along like an overgrown schoolboy, drawing the others with him until Miss Martin laughed aloud and skipped too. After a few awkward moments Lizzie joined them and they skipped along the avenue, the three of them, laughing and whooping and altogether making an undignified spectacle of themselves. It was a good thing any other people in the park were either out of sight altogether or else were so far away that they missed the show. Some of his friends might be interested to see him now, Joseph thought—skipping along a park avenue with his blind daughter and a school headmistress.

Doubtless Miss Martin's pupils and teachers would be interested too.

But Lizzie's carefree delight was worth any loss of dignity.

Miss Martin helped Lizzie off with her spencer when they reached the blanket and the shade, and suggested too that she take off her bonnet. She removed her own hat, as he did his, and set it on the grass. She smoothed her hands over her disordered hair, but it was a hopeless task. It would take a brush and a mirror to repair the damage. She looked utterly charming to him nevertheless.

They ate their tea with healthy appetites, devouring freshly baked buns with cheese and currant cakes and a rosy apple each. They washed it all down with lemonade that was sadly warm but was at least wet and thirst-quenching.

All the while they chattered on about nothing in particular until Lizzie fell silent and remained silent. She was curled up against Joseph's side, and, looking down, he could see that she was fast asleep. He lowered her head to his lap and smoothed a hand over her slightly damp hair.

"I think," he said softly, "you have just given her one of the happiest days of her life, Miss Martin. Probably *the* happiest."

"I?" She touched her bosom. "What have *I* done?"

"You have given her permission to be a child," he said, "to run and skip and lift her face to the sun and shout and laugh."

She stared back at him but said nothing.

"I have loved her," he said, "from the moment I first set eyes on her ten minutes after her birth. I believe I have loved her even more than I would otherwise have done just *because* she is blind. I have always wanted to breathe and eat and sleep for her and would gladly have died for her if it could have made a difference. I have tried to hold her safe in my arms and my love. I have never—"

Foolishly, he could not finish. He drew a deep breath instead and looked down at his child—who was so very nearly not a child any longer. That was the whole trouble.

"I believe that being a parent is not always a comfortable thing," Miss Martin said. "Love can be so terribly painful. I have experienced a little of what it must be like through a few of my charity girls. They have been so very disadvantaged and I desperately want the rest of their lives to be perfect for them. But there is only so much I can do. Lizzie will always be blind, Lord Attingsborough. But she can find joy in life if she wishes and if those who love her will allow it."

"Will you take her?" he asked, swallowing against what felt like a lump in his throat. "I do not know what else to do. Is school the right thing for her, though?"

She did not reply immediately. She was obviously thinking carefully.

"I do not know," she said. "Give me a little more time."

"Thank you," he said. "Thank you for not saying no out of hand. And thank you for not saying yes before you have considered the matter with care. I would rather her not go at all than for it to be the wrong thing. I will care for her somehow no matter what."

He looked back down at his daughter and continued to smooth his hand over her hair. It was ridiculously sentimental to think again that he would willingly die for her. The thing was, he could not. Neither could he live for her. It was a terrifying realization.

And yet somehow he was comforted by Miss Martin's

presence—even though she was not sure she could offer Lizzie a place at her school. She had shown his daughter—and him!—that she could have fun and even twirl about in the heat of the sun without holding on to anyone.

"I have often wondered," he said without looking up, "what would have happened if Lizzie had not been blind. Sonia would have moved on to other admirers and it is altogether possible that I would have carried on with my own life much as before, while supporting the child I had sired but rarely saw—yet I would have believed I was doing my duty by her. I would perhaps have married Barbara and deprived myself of the pull of love to my firstborn. But how impoverished my life would have been! Lizzie's blindness is perhaps a curse to her, but it has been an abundant blessing to me. How strange! I had never realized that until today."

"Blindness need not be a curse to Lizzie either," she said. "We all have our crosses to bear, Lord Attingsborough. It is how we bear those crosses that proves our mettle—or lack of it. You have borne yours and become a better person, and it has enriched your life. Lizzie must be allowed to carry her own burden and triumph over it—or not."

"Ah." He sighed. "But it is that possibility of *or not* that breaks my heart."

She smiled at him as he looked up at her, and it struck him that in fact she was more than just pretty. In fact, she was probably not pretty at all—that was far too girlish and frivolous a term.

"I do believe, Miss Martin," he said without stopping to consider his words, "you must be the loveliest woman it has ever been my privilege to meet."

Foolish and quite untrue words—and yet the truest he had ever spoken.

She stared back at him, her smile suddenly gone, until he lowered his gaze to Lizzie again. He hoped he had not hurt her, made her believe that he had merely been playing the gallant. But he could not think of a way of retrieving his words without hurting her more. The point was, he did not even know quite what he had meant by them himself. She was not lovely in any obvious sense. Not at all. And yet...

Good Lord, he was not becoming infatuated with Miss Claudia Martin, was he? There could be nothing more disastrous. But of course he was not. She had been kind to Lizzie, that was all—and it was impossible not to love her a little as a result. He loved the Smarts for the same reason.

"What happened to the dog?" he asked.

"A home happened—temporarily, at least," she said, "and loving care from all quarters. And your mention of him has given me an idea. May I bring him to visit Lizzie?"

But Lizzie was stirring even as he raised his eyebrows, and he leaned over her and kissed her forehead. She smiled and reached up one hand to touch and pat his face.

"Papa," she said, sounding sleepy and contented.

"It is time to go home, sweetheart," he said.

"Oh, so soon?" she asked, but she did not look unhappy.

"Miss Martin will come and visit you again if you wish," he said. "She will bring her little dog with her."

"A dog?" she said, instantly more alert. "There was one on the street one day a few years ago. Do you remember, Papa? He barked and I was frightened, but then his owner brought him close and I patted him and he panted all over me. But Mother said I might not have one of my own. My stories always have a dog in them."

"Do they? Then we must certainly have this one visit you," he said. "Shall we invite Miss Martin to come too?"

She laughed, and it seemed to him that there was some unaccustomed color in her cheeks.

"*Will* you come, Miss Martin?" she asked. "And will you bring your dog? *Please?* I would like it of all things."

"Very well, then," Miss Martin said. "He is a very affectionate little thing. He will probably lick your face all over."

Lizzie laughed with delight.

But this afternoon was rapidly coming to an end, Joseph thought. They must not be late back. Both he and Miss Martin had the evening visit to Vauxhall to prepare for—and he had a dinner to attend first.

He was sorry the outing was over. He was *always* sorry when his times with Lizzie were at an end. But today had been particularly pleasurable. They felt almost like a family.

But the strange, unbidden thought brought a frown to his face. Lizzie would always be his beloved child, but she would never be part of his *family*. And as for Miss Martin, well...

"Time to go," he said, getting to his feet.

Lady Balderston had invited Joseph to dinner, and it was quickly obvious to him that there were no other guests, that he and the Balderstons and their daughter were to dine *en famille.* And if that fact were not statement enough of his new status as Miss Hunt's almost betrothed, then Lady Balderston's words not long after they sat down were.

"It was extremely obliging of Viscountess Ravensberg to invite Portia to Alvesley Park for the Redfields' anniversary celebrations this summer," she remarked as servants removed the soup plates from the table and brought on the next course.

Ah. It was to be a preeminently family gathering for the fortieth wedding anniversary of the earl and countess. Miss Hunt was already family, then?

"I had not yet informed Lord Attingsborough of the invitation, Mama," she said. "But yes, it is true. Lady Sutton was obliging enough to invite me to call upon Lady Ravensberg with her this afternoon, and while we were there she informed her cousin that I had no plans for the summer other than to go home with Mama and Papa. And so Lady Ravensberg invited me to go to Alvesley. It was all very gratifying."

"Indeed so," Joseph said, smiling at both ladies. "I will be going there too."

"But of course," Miss Hunt said. "I am well aware that I

would not have been invited otherwise. There would have been no point, would there?"

And there was no point in delaying his marriage proposal any longer, Joseph thought. It was obviously merely a formality anyway. The Balderstons and Miss Hunt herself clearly thought so. So did his sister—who nevertheless ought not to have taken matters into her own hands this afternoon.

It was just that he would have liked a little time for courtship.

Balderston was already attacking his roast duck and giving it his full attention. Joseph glanced at him, but now was not the time for plain speaking. He would make an appointment at some other time to speak formally with his future father-in-law. Then he would make an official offer to Miss Hunt, and all would be done. The course of the rest of his life—and hers—would be mapped out.

There was very little time for courtship, then, but there was still some. For the rest of the dinner and the journey to Vauxhall, where they were to meet Lauren and Kit and their party, Joseph focused his attention upon his future bride, deliberately noting again how beautiful she was, how elegant, how refined, how perfect in every way.

He was going to make himself fall in love with her as far as he could, he decided as his carriage proceeded on its way to Vauxhall. He had no desire to enter into a loveless marriage just because his father expected it of him and because circumstances demanded it of him.

"You look particularly lovely tonight," he said, touching the back of her hand and letting his fingers linger on the fine, smooth skin there. "Pink suits your coloring."

"Thank you," she said, turning her head to smile at him.

"I suppose you know," he said, "that your father visited mine in Bath a couple of weeks or so ago."

"Yes, of course," she said.

"And you know the nature of that visit?"

"Of course," she said again.

Her face was still turned to his. She was still smiling.

"You are not in any way upset by it?" he asked her. "You do not feel perhaps that your hand is being forced?"

"Of course not," she said.

"Or that you are being rushed?"

"No."

He had wanted to be sure of that. It was all very well for *him* to accept that he needed a bride and that this woman was the best available candidate. But it took two to make a marriage. He would not have her pressured into marrying him if she would prefer not to.

"I am delighted to hear it," he said.

He would not take the next logical step of asking her to marry him now—he had not yet spoken to her father, and he had the distinct impression that that might matter to her. But he supposed they were one step closer to being officially betrothed.

She did indeed look lovely in pink, a color reflected in her cheeks and highlighted by her shining blond hair. He bent his head to kiss her. But she turned her face before his lips could meet hers so that they grazed her cheek instead. Then she drew a little farther to her side of the carriage. She was still smiling.

"Have I offended you?" he asked after a few moments.

Perhaps she thought kisses inappropriate before an official betrothal.

"You have not offended me, Lord Attingsborough," she said. "It was merely an unnecessary gesture."

"Unnecessary?" He raised his eyebrows and gazed at her perfect profile in the gathering dusk.

The carriage rumbled onto the bridge over the Thames. They would be at Vauxhall soon.

"I do not need to be wooed with such foolishness as kisses," she said. "I am no silly girl."

No, indeed she was not, by Jove.

"Kisses are *foolish*?" He was suddenly amused and bent his head closer to hers again, hoping to coax a smile of genuine amusement from her. Perhaps he had merely flustered her by attempting to kiss her.

"Always," she said.

"Even," he said, "between lovers? Between a husband and wife?"

"I believe, Lord Attingsborough," she said, "that members of polite society ought to be above such vulgarity. Kisses and romance are for the lower orders, who belong there just because they know nothing of wise and prudent alliances."

What the devil? Good Lord!

He was amused no longer.

And it struck him suddenly that in all the years of their acquaintance there had never been any moments of flirtation, any knowing glances, any forbidden touches, any stolen kisses—any of those little gestures between two people who were aware of each other sexually. He could not even remember a time when they had laughed together. There had never been the faintest hint of romance in their relationship.

But all that was about to change, surely.

Or was it?

"You would not welcome my kisses, then?" he asked Miss Hunt. "Ever?"

"I will certainly know my duty, Lord Attingsborough," she said.

Know her ...? The carriage, he realized, was drawing to a halt.

"Are you quite sure," he asked her, "that you really wish for this marriage, Miss Hunt? Now is the time to say so if you do not. I will hold no grudge against you—and I will make sure no shadow of blame falls upon you when I fail to offer for you."

She turned her head to smile at him again.

"We are perfect for each other," she said. "We both know it. We are of the same world and understand its workings and its rules and expectations. We are both past the first blush of youth. If you believe that you must woo me, you are much mistaken."

Joseph felt as if scales had just dropped from his eyes. Could he have been acquainted with her so long and not suspected that she was frigid? But how *could* he have suspected it? He had never tried either to flirt with her or to court her—until now. And yet surely he must be mistaken. Surely it was her innocence and inexperience that spoke. Once they were married . . .

John knocked on the door and then opened it and let down the steps. Joseph vaulted out though he felt somewhat as if his heart was lodged in his shoes. What sort of a marriage could he look forward to? One without any love or warmth at all? But he would not believe it. After all, he felt no deep affection for her now though he was prepared to work on his feelings. She would surely do the same. She had just said that she would know her duty.

"Shall we go in?" he suggested, offering Miss Hunt his arm. "I wonder if the others have arrived yet."

She took his arm and smiled and nodded to another couple who were alighting from their carriage nearby.

Why had he never noticed before this evening that her smile never made her eyes shine? Or was he just imagining things? That nonkiss appeared to have rattled him even if it had not discomposed her.

Peter had met the Duke of McLeith at White's Club during the morning of the previous day and had invited him to dine on the evening of the Vauxhall visit so that Claudia would have an escort.

Claudia was resigned to seeing him again. She was even curious about him. How much had he changed? How much was he the same old Charlie whom she had adored even before her feelings had turned romantic?

She wore the dark blue evening gown that had seen service for a number of special evening events at the school. She had always liked it even though it had never made any pretense to high fashion—or even low fashion, for that matter, she thought with wry humor as Maria styled her hair.

She pushed memories of the afternoon outing firmly from her mind. She would think tomorrow about the decision she was going to have to make concerning Lizzie's schooling—and it was certainly not an easy one. And she would try not to think at all about those startling words Lord Attingsborough had spoken to her—*I do believe, Miss Martin, you must be the loveliest woman it has ever been my privilege to meet.*

The extravagance of the words had been mildly distressing. He surely could not have meant them. And yet they were lovely words from a lovely afternoon that she knew she would remember for the rest of her life.

Charlie proved to be an amiable dinner companion. He told them about his Scottish estate and his travels in the Highlands. He told them about his son. And he regaled Susanna and Peter with anecdotes from his childhood and Claudia's, most of them amusing and all of them true.

Later, he offered his arm to Claudia after they had descended from Peter's carriage outside Vauxhall Gardens, and this time Claudia took it. For years past she had suppressed memories of her childhood with him along with everything that had happened later. Perhaps in future she would be able to separate the two in memory—her girlhood from her young womanhood—and let go some of the bitterness. And bitterness was really all that remained. The pain had gone away long ago.

"Claudia," he said, bending his head closer to hers as they followed Susanna and Peter into the Gardens, "this is all very pleasant indeed. I am happier than I can say to have met you again. And this time we really must not lose touch with each other."

Would they have loved each other for a whole lifetime, she wondered, if he had studied for the law and then married her as planned? Would they have remained close friends as well? It was impossible to know the answers, of course. So much would have been different than it was now. *Everything* would have been different. *They* would have been different. And who could say if that life would have been better or worse than the one she had lived instead?

And then they stepped past the entrance and all else was forgotten.

"Oh, Charlie, look!" she exclaimed in awe.

The long, straight avenue that stretched ahead of them was lined with trees, and all were hung with colored lamps, which looked magical even now when it was not yet fully dark. The paths were crowded with other revelers, all brightly and elegantly clad for the occasion.

"It is rather lovely, is it not?" he said, smiling at her. "I like to hear the old name on your lips, Claudia. I have been nothing but *Charles* since I was eighteen—when I am not simply *McLeith,* that is. Say it again."

He touched her hand on his arm and squeezed it.

But Claudia was not to be distracted. Everyone about them seemed to be in high spirits, and she too smiled. And then they came to a horseshoe-shaped area that was paved and surrounded by columns and open boxes in tiers, all lit by lanterns on the outside, lamps within. Almost all were already occupied, the central one by an orchestra.

Lady Ravensberg was waving to them from one of the lower boxes.

"Peter, Susanna, Miss Martin," she called as they drew closer. "Oh, and the Duke of McLeith is with you. Do come and join us. You are the last to arrive. Now our party is complete."

The party consisted of the viscount and viscountess, the Duke and Duchess of Portfrey, the Earl and Countess of Sutton, the Marquess of Attingsborough and Miss Hunt, the Earl and Countess of Kilbourne, and the four new arrivals.

Claudia felt amusement again at finding herself in such illustrious company. But she was determined to enjoy the evening to the full. Soon she would be back at school, and it was unlikely that she would experience such an evening ever again.

And what an experience it was!

The company was mostly congenial. Though the Suttons virtually ignored Claudia, and Miss Hunt sat at the opposite side of the box and rarely looked her way, everyone else was more than polite. The very sweet and pretty Countess of Kilbourne and the elegant, dignified Duchess of Portfrey engaged her in conversation for some time as did Viscount Ravensberg and his wife. And of course there were Susanna and Peter and Charlie.

But all did not depend upon conversation.

There was supper to be eaten, most notably the thin slices of ham and the strawberries for which Vauxhall Gardens were famous. And there was wine to be drunk. There were other people to watch as they moved by along the main avenue and strolled around by the boxes, stopping to engage some of their occupants in conversation. There was the music to listen to.

And there was the dancing. Although she had not danced in a long while, Claudia participated anyway. How could one possibly resist dancing in the open air with waving lanterns and the moon and stars above to light the ground on which they moved? She was partnered by Charlie, the Earl of Kilbourne, and the Duke of Portfrey.

Eleanor would tease her quite mercilessly about all this when she heard of it.

And if the music and dancing were not enough to fill her cup of pleasure to overflowing, there were the fireworks to look forward to later.

While they waited for that display to begin, Lady Ravensberg suggested a walk, and everyone agreed that it would be just the thing. They all paired off to walk together—the Earl of Kilbourne with his cousin, Lady Sutton, on his arm, Viscount Ravensberg with the Countess of Kilbourne, Peter with the Duchess of Portfrey, the duke with Susanna, the Earl of Sutton with Lady Ravensberg.

"Ah," Charlie said, "I see that everyone is taking a different partner. Miss Hunt, may I have the pleasure?"

She smiled and took his arm.

The Marquess of Attingsborough was finishing a conversation with a couple of acquaintances who had stopped outside the box.

"Go on ahead," he said, waving everyone on their way. "Miss Martin and I will follow in a moment."

Claudia felt a little embarrassed. He really had no choice but to accompany her, did he? But really, if there had been one secret disappointment about the evening so far, it was that there had been no chance to converse or to dance with him. The afternoon picnic seemed as if it must have happened days ago.

I do believe, Miss Martin, you must be the loveliest woman it has ever been my privilege to meet. He had spoken those very words to her a mere few hours ago. And of course, the more she tried to forget, the more she remembered.

And then he was smiling at her and offering his arm.

"I do apologize for the delay," he said. "Shall we chase after the others? Or shall we stroll in more leisurely fashion while you tell me truthfully what you think of Vauxhall?"

They made their way across the main avenue and down a shorter one until they reached another long, wide path, parallel to the first, that was breathtaking in its loveliness. Not only were there lamps hanging among the trees, but the series of stone arches across the path ahead was hung with them too.

"Perhaps," she said, "you expect me to look about with great good sense, Lord Attingsborough, and pronounce my disdain for such frivolous artificiality."

"But you are not going to do it?" He looked down at her with laughing eyes. "You cannot know how delighted I would be to know that you are not always ruled by good sense. This evening I have been chilled by good sense."

"Sometimes," she said, "I prefer to forget I even have such encumbrances as critical faculties. Sometimes I prefer just to *enjoy.*"

"And you are enjoying yourself this evening?" he asked her, guiding her around a largish group of merry revelers who were not looking where they were going.

Their own group was some distance ahead, Claudia could see.

"I am," she said. "Oh, I *really* am. I only hope I can remember all this just as it is so that I can draw out the memories when

I am alone in my quiet sitting room in Bath some winter evening."

He chuckled. "But first you must enjoy it to the last moment," he said. "And *then* remember it."

"Oh, I will," she assured him.

"All is well with McLeith?" he asked her.

"He came to dinner and made himself very agreeable," she told him. "He recounted exploits and episodes of mischief in which we were embroiled as children, and I was reminded of how very much I liked him then."

"You were lovers later?" he asked quietly.

She felt the heat in her cheeks as she remembered almost admitting as much to him in Hyde Park. How could she possibly have said what she had aloud to him—or to anyone?

"Very briefly," she said, "before he left home never to return. We were inconsolable at the knowledge that he had to go to Scotland, that it would be some time before we would see each other again and could be together for the rest of our lives. And so—"

"Such things happen," he said. "And all in all I believe passion—even misguided passion—is preferable to cold indifference. I believe you yourself said something similar to me once."

"Yes," she said just before he drew her firmly to one side of the path to avoid a collision with another careless and noisy group.

"This is undoubtedly a picturesque avenue," he said, "and of course we must remain on it if we are to catch up with the others. But do you *wish* to catch up, Miss Martin, or shall we take one of the quieter paths? They are not as well lit, of course, but it is not a dark night."

"One of the quieter paths, please," she said, and they turned onto one almost immediately and were soon swallowed up by darkness and the illusion of quiet.

"Ah, this is better," he said.

"Yes."

They strolled onward, quiet themselves now that they had

moved away from the crowds. Claudia breathed in the smell of greenery. And even above the distant strains of music and the muted sounds of voices and laughter, she could hear—

"Oh, listen," she said, drawing her hand free of his arm and grasping his sleeve. "A nightingale."

He listened too for several moments as they stood quite still.

"And so it is," he said. "It is not just my daughter who hears the birds, then."

"It is the darkness," she said. "It makes one more aware of sound and smell and touch."

"Touch." He laughed softly. "If you loved, Miss Martin, as you once did, or if at least you intended to marry a certain man, would you object to his touch? To his kiss? Would you call them unnecessary or foolish?"

Claudia was very glad of the darkness then. Her cheeks, she was sure, were aflame.

"*Unnecessary?*" she said. "*Foolish?* Surely neither. I would both want and expect touches—and kisses. Especially if I loved."

He looked about him, and Claudia, realizing that her hand was still on his sleeve, drew it free.

"This very evening," he said, "on the way here, I tried to kiss Miss Hunt—the only time I have ever taken such a liberty. She told me not to be foolish."

"Perhaps," she said, smiling despite herself, "she felt embarrassed or frightened."

"She explained herself at greater length when I questioned her," he told her. "She said that kisses are unnecessary and foolish between two people who are perfect for each other."

A slight breeze was causing the branches overhead to sway and admit faint bars of moonlight to play over his face. Claudia stared at him. Whatever had Miss Hunt meant? How could they be perfect for each other when she did not want his kisses?

"Why are you going to marry her?" she asked.

His eyes moved to hers and stayed there. But he did not answer.

"Do you love her?" she asked.

He smiled. "I think I had better say no more," he said. "I have already said too much when the lady ought to be able to expect some discretion from me. What is it about you that invites confidences?"

It was her turn not to answer.

His eyes were still on hers. Even when the moonlight was not filtering through the trees, the darkness was really not very dark at all.

"Would *you* be embarrassed or afraid," he asked her, "if I tried to kiss *you*?"

She would be both. She was quite sure she would. But it was a hypothetical question.

"No," she said so softly that she was not even sure sound came from her lips. She cleared her throat. "No."

It was *a hypothetical question.*

But as he lifted one hand and touched his fingertips to her cheek while his palm came beneath her chin, sighing as he did so, Claudia realized that perhaps it was not.

She closed her eyes and his lips touched hers.

It was a terrible shock. His lips were warm and slightly parted. She could taste the wine he had drunk and smell his cologne. She could feel the warmth of his hand and of his breath. She could hear the nightingale singing and someone far away shriek with laughter.

And all her insides reacted in such a way that afterward she marveled that she had remained on her feet. Her hands clenched into tight fists at her sides.

It lasted for maybe twenty seconds—maybe not even as long.

But her world was rocked to its very foundations.

As he lifted his head and lowered his hand and took a step back, Claudia firmly repossessed herself of her equilibrium.

"There, you see?" she said, her voice sounding unfortunately brisk and overcheerful. "I was neither embarrassed nor afraid. So there is nothing inherently embarrassing or fearful about you."

"I ought not to have done that," he said. "I am so sor—"

But Claudia's hand shot up, seemingly of its own volition, and she watched herself place two fingers firmly across his lips— those lovely warm lips that had just kissed her own.

"*Don't* be," she said, and her voice was a little less forceful now. It even shook slightly. "If you are sorry, then I will feel that I ought to be too, and I am not sorry at all. It is the first time I have been kissed in eighteen years and will probably be the last time for the rest of my life. I do not want to be sorry, and I do not want *you* to be sorry. Please."

He set his hand over hers and kissed her palm before lowering it to hold against the folds of his neckcloth. Even in the darkness she could see that his eyes were alight with laughter.

"Ah, Miss Martin," he said, "it has been almost *three* years even for me. What sadly deprived mortals we are."

She could not stop herself from smiling back at him.

"In fact," she said, "I would not mind at all if you were to do it again."

She felt oddly as if someone else were speaking through her lips while the real Claudia Martin looked on in shocked amazement. Had she really said what she had just said?

"I would not mind either," he said, and they gazed at each other for long moments before he released her hand and wrapped his arm about her shoulders while the other came about her waist. Claudia curled her own arms about him for lack of anywhere else to put them. And she lifted her face to his.

He was large and hard-bodied and very, very male. For one moment she really was frightened. Mortally so. Especially as he was no longer smiling. And then she forgot about fear and everything else too as she was engulfed in the sheer carnality of being slowly and very thoroughly kissed. Her body bloomed beneath his touch and she was no longer Claudia Martin, successful businesswoman, teacher, and headmistress.

She was simply woman.

She felt the breadth and hard muscles of his shoulders, and one of her hands twined into his thick, warm hair. With her breasts she felt the solid wall of his chest. Her thighs pressed against his. And between her thighs she felt a sharp throbbing that spiraled up inside her right into her throat.

Not that she analyzed each sensation. She merely felt them.

When he opened his mouth over hers, she opened hers too and angled her head and clutched his hair as his tongue came inside her mouth and stroked over every soft, moist surface. When he backed her against the trunk of a tree a mere foot or so behind her, she moved with him, and then she could lean against it while his hands roamed over her breasts and her hips and her buttocks.

When he pressed against her and she could feel the hardness of his arousal, she parted her legs and rubbed against him, wanting nothing more than to feel him inside her, deep inside. Ah, deep.

Yet not for one moment did she forget that it was with the Marquess of Attingsborough that she shared this hot embrace. And not for one moment was she deceived by any illusions. This was for now. Only for now.

Sometimes now was enough.

Sometimes it was everything.

She knew she would never be sorry.

She knew too that she would suffer heartache for a long time to come.

It did not matter. Better to live and hurt than not to live at all.

She felt his withdrawal as soon as he gentled the embrace, kissing her mouth softly and then her eyes and temples as he spread a hand over the back of her head and then brought her face against one of his shoulders, drawing her away from the tree trunk as he did so. And she felt both sorrow and relief. It was time for them to stop this. They were in an almost public place.

She felt the tension of sexual incompletion gradually drain from her body as she wrapped her arms loosely about his waist.

"We will agree, will we," he said after a minute or so of silence, his mouth close to her ear, "not to be sorry for this? And not to allow it to cause discomfort between us when we meet again?"

She did not answer immediately. Then she lifted her head, released her hold on him, and took a step back. As she did so she very consciously donned the persona of Miss Martin, schoolteacher, again, almost as if it were a garment stiffened from disuse.

"Yes to the first," she said. "I am not at all sure about the second. I have the feeling that in the cold light of day I am going to be very embarrassed indeed to come face-to-face with you after tonight."

Good heavens, now that she could *see* him in the semidarkness, it already seemed both incredible and very embarrassing indeed—or *would* seem.

"Miss Martin," he said, "I hope I have not... I cannot..."

She clucked her tongue. She could not let him finish. How humiliated she would be if he said the words aloud.

"*Of course* you cannot," she said. "Neither can I. I have a life and a career and people dependent upon me. I do *not* expect you to turn up on Viscount Whitleaf's doorstep tomorrow morning with a special license in your hand. And if you *did,* I would send you on your way faster than you had come there."

"With a flea in my ear?" he said, smiling at her.

"With *at least* that."

And she smiled ruefully back at him. How very foolish love was, blossoming at an impossible time and with an impossible person. For she was, of course, in love. And it was, of course, quite, quite impossible.

"I think, Lord Attingsborough," she said, "that if I had known what I know now when I stepped inside the visitors' parlor at school to see you standing there, I might have sent you away *then* with a flea in your ear. Though perhaps not. I have enjoyed the past two weeks more than I can say. And I have grown to like you."

It was true too. She really *did* like him.

She held out a hand to him. He took it and shook it firmly. The barriers were being set up between them again, as they absolutely must.

And then she jumped, her hand convulsing about his, as a loud crack broke the near silence.

"Ah," he said, looking up, "how appropriate! The fireworks."

"Oh!" she exclaimed as they both watched a streak of red arch above the trees and sink down out of sight again, roaring as it went. "I have so looked forward to them."

"Come," he said, releasing her hand and offering her his arm. "Let's go back into the open and watch them."

"Oh, yes," she said. "Let's."

And despite everything—despite the fact that something that had hardly started had also ended here tonight—she felt a deep welling of happiness.

She had spoken correctly a minute or two ago. She would not have missed this short stay in London for all the enticements in the world.

And she would not have missed knowing the Marquess of Attingsborough either.

Claudia was seated at the escritoire in the morning room, writing a reply to a letter from Eleanor Thompson, when the butler came to announce the arrival of visitors. The collie, who had been curled up beside her chair, sleeping, scrambled to his feet.

"Her grace, the Duchess of Bewcastle, the Marchioness of Hallmere, and Lady Aidan Bedwyn are waiting below, ma'am," he said. "Shall I show them up?"

Gracious! Claudia raised her eyebrows.

"Lord and Lady Whitleaf are upstairs in the nursery," she said. "Should this message not be delivered to them?"

"Her grace said it was you she has come particularly to see, ma'am," the butler said.

"Then show them up," Claudia said, hastily cleaning her pen and pushing her papers into a neat pile. At least she would be able to tell the duchess that her sister was well. But why would they call upon *her*?

Yet again she had not slept well. But this time it had been entirely her own fault. She had not really wanted to sleep. She had wanted to relive the evening at Vauxhall.

She was *still* not sorry.

The dog greeted the Duchess of Bewcastle and her sisters-in-law with fierce barks and a rush of attack.

"Oh, dear," Claudia said.

"Will he bite my leg off?" the duchess asked, laughing and bending over to pat his head.

"A border collie," Lady Aidan said, bending also. "He is just greeting us, Christine. Look at his tail wagging. And good morning to you too, you sweet little thing."

"He was a mistreated dog I was forced to adopt a couple of days ago," Claudia explained. "I believe all he needs is love—and plenty of food."

"And you are providing both, Miss Martin?" Lady Hallmere looked somewhat surprised. "Do you collect strays as Eve does? But you do collect stray pupils, do you not?"

She held up one hand when Claudia would have made a cutting remark.

"I have one of them as governess to my children," she said. "Miss Wood seems to have captured their interest. It remains to be seen if she can continue to do so."

The ladies took the seats Claudia indicated.

"I do thank you for bringing Miss Bains to town in person, Miss Martin," Lady Aidan said. "She seems a very pleasant, cheerful young lady. Hannah, my youngest, is already very attached to her, even after just one day. Becky is being more cautious. She has lost two governesses to marriage and she adored them both. She is inclined to be resentful of someone new. However, Miss Bains told the girls about her first day at your school in Bath, when she hated everybody and everything and was quite determined never to settle there even though she had agreed to go—and very soon she had them both laughing and begging for more stories about school."

"Yes," Claudia said, "that sounds like Flora. She likes to talk. She studied conscientiously, though, and will be a good teacher, I believe." She patted the dog, who had come back to sit beside her chair.

"I am sure she will," Lady Aidan said. "My husband and I did talk about sending Becky away to school this year, but I really cannot bear the thought of parting with her. It is bad enough that

Davy has to go to school. Bad for me, that is. *He* is having a grand time there, as Aidan said he would."

Claudia, inclined to dislike the woman merely because she was a Bedwyn by marriage, found that she could not do so after all. She even thought that she could detect the slight lilt of a Welsh accent in Lady Aidan's voice.

"I am so glad," the Duchess of Bewcastle said, "that James is still far too young for school. He will go when the time comes, of course, even though Wulfric did not when *he* was a boy. It is an experience he has always regretted missing, and he is determined that none of his sons will remain at home. I just hope that my next child will be a girl, though as a dutiful wife I suppose I should hope for another boy first—the spare to go with the heir or some such nonsense. The next, by the way, should make his or her appearance within seven months or so."

She beamed happily at Claudia, who could not help but like the duchess also—and pity her for being married to the duke. Though she did not appear to be a woman whose spirit had been broken.

"You and Frances both," Claudia said. "The Countess of Edgecombe, that is."

"Really?" The duchess smiled warmly. "How delightful for her and the earl. I suppose she will stop traveling and singing for a while. The world will go into mourning. She has a beautiful, beautiful voice."

The door opened at that moment and Susanna came into the room. All three visitors stood to greet her and the dog rushed about her ankles.

"I hope I have not taken you from your son," the duchess said.

"Not at all," Susanna assured her. "Peter is with him, and the two of them were looking so pleased with each other that I deemed my presence quite redundant. Do sit down again."

"Miss Martin," the duchess said as soon as she had seated herself once more, "I had a brilliant idea earlier this morning. I do occasionally have them, you know. Do not laugh, Eve.

Eleanor has written to say that she will definitely bring ten of the girls from the school to spend part of the summer at Lindsey Hall. I daresay you know that already—she wrote to you before writing to me, did she not? She almost changed her mind when she knew that Wulfric and I will not be away for the whole summer after all. Wulfric turns tyrant when I am increasing and insists that I do as little traveling as possible, and he claims to have lost his appetite for traveling alone. Besides, the Earl and Countess of Redfield are celebrating an anniversary this summer and have invited us to a grand ball at Alvesley Park among other things. It would not be neighborly to be from home on such a grand occasion. However, there is plenty of room and to spare at Lindsey Hall for ten schoolgirls."

Lady Aidan laughed. "And does Wulfric agree with you, Christine?" she asked.

"Of course," the duchess said. "Wulfric always agrees with me, even when he needs a little persuasion first. I reminded him that we had *twelve* girls stay with us last summer for the marriage of Lord and Lady Whitleaf and he was not at all inconvenienced."

"And I was very happy to have them at my wedding," Susanna said.

"My brilliant idea," the duchess said, returning her attention to Claudia, "was that you come too, Miss Martin. I daresay you intend to return to Bath soon, and if the prospect of spending the summer in a school without any children in it is your idea of bliss—as it very well may be—then so be it. But I would love to have you come to Lindsey Hall with Eleanor and the girls and enjoy the pleasures of the countryside for a few weeks. And if any further inducement is necessary, I would remind you that both Lady Whitleaf and Mrs. Butler will be at Alvesley Park. I know they are both particular friends of yours as well as former teachers at your school."

Claudia's first reaction was one of stunned incredulity. Stay at *Lindsey Hall,* setting of one of her worst waking nightmares? With *the Duke of Bewcastle* in residence?

Susanna's eyes were brimming with merriment. It was obvious that she was having the same thought.

"We will be going to Lindsey Hall too for a short while," Lady Aidan said, "as will Freyja and Joshua. You will be able to see how Miss Bains and Miss Wood are settling to their new positions, Miss Martin. Though they will not begin work in earnest until after we have returned home to Oxfordshire and Freyja and Joshua to Cornwall, of course."

So it would not be just Lindsey Hall and the Duke of Bewcastle—it would be the former Lady Freyja Bedwyn too. The idea that she should go was so appalling to Claudia that she almost laughed aloud. And it was surely not her imagination that Lady Hallmere was looking at her with a slightly mocking gleam in her eye.

"Please say you will come," the duchess said. "It will please me enormously."

"Oh, do go, Claudia," Susanna urged.

But Claudia had had a sudden idea, and it was only because of it that she did not say an instant and very emphatic no.

"I wonder," she said. "Would you balk at the idea of *eleven* girls instead of ten, your grace?"

Lady Hallmere raised her eyebrows.

"Ten, eleven, twenty," the duchess said cheerfully. "Let them all come. And bring the dog too. There will be plenty of space for him to run about. And I daresay the children will spoil him quite shamelessly."

"There is another girl," Claudia said. "Mr. Hatchard, my man of business in town here, has mentioned her. He sometimes recommends charity cases to me if he believes I can do something to help the girl."

"I was once one of them," Susanna said. "Have you met this girl, Claudia?"

"Yes." Claudia frowned, hating the lie but finding it necessary. "I am not at all sure she is suitable or that she wishes to attend my school. But . . . perhaps."

The duchess got to her feet.

"You will both be very welcome," she said. "But we must be on our way. This was intended to be a very brief visit, since it is not at all the fashionable hour to call upon anyone, is it? We will see you both at Mrs. Kingston's ball this evening?"

"We will be there," Susanna said.

"Thank you," Claudia said. "I will come to Lindsey Hall, your grace, and help Eleanor care for the girls. I know she hopes to spend some time with her mother while she is there, and now that you intend to remain at home too she will wish to spend time with you as well."

"Oh, splendid!" the duchess said, looking genuinely pleased. "This is going to be a delightful summer."

A delightful summer indeed, Claudia thought wryly. What on earth had she just agreed to? Was this her summer for going back in time to confront past horrors and perhaps exorcise them from her memories?

Peter had just stepped into the room to greet the visitors. He and Susanna went downstairs with them to see them on their way. Lady Hallmere remained behind for a few moments, held perhaps by a very direct look from Claudia.

"Perhaps Edna Wood told you," Claudia said, "or perhaps she did not, that I did not approve of her taking employment with you. It was her own choice to attend an interview and to accept the position, and I must respect her right to do so. But I do not like it, and I do not mind telling you so."

Lady Freyja Bedwyn had been a peculiar-looking girl, with her fair unruly hair, darker eyebrows, dark-toned skin, and rather prominent nose. She still had those features. But somehow they all added up to a striking handsomeness, which Claudia resented. It would have been more just if the girl had grown into an ugly woman.

Lady Hallmere smiled.

"You bear a long grudge, Miss Martin," she said. "I have rarely admired anyone as much as I did you as you marched down the driveway of Lindsey Hall on foot, carrying your baggage. I have admired you ever since. Good morning."

And she was gone in pursuit of her sisters-in-law.

Well!

Claudia sat at the escritoire and scratched the dog's ears. If the woman had intended to take the wind right out of her sails and tie her tongue in knots and mix her metaphors, she had been entirely successful.

But she soon turned her mind back to the Duchess of Bewcastle's invitation and her own bright idea. Did this mean she had made some sort of decision about Lizzie Pickford? She would have to discuss it with the Marquess of Attingsborough, of course. Oh, goodness, she really *was* going to find it embarrassing to come face-to-face with him again. But it must be done. This was business.

Was he planning to attend the Kingston ball? She was going. Susanna and Peter had told her so at breakfast, and somehow she felt caught up in this madness that was the spring Season and swept along on its current. A very large part of her longed to be back at home in Bath, back in her own familiar world.

And a very small part of her remembered that kiss last night and perversely longed to linger here just a little longer.

She sighed and tried to return her attention to the letter she was writing to Eleanor. The dog curled up at her feet and went back to sleep.

When Joseph arrived at the Kingston ball later that evening, the first set was already in progress. He had been delayed by Lizzie's request for one more story and then just one more before she went to sleep. Her need for him was greater now that Miss Edwards was gone.

He stood in the ballroom doorway, looking about him for familiar faces after greeting his hostess. He could see Elizabeth, the Duchess of Portfrey, off to one side, not dancing. He would have joined her, but she was in conversation with Miss Martin. In a craven moment quite unlike him, he pretended not to see them even though Elizabeth had smiled and half raised a hand. He strolled in the opposite direction instead to join Neville, who was watching Lily dance with Portfrey, her father.

"You are scowling, Joe," Neville said, raising his quizzing glass to his eye.

"Am I?" Joseph offered him an exaggerated smile.

"You are still scowling," Neville said. "I know you, remember? You were not supposed to dance the opening set with Miss Hunt, by any chance, were you?"

"Good Lord, no," Joseph said. "I would not have been late if I were. I have been with Lizzie. I looked in at Wilma's this afternoon, almost at the end of her weekly tea. All the other guests were leaving—and so I was fair game for one of her lectures."

"I suppose," Neville said, "she thinks you ought to have secured the opening set with Miss Hunt. I have always been glad, Joe, that Wilma is *your* sister and Gwen mine and not the other way around."

"Thank you," Joseph said dryly. "It was not just that, though. It was my behavior last evening."

"Last evening? At Vauxhall?" Neville raised his eyebrows.

"It seems I neglected Miss Hunt in order to show a misguided kindness to the dowdy schoolteacher," Joseph said.

"Dowdy? Miss Martin?" Neville turned to look toward her. "Oh, I would not say so, Joe. She has a certain understated elegance even if she is not in the first stare of fashion or the first blush of youth. And she is dashed intelligent and well informed. Lily likes her. So does Elizabeth. And so do I. Miss Hunt said much the same as Wilma last evening, though, in Lily's hearing. A trifle insulting to Lauren, who had invited Miss Martin to join the party, Lily thought—and so did I. But I ought not to be saying so to you, I suppose."

Joseph frowned. He had just spotted Miss Hunt. She was dancing with Fitzharris. She was wearing gold net over white silk, and the underdress draped her perfect form to give the look of a Greek goddess. The gown was cut low at the bosom to show off her main assets. Her blond curls were threaded with gold.

"She is going to be at Alvesley," he said. "Wilma wangled an invitation from Lauren in Miss Hunt's hearing, and Lauren, I suppose, had no choice at all. You know how Wilma goes about getting her own way."

"At Alvesley?" Neville said. "I suppose Lauren would have invited her anyway after your betrothal, though. That *is* imminent, I suppose?"

"I daresay," Joseph agreed.

Neville looked at him sharply.

"The funny thing was," Joseph said, "that Wilma's lecture included the detail that while I was entertaining Miss Martin, McLeith was charming Miss Hunt. Wilma was warning me that I might lose her if I am not careful. Apparently they looked very pleased with each other."

"Ha," Neville said. "About to be jilted, are you, Joe? Do you want me to see if I can hasten the process?"

Joseph raised his eyebrows. "Whyever would you think I might want any such thing?" he asked.

Neville shrugged. "Perhaps I just know you too well, Joe," he said. "Lady Balderston is waving this way, and I do not suppose it is at me."

"The dance is ending," Joseph said. "I had better go and join her and ask Miss Hunt for the next set. And what the devil do you mean by saying you know me too well?"

"Let me just say," Neville said, "that I don't think Uncle Webster *does.* Or Wilma. They both think you ought to marry Miss Hunt. Lily thinks just the opposite. I usually trust Lily's instincts. Ah, the dance has ended. Off you go, then."

Nev might have kept his—and Lily's—opinion to himself, Joseph thought irritably as he crossed the floor. It was too late *not* to offer for Miss Hunt even if he so desired. He proceeded to dance with her, trying not to be distracted by Miss Martin, who stood in the line of ladies just two places down the set, smiling across at McLeith, her partner. He had the feeling, though, that she was trying just as hard not to look at *him.* And yet again, as he had been doing at frequent intervals throughout the day, he looked back upon last evening with some incredulity and wondered if it could possibly have happened. Not only had he *kissed* the woman, but he had wanted her with a lust that had almost overpowered all caution and common sense.

It was a good thing they had been in an almost public place or there was no knowing where their embrace might have led.

He danced with Miss Holland next, as he often did at balls this spring because she was so frequently a wallflower, and her mother was too indolent to ensure that she had partners. And then, after introducing her to a blushing Falweth, who could never summon up the courage to choose his own partners, he stood with a group of male acquaintances, chatting genially and watching another vigorous country dance.

As the music drew to a close, he agreed to step into the card room to play a hand or two with a few of his companions. But it struck him that he could not see Miss Martin dancing. She had not danced the first set either. He would hate to see *her* be a wallflower, though she was not, of course, a young girl in search of a husband.

She was sitting on a love seat close to the door, he could see when he looked around, in conversation with McLeith. He was smiling and animated, she paying him close attention. Perhaps, Joseph thought, she was happy after all that she had met her old lover again. Perhaps their long-aborted romance was in the process of being rekindled.

And then she glanced up and looked directly at Joseph in such a way that he realized she had known he was standing there. She looked away hastily.

This was ridiculous, he thought. They were like a couple of pubescent children who had sneaked a kiss behind the stable one day and were consumed with embarrassment about it forever after. They were adults, he and Miss Martin. What they had done last evening had been by mutual consent, and they had both agreed not to be sorry. And when all was said and done, all that had happened was a *kiss*. A rather hot kiss, it was true, but even so . . .

"You go on without me," he told the other men. "There is someone I need to talk to."

And before he could think of an excuse to stay away from her, he strode across the room toward the love seat.

"McLeith? Miss Martin?" he said, nodding genially to them both. "How do you do? Miss Martin, are you free for the next set? Will you dance it with me?" And then he remembered something. "It is a waltz."

A waltz!

Claudia had never danced it though she had watched the steps performed any number of times and had once or twice—well, perhaps more than twice—waltzed about her private sitting room with an imaginary partner.

Now she was being asked to waltz at a *ton* ball?

With the Marquess of Attingsborough?

"I will," she said. "Thank you."

She nodded at Charlie, with whom she had been sitting and conversing for the past half hour after dancing with him earlier.

The marquess was holding out a hand for hers, and she set her own in it and got to her feet. She could instantly smell his cologne and was just as instantly engulfed in embarrassment again.

Just last evening . . .

She squared her shoulders and unconsciously pressed her lips into a tight line as he led her out onto the dance floor.

"I hope I do not make an utter cake of myself," she said briskly as he turned to face her. "I have never waltzed before."

"Never?" She looked up into his eyes just as they filled with laughter.

"I know how to perform the steps," she assured him, feeling heat in her cheeks, "but I have never actually waltzed."

He said nothing and his expression did not change. She laughed out loud suddenly and he tipped his head slightly to one side and looked at her more closely, though what his thoughts might be she could not fathom.

"You may be sorry you asked me," she said.

"As you remarked when you agreed to allow me to escort you to London," he said. "I am still not sorry about that."

"This is different," she said as more couples gathered around them. "I shall try not to disgrace you. Gallantry forbids you to back out now, does it not?"

"I suppose," he said, "I could be overcome by a sudden fit of the vapors or something even more irrefutable, like a heart seizure. But I will not. I confess to a curiosity to see how you acquit yourself during your first waltz."

She laughed again—and then stopped abruptly as he set one hand behind her waist and took her right hand in the other. She raised her free hand to his shoulder.

Oh, my!

Memories of the night before came flooding in, bringing with them more heat to her cheeks. She determinedly thought of something different.

"I need to talk with you."

"Do I owe you an apology?"

They spoke simultaneously. She realized what he had said.

"Absolutely not."

"Do you?"

They spoke together again and then silently smiled at each other.

Any conversation would have to wait. The music was beginning.

There was a minute or so of desperate fright as her mind blanked to the steps she had never danced with a partner. But he was a good leader, she realized when her mind was capable of rational thought again. She knew that he was using the most basic of steps, and by some miracle she was following along without making any ghastly errors. She was also, she realized, counting in her head, though she suspected that her lips might have been moving. She stilled them.

"I do believe," he said, "you are doomed to oblivion, Miss Martin. You will not make a cake of yourself and no one will notice us."

He gave her a mournful look, and she smiled back at him.

"And anyone who does will soon expire of boredom," she said. "We are the least noteworthy couple on the floor."

"Now *that*," he said, "sounds like a challenge to my male pride."

And he tightened his hold on her waist slightly and swung her into a sweeping twirl as they turned one corner of the room.

Claudia only just stopped herself from shrieking. She laughed instead.

"Oh," she cried, "that was wonderful. Do let's try it again. Or is that tempting fate? However did I keep my slippers from beneath your feet?"

"Ahem," he said, clearing his throat. "I believe it had something to do with my skill, ma'am."

And he twirled her again.

She laughed once more at the exhilaration of the dance and at the wonderful novelty of actually joking with a man. She liked him exceedingly. She looked into his eyes to share her pleasure.

And then somehow there was more. More than exhilaration, more than pleasure. There was...

Ah, there were no words.

It was a moment upon which she would live and dream for the rest of her life. She was quite sure of that.

The music played on, the dancers twirled, she and the Marquess of Attingsborough among them, and the world was a wonderful place to be.

"Oh," she said when the music finally slowed, a sure sign that it was about to stop altogether, "is it over already?"

Her first waltz. And doubtless her last.

"Your first waltz is about to become history, alas," he said, echoing her thoughts.

And then she remembered that she needed to speak to him,

that apart from a little light banter at the beginning of the waltz they had danced in silence.

"Oh," she said, "I need to talk with you, Lord Attingsborough. Perhaps sometime tomorrow?"

"Even before the waltz began," he said, "I was eyeing those open French windows with some wistfulness. Now it has become a downright longing. There is a balcony beyond them. And, more important, there is cool air. Shall we stroll out there if you have not promised the next set?"

"I have not," she said, looking toward the open doors and the lamplit darkness beyond. Perhaps after last evening it would not be wise...

But he was offering his arm, and she took it. He steered her through the crowds until they stepped out onto the balcony.

Tonight would be different.

Tonight they had business to discuss.

12

It was indeed cool outside—deliciously so, in fact. But they were not the only ones who had taken advantage of the open doors in order to escape from the heat of the ballroom for a while. There were several people out on the balcony.

"There are lamps lit in the garden," Joseph said. "Shall we go down there and stroll?"

"Very well," she said, using her schoolmistress voice—he wondered if she realized she had two quite distinct voices. "Lord Attingsborough—"

But she stopped talking as he set a hand over hers on his arm, and turned her head to look at him. He had to speak first. Last night needed to be mentioned between them.

"Were you as embarrassed as I earlier this evening?" he asked her.

"Oh, more so," she said with her usual forthright honesty.

"But you are not now?"

"No," she said, "though perhaps it is as well you can no longer see the color of my cheeks."

They were down in the garden, which was not brilliantly lit. He turned them onto a path that wound to the left.

"Good." He chuckled and patted her hand. "Neither am I. I remember with pleasure and am not at all sorry, though I would make abject apologies if I thought they were necessary."

"They are not," she assured him.

He wondered, not for the first time, if she was essentially a lonely woman. But it was perhaps just male arrogance that made him think she might be. She had certainly proved that a woman could lead a full and productive life without a man. But then loneliness was not confined to women, was it? For all the family and friends and friendly acquaintances with whom he was almost constantly surrounded and the busy activities that filled his days, he was basically a lonely man.

Despite Lizzie, whom he loved more than life, he *was* lonely. The admission surprised him. He was lonely for a woman who could touch and fill his heart. But it was unlikely he would ever find her now. He was almost certain that Portia Hunt would never fill the role.

"Shall we sit?" he suggested when they came to a small lily pond with a rustic wooden seat overlooking it from beneath the overhanging branches of a willow tree.

They sat down side by side.

"It is blessedly cool out here," she said. "And quiet."

"Yes."

"Lord Attingsborough," she said, resuming her brisk tone, "Miss Thompson, the teacher you saw the morning we left Bath, the older of the two, is taking ten of our charity girls to Lindsey Hall for part of the summer. She is the Duchess of Bewcastle's sister, you know."

"Ah," he said, the image of Bewcastle entertaining ten schoolgirls at his table dancing across his mind.

"The duchess has invited me to join them," she said.

He felt instant amusement, remembering what she had told him about her experiences as a governess there. He turned his head to grin at her. Her face was faintly visible in the beam of a lamp hanging in the tree.

"To *Lindsey Hall*?" he said. "With *Bewcastle* in residence? Are you going?"

"I have said yes," she told him, staring at the water as if it had somehow offended her. "Lady Hallmere is going to be there too."

He chuckled softly.

"I said yes because I had an idea," she said. "I thought perhaps it would be a good thing for me to take Lizzie there with me."

He sobered instantly. He felt a sudden chill. He had been hoping fervently that she would consider school a possibility for his daughter. He had also been hoping, he realized now, that she would *not*. The real chance that he might have to part with Lizzie for months at a time smote him.

"It might be a good trial," she said. "She needs air and exercise and...*fun*. She will surely get some of all three at Lindsey Hall. She will meet Eleanor Thompson and ten of the girls from the school. She will be with me daily. It will give us all a chance to discover whether schooling will be of any benefit to her and whether Eleanor and I can offer her enough to make the experience—and the fees—worthwhile. And yet it will all be done in the relaxed atmosphere of a holiday."

He could not fault any of her reasoning. It sounded like an eminently sensible suggestion. But his stomach clenched with something that felt like panic.

"Lindsey Hall is a large place," he said. "And the park is large. She would be intolerably bewildered."

"My *school* is large, Lord Attingsborough," Miss Martin said.

But that would be different. Would it not?

He leaned forward on the seat, rested his elbows on his knees, his hands hanging loose between them. He lowered his head and closed his eyes. There was a lengthy silence between them while the sounds of music and voices and laughter coming from the ballroom wafted on the air. She was the one who spoke first.

"You conceived the idea of sending Lizzie to school," she said, "not because it would solve the problem of who was to take care of her and not because you wished to be rid of her—though I believe those are what you fear are your motives. You need not fear any such thing. I have seen how you love her. No child has ever been more loved."

She was using her other voice—her pure woman's voice.

"Then why do I feel I am betraying her?" he asked.

"Because she is blind," she said. "And because she is illegitimate. And you wish to protect her from the consequences of both by smothering her with your love."

"*Smothering,*" he said, a dull ache in his heart. "Is that what I do to her? Is that what I have always done?"

He knew she was right.

"She has as much right to live as anyone else," she said. "She has as much right to make her own decisions, to explore her world, to dream of her future, and to work to bring those dreams true. I am not at all sure school is the right thing for her, Lord Attingsborough. But it may very well be the best thing under the circumstances."

The circumstances being that Sonia was dead and he was about to marry Portia Hunt and there would be very little place for his daughter in his life.

"What if she does not want to go?" he asked.

"Then her wishes must be respected and some other option found," she said. "This is my condition, you see—if, that is, you approve my plan. Lizzie must agree to it too. And if at the end of the summer I decide to offer her a place at my school, then Lizzie must be the one to accept or reject it. That is always my condition. I have told you that before."

He rubbed his hands over his face and sat up.

"You must think me a very sorry creature, Miss Martin," he said.

"No," she said. "Merely a concerned and loving father."

"I do not always *feel* like one," he said. "I have seriously considered taking her to America with me and setting up a new life there. I could be with her all the time. We would both be happy."

She did not reply, and he felt foolish. He had *thought* of taking Lizzie to America, it was true, but he had always known that he would not actually do it—that he *could* not. He would be Duke of Anburey one day, and many lives would be dependent upon him and many duties incumbent on him.

The notion of freedom of choice was often an illusion.

And then a thought struck him and he was surprised it had not occurred to him sooner.

"But I will be close by," he said, lifting his head and turning to look at her. "I am going to be at Alvesley Park for the Earl and Countess of Redfield's anniversary. Alvesley is only a few miles from Lindsey Hall. Did you know that?"

"Yes, I did," she said. "I also knew of the party because Susanna and Peter are going there. I had not realized you were to be there too, though."

"I will be able to see Lizzie," he said. "I will be able to spend time with her."

"Yes, if you wish," she said, looking steadily back at him.

"*If I wish?*"

"Your family and friends may wonder at your interest in a mere charity girl from my school," she said.

"A *charity* girl?" He frowned. "I will pay double your fee, Miss Martin, if Lizzie is willing to go to your school and is likely to be happy there."

"I told the duchess that the girl I may take with me is a charity case recommended by Mr. Hatchard," she said. "I take it you do not wish the truth to be known?"

He stared at her in some anger before turning his head away and closing his eyes. His mother and father, Wilma, Kit's family, Bewcastle's family—all would be offended if they discovered that his daughter was at Lindsey Hall while he was at nearby Alvesley. Not to mention Portia Hunt. Gentlemen just did not expose their illegitimate offspring to their very legitimate families and acquaintances.

"And so I must behave as if I am ashamed of the most precious person in my life?" he asked.

It was, of course, a rhetorical question. She did not answer it.

"I will see her there and spend time with her, regardless," he added. "Yes, it is agreed, then, Miss Martin. Lizzie will go to Lindsey Hall—if she will say yes, of course, and you and she and Miss Thompson will decide among you whether she will then go on to school in Bath."

"You are *not,* you know," she said, "agreeing to her execution, Lord Attingsborough."

He turned his head to look at her again and laughed softly but without humor.

"You must understand," he said, "that my heart is breaking."

Too late he heard the sentimental hyperbole of his words and wondered if they could possibly be true.

"I do," she said. "Now, I must meet Lizzie again. I must have a talk with her and see if I can persuade her to come to Lindsey Hall to spend a few weeks of the summer with some other girls and me. I do not know for certain how she will answer, but I believe there is more to your daughter than you have been willing to recognize, Lord Attingsborough. You have been blinded by love."

"A nice irony, that," he said. "Tomorrow, then? In the afternoon? At the same time as usual?"

"Very well," she said. "And I will, if I may, bring the dog with me. He is a friendly little thing, and she may like him."

She was still sitting as before. With her face half in light, half in shadow she looked very appealing. It was hard to remember his first impression of her when she had stepped inside the visitors' parlor at her school, looking stern and humorless.

"Thank you," he said. He reached out and covered her hands with one of his own. "You are very generous."

"And perhaps very foolish," she said. "How on earth can I offer any sort of an education to someone who cannot see? I have never thought of myself as a wonder worker."

He had no answer for her. But he curled his fingers about one of her hands and raised it to his lips.

"Even for what you have done and are prepared to do I thank you," he said. "You have looked upon my daughter not just as an illegitimate child who has the additional disadvantage of being blind, but as a person worthy of a meaningful life. You have persuaded her to run and laugh and shout with glee just like any other child. Now you are prepared to give her a summer of fun that has surely always been beyond her wildest dreams—or mine."

"I believe," she said, "that if I were a Papist I would be eligible for sainthood, Lord Attingsborough."

He loved her dry humor and chuckled softly.

"I believe the music has stopped," he said, pausing for a moment to listen. "And it was the supper dance. May I escort you to the supper room and fill a plate for you?"

She took her time about answering. Her hand was still in his on his lap, he realized.

"We waltzed together," she said, "and then left the ballroom together. Perhaps we would create the wrong impression if we sat at supper together too. Perhaps you ought to go and sit with Miss Hunt, Lord Attingsborough. I will remain here for a while. I am not hungry."

To the devil with Miss Hunt, he almost said aloud. But he stopped himself in time. She had done absolutely nothing to deserve such open disrespect, and indeed it could be said that he had neglected her somewhat this evening. He had danced with her only once.

"You are afraid," he said, "that people will think I am dallying with you?"

She turned her face, and he could see that she looked suddenly amused.

"I very much doubt anyone would think that," she said. "But they might very well think that I am angling for *you.*"

"You belittle yourself," he said.

"Have you looked at yourself in a glass lately?" she asked him.

"And have *you?*"

She smiled slowly.

"You are gallant," she said, "and kind. I am *not* angling for you, you may be relieved to know."

He raised her hand to his lips again and then, instead of releasing it, he laced their fingers together and rested their hands on the seat between them. She made no comment and did not try to snatch her hand away.

"If you are not hungry," he said, "I will sit here with you until the dancing starts again. It is pleasant here."

"Yes," she said.

And they sat there for a long time just as they were, without speaking. Almost everyone else must have gone for supper, including the orchestra. Apart from a few stray voices coming from the direction of the balcony, they might have been all alone. The lamplight beamed across the small pond, outlining a few lily pads. A slight breeze caused the fronds of the willow tree to sway before them. The air was cool—and then perhaps a little more than just cool. He felt her shiver.

He released her hand and removed his evening coat—not an easy thing to do when it had been made fashionably form-fitting. He set it about her shoulders and kept his hand there, to hold it in place. With his other hand he took hers again.

Neither of them spoke a word. She made no objection to his arm about her shoulders or her hand in his. Beneath his touch she was neither stiff nor yielding.

He relaxed.

The extraordinary notion occurred to him—not for the first time—that perhaps he was falling ever so slightly in love with Miss Claudia Martin. But it was an absurd idea. He liked her. He respected her. He was grateful to her. There was even a touch of tenderness mingled in with the gratitude because she had shown so much kindness to Lizzie without demonstrating any moral outrage toward him for having begotten an illegitimate child.

He was comfortable with her.

Those feelings did not equate with love.

But there *had* been last evening.

If she had turned her head, perhaps he would have kissed her again. He was glad she did not—perhaps.

At last he could hear the orchestra tuning their instruments. And once again he thought about Miss Hunt, to whom he was honor-bound to make a marriage offer.

"The dancing will be resuming soon," he said.

"Yes," she said, and she got to her feet a moment before he did.

He struggled back into his coat. His valet would probably weep if he could see how his shirt wrinkled beneath it.

He offered his arm and she took it before they walked in the direction of the ballroom. He stopped after they had climbed the steps to the balcony.

"I will come for you tomorrow, then?" he asked her. "At the same time?"

"Yes," she said, lifting her eyes to his.

He could see them clearly in the light spilling from the ballroom. Wide and intelligent as always, they also looked something else now. Something he could not quite identify. They looked very deep, as if he could fall into them if he chose.

He nodded to her and indicated with one hand that she should precede him into the ballroom. He hung back for a moment or two after she had stepped inside. He hoped no one had noticed how long they had been together.

He would not willingly sully her reputation.

Or willingly humiliate Miss Hunt.

Lily Wyatt, Countess of Kilbourne, sat next to Lauren Butler, Viscountess Ravensberg, at supper, and the two of them engaged in a private conversation while the group with which they sat conversed more loudly with one another.

"Neville told me earlier," Lily said, "that you have invited Miss Hunt to Alvesley for the anniversary celebrations."

Lauren pulled a face. "Wilma brought her visiting," she said, "and dropped hints so broad that even a person with no brain could not have failed to understand. And so I invited her. But it hardly signifies, does it? By then she and Joseph will surely be betrothed. It is no secret, is it, why Uncle Webster summoned him to Bath."

"You do not like her either?" Lily asked.

"Oh, I do not," Lauren admitted, "though I would be hard put to it to explain why. She is too—"

"Perfect?" Lily suggested, understanding that Lauren had not overheard Miss Hunt questioning her taste in inviting a mere schoolteacher to share the box at Vauxhall with her betters. "Wilma has been scolding Joseph for allowing her to walk with the Duke of McLeith last evening while he played the gallant to Miss Martin. She is afraid that they fancy each other."

"Miss Hunt and the duke?" Lauren said, her eyes widening with incredulity. "Surely not. He seems an amiable man."

"A comment that says volumes," Lily said. "But I cannot help but share your feelings, Lauren. Miss Hunt reminds me of Wilma but worse. At least Wilma dotes on her boys. I cannot imagine Miss Hunt doting upon anyone, can you? I thought perhaps you and I could—"

But a light had come into Lauren's eyes and she interrupted.

"Lily," she said, "you are not plotting to play matchmaker—and match*breaker,* are you? Can I play too?"

"You could invite the duke to Alvesley as well," Lily said.

"To a *family* celebration?" Lauren raised her eyebrows. "Would it not seem odd?"

"Use your ingenuity," Lily suggested.

"Oh, dear, do I have any?" Lauren laughed. But then she brightened. "Christine told me earlier today that Miss Martin is going to Lindsey Hall for part of the summer—Christine's sister is taking some girls from the school there for a holiday. The Duke of McLeith and Miss Martin grew up in the same house like brother and sister and have just found each other again after years and years of separation. He in particular is very delighted about it, and I daresay she is too. Perhaps I could suggest that he might like to be close to her for a few weeks of the summer before he returns to Scotland and she goes back to Bath."

"Brilliant," Lily said. "Oh, do it, Lauren, and then we will see what can be accomplished."

"This is fiendish," Lauren said. "And do you know what Susanna believes? She thinks Joseph might be a little sweet on Miss Martin. He has taken her driving several times and has spent time with her at several entertainments, including last evening at Vauxhall. They were waltzing together earlier. Where is he now, do you know? And where is she?"

"It is the most unlikely romance imaginable," Lily said. But her eyes gleamed. "But oh, goodness, Lauren, she just might be perfect for him. No one else ever has been. Miss Hunt certainly is not."

"Wilma would turn purple in the face," Lauren added.

They grinned at each other, and Neville, Earl of Kilbourne, who was just out of earshot, pursed his lips and looked innocent.

13

Claudia and Susanna had just returned from a visit to Hookham's library the following morning when the Duke of McLeith called at the house. He was admitted to the morning room, where Claudia was sitting alone, leafing through the book she had just borrowed. Susanna had gone up to the nursery to see Harry.

"Claudia," he said, advancing across the room after the butler had announced him and the collie had rushed across the room to bark at him and then wag his tail. "Your dog?"

"I believe it is more a case of my being his person," she said as he tickled him behind one ear. "Until I can find a good home for him, I am his."

"Do you remember Horace?" he asked.

Horace! He was a spaniel she had adored as a child. He had followed her everywhere, like a floppy-eared shadow. She smiled as they both took a seat.

"Viscount and Viscountess Ravensberg spoke with me last evening before I left the ball," he said. "They invited me to spend a few weeks at Alvesley Park before returning to Scotland. Apparently there is to be a large gathering there for the Earl and Countess of Redfield's anniversary. I must confess I was surprised—I did not think I had a sufficient acquaintance with them to merit such a distinction. However, the viscountess explained that you were going to be staying at Lindsey Hall nearby and that I might be glad of a few weeks in which to enjoy your company again after so long."

He paused and looked inquiringly at Claudia.

She clasped her hands in her lap and looked back at him without comment. Susanna and all her friends seemed charmed by the story he had told—which was quite true, though it was not by any means the whole truth. She had once loved him with all the ardor of her young heart. But though the days of their court-ship had been innocent and decorous, their parting had been neither.

She had given her virginity to Charlie out on a deserted hill-top behind her father's house.

He had sworn that he would come back for her at the earliest opportunity to make her his bride. He had sworn too, holding her tightly to him while they had both wept, that he would love her forever, that no man had ever loved as he loved. She had said much the same in return, of course.

"So," he said, "what do you think? Shall I accept? We have had so little chance to talk since we met again, yet there is so much to say. There is so much reminiscing still to do and so much getting to know each other again. I believe I like the new Claudia every bit as much as I liked the old. But we had happy times to-gether, did we not? No real brother and sister could have been more contented with each other's company."

She had carried anger inside her for such a long time that she sometimes thought it was gone, over with, forgotten. But some long-ago feelings ran so deep that they became part of one's very being.

"We were *not* brother and sister, Charlie," she said briskly, "and we certainly did not think of ourselves as such for the year or two before you went away. We were in love." She kept her eyes on him as the dog settled across her feet and sighed with contentment.

"We were very young," he said, his smile fading.

"There is a perception among the not-so-young," she said, "that the young are incapable of loving, that their feelings are of no significance."

"Young people lack the wisdom that age brings," he said. "It was almost inevitable that we develop romantic feelings for each other, Claudia. We would have grown out of them. I had almost forgotten."

She felt a deep rage—not for herself as she was now, but for the girl she had been. That girl had suffered inconsolably for years.

"We can laugh about it now," he said.

He smiled. She did not.

"I am not laughing," she said. "*Why* did you forget, Charlie? Because I meant so little to you? Because remembering was too uncomfortable for you? Because you felt guilty about that last letter you wrote me?"

I am a duke now, Claudia. You must understand that that makes a great deal of difference.

. . . I am a duke . . .

"And have you forgotten also that we were actually lovers on one occasion?" she asked him.

A dull flush crept up his neck and into his cheeks. She willed herself not to flush too. But she would not look away from his eyes.

"That was unwise," he said, rubbing a hand over the back of his neck as if his neckcloth had suddenly become too tight. "It was unwise of your father to give us so much freedom. It was unwise of you when I was going away and there might have been consequences. And it was unwise of me—"

"Because," she suggested when he hesitated, "there might have been consequences and they might have caused complications to your new life—as your final letter made very clear?"

I must not be seen to associate too closely with people who are beneath my notice. I am a duke now . . .

"I had not realized, Claudia," he said with a sigh, "that you were bitter. I am sorry."

"I left bitterness behind a long time ago," she said, not sure that was strictly true. "But I cannot allow you to continue treating me with hearty delight as your long-lost sister, Charlie, without forcing you to remember what you have so conveniently forgotten."

"It was not easy," he said, sitting back in his chair and dropping his eyes from hers. "But I was just a boy, and suddenly I was faced with duties and responsibilities and a whole life and world I had never even dreamed of."

She said nothing. She knew he spoke the truth, and yet . . .

And yet all that did not excuse the cruelty of his final rejection. And how could she tell herself that she had let go of the hurt and bitterness when she had hated, hated, *hated* all men with the title of duke since then?

"Sometimes," he said, "I have wondered if it was all worth the sacrifices I was forced to make. My dream of a career in the law. You."

Again she said nothing.

"I behaved badly," he admitted at last, getting abruptly to his feet and crossing the room to look out the window. "Do you think I did not realize that? And do you think I did not suffer?"

She did understand. She had always understood the inner turmoil he must have lived through. But some things, if not beyond forgiveness, were at least beyond bland excusing.

She had destroyed that last letter, along with all the others that had preceded it, a long time ago. But she believed she could *still* recite it from memory if she chose to do so.

"If it is any consolation to you, Claudia," he said, "I did not have a happy marriage. Mona was a shrew. I spent as much time from home as I could."

"The Duchess of McLeith is not here to speak up for herself," she said.

"Ah," he said, turning to look at her again, "I see you are determined to quarrel with me, Claudia."

"Not quarrel, Charlie," she said, "merely have some truth spoken between us. How can we go on if we allow ourselves distorted memories of the past?"

"We *can* go on, then?" he asked her. "Will you forgive me for the past, Claudia? Put it down to youth and foolishness and the pressures of a life for which I had had no preparation?"

It was not much of an apology. Even as he made it he also made an excuse for himself. Was youth less accountable than age? But there had been many years of close friendship and a few of love and one afternoon of intense passion. And a year of yearning love letters before the final one that had broken her heart and shattered her world and her very being. Perhaps it was foolish to base her whole opinion of him now on that one letter. Perhaps it was time to forgive.

"Very well," she said after a few moments of silence, and he came toward her to take one of her hands in his and squeeze it.

"I made the biggest mistake of my life when—" he began. "But never mind. What shall I do about this invitation?"

"What do you wish to do?" she asked.

"I wish to accept," he told her. "I like the Ravensbergs and their family and friends. And I want to spend more time with you. Let me come, Claudia. Let me be your brother again. No, not brother. Let me be your *friend* again. We were always friends, were we not? Even at the end?"

To which ending did he refer?

"I lay awake much of last night," he said, "wondering what I ought to do and realizing how my life was impoverished the day I left your father's home and you. And then I knew that I could not accept the invitation unless you said I might."

She had lain awake much of the night too, but she did not believe she had once thought of Charlie. She had thought of two people sitting beneath a willow tree beside a lily pond at night, his coat warm from his body heat about her shoulders, his arm holding it in place, her hand in his, not saying a word to each other for almost half an hour. It was a memory every bit as intense as that of their kiss in Vauxhall Gardens. Perhaps more so. The latter had been about lust. The former had not. She did not care to think of what it *had* been about.

"Go to Alvesley, then," she said, drawing her hand free of

his. "Perhaps we can create new memories for the future while we are there—kinder memories."

She felt a lump form in her throat when he smiled at her—an eager smile that reminded her of the boy he had once been. She had never even dreamed that that boy could be cruel. Was she doing the right thing, though? Was it wise to trust him again? But it was mere friendship he asked for. It might be good to be his friend again, finally to put the past behind her.

"Thank you," he said. "I will not keep you any longer, Claudia. I will go back to my rooms and send an acceptance note to Lady Ravensberg."

After he had left, Claudia looked at the library book again. She did not open it, though. She smoothed her hand over the leather cover until the dog jumped up beside her and set his head in her lap.

"Well, *Horace*," she said aloud, patting his head, "I feel as if I am riding a gigantic rocking horse of emotions. It is not a comfortable feeling at all for someone my age. Indeed, if Lizzie Pickford will not come to Lindsey Hall with me, I believe I may well go straight home to Bath after all and to the devil with Charlie—if you will pardon the shocking language. *And* the Marquess of Attingsborough. But what on earth am I to do about you?"

He raised his eyes to hers without moving his head, and sighed deeply while thumping his tail on the sofa.

"Exactly!" she agreed. "You males all think yourselves irresistible."

Some cousins of Lady Balderston's had arrived in town from Derbyshire, and Joseph had been invited to dine with the family and accompany them to the opera later.

He still had not made an appointment to speak with Balderston, but he would. Perhaps tonight. His procrastination was becoming something of an embarrassment to him.

And perhaps this evening he would try again to woo Portia

Hunt. There must be a softer side to her than she had shown on the way to Vauxhall, and he must find it. He knew that ladies on the whole found him both charming and attractive even though he rarely used that fact to flirt or dally. *Rarely* being the key word. He was uncomfortable about his dealings with Miss Martin. And yet they had not felt like either flirtation or dalliance. He hated to think what they *had* felt like.

And so he was in something of a grim mood all morning while sparring at Gentleman Jackson's boxing saloon. By the time he arrived at Whitleaf's house on Grosvenor Square in the afternoon, he was determined to be all business. He was taking Miss Martin to see Lizzie, to make her a proposition for the summer, to allow her to decide for herself. His own involvement need be only very minimal.

She was dressed simply as usual in the dress she had worn to the picnic, though it had been ironed since then. She wore the same straw hat too. She was holding the dog in her arms as she came downstairs at the butler's summons.

She looked like someone he must have known all his life. She looked like a little piece of home—whatever the devil his mind meant by presenting him with that odd idea.

"We are both ready," she said briskly.

"Are you sure you wish to take the dog driving, Claudia?" Whitleaf asked her. "You are quite welcome to leave him here with us."

"He can do with the airing," she said. "But thank you, Peter. You are remarkably kind considering the fact that you had little choice but to take him in or boot me out." She laughed.

"Go and enjoy yourself, then," Susanna told her, though it was at him she looked, Joseph saw, a speculative look in her eyes.

For the first time it struck him that, not knowing the true nature of Miss Martin's drives with him, she and Whitleaf must wonder what the devil he was up to—especially as they probably knew that he was to all intents and purposes a betrothed man. He had put Miss Martin in an awkward position, he realized.

They proceeded on their way in his curricle though the weather was not quite as warm as it had been recently. There were a few clouds to take the edge off the heat when they covered the sun.

"Where did you tell Susanna you were going this afternoon?" he asked.

"For a drive in the park," she said.

"And the other times?"

"For a drive in the park." She concentrated her attention on the dog.

"And what has she had to say about all these drives?" he asked.

He turned his head in time to see her flush before lowering her head.

"Oh, nothing," she said. "Why should she say anything?"

They must think he was dallying with her while courting Miss Hunt. And the devil of it was that they were not far off the mark. He grimaced inwardly. This must all be very distressing for her.

They lapsed into silence. But silence today must be avoided at all costs, he decided after a few moments, and it seemed that she agreed. All the rest of the way to Lizzie's they talked cheerfully about books they had both read. But it was not stilted, awkward talk, as he might have expected. It was lively and intelligent. He could have wished that the journey were longer.

Lizzie was in the upstairs parlor waiting for him. She hugged him with both arms wound about his neck, as she usually did, and then cocked her head to one side.

"You have someone with you, Papa," she said. "Is it Miss Martin?"

"It is," he said, and watched her face brighten.

"And not just me," Miss Martin said. "I have brought someone else to meet you, Lizzie. At least, he is *almost* a someone. I have brought Horace."

Horace? Joseph shot her an amused glance, but her attention was all focused upon his daughter.

"You brought your *dog*!" Lizzie cried just as the collie decided to bark.

"He wants to be friends," Miss Martin explained as Lizzie recoiled. "He absolutely will not hurt you. I have a firm hold on him anyway. Here, let me take your hand."

She did so and brought it to the dog's head and smoothed it down over his back. The dog turned his head and licked her wrist. Lizzie snatched back her hand but then shrieked with laughter.

"He *licked* me!" she cried. "Let me feel him again."

"He is a border collie," Miss Martin explained as she took Lizzie's hand again and guided it to the dog's head. "One of the most intelligent of dogs. Collies are often used to guard sheep, to stop them from wandering, to round them up when they do, to lead them back to the fold when they have been out in the fields or in the hills grazing. Of course Horace is not much more than a puppy and has not been fully trained yet."

Joseph went to open the parlor window and stood there, watching his daughter fall in love. Soon she was seated on the sofa with the dog beside her, panting with delight as she explored him with sensitive, gentle hands and laughing as he licked first one of her hands and then her face.

"Oh, Papa," she cried, "look at me. And look at Horace."

"I *am* looking, sweetheart," he said.

He watched Miss Martin too as she sat beside his child, on the other side of the dog, petting him with her and telling Lizzie the story of how she had acquired him, embellishing it considerably so that it seemed much more comical than it had been in reality. It seemed to Joseph that she was entirely engrossed in her conversation with his daughter, that she had forgotten his presence. It was very easy to see how she had become a successful teacher and why he had sensed a happy atmosphere at her school.

"I remember your telling me," Miss Martin said, "that all the stories you make up have a dog in them. Would you like to tell me one of those stories and have me write it down for you?"

"Now?" Lizzie asked, laughing as she drew back her head from another enthusiastic licking.

"Why not?" Miss Martin said. "Perhaps your papa will find paper and pen and ink for me."

She looked at him with raised eyebrows, and he left the room without further ado. When he came back, they were both sitting on the floor, the dog between them on his back, having his stomach rubbed. Both Lizzie and Miss Martin were chuckling, their heads close together.

Something stirred deep inside Joseph.

And then Miss Martin sat at a small table writing while Lizzie told a lurid tale of witches and wizards practicing their evil arts deep in a forest where an unfortunate little girl got lost one day. As trees closed about her to imprison her and tree roots thrust upward to trip her and grew tentacles to wrap about her ankles to bring her down, and as thunder crashed overhead and other dire catastrophes loomed, her only hope of escape was her own intrepid heart and a stray dog that appeared suddenly and attacked everything except the thunder and finally, bleeding and exhausted, led the girl to the edge of the wood, from where she could hear her mother singing in her garden full of sweet-smelling flowers. It seemed the thunderstorm had not spread beyond the forest.

"There," Miss Martin said, setting her pen down. "I have it all. Shall I read it back to you?"

She proceeded to do so. Lizzie clapped her hands and laughed when she had finished.

"That is my story *exactly*," she said. "Did you hear it, Papa?"

"I did," he said.

"You will be able to read it to me," she said.

"And so I will," he agreed. "But not at bedtime, Lizzie. Perhaps *you* could sleep afterward, but I am sure *I* would not. I am still shaking in my boots. I thought they would both perish."

"Oh, Papa!" she said. "The main characters in stories always live happily ever after. You know that."

His eyes met Miss Martin's. Yes, in stories, perhaps. Real life was often different.

"Perhaps, Lizzie," he said, "we could take Miss Martin out to the garden and you can name all the flowers for her. The dog can come too."

She jumped to her feet and reached out an arm to him.

"Come with me to fetch my bonnet," she said.

He took one step toward her and then stopped.

"Be my clever girl and go and fetch it without me," he said. "Can you do it?"

"Of course I can." Her face lit up. "Count to fifty, Papa, and I will be back. Not too fast, though, silly," she added, laughing with glee as he began rattling off numbers.

"One . . . two . . . three," he began again more slowly as she left the room. After a moment the dog scrambled to his feet and went after her.

"She really is capable of a great deal, is she not?" he said. "I have been remiss. I ought to have arranged something for her much sooner than this. It is just that she has been a very young child, and love and protection seemed enough."

"Don't blame yourself," Miss Martin said. "Love is worth more than any one other gift you could give her. And it is not too late. Eleven is a good age for her to discover that she has wings."

"With which to fly away from me?" he said with a rueful smile.

"Yes," she agreed, "and with which to fly back to you again."

"Freedom," he said. "Is it possible for her?"

"Only she can decide that," she said.

But he could hear Lizzie's returning footsteps on the stairs.

". . . forty . . . forty-one . . . forty-two . . ." he said loudly.

"Here I am!" she shrieked from outside the door, and then she appeared in the doorway, flushed and excited, eyelids fluttering while the dog rushed past her. "And here is my bonnet." She waved it from one hand.

"Oh, bravo, Lizzie," Miss Martin said.

Love tightened in Joseph's chest almost like pain.

They spent an hour in the garden before Mrs. Smart brought out the tea tray. Lizzie engaged in one of her favorite games, bending over flowers and feeling them and smelling them before identifying them. Sometimes she clasped her hands behind her and played the game from the sense of smell alone. Miss Martin tried it too, her eyes closed, but she made as many errors as correct identifications and Lizzie laughed with glee. She also listened attentively as Miss Martin gave her a lesson in botany, pointing out parts and qualities of each plant while Lizzie felt to see what she was talking about.

Joseph sat watching. He almost never had the leisure simply to observe his daughter. Usually when he visited he was the whole focus of her world. Today she had Miss Martin and the dog, and while she frequently called to him to be sure that he had noticed something, she was clearly reveling in their company.

Is this what family life might have been like, he wondered, if he had been free to marry as a younger man—when he met and fell in love with Barbara? Would he have delighted in his wife and children as he was delighting in Miss Martin and Lizzie? Would there have been this contentment, this happiness?

Their heads were touching as they bent over a pansy. Miss Martin set one arm loosely about Lizzie's waist, and Lizzie set her arm about Miss Martin's shoulders. The dog woofed around them before racing off to chase a butterfly.

Good Lord, Joseph thought suddenly. Dash it all, this line of thought just would not do. This was exactly what he had resolved not to do this afternoon.

He would have his family life. The wife and mother would not be either Barbara or Miss Martin, and none of the children would be Lizzie. But he *would* have it. He would begin wooing Portia Hunt in full earnest this evening. He would call upon Balderston tomorrow and then make her a formal offer. Surely she would relax more once they were officially betrothed. Surely she must want some affection, some warmth, some family closeness, out of her marriage too. *Of course* she must.

The tea tray arrived to interrupt his thoughts, and the ladies came to sit down. Miss Martin poured the tea.

"Lizzie," she said after handing about the cups and the pastries, "I would like to see you get more fresh air during the summer. You enjoyed the afternoon in Richmond Park, did you not? I would like to see you walk and run and skip again and find more flowers and plants than you yet know. I would like you to come into the country with me for a few weeks."

Lizzie, who was sitting beside Joseph, felt for him with the hand that was not holding her plate. He took it in a firm grasp.

"I do not want to go to school, Papa," she said.

"This is not school," Miss Martin explained. "One of my teachers, Miss Thompson, is going to take ten of the girls from the school to Lindsey Hall in Hampshire for a few weeks. It is a large mansion in the country with a huge park around it. They are going there for a holiday, and I am going too. Some of my girls, you see, do not have parents or homes and so must stay with us during holiday times. We try to give them a good time with lots of activities and lots of fun. I thought you might like to come with me."

"Are you going too, Papa?" Lizzie asked.

"I will be going for a while to a house nearby," he said. "I will be able to come and see you."

"And who will take me?" Lizzie asked.

"I will," Miss Martin said.

He looked closely at Lizzie. All the faint color the hour outdoors had brought into her cheeks had faded.

"I am afraid," she whispered.

He squeezed her hand more tightly. "You do not have to go," he said. "You do not have to go anywhere. I will find someone else to come and live here and be your companion, someone you will like, someone who will be kind to you."

Perhaps Miss Martin would disagree with him. Perhaps she would think that he should insist that his daughter find her wings, that he should push her out of the nest, so to speak.

But she said nothing. And actually she had said just the opposite, had she not? She had told him that Lizzie must decide for herself.

"Those girls would hate me," Lizzie said.

"Why would they?" Miss Martin asked.

"Because I have a home and a papa," Lizzie said.

"I do not believe they will hate you," Miss Martin said.

"I would not say anything about having a papa," Lizzie said, brightening. "I would pretend to be just like them."

Which was exactly the way Miss Martin had described her to the Duchess of Bewcastle—as a charity girl brought to her attention by her man of business. And he was not going to speak up in protest? Was he really ashamed of her, then? Or was he just bowing to what society expected of any gentleman?

"Would they do things with me?" the child asked, turning her face in Miss Martin's direction. "Would they think me a nuisance?"

Yet again Joseph admired Miss Martin's honesty. She did not rush immediately into a denial.

"We will have to find out," she said. "They will certainly be polite. They learn good manners at my school. But it will be up to you to make friends."

"But I have never *had* friends," Lizzie said.

"Then this will be your chance to make some," Miss Martin told her.

"And I would come back here after a few weeks?" Lizzie asked.

"If you chose," Miss Martin said.

Lizzie sat very still, no longer touching Joseph. Her hands fidgeting in her lap showed her agitation. So did the fact that she rocked back and forth as she sometimes did when she was deeply troubled. Her eyelids fluttered and her eyes wandered beneath them. Her lips moved silently.

Joseph resisted the urge to gather her up in his arms.

"But I am so afraid," she whispered again.

"Then you will remain here," he said firmly. "I will start looking immediately for a new companion."

"I did not mean I would not *go*, Papa," she said, "only that I am *afraid*."

She continued to rock and fidget while Miss Martin said nothing and Joseph felt resentful of her—quite unjustifiably, of course.

"I have learned all about courage from some of the stories you have told me, Papa," Lizzie said at last. "You can only show courage when you are afraid. If you are not afraid, there is no need of courage."

"And you have always wanted to do something courageous, Lizzie?" Miss Martin asked. "Like Amanda in your story, when she might have escaped from the forest earlier if she had not stopped to rescue the dog from the rabbit snare?"

"But it is not just for fighting witches and evil, is it?" Lizzie said.

"It is also for stepping into the unknown," Claudia said, "when it would be easier to cling to what is familiar and safe."

"I think, then," Lizzie said after another short silence, "I will be courageous. Will you be proud of me if I am, Papa?"

"I am *always* proud of you, sweetheart," he said. "But yes, I would be especially proud if you were to be brave enough to go. And I would be very happy if it turned out that you enjoyed yourself as I daresay you would."

"Then I will go," she said decisively, and abruptly stopped rocking. "I will go, Miss Martin."

Then she turned sharply to paw at Joseph's arm and scrambled onto his lap to hug him tightly and hide against him.

His arms closed about her and he tipped back his head and closed his eyes. He swallowed, feeling absurdly close to tears. When he opened his eyes, he could see that Miss Martin was watching them steadily, looking like a disciplined teacher again—or like his very dear friend.

Without thinking he stretched one arm across the table

between them and, after looking at his hand for a moment, she set her own in it.

Ah, sometimes life was bitterly ironic. He felt again as if he had found a family where there could be none—just when he was honor-bound to offer for a woman who wanted never to be kissed.

His hand closed about Miss Martin's and squeezed tightly.

Late one afternoon two weeks later Claudia was dressed in her old faithful blue evening gown and was styling her hair herself, having declined the Duchess of Bewcastle's kind offer of the services of a maid. She was feeling unaccountably depressed when she had every reason to feel just the opposite.

She was being treated as a favored guest at Lindsey Hall rather than as a teacher in charge of a largish group of charity schoolgirls. And within half an hour she would be on her way with the Bedwyn family to a celebratory dinner and social evening at Alvesley Park. She would see Susanna there. She would also see Anne, who had arrived from Wales with Sydnam and their children just yesterday.

The journey from London a few days ago had proceeded uneventfully, though Lizzie had been tearful for a while after leaving the house and her father and had clung to Claudia the whole way. But Susanna and Peter, with whom they had traveled, had been kind to her, the dog had snuggled up beside her, and she had been more than thrilled when the carriages had stopped and Harry's nurse had brought him forward to his mother and Lizzie had been allowed to touch his little hand and smooth her hand over his downy head.

It had been good to see Eleanor Thompson again and the girls she had brought to Lindsey Hall, and they had all seemed genuinely glad to see her. They had greeted Lizzie with caution and curiosity, but on the very first evening Agnes Ryde, the most dominant of the girls and sixteen years old, had decided to take the new girl under her wing, and Molly Wiggins, the youngest and most timid, had chosen Lizzie as her particular friend and taken her firmly by the hand. She had promptly offered to brush Lizzie's hair and had borne her off to the room they were to share, while Agnes took her other arm.

It had been good to see Flora and Edna again, and to discover that both seemed quite blissfully happy with their new lot in life and eager to show off a little for their former schoolmates.

The duchess had been amiable. So had Lord and Lady Aidan Bedwyn, the Earl and Countess of Rosthorn—the countess was the younger of two Bedwyn sisters—and the Marquess of Hallmere. The Duke of Bewcastle had been polite. He had even engaged Claudia in conversation for all of ten minutes at dinner one evening, and she had not been able to fault his manners. And Lady Hallmere had actually come striding across the lawn from the stables one morning dressed in her riding habit and had bidden Claudia a good morning before talking briefly with Molly and Lizzie, who were laboriously making daisy chains. The dog meanwhile had been chasing his tail and any flying creature that was incautious enough to venture into his space.

Lady Hallmere acted like a queen condescending to the lowliest of her subjects, Claudia had thought unkindly until she had chastised herself for unfairness. The woman could easily have ignored them altogether. And her words in London had chastened Claudia somewhat—*you bear a long grudge, Miss Martin.*

Charlie had ridden over from Alvesley each day, and once they had gone for a long walk about the lake and talked without stopping. It had felt quite like old times—well, perhaps not quite. He had been a hero in those long-ago days, an idol, someone incapable of doing anything wrong or remotely ignoble. Now she had no illusions about him. He was a man, like all others, with human weaknesses. But it felt undeniably good to be with him again, to talk with him. She was not sure she could ever really trust him again, but then she was not being called to trust. Just to enjoy a resumption of their friendship.

And then had come the invitation to go to Alvesley with everyone else except Eleanor, who had volunteered to remain behind with the girls, something that was hardly a sacrifice, she had insisted to both Claudia and her sister, since she found most social entertainments a colossal bore.

And of course, Claudia thought as she set down her brush and got to her feet and picked up her paisley shawl, it was that invitation and the reason behind it that was responsible for the dip in her mood. It was indeed to be a celebratory dinner even though it was a whole week before the planned anniversary party for the Earl and Countess of Redfield.

This celebration was for a new betrothal.

Miss Hunt's to the Marquess of Attingsborough.

And it was a massive case of self-deception to tell herself that it was an *unaccountable* depression that she felt.

She was going to Alvesley, then, to celebrate his betrothal. She might easily have avoided going, she supposed, but she had decided that it would be cowardly to stay away. And it had never been her nature to avoid reality. Besides, she was genuinely looking forward to seeing Anne and Susanna.

An hour or so later, when she arrived at Alvesley with the Lindsey Hall party, she was immediately engulfed in a great bustle of greetings. But within moments she found herself caught up in the arms of a laughing Anne. And suddenly she was very glad indeed that she had come.

"Claudia!" Anne cried. "Oh, how good it is to see you. You are looking very well indeed and have been taking London by storm, if Susanna is to be believed."

Claudia laughed. "Somewhat of an exaggeration," she said. "Anne, you look wonderful. You look as if you are bursting with good health. But your face is not *sun*-bronzed, is it?"

"It is the sea air," Anne explained. "Sydnam would have it that it is also the *Welsh* air."

He was standing beside her, and Claudia offered him her hand, remembering to give her left as he had no right arm. He smiled as he shook it—his rather charming, lopsided smile, as burns to the right side of his face had damaged the nerves there.

"Claudia," he said, "it is good to see you again."

Anne linked an arm through his and looked at Claudia with shining eyes.

"We have wonderful news," she said, "and have been telling everyone who is willing to listen." She looked up at her husband and laughed. "Or rather *I* have been telling everyone. Sydnam is far too modest. He is to have three of his paintings hung at the Royal Academy in the autumn. Have you ever heard anything more exciting?"

There was a shriek from nearby and the Countess of Rosthorn dashed up to Sydnam Butler and hugged him tightly.

"Syd!" she cried. "Is it *true*? Oh, I am so happy I could weep. And look, that is just what I am doing. Silly me. I knew you could do it. I just *knew*. Gervase, do come and hear this, and please bring a handkerchief with you."

Mr. Butler had been a talented artist before losing his right arm and eye during the Peninsular Wars. After that he had devoted himself to becoming a good steward, having persuaded the Duke of Bewcastle into giving him a post at his estate in Wales. But soon after his marriage to Anne two years ago, Sydnam had started to paint again, under her encouragement, using his left hand and his mouth.

Claudia took Anne's arm and squeezed it.

"I am so happy for both of you, Anne," she said. "How is my boy David? And Megan?"

David Jewell was Anne's son, born nine years before she met Mr. Butler. When Anne had taught at the school in Bath, David had lived there too. After they left, Claudia had missed him almost as much as she had missed Anne.

But she scarcely heard Anne's reply. She had spotted the Marquess of Attingsborough, who was speaking with the Duchess of Bewcastle and Lady Hallmere. He looked tall and imposing and handsome. He was also smiling and looking very happy.

He looked like a stranger, Claudia thought. And yet, even as she thought it, his eyes met hers across the crowded hallway and he looked again like the man who had become strangely dear to her during the course of a couple of weeks in London.

He was making his way toward her, she could see a moment later. She turned away from Anne to meet him.

"Miss Martin," he said, offering his hand.

"Lord Attingsborough." She set her hand in his.

"How is Lizzie?" He had lowered his voice.

"She is doing remarkably well," Claudia told him. "She has made friends and daisy chains. And Horace has shown no loyalty whatsoever—he has abandoned me to become her shadow. The duke's head groom is making a collar and leash for him so that Lizzie can hold it and be led about. I believe the dog knows that she needs protection and will learn to be invaluable to her after some training."

"Daisy chains?" He raised his eyebrows.

"They are well within her capabilities," she said. "She can find and identify daisies in the grass, and making the chains is really quite easy. She has been going about bedecked with gar-lands and coronets."

He smiled. "And friends?"

"Agnes Ryde, the most fierce of my pupils, has become her self-appointed guardian," Claudia told him, "and Molly Wiggins and Doris Chalmers are vying for the position of best friend. I be-lieve the contest was won early, though, since Molly had the idea first and shares a room with Lizzie. They have become virtually inseparable."

He beamed at her. But before either of them could say more Miss Hunt, looking lovely in pink, appeared at his side and took his arm. She smiled at him after favoring Claudia with a dis-tant nod.

"You must come and speak with the Duke and Duchess of

Bewcastle," she said. "They are over there, talking with Mama and Papa."

He bowed to Claudia and turned away with his betrothed.

Claudia firmly shook off the depression that had been hovering over her all day. It was really quite demeaning—not to mention silly—to be coveting someone else's man. Susanna, smiling brightly in welcome, was coming toward her from one side and Charlie, smiling just as warmly, was approaching from the other. She had every reason in the world to be cheerful.

And truly she *was*.

Joseph really was feeling reasonably happy. His marriage offer had, of course, been favorably received by both Balderston and Portia herself. Lady Balderston had been ecstatic.

The wedding was to be celebrated in the autumn in London. That had been decided by Lady Balderston and Portia between them. It was a pity, they had both agreed, that it could not take place at a more fashionable time of the year when all the *ton* would be in town, but it was far too long to wait until next spring, especially given the indifferent health of the Duke of Anburey.

The talk ever since—whenever Joseph was within hearing distance, anyway—had been all of guest lists and bride clothes and wedding trips. It all gave him renewed hope that his marriage would be a good one after all. Of course, all the bustle of wedding plans and then the removal to Alvesley had made it impossible for him to spend any private time with his betrothed, but that situation would surely be rectified after this evening's celebrations were over. And it was undeniably good to see almost all his family gathered for the occasion, including his mother and father, who had come from Bath. Lord and Lady Balderston were there too, though they were to leave tomorrow, before the anniversary celebrations began in earnest.

As good manners dictated, Portia did not remain at his side

after dinner, when everyone gathered in the drawing room. She sat sipping her tea with Neville and Lily and McLeith. Nev had beckoned her over, somewhat to Joseph's surprise. He knew that neither he nor Lily really liked her yet. Perhaps they were making an effort to get to know her better.

Only one thing threatened to lower his spirits—well, perhaps two if he included the presence of Miss Martin, of whom he had grown far too fond while they were both in London. He was missing Lizzie dreadfully. She was tantalizingly close there at Lindsey Hall, making friends and daisy chains and shadowed by a border collie. He wanted to be there, tucking her into bed, reading her a story. Yet society decreed that a man's illegitimate offspring be kept not only away from his family but also a secret from them.

"You are wool-gathering, Joseph," his cousin Gwen, the widowed Lady Muir, said as she came to sit beside him.

"What gives society its power, Gwen?" he asked.

"An interesting question," she said, smiling at him. "Society is made up of individuals—and yet it does have a collective entity all its own, does it not? What gives it its power? I don't know. History, perhaps? Habit? A combination of the two? Or the collective fear that if we relax any of its stringent rules we will be overrun by the dreaded lower classes? The specter of what happened in France still looms large, I suppose. It is all absurd, though. That is why I stay away from society as much as I can. Do you have a particular problem with it?"

He almost confided in her. What would she say if he told her about Lizzie, as he had told her brother long ago? He was almost convinced that she would be neither shocked nor unsympathetic. But he could not do it. She was his cousin and his friend—but she was also a lady. He countered her question with one of his own.

"Do you ever wish," he asked, "that you could move away to the farthest corner of the world and start a new life, where no one knows you and there are no expectations of you?"

"Oh, yes, of course," she said, "but I seriously doubt there is such a corner." She touched his hand and lowered her voice. "Are you regretting this, Joseph? Did Uncle Webster force you into it?"

"My engagement?" He laughed lightly. "No, of course not. Portia will make an admirable duchess."

"And an admirable wife too?" She looked closely at him. "I do want to see you happy, Joseph. You have always been my favorite cousin, I must confess. My favorite *male* cousin, at least, since I cannot claim to have loved you more than I do Lauren. But then Lauren and I grew up more as sisters than cousins."

As if summoned by the mention of her name, Lauren joined them at that moment, bringing Miss Martin with her.

"Gwen," she said after a few minutes, "come to the supper room with me for a minute, will you? There is something upon which I need your opinion."

Neville and Lily were leaving the room via the French windows, Joseph could see. They were taking Portia and McLeith with them, presumably for a stroll outside.

And so they were virtually alone together again, he and Miss Martin. She was wearing a dark blue gown that he had seen more than once in London. Her hair was dressed as severely as it ever had been. Once again she looked unmistakably a schoolteacher, remarkably plainly turned out in contrast with all the other ladies. But he could no longer see her with the old eyes. He could see only the firmness of character, the kindness, the intelligence, the . . . yes, the *passion* for life that had endeared her to him.

"Are you happy to be back with some of your pupils?" he asked her.

"I am," she said. "It is with them I belong."

"I want to see them," he said. "I want to see Lizzie."

"And she wants to see you," she told him. "She knows you are here, not far away from her. At the same time, she is convinced that the girls will no longer like her if they know she has a father, and such a wealthy one. She has told me that if you come she will pretend not to know you. She thinks it would be a funny game."

And of course it would suit his purposes admirably. But he felt grim at the very thought that for different reasons they must hide their relationship from others.

Miss Martin touched his hand, just as Gwen had done a few minutes ago.

"She is really quite happy," she told him. "She thinks of these weeks as a marvelous adventure, though she told me last night that she still does not want to go to school. She wants to go home."

He felt strangely comforted by the thought—strange when it would be far more convenient for him if she went away.

"She may change her mind," she said.

"Is she educable, then?" he asked her.

"I think she may be," she said, "and Eleanor Thompson agrees with me. It would take some ingenuity, of course, to fit her into our routine with tasks that are both meaningful and possible for her, but we have never shunned a doable challenge."

"What personal satisfaction do you draw from your life?" he asked, leaning a little closer to her. And then he wished fervently that he had not asked such an impulsive and impertinent question.

"There are many persons in my life, Lord Attingsborough," she said, "whom I can love in both an abstract, emotional sense and in practical ways. Not everyone can say as much."

It was not a good enough answer.

"But does there not have to be one special someone?" he asked her.

"Like Lizzie for you?" she asked.

It was not what he had meant. Even Lizzie was not enough. Oh, she was, she *was*—but . . . But not for that deep core of himself that craved a mate, an equal, a sexual partner.

He completely forgot for the moment that he already had such a person in his life. He had a betrothed.

"Yes," he said.

"But it is not what you meant, is it?" she asked him, searching his eyes with her own. "We are not all fated to find that special someone, Lord Attingsborough. Or if we are, sometimes we are fated also to lose that person. And what do we do when it happens? Sit around moping and feeling tragic for the rest of our lives? Or find other people to love, other people to benefit from the love that wells constantly from within ourselves if we do not deliberately stop the flow?"

He sat back in his chair, his eyes still on her. Ah, but he did indeed have that special someone in his life. But only on the periphery of it—and always to remain there. She had come too late. Though there would never have been the right time, would there? Miss Martin was not of his world—and he was not of hers.

"I choose to love others," she said. "I love all my girls, even those who are least lovable. And, believe me, there are plenty of those." She smiled.

But she had admitted to what he had always suspected, always sensed in her. She was an essentially lonely woman. As he was essentially lonely—on the very evening when a large company of relatives and friends had gathered to celebrate his betrothal and he had persuaded himself that he was happy.

He was going to have to make this up to Portia. He was going to have to love her with all the deliberate power of his will.

"I must try to emulate you, Miss Martin," he said.

"It is perhaps enough," she said, "that you love Lizzie."

Ah, she knew, then. Or she knew, at least, that he did not love Portia as he ought.

"But is it enough that I will not acknowledge her publicly?" he asked.

She tipped her head slightly to one side and thought—a characteristic reaction of hers when other persons might have rushed into a glib answer.

"I know you feel guilty about that," she said, "and perhaps with good reason. But not for the reason you always fear. You are *not* ashamed of her. I have seen you with her and I can assure you of that. But you are trapped between two worlds—the one you have inherited and to which you are firmly committed by the fact that you are the heir to a dukedom, and the one you made for yourself when you created Lizzie with your mistress. Both worlds are important to you—the one because you are impelled by duty, the other because you are enmeshed in love. And both are worlds that will pull at you forever."

"Forever." He smiled ruefully at her.

"Yes," she said. "Duty and love. But especially love."

He was about to reach out for her hand, forgetting his surroundings again, when Portfrey and Elizabeth joined them. Elizabeth wanted to know about the little blind girl she had heard Miss Martin had brought to Lindsey Hall.

Miss Martin told her about Lizzie.

"How very brave and admirable of you, Miss Martin," Elizabeth said. "I would love to meet her and all your other charity girls too. May I? Or would it appear to be an intrusion, as if I thought them merely an amusing curiosity? Lyndon and I have extended the school at home so that all local children are eligible to attend, but I have toyed with the idea of making it also a boarding school to accommodate children from farther distances."

"I think," Miss Martin said, "the girls would be delighted to meet you."

"I have just persuaded Miss Martin to let me come on the same errand," Joseph said. "I met two of her former pupils when I escorted them and her to London several weeks ago, and now they are at Lindsey Hall too, one as governess to the Hallmere children, the other as governess to Aidan Bedwyn's children."

"Ah," Elizabeth said, "then we will go together, Joseph. Will tomorrow afternoon suit you, Miss Martin, weather permitting?"

And so it was arranged—as simply as that.

Tomorrow he would see Lizzie.

And Miss Martin again.

Lily and Neville were coming inside, he noticed.

Portia and McLeith remained outside.

When she came back in, Joseph thought, he was going to have to spend the rest of the evening with her, perhaps in private conversation if it could be arranged. He was going to love her, by Jove, even if he could never *fall* in love with her. He owed her that much.

Miss Martin got to her feet, bade him good night, and went to join the Butlers and the Whitleafs. Soon she was glowing with animation.

Some of the older girls had gone out for a walk. One of the younger ones was playing quietly and ploddingly on the spinet in the schoolroom at Lindsey Hall. Another read silently to herself, curled up on the window seat. A third was embroidering a large daisy across the corner of a cotton handkerchief. Molly was reading aloud from *Robinson Crusoe*, and Becky, Lady Aidan's elder daughter, was listening with rapt attention. Claudia was teaching Lizzie to knit, having cast on twenty stitches and knitted up a few rows to get her started. The collie lay at their feet, his head on his paws, his eyes turned upward.

Claudia looked up when the door opened. It was Eleanor, who had been enjoying a prolonged breakfast with the duchess.

"Miss Martin," she said, "the Duke of McLeith has ridden over from Alvesley again and wishes to see you. I will stay with the girls while you are gone. Oh, Lizzie is learning to knit, is she? Let me see if I can help. And I do apologize, Molly. I have interrupted your reading. Please continue."

Her eyes twinkled at Claudia. They had had a long talk after Charlie's last visit. Eleanor was convinced that his interest was more than just fraternal.

Claudia found him in the morning room downstairs, in conversation with the Duke of Bewcastle and Lord Aidan. Both withdrew soon after her arrival.

She sat. Charlie did not. He crossed the room to the window

instead and stood looking out. His clasped hands tapped against his back.

"Ever since you forced me to remember," he said, "the floodgates of memory have opened, Claudia. Not just remembered *events*, which are relatively easy to forget, but remembered *feelings*, which never can be. They can only be suppressed. In the last week I have done nothing but remember how wretchedly unhappy I was after I left you, and how totally unable I was to come back to face you when I felt obliged to marry someone else. I really had no choice, you know. I had to marry—"

"Someone from your own world," she said, interrupting him. "Someone who would not shame or embarrass you with the inferiority of her birth and manners."

He turned his head to look at her.

"That was not it," he said. "I never thought those things about you, Claudia."

"Did you not?" she said. "Was it someone impersonating your handwriting who wrote that final letter to me, then?"

"I did not write those things," he protested.

"You were sorry to be so plain with me," she said, "but really you ought not to have been taken to live with Papa and me in the first place since there was always the possibility that you would inherit a dukedom one day. You ought to have been given a home and upbringing more suited to your station. The fact that you had lived with us all those years had put you in an awkward position with your peers. I must understand why you felt it necessary to break off all connection with me. You were a *duke* now. You must not be seen to associate too closely with people who were beneath your notice. You were to marry Lady Mona Chesterton, who was everything a duchess and your wife ought to be."

"Claudia!" He looked pale and aghast. "I did not write those things."

"Then I wonder who did," she said. "Losing someone one loves is one of the worst things that can happen to anyone, Charlie. But to be rejected because one is inferior, because one is despised, because one simply is not good enough...It took me years to gain back my self-respect, my self-confidence. And to put the pieces of my heart back together. Do you *wonder* that I was less than delighted to see you again in London a few weeks ago?"

"Claudia!" He passed a hand through his thinning hair. "My God! I must have been so upset that I was out of my mind."

She did not believe it for a moment. Becoming a *duke* had gone to his head. It had made him conceited and arrogant and any number of other nasty things she would never have suspected him capable of.

He sat down on a chair close to the window and stared at her.

"Forgive me," he said. "Lord, Claudia, forgive me. I was even more of an ass than I remember. But you *did* recover. You did magnificently well, in fact."

"Did I?" she said.

"You proved," he said, "that you were the strong person I always knew you were. And I have paid my dues to whatever power decreed that I be snatched from my familiar life—twice, once when I was five and once when I was eighteen—and plunged into a completely alien one. There is no longer any reason, though, why either of us cannot return to where we were when I was eighteen and you were seventeen. Is there?"

What exactly did he mean? Return to *what*?

"I have a life," she said, "that involves responsibility to others. I have my school. And you have duties to others that only you can perform. You have your son."

"There is no obstacle," he said, "that cannot be overcome. We have been apart for eighteen years, Claudia—half my life. Are we going to remain apart for the rest of our lives too just because you have a school and I have a son—who, by the way, is almost grown up? Or will you marry me at last?"

She very much feared afterward that her jaw had dropped.

If only she had seen this coming, she thought—if only she had believed Eleanor—she might have prepared herself. Instead she stared stupidly and mutely at him.

He came across the room to her and bent over her to take both her hands in his.

"Remember how we were together, Claudia," he said. "Remember how we loved each other with the sort of all-consuming passion the very young are not afraid of. Remember how we made love up on that hill—surely the only time in my life I have really *made love*. It has been a long, weary time, but it is not too late for us. Marry me, my love, and I will make up for that letter and for the eighteen years of emptiness in your life."

"My life has not been empty, Charlie," she told him.

Though it had been—in some ways at least.

He looked into her eyes. "Tell me you did not love me," he said. "Tell me you *do* not love me."

"I did," she said, closing her eyes. "You know I did."

"And you do."

She felt dreadfully upset, remembering that long-ago love, its physical consummation, and the anguish of the yearlong separation and then its cruel, abrupt ending. It was not possible to go back, to forget that even as boy he had been capable of destroying the one person he had professed to love more than life.

Besides, it was too late for him.

He was the wrong man.

"Charlie," she said, "we have both changed in eighteen years. We are different people."

"Yes," he agreed. "I have less hair and you are a woman rather than a girl. But at heart, Claudia? Are we not the same as we ever were, the same as we always will be? You have never married even though you had plenty of would-be suitors even before I left home. That tells me something. And I have admitted to you that I was never happy with Mona, though I was rarely unfaithful to her."

Rarely? Oh, Charlie!

"I cannot marry you," she said, leaning a little toward him. "If we had married then, Charlie, we would have grown together and I daresay I would have loved you all my life. But we did not marry then."

"And love dies?" he asked her. "Did you ever love me truly, then?"

She felt a spurt of anger. Had *he* truly loved *her*?

"Some forms of love die," she said. "If they are not fed, they die. I have gradually been coming to like you again since we met in London—as the friend you were through our childhood."

His jaw was hard-set as she remembered its being whenever he was angry or upset.

"I have spoken too soon," he said. "I must confess that the violence of my feelings has surprised even me. I will give you time to catch up with me. Don't say an outright no today. You already have, but let us agree to forget that you spoke the words. Give me time to woo you—and to make you forget what I once wrote to you."

He released her hands after squeezing them.

"Goodness, Charlie," she said, "look at me. I am a thirty-five-year-old spinster schoolteacher."

He smiled slowly.

"You are Claudia Martin," he said, "that bold, vital girl I loved, now masquerading as a spinster schoolteacher. *What a lark,* you would have said then if you could have looked ahead."

If she could have looked ahead, she would have been consumed with horror.

"It is no masquerade," she said.

"I beg to disagree," he told her. "I had better go now—I am expected back at Alvesley for luncheon. But I will come again if I may."

But after he had gone she stared at her hands in her lap. How very strange life could be. For years and years now her school had been her whole world, all thoughts of love and romance and marriage long suppressed. Yet she had made the seemingly harmless decision to accompany Flora and Edna to London so that she could talk to Mr. Hatchard in person and her whole world—her whole *universe*—had changed.

She wondered in some trepidation how she was going to be

able to recapture the relative contentment and tranquillity of her life when she returned to Bath.

There was a tap on the door and it opened to reveal Eleanor.

"Ah, you *are* still here," she said, coming inside. "I have just seen the duke riding away. Louise is still playing the spinet, but the others have gone outside—except Molly and Lizzie. Becky has taken them to the nursery to meet her little sister, Hannah, and her new governess as well as numerous cousins, all of whom are very young. Lizzie is doing very well, Claudia, even if you did find her crying to herself in her bed this morning."

"This is all very bewildering but very exciting for her," Claudia said.

"Poor girl," Eleanor said. "One wonders what her life has been like until now. Did Mr. Hatchard say?"

"No," Claudia said.

"The Duke of McLeith did not stay long this morning," Eleanor said.

"He asked me to marry him," Claudia told her.

"*No!*" Eleanor looked at her, arrested. "And ... ?"

"I said no, of course," Claudia said.

"*Of course?*" Eleanor sat down in the nearest chair. "Are you quite sure, Claudia? Is it because of the school? I have never mentioned this to you because it seemed inappropriate, but I have often thought how I would not mind if it were mine. And I do believe I would be able to run it in a manner worthy of you. I mentioned it to Christine at one time and she thought it a wonderful idea and even said she would sponsor me with a loan or an outright gift if I would accept one—and if the time ever came. And Wulfric, who was reading a book at the time, looked up and said it would certainly be a gift. So if your refusal had anything to do with misgivings about—"

"Oh, Eleanor," Claudia said, laughing, "it did not, though I suppose it might have if I had wanted to say yes."

"But you did not?" Eleanor asked. "He is so very amiable, and he seems inordinately fond of you. And he must have pots of money, if one wants to be mercenary about such matters. Of course he *is* a duke, which puts him at a horrid disadvantage, poor man."

"I loved him once," Claudia admitted, "but no longer. And I am comfortable and really quite happy with my life as it is. The time when I might have thought of marriage is long past. I prefer to keep my independence even if my fortune *is* minuscule."

"As I do," Eleanor said. "I loved once too—quite passionately. But he was killed in Spain during the wars and I have never been tempted to find someone to replace him in my affections. I would rather be alone. If you should ever change your mind, though, know that concerns for the school need not stand in your way."

She laughed, and Claudia smiled.

"I will remember that," she said, "if I should ever fall violently in love with someone else. Thank you, Eleanor."

The morning clouds had moved off by noon. As a result several other people decided to ride with Joseph and Elizabeth from Alvesley to Lindsey Hall—Lily and Portfrey and Portia and three of Kit's cousins. Lily tried to persuade McLeith to come too, but he had been over during the morning.

A large number of people were out of doors at Lindsey Hall, Joseph could see as they rode up the driveway, including surely all the children—and the visiting schoolgirls. His eyes searched their number eagerly even before he was close enough to distinguish individuals.

He left his horse at the stables, as did all the others, and walked across the lawn with Portia, Lily, and Elizabeth while the others made their way toward the house.

The schoolgirls were dancing about a makeshift maypole, to the accompaniment of vocal music by one of their number and a great deal of laughter and confusion. Joseph could see no sign of Lizzie until he realized with a start that she was one of the dancers. Indeed, it was she who was causing the confusion—and the laughter.

She was clinging to one of the ribbons with both hands, and she was dancing about the maypole with vigorous, ungainly steps while Miss Martin moved behind her, her hands on Lizzie's waist. She was laughing too. She was also bonnetless and disheveled and flushed.

Lizzie was shrieking with louder laughter than anyone else.

"How very charming," Elizabeth said without any apparent irony.

"Is that the *blind* girl I have heard about?" Portia asked of no one in particular. "She is spoiling the dance for the others. And she is making a spectacle of herself, poor girl."

Lily was simply laughing. She clapped her hands in time to the music.

And then several of the girls noticed the new arrivals and the dance came to an end as they all stopped and stared and then bobbed curtsies.

Lizzie clutched Miss Martin's skirt.

"Maypole dancing in July?" Lily cried. "But why not? What a grand idea."

"It was Agnes's idea," Miss Martin explained, "instead of the ball game we were going to play. It was her way of including Lizzie Pickford, who has joined us for the summer holiday."

Her eyes met Joseph's briefly.

"Lizzie has been able to hold on to the ribbon," she continued, "and dance in a circle with everyone else without colliding with anyone or getting lost."

"She ought to be taught the proper steps, then," Portia said, "so that she may look more graceful."

"I thought she was doing remarkably well," Elizabeth said.

"So did I," Joseph said.

Lizzie cocked her head and her face lit up, and he almost wished that she would cry out his name and reach out her arms to him and put an end to this distasteful charade.

But then she smiled and raised her face to Miss Martin, a look of gleeful mischief there. Miss Martin set an arm about her shoulders.

"Do carry on," Elizabeth said. "We did not mean to disturb you."

Some of the younger children, Joseph could see—not the schoolgirls—were tackling Hallmere on the grass and shrieking with delight. Lady Hallmere was egging them on. The dog, tethered to a tree close to the maypole, was sitting and placidly watching, his tail thumping on the grass. The duchess was hurrying toward them from a distant cluster of infants.

"I believe we are all out of breath," Miss Martin said. "It is time for something less strenuous."

"Ball?" one of the older girls suggested.

Miss Martin groaned, but the lady Joseph recognized as Miss Thompson, the teacher who had appeared outside the school in Bath, had come up with the duchess.

"I will supervise a game for anyone who wants to play," she said.

"Horace has a new collar and leash," Lizzie announced loudly. "I hold on and he takes me about and I don't run into things or fall down."

"How very clever, dear," Elizabeth said kindly. "Perhaps you could show us."

"That child," Portia said sotto voce to Joseph, "ought to learn to speak when she is spoken to. Blindness is surely no excuse for bad manners."

"But perhaps childish exuberance is," he said, watching as Lizzie turned and groped with one hand until Miss Martin untied the dog and set the loop of the leather leash in her hand. It took all his willpower not to rush forward to help.

"I will come walking with you if you wish, Lizzie," a girl about her own age said, taking her free hand.

Lizzie looked in his general direction.

"Would you like to come too . . . sir?" she asked.

"Well, really!" Portia exclaimed. "What impudence."

"I would be delighted," he said. "Miss . . . Pickford, is it?"

"Yes." She laughed with glee.

"And Miss Martin must go too," Lily suggested.

"The rest of us will remain here and be lazy," the duchess said. "And then we will go into the house for tea. How delighted I am to see you all."

The dog moved off at a trot and Lizzie and the other girl shrieked with laughter again as they set off in his wake. But he seemed to understand the charge with which he had been entrusted and slowed to a walk as he made his way toward the driveway and then crossed it, making a wide loop about the large stone fountain that stood before the main doors. He also steered well clear of all the trees, leading them toward the other side of the house.

"I hope, Miss Martin," Joseph said, clasping his hands at his back, "you are not too attached to that dog. I cannot see Lizzie being willing to part with him at the end of the summer. He is looking remarkably healthy. Has his weight doubled, or is that just my imagination?"

"Your imagination, thank goodness," she said. "But his ribs are no longer visible, and his coat has acquired a sheen."

"And Lizzie," he said. "Can that possibly be her, walking hand in hand with another girl, being drawn along by a dog? And dancing earlier about a maypole?"

"And knitting this morning," she said, "though I believe she dropped more stitches than she worked."

"How can I ever thank you?" he asked, looking down at her.

"Or I you?" She smiled back at him. "You have challenged me. Sometimes one becomes blinded by routine—ah, pun unintentional."

They were making their way, he could see, toward a largish lake. He lengthened his stride, but Miss Martin caught his arm.

"Let us see what happens," she said. "I think it very unlikely that Horace will march straight into the water, and if he does, Molly certainly will not."

But the dog stopped well short of the bank, and the girls

stopped too. The child called Molly then led Lizzie forward, and they both went down on their knees and touched their hands to the water, Lizzie tentatively at first.

Joseph moved up beside them and squatted down next to his daughter.

"There are some stones along the bank," he said, picking one up. "If you toss them into the water, the farther out the better, you can hear them plop. Listen!"

And he demonstrated while Molly looked at him with fright and Lizzie turned her head and inhaled in such a way that he knew she was breathing in his familiar scent. But she smiled when she heard the stone plop into the water and reached for his hand.

"Help me to find a stone," she said.

He squeezed her hand and she squeezed back, but from the mischievous smile on her face he knew she was enjoying the game of secrecy.

For the next few minutes she hurled the stones he helped her find. The other girl overcame her fright and threw some too. They both laughed whenever a stone fell with a particularly loud plop into the lake. But finally Lizzie had had enough.

"Shall we go back to the others, Molly?" she asked. "Perhaps you want to join in the ball game. I don't mind. I'll sit and listen."

"No, I'll watch it with you," Molly said. "I can never catch a ball."

"Miss Martin," Lizzie said, "will you and P— and this gentleman stay here while we go? I want to show you that we can do it on our own. Do you think we can, sir?"

"I shall be vastly impressed if you can," he said. "Off you go, then. Miss Martin and I will watch."

And away they went, the dog in the lead.

"Is she sprouting wings so quickly?" he asked ruefully when they were out of earshot.

"I believe she is," Miss Martin said. "I hope she does not grow overbold too soon. I do not expect it, though. She knows she needs Molly or Agnes or one of the other girls—and Horace, of course. This summer will be a very good experience for her."

"Let's sit for a little while, shall we?" he suggested, and they sat side by side on the bank of the lake. She drew up her knees and wrapped her arms about them.

He picked up one more stone and bounced it across the water.

"Oh," she said, "I used to be able to do that when I was a girl. I still remember the memorable occasion when I made a stone bounce six times. But I had no witness, alas, and no one ever believed me."

He chuckled. "Your pupils are fortunate indeed to have you for a headmistress," he said.

"Ah, but you must remember that this is a holiday," she told him. "I am rather different during term time. I am a stern task-mistress, Lord Attingsborough. I have to be."

He remembered how all the senior girls had fallen silent as soon as she stepped out onto the pavement just before she left Bath with him.

"Discipline can be achieved without humor or feeling," he said, "or with both. You achieve it *with*. I am quite sure of that."

She hugged her knees and did not answer.

"Do you ever wish for a different life?" he asked her.

"I could have had one," she said. "Just this morning I had a marriage offer."

McLeith! He had ridden over here this morning to call on her.

"McLeith?" he said. "And *could have*? You said no, then?"

"I did," she said.

He was damnably glad.

"You cannot forgive him?" he asked.

"Forgiveness is not a straightforward thing," she said. "Some things can be forgiven but never quite forgotten. I *have* forgiven him, but nothing can ever be the same between us. I can be his friend perhaps, but I can never be more than that. I could never trust that he would not do something similar again."

"But you do not still love him?" he asked.

"No."

"Love does not last forever, then?"

"He asked me the same thing this morning," she said. "No, it does not—not love that has been betrayed. One realizes that one has loved a mirage, someone who never really existed. Not that love dies immediately or soon, even then. But it *does* die and cannot be revived."

"I never thought I would stop loving Barbara," he told her. "But I did. I look upon her fondly whenever I see her, but I doubt I could love her again even if we were both free."

She was looking directly at him, and he turned his head to look back.

"It is a consolation," she said, "to know that love dies eventually. Not a very strong consolation at first, it is true, but *some* comfort nevertheless."

"Is it?" he asked softly.

He did not know if she was talking about them. But the air suddenly seemed charged between them.

"No," she said, her voice almost a whisper. "Not at all really. What absurdities we sometimes speak. Future indifference is no consolation for present pain."

And when he leaned toward her and set his lips to hers, she did not draw away. Her lips trembled against his and then pressed back against them and parted as his tongue pushed between them and into the warm cavity of her mouth.

"Claudia," he said a few moments later, closing his eyes and touching his forehead to hers.

"No!" she said, withdrawing and getting to her feet. She stood looking out over the lake.

"I am so sorry," he said. And he was too—sorry for what he had done to her and for the disrespect he had shown Portia, to whom he was betrothed. Sorry for his lack of control.

"I wonder if it is a pattern doomed to repeat itself every eighteen years or so of my life," she said. "A duke and a duke-in-waiting choosing a bride for her suitability for the position and leaving me behind to grieve."

Oh, dash it all! He drew a slow breath.

"And *what* have I said?" she asked him. "What have I just admitted? It does not matter, though, does it? You must have guessed. How pathetic I must seem."

"Good God!" he cried, getting to his feet too and standing a short distance behind her. "Do you think I kissed you because I pity you? I kissed you because I—"

"*No!*" She swung around, holding up one hand, palm out. "Don't say it. Please don't say it even if you mean it. Either way, I could not *bear* to hear it spoken aloud."

"Claudia..." he said softly.

"*Miss Martin* to you, Lord Attingsborough," she said, lifting her chin and looking very much the schoolmistress again despite her disheveled appearance. "We will forget what happened here and what happened at Vauxhall and at the Kingston ball. We will *forget.*"

"Will we?" he said. "I am so sorry to have upset you like this. It was inexcusable of me."

"I am not blaming you," she said. "I am quite old enough to know better. I will never even be able to convince myself that I fell prey to the lures of a practiced rake, though that is what I expected you to be when I first set eyes on you. Instead you are a gentleman whom I like and admire. That has been the whole problem, I suppose. And I am prattling. Let us return or everyone—Miss Hunt in particular—will be wondering what I am up to."

And yet, he thought as they made their way back to the far lawn, not touching and not talking, they could be no more than a few minutes behind the girls.

Minutes that had done infinite damage to both their lives. No longer could he even pretend that he did not love her. No longer could she pretend that she did not love him.

And no longer would they be able to trust themselves to be alone together.

He felt his loss like a hard fist to the stomach.

16

*After their return from Lindsey Hall, Joseph and Portia sat to-*gether in the formal flower garden to the east of the house. He was feeling mortally depressed. For one thing he had spent very little time with Lizzie, and the deception, though it had seemed to amuse her, had been distasteful to him. For another thing, he and Claudia Martin must now stay away from each other. No longer could he enjoy even her friendship.

And for a third thing he had been able to discover no warmth, no compassion, no generosity, no spark of passion, beneath the beautiful, dignified, perfect appearance Portia presented to the world. And he *had* tried.

"I am pleased that you enjoy riding," he had told her on the way back to Alvesley. "It is one of my favorite activities. It will be something we can do together."

"Oh," she had replied, "I will not expect you to be hanging about me all day when we are married, just as I will not be hanging about you. We will both have our duties and our pleasures to keep us busy."

"And those pleasures cannot be found in each other's company?" he had asked her.

"When necessary," she had said. "We will entertain a great deal, of course, especially when you become the Duke of Anburey."

He had persisted. "But *private* pleasures? Walking together, dining together, even just sitting and reading or conversing together? Will there not be time for them too? Will we not *make* time for them?" He had *not* added the idea of making love as another private pleasure in which they might choose to indulge after they married.

"I imagine," she had said, "that you will be a busy man. I am sure I will be busy with all the duties of being the Marchioness of Attingsborough and later the Duchess of Anburey. I will not expect you to feel obliged to amuse me."

He had not pursued that line of conversation.

He had tried, now, here in the garden, to get her to relax and enjoy with him the beauty that surrounded them.

"Listen!" he had said just a few minutes ago, holding up one hand. "Have you ever thought about how much we miss in life from being endlessly busy? Listen, Portia."

There was a stream at the bottom of the flower garden with a rustic wooden bridge crossing it and wooded hills beyond. And, sure enough, the birds in the trees here were as busy with their summer chorus as those in Richmond Park had been. He could also hear the gurgle of the stream. And he could feel the warmth of the summer air. He could smell the flowers and the water.

She had maintained a polite silence for a few moments.

"It is by being busy, though," she had said then, "that we prove ourselves worthy of our humanity. Idleness is to be avoided, even despised. It reduces us to the level of the bestial world."

"Like Lizzie Pickford's dog sitting beside the maypole waiting to take her safely wherever she wished to go?" he had asked with a smile.

It had been a mistake to mention that particular animal.

"That child," she had said, "ought not to have been rewarded for being so forward when she was in company with her betters. Blindness is no excuse. It was very good of you to go walking with her to the lake, and the Duchess of Bewcastle made a point of commending your kindness and good nature, but she must surely have wondered if you had not shown some lack of discrimination."

"Discrimination?"

"Her own son, the Marquess of Lindsey, was outdoors with

her," she had pointed out to him, "as were the children of the Marquess of Hallmere and the Earl of Rosthorn and Lord Aidan Bedwyn. Perhaps it would have been more appropriate to turn your attention to one of them."

"None of them asked me to go walking with them," he had said. "And none of them was blind."

And none of them was his own child.

"The Duchess of Bewcastle is a very amiable lady," she had said. "I cannot help wondering, though, if the duke does not regret condescending to marry her. She was once a teacher in a village school. Her father was once a teacher. Her sister teaches at Miss Martin's school in Bath. And now she has all those charity girls staying at Lindsey Hall and speaks of them as if they give her as much pleasure as the children of the duke's own family. They ought not to be there. For their own good they ought not."

"For their own good?"

"They need to learn their proper station in life," she had said. "They must learn the distinctions between themselves and their betters. They must learn that they do not belong in places like Lindsey Hall. It is really quite cruel to them to allow them to spend a holiday here."

"They ought to remain at the school, then," he had said, "kept busy with mending and darning and fed bread and water?"

"It is not what I mean at all," she had told him. "You must surely agree with me that those girls ought not even to be at a school with other, paying pupils. Those others are only the daughters of merchants and lawyers and physicians, I daresay, but even so they are middle class, not lower, and there is a definite distinction."

"You would not want to see your own daughter go there, then?" he had asked.

She had turned her head to look at him and laughed. She had looked genuinely amused.

"Our own daughters," she had said, "will be educated at home, as I am sure you would expect."

"By a governess who may have been educated at Miss Martin's school or one like it?"

"Of course," she had said. "By a servant."

And so now, a mere few moments later, in another silence, Joseph felt his spirits slide all the way down to the soles of the riding boots he was still wearing. There was no hope, no ray of light, ahead. He ought to have insisted upon a decent period of courtship before committing himself to offering for her. He ought...

But there was no point in such thoughts. The reality was that he was betrothed to Portia Hunt. He was as firmly bound to her as if the nuptials had already been solemnized.

The sound of feminine voices in merry conversation with one another came from the terrace behind them, and soon Lauren and Gwen and Lily and Anne Butler stepped into the garden.

"Ah, your peace is being invaded," Lauren called when she saw them. "We are going to climb to the top of the hill and admire the view. Have you been up there?"

"We have just been relaxing here," Joseph said with a smile.

"We are going to sit up there and make *plans*," Lily said.

"Plans?" Portia asked.

"For a picnic the day before the anniversary celebrations," Lily explained. "Elizabeth and I have been telling everyone about the delightful scene that met our eyes when we arrived at Lindsey Hall earlier, children everywhere, all enjoying themselves enormously."

"And it struck my mother-in-law and me," Lauren said, "that there are lots of children here too and yet all the official celebrations virtually exclude them. And so we decided on the spot to organize a children's picnic for the day before the ball."

"How delightful," Portia murmured.

"But now we have to plan it," Mrs. Butler said. "And because I was once a teacher, I am expected to be an expert."

"Lauren and Lady Redfield are going to invite all the children from Lindsey Hall too," Gwen said. "And some of the other children from the neighborhood. There will be an army."

"Miss Martin's girls too?" Joseph asked. He had been wondering how he could arrange to see Lizzie again.

"But of course not," Portia said, sounding shocked.

"But of course," Lily said simultaneously. "They were a delight, were they not, Joseph, all dancing about the maypole? And that little blind girl was quite undaunted by her affliction."

"Lizzie?"

"Yes, Lizzie Pickford," she said. "Lauren is going to invite them all."

"Alvesley may never be the same," Lauren said with a laugh. "Not to mention us."

Joseph, smiling back at her, could remember a time when Lauren had been every bit as straitlaced and apparently lacking in humor as Portia. Love and her marriage to Kit had transformed her into the warmhearted woman she was now. Was there a glimmering of hope for him after all? He must persevere with Portia. He must find a way to her heart. He *must*. The alternative was too dreadful to contemplate.

"Do you want to come up with us?" Gwen suggested, looking at Portia.

"The sun is rather too hot," Portia said. "We will return to the house."

The ladies proceeded on their way across the bridge and onto the path that would take them up the rather steep slope. Even Gwen was undaunted, despite a rather heavy limp, the permanent aftereffect of a riding accident that had happened during her marriage, before Muir died.

"It is to be hoped," Portia said as they rose to their feet and he offered her his arm, "that they plan the picnic very carefully indeed, though it is kind of Lady Ravensberg and Lady Redfield to think of it. There is nothing worse than children being allowed to run wild."

"Nothing worse for the adults in charge of them, perhaps," he said, chuckling. "Nothing more blissful for the children themselves."

Would Lizzie come? he wondered.

And would Claudia Martin come?

For four days Claudia did not set eyes upon the Marquess of Attingsborough. For herself she was very glad indeed. She must forget him—it was as stark and as simple as that—and the best way to do that was never to set eyes on him again.

But Lizzie grieved.

Oh, outwardly she seemed to be thriving. She was looking less pale and thin than she had. She had friends willing to take her about and read to her. She had music to listen to since some of the girls liked to take a turn at the spinet and several liked to sing. Claudia tried telling her stories from history and then asking her questions later. The not unsurprising discovery was that Lizzie had a sharp memory. She was certainly not uneducable. She dictated two more of her own stories, one to Claudia and one to Eleanor, and never tired of having them read back to her. She liked to knit, though her inability to see a dropped stitch or to pick it up if someone else pointed it out was a problem yet to be solved.

She had the dog as a constant companion and increasingly as a guide. Indeed, she was becoming bolder every day, taking short walks with just the dog while Claudia or Molly or Agnes trailed along behind in case they were needed and sometimes went ahead to lead Horace in the desired direction.

She was even something of a favorite with the duchess and her other guests, who often made a point of speaking with her and sometimes included her in their activities when the other girls were engaged in a game in which she was unable to participate. Lord Aidan Bedwyn took her riding with him one day while his older children rode their own mounts and his young daughter rode with her mother.

But despite it all Lizzie grieved.

Claudia found her one afternoon when the other girls had

gone out with Eleanor on a lengthy nature hike, curled up on her bed in her room. Her cheeks were wet with tears.

"Lizzie?" Claudia said, seating herself beside the bed. "Are you sad at being left behind? Shall we do something together?"

"Why does he not come back?" Lizzie wailed. "Is it something I did? Is it because I called him *sir* instead of *Papa*? Is it because I asked him to wait at the lake with you so that I could show him I was able to find my way back to the house with just Horace and Molly?"

Claudia smoothed a hand over Lizzie's hot, untidy hair.

"It is nothing you did," she said. "Your papa is busy at Alvesley. I know he is missing you as much as you miss him."

"He is going to send me to your school," Lizzie said. "I *know* he is. He is going to marry Miss Hunt—he told me so when I was still at home. Is she the lady who said I was a clumsy dancer? Papa is going to send me to school."

"And you do not want to go?" Claudia asked. "Even though Molly and Agnes and the other girls will be there, and Miss Thompson and I?"

"I want to be home with Papa," Lizzie told her. "And I want you and Horace to come as you did before, only more often. Every day. And I want Papa to stay the night *every* night. I want...I want to be *home*."

Claudia continued smoothing a hand over her hair. She said nothing though her heart ached for a child who wanted only what ought to be every child's right. After a few minutes Lizzie was asleep.

But the very next day Claudia was able to seek her out with altogether more cheerful news. She had just heard it herself from Susanna and Anne, who had come over from Alvesley with Lady Ravensberg. And Lizzie, Claudia had decided, would be the first of the girls to hear. She was standing by the fountain with Molly despite the fact that it was a chilly, windy day that threatened rain. They were trailing their hands in the water and sometimes stretching out their arms to feel the spray. They were giggling.

"You girls will all be going to Alvesley Park tomorrow," Claudia said as she came up to them. "You have been invited with all the children to a picnic."

"To a *picnic,*" Molly said, her eyes as wide as saucers, the fountain and the water forgotten. "*All* of us, miss?"

"All of you," Claudia said, smiling. "Will that not be a wonderful treat?"

"Do the others know?" Molly asked, her voice just a little lower than a shriek.

"You are the first to be told," Claudia said.

"I am going to tell them," Molly cried, and she went dashing off to find the other girls, leaving Lizzie behind.

Lizzie's face was turned up and seemed lit from within.

"I am to go too?" she asked. "To *Alvesley?* Where Papa is?"

"You are indeed," Claudia told her.

"Oh," Lizzie said softly. And she stooped down and felt for Horace, who was sitting quietly beside her, and took the leash in her hand. "Will he be glad to see me?"

"I expect he is counting the hours," Claudia said.

"Take me to my room, Horace," Lizzie said. "Oh, Miss Martin, how many hours *is* it?"

Horace, of course, was not *that* good a guide, though he might learn in time. He was always careful to see that Lizzie ran against no obstacle, but he had no particular sense of direction despite Lizzie's great faith in him. Claudia led the way indoors and upstairs, and Horace trotted after her, bringing Lizzie along behind. But it always pleased the girl to think she was becoming independent.

She could not get to sleep that night. Claudia had to sit beside her bed and read one of her stories aloud and pat her hand while Horace curled up against her.

Claudia doubted she would sleep either. She had decided reluctantly that she must go with the girls to Alvesley—it was too much to expect Eleanor to take the responsibility entirely on her own shoulders. But she really, *really* did not want to go. She had been concentrating very hard on making plans for the coming school year and upon renewing her acquaintance with Charlie, who still rode over to Lindsey Hall every day.

But now she was going to have to see the Marquess of Attingsborough once more. It was pointless to hope that he would stay away from the children's picnic. She knew he must be pining for Lizzie as much as she was for him.

Was it just her imagination that heartbreak was worse the second time around? Probably, she admitted. At the age of seventeen she had wanted to die. This time she wanted to *live*—she wanted her life back as it had been until the afternoon she had stepped all unwittingly into the visitors' parlor at school to discover the Marquess of Attingsborough standing there.

And she would get that life back. She would live and prosper and be happy again. She *would*. It would just take some time, that was all.

But having to see him again was not going to help.

Joseph's yearning to see Lizzie again was like a gnawing physical ache. Every day he had been on the verge of riding over to Lindsey Hall. He had restrained himself partly because he would have been unable to think of an excuse to see her even if he did go there, and partly because he owed it both to Claudia Martin and to Portia—not to mention himself—to stay away.

But it was only partly of Miss Martin he was thinking when the carriages from Lindsey Hall arrived all in a cavalcade together on the afternoon of the picnic, and half the guests at Alvesley and almost all the children stepped outside onto the terrace to greet the new arrivals as they began to spill out of the carriages. Soon there was a noisy, shrieking melee of adults and children, the latter darting about among adult legs in search of comrades and potential new friends and addressing one another with the sort of volume they might have used if they were five miles apart.

Joseph, who was out there too, spotted Claudia Martin as she climbed down from one of the conveyances. She was wearing a cotton dress he had seen before in London and her usual straw hat. She was also wearing a severe, almost grim expression, which suggested that she would rather be anywhere else on earth than where she was. She turned back to the carriage to help someone else down.

Lizzie! All decked out in her best white dress with her hair tied high behind with a white bow.

He hurried forward.

"Allow me," he said, and he reached up into the carriage, took his daughter by her slender waist, and lifted her down.

She inhaled deeply.

"Papa," she murmured.

"Sweetheart—"

The dog jumped out and ran around them, barking, and Molly came down the steps behind him.

"Thank you, sir," Lizzie said more loudly, lifting a mischievously smiling face toward his. "Are you the gentleman who walked to the lake with us last week?"

"I am indeed," he said, clasping his hands behind him. "And you are . . . Miss Pickford, I believe?"

"You remembered." She giggled—a happy, girlish sound.

And then other girls came spilling out of the carriage, and one of the older ones took Lizzie by one hand while Molly took the other. They bore her off to another carriage, which held the remainder of their number with Miss Thompson.

Joseph looked at Miss Martin. It seemed somewhat incredible that he had kissed this stern woman on two separate occasions and that he loved her. Yet again she looked the forbidding, quintessential spinster schoolteacher.

And then her eyes met his, and it was incredible no longer. There were depths behind those eyes that drew him instantly beyond the surface armor she had put on to the warm, passionate woman within.

"Hello, Claudia," he said softly before he could frame an altogether more appropriate greeting.

"Good afternoon, Lord Attingsborough," she said briskly. And then she looked beyond his shoulder and smiled. "Good afternoon, Charlie."

Someone was tugging at the tassel on Joseph's Hessian boot. He looked down to see Wilma and Sutton's youngest, who proceeded to lift both his arms in the air.

"Uncle Joe," he commanded. "Up."

Uncle Joe obligingly stooped down to pick him up and settle him astride his shoulders.

The empty carriages from Lindsey Hall were moving off to be replaced by other carriages bringing children and adults from neighboring homes. Ten minutes or so later a veritable army—to use Gwen's analogy—of children was making its disordered way toward the picnic site on a wide expanse of lawn beside the lake to the right of the house, the older ones rushing ahead, toddlers riding shoulders, babies bouncing or sleeping in arms.

They might all be deafened by the noise before the afternoon was over, Joseph thought cheerfully.

Lizzie and Molly and the older girl were *skipping*, he noticed.

17

It was very brave of the Earl and Countess of Redfield and of Lord and Lady Ravensberg to have organized a picnic on such a grand scale just the day before the anniversary celebrations, Claudia thought as the afternoon progressed. For of course, parents had come as well as children. There were probably at least as many people milling about the lawn west of the house as there would be in the ballroom tomorrow evening.

It would have been very easy to avoid the Marquess of Attingsborough amid all the crowds if they had not both been keeping a careful eye upon Lizzie.

It was unnecessary to be overvigilant. Lizzie, shadowed by Horace but not needing him as a guide, was having the time of her life. Lady Redfield, the Duchess of Anburey, Mrs. Thompson, and a few of the other older ladies, who were sitting together on chairs that had been placed beneath the shade of a group of trees, would gladly have taken her under their wing and indeed did draw her down to sit with them for a few minutes. But she was not forgotten by everyone else. Soon Molly and a few other girls drew her away to introduce her to David Jewell, who had been openly delighted to meet some of his old school friends again and tell them all about his life in Wales. They took her with them to sit by the lake for a while.

A few of the gentlemen organized a cricket game after tea for any children who were interested, and a number of Claudia's girls joined in as well as David. Molly would not play and Lizzie could not, but they stood for a while, Molly watching and explaining to Lizzie what was happening. And then there was an extraordinary moment when Lady Hallmere—the sole lady involved in the game—went in to bat. She made a great show of settling herself in before the wickets and blocked two of the balls bowled at her by Lord Aidan Bedwyn while her team cheered and his jeered. But before he could bowl to her again, she straightened up and looked consideringly at the two girls.

"Wait," she declared. "I need help. Lizzie, come and bat with me and bring me better fortune."

And she strode over to Lizzie, took her by the hand, and led her back to stand before the wickets while Claudia caught Horace by the collar and held him back. Lady Hallmere leaned down to explain something to the girl.

"Yes!" Agnes Ryde cried as she awaited her turn. "Lizzie is going to bat. *Come on, Lizzie!*"

For the moment there was a suspiciously Cockney flavor to her accent.

Claudia watched with a frown as Lady Hallmere nestled in behind Lizzie, settled all four of their hands about the bat handle, and looked up at Lord Aidan.

"Right, Aidan," she called, "bowl us your best. We are going to hit it for a six, are we not, Lizzie?"

Lizzie's face was bright with excitement.

Claudia turned her head briefly to see that the Marquess of Attingsborough, who had been tossing a never-ending line of very young children up in the air one at a time and catching them, was watching intently.

Lord Aidan came loping in halfway down the pitch before bowling the ball very gently at the bat. Lady Hallmere, her hands clasped over Lizzie's, drew back the bat, missing the wickets behind it by a hair, and swung at the ball, hitting it with a satisfyingly loud crack.

Lizzie shrieked and laughed.

The ball soared into the air and straight into the outstretched hands of the Earl of Kilbourne, who inexplicably failed to catch it but fumbled it awkwardly and eventually allowed it to fall to the ground.

But Lady Hallmere had not waited for what had seemed like an inevitable out. She had grabbed Lizzie about the waist and gone tearing down the pitch with her and back again to score two runs.

She was laughing. So was Lizzie, loudly and helplessly. Their team cheered wildly.

The marquess was laughing too and applauding and whistling.

"Oh, well done, Miss Pickford," he called.

And then Lady Hallmere bent down to kiss Lizzie's cheek, and the Duchess of Bewcastle came to take her by the hand and lead her off to participate in another game.

Claudia, still standing there watching, caught Lady Hallmere's eye, and for an uncomfortable moment their glances held. And then Lady Hallmere raised her eyebrows, looking haughty in the process, and turned her attention back to the cricket game.

That had been a gesture of pure kindness, Claudia was forced to admit, however unwillingly. It was a somewhat disturbing realization. For most of her life, it seemed, she had hated and despised the former Lady Freyja Bedwyn. She did not even want to think now that perhaps the woman had changed, at least to a certain degree. *You bear a long grudge, Miss Martin.*

The duchess was forming a number of the smallest children into a circle. She set Lizzie between two of them, joining their hands, and took her own place between two other children to play ring-around-the-rosy.

"Ho," the Marquess of Attingsborough called just before they began, running up with a small girl riding on one of his shoulders—he was hatless, and she was clinging to his hair, "let us in too."

And he swung the little girl to the ground and took a place between her and Lizzie, who set her hand in his and turned her face up to him, looking as if all the sunshine had poured into her being. He beamed back down at her with such tenderness that Claudia was amazed everyone did not instantly *know*.

The group circled about, chanting and then all falling down on cue in shrieking delight before scrambling back to their feet, joining hands, and beginning the game all over again. Except that Lizzie and her father never did release hands. Instead they fell and laughed together while Lizzie positively glowed with excitement and happiness.

Claudia, standing watching with Susanna while Anne, holding young Megan in her arms, stood with Sydnam, cheering for David, who was up to bat in cricket, felt very close to tears though she was not at all sure why. Or perhaps she was, but there was a confusing number of causes and she did not know which was uppermost.

"Lizzie is a delightful child," Susanna said. "She has become everyone's pet, has she not? And is not Joseph a good sport? He has been playing with the younger children all afternoon so far. I am so sorry he is going to marry Miss Hunt. I thought perhaps you and he ... But never mind. I still have high hopes of the Duke of McLeith even though you *have* refused him once."

"You are a hopeless and impractical romantic, Susanna," Claudia said.

But it was very hard to imagine the Marquess of Attingsborough and Miss Hunt being happy together. Although she had come to the picnic, Miss Hunt had kept herself aloof from all the children and their activities, sitting somewhat removed from everyone else with the Earl and Countess of Sutton and two guests from Alvesley whom Claudia did not know. And Claudia could not help remembering the marquess's telling her at Vauxhall that Miss Hunt thought kisses foolish and unnecessary.

He looked more handsome and charming than ever frolicking with the very young and beaming happily at his daughter.

He deserved better than Miss Hunt.

And then Charlie came strolling up to stand with her and Susanna.

"I doubt I have ever seen so many children so blissfully happy all at one time," he said. "Everything has been very well organized, has it not?"

Indeed it had. In addition to the numerous games before tea and cricket and ring-around-the-rosy after, there was a game of statues in progress, organized by Eleanor and Lady Ravensberg. The Countess of Rosthorn was giving an archery lesson to a few of the nearly grown-up children. The Marquess of Hallmere and another gentleman were giving boat rides. A few children were playing their own private game on the bank of the lake, watched over by the older ladies. A few others were climbing trees. Some babies were being amused by parents or grandparents.

No guests showed any sign yet of wishing to take their leave.

"Claudia," Charlie said, "shall we take a stroll along by the lake?"

Her presence at the picnic site was unnecessary, Claudia thought, looking about. There was plenty of supervision for all her girls. Susanna was smirking her encouragement.

And she needed to get away, if only for a few minutes. Indeed, she wished she had not come at all. It had been obvious to her for most of the afternoon that she might easily have stayed away altogether.

"Thank you," she said, "that would be pleasant."

And it was too. She enjoyed both the walk in sunshine and picturesque surroundings and the company. During the past few days she and Charlie had become friends again. As well as reminiscing about their childhood, he talked a great deal about his life as Duke of McLeith. She talked about her life at the school. They shared ideas and opinions. The old easy camaraderie had returned to their relationship. He had made no further reference to his marriage proposal at Lindsey Hall. He was, it seemed, content to settle for friendship.

Children did not tire easily. When Claudia and Charlie returned from their walk after half an hour, there was still a vast crowd of them milling about the large lawn area, involved in some game or another while adults participated or supervised or sat watching and conversing with one another.

It was a relief to Claudia to notice that the Marquess of Attingsborough was missing. And it was an annoyance to discover that he was the first person she looked for. The next person was Lizzie. Her eyes searched everywhere twice before she came to the conclusion that the child was simply not there.

Her stomach performed an uncomfortable flip-flop.

"Where is Lizzie?" she asked Anne, who was close by with Megan.

"She is holding Harry," Anne said, pointing toward Susanna— who was holding Harry herself while Peter squatted beside her chair, his hand resting on the baby's head while he smiled up at his wife. "Oh, she *was* holding Harry."

"Where is Lizzie?" Claudia asked more urgently of no one in particular.

"The blind girl?" Charlie asked, cupping her elbow with one hand. "Someone is always looking after her. Don't worry."

"*Where is Lizzie?*"

"Morgan is letting her hold the bow and arrows, Miss Martin," Lady Redfield called.

But Lady Rosthorn, Claudia could see, was shooting an arrow at a target while an admiring group of young people looked on—and Lizzie was not among them.

She must have gone somewhere with her father.

"Oh," the Dowager Countess of Kilbourne said. "I believe she went for a walk with Miss Thompson and a group of other girls from your school, Miss Martin. May I commend you on the girls? They all have excellent manners."

"Thank you," Claudia said, sagging with relief while Charlie squeezed her elbow solicitously. And indeed she could see now that Eleanor was missing from the crowd too as were a few of her girls. Lizzie had gone walking with them. Horace must have gone too.

Charlie guided her to an empty chair, and even as she seated herself she could see the Marquess of Attingsborough making his way back to the picnic site with Miss Hunt on his arm. The Earl and Countess of Sutton and another couple were with them. Lizzie was not, of course.

But just as Claudia was beginning to relax, chiding herself for becoming so frightened when Lizzie had a dozen or more chaperones to watch her, she could see Eleanor and her group returning from their walk to the east of the house.

Eleanor, Molly, Doris, Miriam, Charlotte, Becky—Lord Aidan's daughter—an unknown girl, another, David Jewell, Davy—Becky's brother...

Claudia got to her feet, searching the group more intently as it came closer.

Lizzie was not among them.

"Where is Lizzie?"

No one answered.

"Where is Lizzie?"

Lizzie had been feeling blissfully happy. She had come to Alvesley with eager anticipation, knowing that her papa was staying here. But she had not expected too much. For one thing, she did not want her new friends to stop liking her, and they might if they knew that she had a rich father who loved her. And so she was going to have to be careful not to give the game away. But she knew too that her papa would not want openly to acknowledge her. She knew that she was the bastard child of a nobleman and an opera dancer—her mother had made that very clear to her. She knew that she could never belong in her papa's world, that she must never openly appear there. And she knew that he was about to marry a lady, someone from his own world—something her mother had always said would happen one day.

She had not expected too much of the picnic, then. She had been happy just to have him lift her down from the carriage and to hear him cheer for her when she hit the cricket ball with Lady Hallmere's help. Her cup had run over with joy when he had come to play ring-around-the-rosy with her, as he had done sometimes when she was a little girl at home. He had held her hand and laughed with her and fallen on the grass with her. And when the game was over, he had kept hold of her hand and told her that he would take her for a boat ride.

Her heart had been fairly bursting with happiness.

And then a lady had spoken to him in a voice Lizzie had not liked and told him that he was neglecting Miss Hunt and she was close to fainting from the heat and he must come up to the house with them immediately and sit in the cool for a while. And he had sighed and called the lady Wilma and told Lizzie that the boat ride must wait until later but that he would not forget.

But he *would* forget, Lizzie decided after he had gone. Or if he did not, the lady called Wilma and Miss Hunt would make sure that he did not play with her anymore.

She wanted Miss Martin, but when she asked Lady Whitleaf, who came to take her by the hand, she discovered that Miss Martin had gone for a walk but would be back soon.

Lady Whitleaf let her hold Harry, something she had not done before, and she almost wept with happiness. But after a minute or two he grew cross and Lady Whitleaf said she had to go and feed him. Then Lady Rosthorn asked her if she would like to come and examine the bows and arrows and listen to the whistle they made when they were shot and the thumping sound they made as they sank into the target.

Miss Thompson asked her almost at the same moment if she would like to go for a walk with a few of the other children, but Lizzie was feeling a little depressed and said no. But then a few minutes later, when Lady Rosthorn and some other people were shooting the arrows, she was sorry she had not gone. It would have passed the time until her papa came back from the house— *if* he came. And until Miss Martin came back from her walk.

And then Lizzie had an idea. It was something that would make her very proud of herself—and it would surely make her papa and Miss Martin proud of her too.

Miss Thompson's group could not have gone very far yet.

Lizzie tightened her hold on Horace's leash and bent down to talk to him. He panted eagerly back into her face so that she wrinkled her nose and laughed.

"Go find Miss Thompson and Molly, Horace," she said.

"Are you going somewhere, Lizzie?" Lady Rosthorn asked.

She would insist upon coming with her, Lizzie thought, and that would spoil everything.

"I am going to join my friends," she said vaguely.

At the same moment someone was asking Lady Rosthorn for help with holding a bow.

"And you can find them on your own?" Lady Rosthorn asked. But she did not wait for an answer. "Good girl."

And Horace—with Lizzie in tow—was off. Lizzie knew there were lots of people at the picnic. She knew too that there were constant and constantly changing activities. She hoped no one would notice her go and catch up to her to escort her to join the walk. She could do it on her own. Horace was her guide. He could take her wherever she wished to go.

She breathed more easily when the crowd was left behind and no one had hailed her or come dashing up behind her. She even smiled and laughed.

"Go find them, Horace," she said.

After a while there was no longer grass beneath her feet but the hardness of a path or driveway. Horace led the way along it rather than across—the hard surface remained beneath her feet.

It did not take long for the initial euphoria of the adventure to wear off. The walking group must have had far more of a head start than she had realized. There was no sound of them. Once she drew Horace to a halt and listened and called Miss Thompson's name, but there was no sound and no answer.

Horace drew her onward until she felt and heard hollowness beneath her feet and realized that she must be on a bridge. She groped her way sideways until she felt a stone balustrade. She could hear water rushing below.

When they had been coming from Lindsey Hall in the carriage earlier, she had heard the wheels rumbling over a bridge—and Miss Martin had confirmed her observation.

Was it likely the walkers had crossed this bridge? Was Horace leading her to them? Or had they gone somewhere else?

Was she lost?

For a moment she felt panic well inside her. But that would be silly. She knew from stories her papa had read to her that heroines did not panic but were very brave. And all they had to do was turn around and go back the way they had come. Horace would know the way back. And once they were close, she would hear the sound of voices.

She bent down to talk to Horace, but at the same time she got her foot caught in the leash and tipped over until she was sprawled on the ground. She did not hurt herself. Horace came close to make bleating noises and to lick her face and she put her arms about his neck and hugged him.

"You silly dog," she said. "You have come the wrong way. You are going to have to lead me back again. I hope nobody will have noticed that we were gone. I shall feel very foolish."

But the trouble was that by the time she got to her feet and brushed her hands over her best dress to make sure no grit clung to it and repossessed herself of the dog's leash, she was not sure which direction she was facing.

She let Horace decide. She pulled a little on his leash.

"Take us back," she commanded.

It did not take her long to realize that they had gone the wrong way. She could feel the coolness of shade on her face and arms and sensed that it was not just that the sun had gone behind clouds but that there were trees overhead—she could smell them.

There had been no trees the other side of the bridge.

And then Horace must have seen or heard something off to one side of the driveway and went darting off over rough ground and among the trees—that was soon obvious to Lizzie—dragging her with him. He barked excitedly.

And then he was moving too fast for her and she let go of the leash.

She found the trunk of a tree and clung to it. She realized, as her hair came cascading down about her face, that she had lost her hair ribbon.

It was without doubt the most frightening moment of her life.

"Miss Thompson!" she yelled. "Molly!"

But she had known some time ago that this was not the way Miss Thompson and the girls had come.

"Papa!" she shrieked. *"Papa!"*

But Papa had gone to the house with Miss Hunt.

"Miss Martin!"

And then Horace was pushing at her elbow with his cold nose and whining at her. She could feel his leash swinging against one of her legs.

"Horace!" She was sobbing, she realized as she caught hold of the leash. "Take me back to the driveway."

If she could just get back there, she would stay on it. Even if she chose the wrong way to walk, she would surely get somewhere eventually, or someone would find her. It was not far away.

But *which* way?

Horace led her onward, much more carefully than before. He seemed intent upon making sure that she did not collide with any of the trees or trip over any of their roots. But after what must have been several minutes, they had not arrived back at the driveway. They must be going deeper into the woods.

Lizzie thought about her story, the first one Miss Martin had written down for her. Panic was hard to hold back. She was sobbing out loud.

And then Horace stopped, panting as if in triumph and Lizzie, feeling with her free hand, felt a stone wall. At first she thought that by some miracle they had arrived at the house, but she knew it was impossible. She felt along the wall until she encountered first a door frame and then a wooden door and then the doorknob. She turned it, and the door opened.

"Hello," she called, her voice teary and shaking. She was thinking of witches and wizards. "Hello. Is anyone there?"

No one was. There was no answer, and she could hear no breathing except her own and Horace's.

She stepped inside and felt about.

It was just a small hut, she discovered. But it had some furniture in it. Did someone live here? If so, perhaps they would come home soon and tell her which way to go. Perhaps they would not be evil people but would be kind. There were not really evil people or witches, were there?

She was still sobbing aloud. She was still consumed by terror. She was still trying to be sensible.

"Please come home," she sobbed to the unknown owners of the little hut. "Please come home. *Please!*"

She could feel a bed covered with blankets. She lay down on top of them and curled up into a ball, one fist stuffed against her mouth.

"Papa," she wailed. "Papa. Miss Martin. Papa."

Horace jumped up beside her and whined and licked her face.

"Papa."

Eventually she slept.

18

Joseph sat in the drawing room at Alvesley for all of half an hour, conversing with Portia, Wilma and George, and the Vreemonts, cousins of Kit's. It was admittedly cooler indoors and a great deal quieter, but he was annoyed nonetheless.

For one thing, Portia said nothing about feeling faint from the heat and looked a little surprised when he asked solicitously about her health. It had all been Wilma's little ruse, of course, to draw him away. She would have considered it his duty to pay more attention to his betrothed despite the fact that the whole entertainment had been planned for the children and most of the other adults were exerting themselves to amuse them.

For another thing, he had had to break his promise to take Lizzie for a boat ride. He would do it as soon as they returned, but even so he was powerfully reminded that she was always going to have to take second place to his legitimate family, to be fitted in for his attention whenever they did not need him.

For a third thing, he had felt like planting McLeith a facer when he had taken Claudia Martin walking. The man was going to wear down her resistance and persuade her to marry him—which conclusion ought to have made Joseph rejoice. It seemed to him more and more as he thought of it that she yearned for love and marriage and a marital home despite all she said about being happy with her school and her lonely existence as its headmistress.

But he had wanted to plant McLeith a facer.

They made their way back to the picnic site eventually. He was going to take Lizzie boating as soon as possible. It would not seem strange that he do so—a number of the other adults had been entertaining her, making sure that she was involved with various activities and was enjoying herself.

But just as they were approaching the picnic site and he was looking eagerly about for his daughter, a voice spoke loudly above all the hubbub of other voices—it was the strident voice of a schoolmistress accustomed to making herself heard above a tumult of schoolgirl chatter.

"Where is Lizzie?" Miss Martin wanted to know.

She was getting up from a chair beside McLeith's, Joseph could see.

He was instantly more alert.

"Where is Lizzie?"

Her voice was louder now, less controlled, more panicked.

"Good God!" he exclaimed, pulling his arm free of Portia's and hurrying forward. "Where is she?"

A hasty glance around failed to find her. So did another.

Everyone had been alerted by the cry, and everyone was looking around and speaking.

"She is playing circle games with Christine."

"That was ages ago."

"She is with Susanna and the baby."

"No, she is not. That was some time ago. I had to go and feed Harry."

"Perhaps she went for a ride in a boat."

"Lady Rosthorn took her over to be with the archers."

"She must have gone walking with Eleanor and a crowd of the older children."

"No, she did not. She came with me instead to examine the bows and arrows. And then she went to join some of her friends."

"She is definitely not with Miss Thompson. Look, they are coming back and she is not with them."

"She must have gone up to the house."

"She must have..."

"She must have..."

All the time Joseph looked wildly about him.

Where was Lizzie?

Panic seized him and pounded through his veins, robbing him of breath and any chance for rational thought. He was at Claudia Martin's side without even knowing how he had got there and was clutching her by the wrist.

"I have been at the house," he told her.

"I went for a walk." She stared at him, not a vestige of color in her cheeks.

They had left Lizzie alone.

It was Bewcastle who took charge of the situation, followed closely by Kit.

"She cannot have gone far," Bewcastle said, materializing from somewhere and standing in their midst with such a commanding presence that they all fell quiet—even most of the children—though he had not noticeably raised his voice. "The child has wandered away and cannot find her way back. We need to fan out—two to follow the lake this way, two that, two to go in the direction of the stables, two to go to the house, two to..."

He continued to marshal them all, like a general with his troops.

"Syd," Kit said, "go straight to the stables and look there. You know all the hiding places. Lauren and I will go to the house—we know it best. Aidan, go..."

Joseph strode to the water's edge and gazed out at a returning boat, one hand shielding his eyes. But neither of the two children in it was Lizzie.

"Lizzie!" He threw back his head and bellowed her name.

"She cannot have gone far."

The voice, soft and shaking, came from beside him, and he realized that he still had a death grip on her wrist.

"She cannot have gone far," Claudia Martin said again, and it was obvious to him that she was trying desperately to get herself under control—a schoolmistress who was accustomed to dealing with crises. "And she must have Horace with her—he is nowhere in sight either. She believes he is able to take her wherever she wants to go."

People—both adults and children—were fanning off in all directions, many of them calling Lizzie's name. Even the Redfields, Joseph could see, and his mother and father and Aunt Clara were joining the search.

He was paralyzed by panic and indecision. He wanted more than anyone to begin the search, but where was he to go? He wanted to go in every direction at once.

Where was she? Where *was* she?

And then his heart lurched as he realized what Bewcastle and Hallmere were doing not far away. They were both hauling off their boots and stripping to the waist. And then they both dived into the lake.

The implication was so terrifying that it jolted Joseph into motion.

"She cannot be in there," Claudia Martin said in a voice so shaky that it was virtually unrecognizable. "Horace would be running around loose."

He grabbed her hand.

"We must look for her," he said, turning his back resolutely on the water.

Wilma and Portia were right there in front of them.

"I am very sorry, Miss Martin," Portia said. "But really you ought to have been watching her more carefully. You are in charge of all these charity girls, are you not?"

"A blind girl has no business being here at all," Wilma added.

"Hold your tongues!" Joseph said harshly. "Both of you."

He did not wait to either see or hear their response. He hurried away with Claudia.

But where was there to hurry *to*?

"Where can she possibly have gone?" Claudia asked, though clearly she did not expect an answer. She clung to his hand as tightly as he clung to hers. "Where would she have tried to go? Let us *think*. To join you in the house?"

"Doubtful," he said, seeing Lauren and Kit, also hand in hand, hurry toward it.

"To find Eleanor and the others, then?" she asked.

"They went past the front of the house while I was there," he said. "They went toward the little bridge and the wilderness walk beyond."

"They would have seen her if she had gone in that direction," she said. "So would you. There are four searchers going that way anyway. There is no point in our following them."

They had come to the driveway and stood there in horrible indecision again. Lizzie's name was echoing from every direction. But there were no cries from anyone to indicate that she had been found.

Joseph drew a few steadying breaths. Continued panic would get him nowhere.

"The only direction no one has taken," he said, "is the one out of Alvesley."

She looked to their right, down the long sweep of lawn and driveway to the roofed Palladian bridge across the river and the woods beyond.

"She would surely not have gone that way," she said.

"Probably not," he agreed. "But would the dog?"

"Oh, dear God," she said. "Dear God, where is she?" Her eyes filled with tears and she bit her lip. "Where is she?"

"Come," he said, turning with her to stride resolutely down the driveway. "There is nowhere else left to look."

"How could this have happened?" she asked.

"I went to the house," he said harshly.

"I went for a walk."

"I ought not to have let her leave home in London," he said. "She has always been safe there."

"I ought not to have taken my eyes off her," she said. "She was my only reason for coming this afternoon. She was my responsibility. Miss Hunt was quite right to scold me."

"Let us not start blaming ourselves or each other," he said. "She had numerous chaperones this afternoon. Everyone was keeping an eye on her."

"That was the whole trouble," she said. "When everyone is looking after someone, no one really is. Everyone assumes she is with someone else. I ought to know that from experience at school. Oh, Lizzie, where *are* you?"

They stood inside the bridge for a few moments, looking out in all directions, desperately hoping for a sign of the missing Lizzie.

But why was she not answering any of the calls? Joseph could still hear them from where he stood.

"*L-i-z-z-i-e!*" he yelled from one side of the bridge, cupping his hands about his mouth.

"*Lizzie!*" Claudia called from the other side.

Nothing.

His knees felt weak under him suddenly and he almost staggered.

"Do we go on?" he asked, looking beyond the bridge to where the driveway wound its way through the woods. "Surely she could not have come so far."

Perhaps she was back at the lake. He felt an overwhelming need to go back there to see.

"We must go on," Claudia said, crossing the width of the bridge and grasping his hand again. "What else is there to do?"

Their eyes met and then for a brief moment she pressed her forehead against his chest.

"We will find her," she said. "We will."

But *how*? And *where*? If she really had come this way, would she finally end up in the village? Would someone there stop her and care for her until word could be sent to Alvesley?

What if she had turned off the driveway and got lost in the woods?

"*Lizzie!*" Joseph shouted again.

He had stopped walking at an amazingly fortunate moment.

Claudia turned her head, and then she uttered a wordless exclamation and pulled on his hand.

"What is that?" she said, pointing. And as they drew closer to a white streamer caught on a lower branch of a tree, she cried out joyfully. "It is Lizzie's hair ribbon. She *did* come this way."

He disentangled it and pressed it to his mouth, closing his eyes very tightly as he did so.

"Thank God," she said. "Oh, thank God. She is not at the bottom of the lake."

He opened his eyes and they gazed bleakly at each other. They had both been harboring the same fear ever since seeing Bewcastle and Hallmere diving in.

"*Lizzie!*" he called into the woods.

"*Lizzie!*" she called.

There was no answer. And how could they know which way she had gone? How could they go after her without themselves getting lost? But there was, of course, no question of standing still—and no thought of going back to recruit more help, especially from Kit or Sydnam, who would know the woods.

They pressed onward, stopping frequently to call Lizzie's name.

And finally there was a rustling among the trees ahead and then a joyful woofing—and there came Horace, all wiggling rear end and wagging tail and lolling tongue.

"Horace!" Claudia went down onto her knees to hug him, and he licked her face. "Where is she? Why have you left her? Take us to her this minute."

At first it seemed that he wanted to do nothing more than jump up against her skirt and play, but she wagged a stern finger at him and then took the ribbon from Joseph's hand and waved it under the dog's nose.

"Find her, Horace. Take us to her," she commanded.

And he turned with a bark as if this were the best game of the afternoon, and went racing off through the trees. Joseph took Claudia by the hand again, and they went hurrying after him.

There was a little building—a gamekeeper's hut—not far ahead. It looked to be in good repair. The door was ajar. Horace rushed inside.

Joseph stepped up to the door, almost afraid to hope. Claudia clung to his hand and pressed against his side as he pushed the door wider and peered inside. It was dark, but there was just enough light to see that the place was decently furnished and that on a narrow bed against one wall his daughter was curled up asleep, Horace panting and grinning at her feet.

Joseph turned his head, grasped Claudia about the waist, drew her tightly against him, and wept into the hollow between her neck and shoulder. She clung to him.

And for the merest moment as he drew free, they gazed deeply into each other's eyes and his wet mouth touched hers.

And then he was inside the hut and kneeling on the floor beside the bed and touching his trembling hand to Lizzie's head, moving the hair gently from her face. If she had been sleeping, she was sleeping no longer. Her eyes were tightly shut. She was sucking on her fist. Her shoulders were hunched and tense.

"Sweetheart," he murmured.

"Papa?" She lowered her fist and inhaled. "Papa?"

"Yes," he said. "We have found you, Miss Martin and I. You are quite safe again."

"Papa?"

She wailed then, a high keening sound, and launched herself at him until she had a death grip about his neck. He picked her up and turned to sit with her cradled on his lap. He reached up without thought and drew Claudia down to sit beside them. She stroked Lizzie's legs.

"You are safe," she said.

"Miss Thompson took Molly and some others for a walk," Lizzie said in a fast, breathless voice. "They asked me to go but I said no, but then I wished I had said yes because you had gone to the house, Papa, and Miss Martin had gone for a walk. I thought Horace and I could catch up. I thought you would be proud of me. I thought Miss Martin would be proud of me. But Horace could not find them. And then there was a bridge and then I fell down and did not know which way to go and then there were the trees and Horace ran away and I tried to be brave and I thought about witches but I knew there were none, and then Horace came back and we came here but I did not know who lived here or if they would be kind or cruel and when you came I thought it was them and perhaps they would eat me alive though I know that is silly and—"

"Sweetheart." He kissed her cheek and rocked her back and forth while she sucked on her fist again—something she had not done to his knowledge since she was four or five. "There are only Miss Martin and I here with you."

"But how very, very brave you were, Lizzie," Claudia said, "to venture off on your own and then not to panic when you got lost. We will certainly have to train Horace more before you try any such thing again, but I am enormously proud of you anyway."

"I am *always* proud of you," Joseph said. "But especially today. My little girl is growing up and becoming independent."

She had stopped sucking her fist. She snuggled against him and yawned hugely. She had had so much fresh air and exercise today that it was no wonder she was exhausted—even apart from the terrible fright she had had.

He continued to rock her as he used to do when she was a baby and small child. He tipped back his head and closed his eyes. He could feel tears pooling in them again—and then one spilling over to trickle down his cheek.

He felt a feather-light touch to the same cheek and opened his eyes to see Claudia brushing the backs of her fingers across it to dry the tear.

They gazed at each other, and it seemed to him that he could see past her eyes into her mind, into her deepest self, into her soul. And he rested there.

"I love you," he said, intending to speak aloud though no sound passed his lips.

She read his lips anyway. She drew back an inch or two, her

chin lifted a fraction, and her own lips pressed together into an almost-stern line. But her eyes did not change. Her eyes *could* not change. They were the window through the armor she tried to don. Her eyes answered him though the rest of her denied what they said.

I love you too.

"We had better get Lizzie back to the picnic," he said, "and set everyone's minds at rest. Everyone will still be searching for her."

"For me?" Lizzie said. "They are searching for *me*?"

"Everyone has fallen in love with you, sweetheart," he said, kissing her cheek again and getting to his feet with her in his arms. "And I must say I cannot blame them."

It was obvious to him as soon as they stepped outside the hut and Claudia shut the door behind them that there was a faint path leading from it. The hut was furnished and clean and comfortable. It made sense that it was used often and that the user or users would have worn a path, probably from the driveway. They followed it and sure enough, in no time at all, it seemed, they were back on the driveway, within sight of the bridge.

Claudia went a little way ahead of him across the bridge and waved her arms and called out to a few groups of people who were in sight. It was obvious they read her message. The search was over—Lizzie had been found.

By the time they approached the lake, everyone was waiting expectantly for them and Lizzie was half asleep. Horace bounded ahead, panting and woofing.

They received a hero's welcome. Everyone wanted to touch Lizzie, to ask if she had taken any harm, to ask what had happened, to explain how they had searched and searched and almost given up hope.

"Your arms must be tired from carrying her, Attingsborough," Rosthorn said. "Let me take her from you. Come, *chérie*."

"No," Joseph said, tightening his hold. "Thank you, but she is fine where she is."

"She really ought to be taken back to Lindsey Hall immediately," Wilma said. "Such a fuss, and it has threatened to ruin this splendid picnic. You really ought to have been doing your duty, Miss Martin, and keeping an eye on the girl instead of going walking with your betters."

"Wilma," Neville said, "stuff it, will you?"

"Well, *really*!" she said. "I demand an apol—"

"This is absolutely not the time for cruelty and recriminations," Gwen said. "Be quiet, Wilma."

"But it really ought to be said," Portia added, "that it is disrespectful to Lady Redfield and Lady Ravensberg to have brought *charity* pupils to mingle with such a gathering and then to have left them to the chaperonage of someone else. And a *blind* charity girl is the outside of enough. We really ought—"

"Lizzie Pickford," Joseph said in a firm, clear voice to an attentive audience that consisted of his father and mother, his sister, his betrothed, and numerous relatives, acquaintances, and strangers, "is *my daughter*. And I love her more than life itself."

He felt Claudia's hand on his arm. He lowered his head to kiss Lizzie's upturned face. He felt Neville's hand grasp his shoulder and squeeze hard.

And then he became aware of an awful silence that overlaid the sounds of children at play.

19

The words Lady Sutton and Miss Hunt spoke cut Claudia like a knife. Though they were spitefully uttered, she was utterly defenseless against them. She had been terribly to blame. She had been walking with Charlie—ah, yes, *with her betters*—when she should have been keeping an eye on Lizzie.

But perhaps even more than personal insult and guilt, she felt a deep and impotent anger to hear her precious charity girls spoken of so disparagingly in their hearing. And yet she could say nothing in their defense either. Perhaps Lady Ravensberg might have done so and informed Miss Hunt that they were here by her specific invitation. But the Marquess of Attingsborough spoke first.

Lizzie Pickford is my daughter. And I love her more than life itself.

Anger and guilt were forgotten in deep distress. Claudia set a hand on his arm and looked at Lizzie in some concern.

Most of the younger children played on with the indefatigable energy of their age and a total unawareness of the drama unfolding around them. But somehow the noise they made only accentuated the awful silence that fell over everyone else.

The lame and pretty Lady Muir spoke first.

"Oh, Wilma," she said, "*now* see what you have done. And you too, Miss Hunt. Oh, really, it is too bad of you."

"Miss Martin's schoolgirls," the Countess of Redfield said, "are here at my express invitation."

"And at mine," Lady Ravensberg added. "It has been a delight to have them. *All* of them."

But everyone fell silent again as the Duke of Anburey got to his feet.

"*What* is this?" he asked, frowning ferociously, though it did not seem that he expected an answer. "A son of mine making such a vulgar admission in such company? Before Lord and Lady Redfield in their own home? Before his mother and his sister? Before his *betrothed*? Before the whole world?"

Claudia lowered her hand to her side. Lizzie turned her face into her father's waistcoat.

"I have never been more insulted in my life than I have been this afternoon," Miss Hunt said. "And now I am expected to bear *this*?"

"Calm yourself, my dear Miss Hunt," the Countess of Sutton said, patting her arm. "I am deeply ashamed of you, Joseph, and can only hope that you spoke in the heat of the moment and are already feeling properly remorseful. I believe a public apology to Papa and Miss Hunt and Lady Redfield is in order."

"I do apologize," he said, "for the distress I have caused and for the manner in which I have finally acknowledged Lizzie. But I cannot be sorry for the fact that she is my daughter. Or for the fact that I love her."

"Oh, Joseph," the Duchess of Anburey said. She had got to her feet with her husband and was walking toward her son. "This child is *yours*? Your daughter? *My granddaughter?*"

"Sadie!" the duke said in a forbidding tone.

"But she is beautiful," she said, touching the backs of her knuckles to Lizzie's cheek. "I am so happy she is safe. We were all dreadfully worried about her."

"Sadie," the duke said again.

Viscount Ravensberg cleared his throat.

"I suggest," he said, "that this discussion be removed indoors, where those people who are most nearly concerned may be afforded some privacy. And Lizzie probably needs to be taken out of the sun. Lauren?"

"I'll go ahead," the viscountess said, "and find a quiet room where she may lie down and rest. She looks quite exhausted, poor child."

"I will put her in my room if I may, Lauren," the Marquess of Attingsborough said.

The Duke of Anburey was already taking the duchess by the arm and turning her in the direction of the house. Miss Hunt gathered up her skirt and turned to follow. Lady Sutton linked an arm through hers and went with her. Lord Sutton walked on Miss Hunt's other side.

"Shall I carry her for you, Joe?" the Earl of Kilbourne offered.

"No." The marquess shook his head. "But thank you, Nev."

He took a few steps in the direction of the house but then stopped and looked back at Claudia.

"Come with us?" he said. "Come and watch Lizzie for me?"

She nodded and fell into step beside him. What an awful ending to the picnic for those who were left behind, she thought. But perhaps not. It was certainly a picnic no one was going to forget in a hurry. It would doubtless be the subject of animated conversation for days, even weeks to come.

It was a solemn procession that made its way to the house, except for Horace, who darted ahead and raced back, all panting breath and lolling tongue as if this were a new game devised entirely for his amusement. Viscount and Viscountess Ravensberg came along behind them and caught up with the marquess when they were near the house.

"Where did you find her, Joseph?" the viscountess asked softly.

"There is a little hut in the woods on the other side of the bridge," the marquess said. "She was in there."

"Ah," the viscount said, "we must have forgotten to lock it the last time we were there, Lauren. We sometimes do forget."

"And thank heaven we did," she said. "She is so sweet, Joseph, and of course she looks like you."

And then they all reached the house, and the viscount directed everyone to the library.

The marquess did not follow them. He led the way upstairs, and Claudia went with him to his room, a large, comfortable guest chamber overlooking the eastern flower garden and the hills beyond. Claudia drew back the covers from the canopied bed, and he set Lizzie down in the middle of it. He sat beside her and held her hand.

"Papa," she said, "you *told* them."

"Yes," he said, "I did, did I not?"

"And now," she said, "everyone will hate me."

"My mother does not," he said, "and Cousin Neville does not. Neither does Cousin Lauren, who just told me you are sweet and look like me. If you had had eyes to see a few minutes ago, you would have seen that most people were looking at you with liking and sympathy—and happiness that you were safe."

"*She* hates me," she said. "Miss Hunt."

"I think," he said, "it is me she hates at the moment, Lizzie."

"Will the girls hate me?" she asked.

It was Claudia who answered.

"Molly does not," she said. "She was weeping just now because she was so happy to see you again. I cannot speak for the others, but I will say this. I am not sure it is a good idea to try to win love by pretending to be what we are not—you are not an orphaned charity girl, are you? It is perhaps better for all of us to risk being loved—or not—for who we really are."

"I am Papa's daughter," Lizzie said.

"Yes."

"His *bastard* daughter," she added.

Claudia saw him frown and open his mouth to speak. She spoke first.

"Yes," she agreed. "But that word suggests someone who is resented and unloved. Sometimes our choice of words is important, and one of the wonders of the English language is that there are often several words for the same thing. It would be more appropriate, perhaps, to describe yourself as your papa's illegitimate daughter or—better yet—as his love child. That is exactly what you are. Though it is not necessarily *who* you are. None of us can be described by labels—even a hundred labels or a thousand."

Lizzie smiled and lifted a hand to stroke her father's face.

"I am your *love* child, Papa," she said.

"You certainly are." He caught her hand and kissed the palm. "And now I must go downstairs, sweetheart. Miss Martin will stay with you, though I daresay you will be asleep in no time. You have had a busy day."

She yawned hugely as if to prove him right.

He got to his feet and looked at Claudia. She smiled ruefully at him. He half shrugged his shoulders and left the room without another word.

"Mmm," Lizzie said as Horace jumped up onto the bed to curl up against her, "the pillow smells of Papa."

Claudia looked directly at Horace, who gazed back in perfect contentment, his head on his paws. If she had not rushed to his defense in Hyde Park that afternoon, she thought, all this would very probably not have happened. How strange a thing fate was and the chain of seemingly minor, unrelated events that all led inexorably to some major conclusion.

Lizzie yawned again and was almost instantly asleep.

And what now? Claudia wondered. Was she going to take Lizzie back to school with her when she and Eleanor and the other girls returned to Bath within the next week or so? Even though she knew that Lizzie did not want to go? Did either of them have any other choice now? What other option was there for the child? Claudia could only imagine what was transpiring downstairs in the library. And what choice did *she* have? She loved Lizzie.

There was a soft tap on the door about ten minutes later, and Susanna and Anne opened it and tiptoed inside without waiting for an answer.

"Oh," Susanna said softly, looking toward the bed, "she is asleep. I am glad for her sake. She looked in shock out there at the lake."

"The poor dear child," Anne said, looking toward Lizzie too.

"This has been a sad ending to the afternoon for her. Yet earlier she enjoyed herself so much. A few times I was close to tears just watching her have fun."

The three of them sat close to the window, some distance from the bed.

"Everyone is leaving," Susanna said. "The children must all be exhausted. It is almost evening already. They have played for hours without stopping."

"Lizzie was afraid," Claudia said, "that everyone must hate her now."

"Quite the contrary," Anne said. "It was a rather shocking revelation, especially for Lauren and Gwen and the rest of Lord Attingsborough's family, but I do believe most people are secretly charmed by the fact that she is his daughter. Everyone had fallen for her anyway."

"I have been wondering," Claudia said, "if Lizzie and I will still be welcome at Lindsey Hall. I did bring her there under false pretenses, after all."

"I overheard the Duke of Bewcastle remark to the duchess," Susanna said, "that some people deserve their comeuppance and it is gratifying to see them get it. It was obvious he was referring to Lady Sutton and Miss Hunt."

"And Lady Hallmere declared quite openly," Anne said, "that the marquess's revelation was quite the most splendid moment of this or any afternoon she can remember. And everyone wanted to know if anyone else knew what had happened to Lizzie to cause her to get lost, and where you found her. Where *did* you find her?"

Claudia told them.

"I suppose," Susanna said, "you visited Lizzie in London, Claudia."

"Several times," Claudia said.

"As I thought," Susanna said with a sigh. "There goes my theory that Joseph was sweet on you when he took you driving so often. Perhaps it is just as well, though. Your romance would have had a tragic ending, would it not, since he was bound to offer for Miss Hunt. Though my opinion of her deteriorates every day."

Anne was looking closely at Claudia.

"I am not so sure tragedy *has* been averted, Susanna," she said. "Even apart from his looks, the Marquess of Attingsborough is an enormously charming gentleman. And any man's appeal can only be enhanced when he is seen to be devoted to his child. Claudia?"

"What nonsense!" Claudia said briskly, though she still kept her voice low. "It is pure business between me and the marquess. He wishes to place Lizzie at my school, and I have brought her here with Eleanor and the other girls as a trial. There is nothing else between us. Nothing at all."

But both her friends were looking at her with deep sympathy in their eyes, just as if she had confessed to an undying passion for the man.

"Oh, Claudia," Susanna said, "I am *so* sorry. Frances and I made a joke of it in London, I remember, but it was not funny at all. I am so sorry."

Anne merely leaned forward and took hold of Claudia's hand and squeezed.

"Well," Claudia said, her voice still brisk, "I always did say dukes were nothing but trouble, did I not? The Marquess of Attingsborough is not a duke yet, but I ought nonetheless to have run a thousand miles the moment I set eyes on him."

"And that was *my* fault," Susanna said.

And now she could no longer deny the truth to them, Claudia thought. She would be the object of their pity forever after. She squared her shoulders and pressed her lips together.

When a footman opened the library door and Joseph stepped inside, it was to find his mother and father alone there. His mother was seated beside the fireplace. His father was pacing, his hands clasped behind his back, though he stopped when he saw his son, a frown causing a deep crease between his brows.

"Well?" he said after they had all regarded one another silently for a few seconds. "What do you have to say for yourself?"

Joseph stood where he was, just inside the door.

"Lizzie is my daughter," he said. "She is almost twelve years old though she looks younger. She was born blind. I have housed and supported her all her life. I have been part of her life from the beginning. I love her."

"She seems like a very sweet child, Joseph," his mother said. "But how very sad that she is—"

The duke quelled her with a look.

"I did not ask, Joseph," he said, "for a history. *Of course* you have taken responsibility for the support of your bastard child. I would expect no less of a gentleman and a son of mine. What I *do* need to have explained is the presence of the child in this neighborhood and her appearance at Alvesley this afternoon where she was bound to be seen by your mother and your sister and your betrothed."

As if Lizzie were somehow contaminated. But of course she was in the minds of polite society.

"I am hoping to place her at Miss Martin's school," he explained. "Her mother died at the end of last year. Lauren invited Miss Martin and Miss Thompson to bring the girls to the picnic this afternoon."

"And you did not think to inform them," his father asked, his face ruddy with anger, a pulse beating visibly at one temple, "that it would be the depths of vulgarity to bring the blind child with them? Do not attempt an answer. I do not wish to hear it. And do not attempt an explanation of your appalling outburst after Wilma and Miss Hunt had reprimanded that schoolteacher. There can *be* no explanation."

"Webster," Joseph's mother said, "do calm yourself. You will make yourself ill again."

"Then you will know, Sadie, at whose door to lay the blame," he said.

Joseph pursed his lips.

"What I *do* demand," his father said, turning his attention back to his son, "is that neither your mother nor Wilma nor Miss Hunt ever hear another word of your private affairs after today. You will apologize to your mother in my hearing. You will apologize to Wilma and to Lady Redfield and Lauren and the Duchess of Bewcastle, whose home you have sullied quite atrociously. And you will make your peace with Miss Hunt and assure her that she will never hear the like from you again."

"Mama," Joseph said, turning his attention to her. She held her hands clasped together at her bosom. "I have caused you distress today, both at the picnic and now. I am deeply sorry."

"Oh, Joseph," she said, "you must have been more frantic than any of us when that poor child was missing. Did she take any harm?"

"Sadie—" the duke said, frowning ferociously.

"Shock and exhaustion, Mama," Joseph said. "No physical injuries, though. Miss Martin is sitting with her. I expect she is asleep by now."

"Poor child," she said again.

Joseph looked back at his father.

"I will go and find Portia," he said.

"She is with your sister and Sutton in the flower garden," his father told him.

It was *he* his father had been censuring, Joseph reminded himself as he left the library—his behavior in allowing Lizzie to be brought to Lindsey Hall and to Alvesley Park today, where she would necessarily be in company with his family and betrothed. And his behavior in allowing himself to be goaded into admitting publicly that Lizzie was his daughter.

It was not Lizzie herself he had been censuring. But dash it all, it felt very much as if that had been the case.

...your bastard child...

...the blind child...

And he almost felt that he ought to be ashamed. He had broken the unwritten but clearly understood rules of society. His *private affairs,* his father had called his secrets, as if every man was expected to have them. But he *would* not be ashamed. If he admitted he had done wrong, then he was denying Lizzie's right to be with the other children and with him.

Life was *not* easy—today's profound thought!

He found Portia, as his father had told him, sitting in the flower garden with Wilma and Sutton. Wilma looked at him as if she wished she could convert her eyes into daggers.

"You have insulted us all quite intolerably, Joseph," she said. "To have made such an admission when so many people were listening! I have never been more mortified in my life. I hope *you* are ashamed."

He wished he could tell her to stuff it, as Neville had done earlier, but she had the moral high ground. Even for Lizzie's sake, his admission had been rash and inappropriate.

Except that the words had been more freeing than any others he had ever uttered, he realized suddenly.

"And *what* do you have to say to Miss Hunt?" Wilma asked him. "You will be very fortunate indeed if she will listen."

"I think, Wilma," he said, "that what I have to say and what she says in reply ought to be private between the two of us."

She looked as if she was going to argue. She drew breath. But Sutton cleared his throat and took her by the elbow, and she turned without another word and stalked back in the direction of the house with him.

Portia, still in the primrose yellow muslin dress she had worn to the picnic, looked as fresh and as lovely as she had at the beginning of the afternoon. She also looked calm and poised.

He stood looking down at her, feeling his dilemma. He *had* wronged her. He had humiliated her in front of a large gathering of his family and friends. But how could he apologize to her without somehow denying Lizzie anew?

She spoke first.

"You told Lady Sutton and me to hold our tongues," she said.

Good Lord! *Had* he?

"I do beg your pardon," he said. "It was when Lizzie was

missing, was it? I was frantic with worry. Not that that was any excuse for such discourtesy. Do please forgive me. And, if you will, for—"

"I do not wish to hear *that name* again, Lord Attingsborough," she said with quiet dignity. "I will expect you to have her removed from here and from Lindsey Hall by tomorrow at the latest and then I will choose to forget the whole unfortunate incident. I do not care where you send her or the others like her or the...*women* who produced them. I do not need or wish to know."

"There are no other children," he said. "Or mistresses. Has this afternoon's revelation led you to believe that I am promiscuous? I assure you I am not."

"Ladies are not fools, Lord Attingsborough," she said, "however naive you may think us. We are perfectly well aware of men's animal passions and are quite content that they slake them as often as they please, provided it is not with us and provided we know nothing about it. All we ask—all *I* ask—is that the proprieties be observed."

Good Lord! He felt chilled. Yet surely the truth would make her feel somewhat better, make her less convinced that she was about to marry an animal in the thin guise of a gentleman.

"Portia," he said, gazing down at her, "I believe very firmly in monogamous relationships. After Lizzie was born, I remained with her mother until her death last year. That is why I have not married before now. After our marriage I will be faithful to you for as long as we both live."

She looked back at him, and it struck him suddenly that her eyes were very different from Claudia's. If there was anything behind them, any depth of character, any emotion, there was certainly no evidence of it.

"You will do as you please, Lord Attingsborough," she said, "as all men are entitled to do. I ask only that you exercise discretion. And I ask for your promise that that blind girl will be gone from here today and from Lindsey Hall tomorrow."

That blind girl.

He strolled a few feet away from her and stood looking at a

bed of hyacinths growing against a wooden trellis, his back to her. It was a reasonable request, he supposed. To her—probably to everyone at Alvesley and Lindsey Hall—it must seem that keeping Lizzie close was in extremely poor taste.

Except that Lizzie was a person. She was an innocent child. And she was his.

"No," he said, "I cannot make that promise, I'm afraid, Portia."

Her silence was more accusing than words would have been.

"I have observed the proprieties for all these years," he said. "My daughter had a mother and a comfortable home in London, and I could see her whenever I wished, which was every day when I was in town. I told no one about her except Neville, and never took her where we would be seen together. I accepted that that was the way it must be. I never had real cause to question society's dictates until Sonia died and Lizzie was left alone."

"I do not wish to hear this," Portia said. "It is quite improper."

"She is not quite twelve," he said. "She is far too young for any independence even if she were not blind."

He turned to look at her.

"And I love her," he said. "I cannot banish her to the periphery of my life, Portia. I will not. But my worst mistake, I realize now, was not telling you about her sooner. You had a right to know."

She said nothing for a while. She sat as still as any statue, delicate and lovely beyond belief.

"I do not believe I can marry you, Lord Attingsborough," she said then. "I had no wish to know of any such child and am only amazed that you think now you ought to have informed me about that dreadful creature, who cannot even *see*. I will not hear any more about her, and I will not tolerate knowing that she remains here or even at Lindsey Hall. If you cannot promise to remove her, and if you cannot promise that I will never hear of her again, I must withdraw my acceptance of your offer."

Strangely, perhaps, he was not relieved. Another broken engagement—even if it would be obvious to the *ton* that she was blameless in both—would surely render her almost unmarriage-able. And she was no young girl. She must be in her middle twenties already. And in the eyes of society, her demands would appear quite reasonable.

But—*that dreadful creature...*

Lizzie!

"I am sorry to hear it," he said. "I beg you to reconsider. I am the same man you have known for several years. I fathered Lizzie long before I knew you."

She got to her feet.

"You do not understand, Lord Attingsborough, do you?" she said. "I *will not* hear her name. I will go now and write to Papa. He will not be pleased."

"Portia—" he said.

"I believe," she said, "you no longer have any right to use that name, my lord."

"Our engagement is off, then?" he asked her.

"I cannot imagine anything that would make me reconsider," she told him, and turned to walk back to the house.

He stood where he was, watching her go.

It was only when she had disappeared from sight that he felt the beginnings of elation.

He was free!

20

Claudia returned to Lindsey Hall without Lizzie. By the time the Marquess of Attingsborough returned to his room, she was fast asleep and it seemed very possible that she would sleep all night if left undisturbed. Lady Ravensberg offered to have a truckle bed set up for him in the dressing room.

He also insisted upon escorting Claudia back to Lindsey Hall in his own carriage—the guests from there had returned home long ago, of course. The viscountess, Anne, and Susanna all promised to watch Lizzie until his return.

Claudia tried to insist upon going alone, but he would not hear of it. Neither would Anne and Susanna, who reminded her that it was now evening. And heaven help her, Claudia thought as they descended the staircase together and stepped out onto the terrace, where the carriage awaited them, she was not going to argue the point.

Viscount and Viscountess Ravensberg were out there, as was Lady Redfield.

"Miss Martin," the countess said, "I hope you will disregard everything that Lady Sutton and Miss Hunt said earlier. My husband and I have been delighted to entertain both you and the girls from your school—*including* Lizzie Pickford—and you were not neglecting your duties by walking with your childhood friend, the Duke of McLeith. We were all watching her and so we were all responsible for letting her wander away."

"Miss Martin was certainly not to blame," the Marquess of Attingsborough said. "When she went walking I was playing with Lizzie. She had every reason to believe that I would keep her safe."

He handed Claudia into the carriage and climbed in after her.

"Miss Martin," the viscountess said, leaning into the carriage before the door was closed, "you *will* come to the anniversary ball tomorrow, will you not?"

Claudia could think of nothing she would like less.

"Perhaps it would be better," she said, "if I were to stay away."

"You must not," the viscountess said. "You would thereby suggest to some of our guests that they have more power to decide who is welcome at our home than we have."

"Lauren is quite right, Miss Martin. Please come," the countess said. Her eyes twinkled. "You do not look to me like a lady who lacks courage."

The viscount, when Claudia caught his eye, winked.

"You are all most kind," Claudia said. "Very well, then, I will come."

What she *really* wanted to do, she thought, was return to Lindsey Hall alone, pack her bags, and leave at first light. As the door closed and the carriage moved forward, she thought of the last time she had left Lindsey Hall. How she would love to repeat that exit!

The carriage suddenly seemed to be filled with just the two of them—the very same carriage in which he had taken refuge from the rain on the road from Bath when she had been uncomfortably aware of his masculinity. She was aware again, though of far more than just that.

And she remembered what—incredibly—she had almost forgotten in the emotional turmoil of the past hour or so. While they had been sitting on the bed in that little hut in the woods he had spoken to her without any sound—with only lip movements. But she had heard loudly and clearly.

I love you, he had told her.

Heartache, she thought, was very likely to turn to heartbreak before this was all over. And that was an optimistic assessment of the future. It *would* turn to heartbreak. Indeed, it already had.

"Miss Hunt has broken off our engagement," he said as the carriage wheels rumbled onto the Palladian bridge.

Sometimes even a short sentence did not have the power to impress itself upon the mind all at once. It was as if she heard the words separately and needed a few moments to piece them together and know what he was telling her.

"Irrevocably?" she asked.

"She told me," he said, "that she cannot imagine anything that would cause her to change her mind."

"Because you have an illegitimate child?" she asked.

"Apparently," he said, "that is not the reason at all. She does not care if I have any number of mistresses and children. Indeed, she seems to expect it of me—as she expects it of all men. It is the fact that I broke one of the cardinal rules of polite society by acknowledging Lizzie's relationship to me that has offended her. My refusal to have her removed from Alvesley tonight and Lindsey Hall tomorrow and never to mention her ever again is what caused her to inform me that she could not marry me."

"Perhaps," she said, "on cooler reflection she will change her mind."

"Perhaps," he agreed.

They did not speak for a while.

"What next, then?" she asked. "What will happen to Lizzie? Eleanor and I are agreed that she is educable and adaptable and eager to learn. It would be a pleasure to take on the challenge of having her at the school. However, I am not sure it is what Lizzie wants even though I know she had been enjoying the company and the activities."

"What I have wanted to do from the moment of Sonia's death," he said, "is move Lizzie to Willowgreen, my home in Gloucestershire. It has always seemed an impossible dream, but maybe now I can make it a reality. The secret is out after all, and I find that I do not care the snap of two fingers what society thinks of me. And society is often not half the villain we sometimes expect it to be. Anne and Sydnam Butler have her son with them at Alvesley. He was born out of wedlock nine years before they met each other—but of course, you know all about that. David Jewell is treated here no differently from all the other children."

"Oh," Claudia said, "I think Willowgreen—the country—would be perfect for Lizzie."

She felt a nameless longing—which would not remain nameless if she allowed her thoughts to dwell upon it.

"What provision would you make for her education?" she asked.

"I would hire a companion and governess for her," he said. "But I would be able to spend a great deal of my own time with her. I would teach her about the countryside, about plants and animals, about England, about history. I would hire someone to teach her to play the pianoforte or the violin or the flute. Perhaps in a year or two's time she would be more ready for school than she is now. In the meantime I would be able to remain at home for far longer spells than I have been able to do with her in London. I would be less idle, more meaningfully employed. You might even come to approve of me."

She turned her head to look at him. The carriage was just drawing clear of the trees at the bottom of the driveway and passing through the gates. His face was lit by the slanting rays of the sun, which was low in the sky. She noticed that he spoke hypothetically, as if he did not really believe in his freedom.

"Yes," she said, "perhaps I might."

He smiled slowly at her.

"Though I already *do* approve of you," she said. "You have not spent so much time in London for frivolous reasons. You have done it for love. There is no nobler motive. And now you have acknowledged your daughter publicly. I approve of that too."

"You look," he said, "like the prim schoolteacher who first greeted me in Bath."

"That," she said, folding her hands in her lap, "is who I am."

"Was it not you," he said, "who told my daughter just a short while ago that no one can be summed up by labels alone?"

"I have a rich life, Lord Attingsborough," she told him. "I have made it myself, and I am happy with it. It is as different from the life I have lived during the past few weeks as it could possibly be. And I cannot wait to return to it."

She had turned her head away to look out through the window.

"I am sorry," he said, "for the turmoil I have brought into your life, Claudia."

"You have brought nothing that I have not allowed," she told him.

They lapsed into silence after that, a silence that was fraught with tension and yet was curiously companionable too. The tension, of course, was sexual. Claudia was well aware of that. But it was not lust. It was not just the desire to embrace and perhaps go beyond mere embraces. Love lent a comforting touch to the atmosphere, and yet it was a love that might yet be tragic. Miss Hunt might yet change her mind.

And if she did not?

But Claudia's mind could not move beyond that stumbling block.

The Duke and Duchess of Bewcastle stepped out through the front doors of Lindsey Hall as the carriage rounded the great fountain and drew to a halt.

"Oh," the duchess said when the coachman had opened the door and let down the steps, "the Marquess of Attingsborough has accompanied you, Miss Martin. I am so glad. We have worried about you coming alone. But Lizzie is not with you?"

"She is sleeping," the marquess explained to her as he stepped out and turned to hand Claudia down. "I thought it best not to disturb her. I will take her away from there tomorrow—to another destination if you wish."

"Other than Lindsey Hall, you mean?" the duchess said. "I most certainly hope not. This is where she belongs until Eleanor and Miss Martin leave for Bath. I invited her here."

"I have thought that perhaps I ought to leave tomorrow too," Claudia said.

"Miss Martin." It was the duke who spoke. "You are not planning to leave us in the manner you chose last time, it is to be hoped? It is true that Freyja credits the chagrin and guilt she felt at that time with turning her into a tolerable human being, but I could draw no such comfort from the incident—especially after I had heard that Redfield took you and your heavy valise up in his carriage because you would not take mine."

He spoke haughtily and somewhat languidly, and his hand closed about the handle of his quizzing glass and half raised it to his eye.

The duchess laughed. "I *wish* I could have seen that," she said. "Freyja was telling us about it during the drive back from Alvesley. But, come inside, both of you, and join everyone else in the drawing room. And if you are afraid, Lord Attingsborough, that you will meet disapproving frowns there, then you do not know the Bedwyn family—or their spouses. Does he, Wulfric?"

"Indeed," the duke said, raising his eyebrows.

"I will not come in," the marquess said. "I must return to Alvesley soon. Miss Martin, would you care to take a stroll with me first?"

"Yes," she said. "Thank you."

She was aware of the duchess smiling warmly at them as she took the duke's arm and turned to go back into the house with him.

Joseph was not well acquainted with the park about Lindsey Hall. He turned in the direction of the lake, where the dog had led Lizzie almost a week ago. They walked in silence, he with his hands at his back, she with her hands clasped at her waist.

They stopped when they came to the water's edge, close to

where he had shown Lizzie how to hurl pebbles so that she could hear them plop into the lake. The remains of the sunset made the water luminous. The sky stretched above, light at the horizon, darker overhead. Stars were already visible.

"It is altogether possible that my father and my sister will persuade Portia that it is not in her best interests to end her betrothal," he said.

"Yes."

"Though she *did* say nothing could change her mind," he added, "and I will not compromise. Lizzie will remain a visible part of my life. But it is a terrible thing for a lady to end an engagement—especially twice. She may reconsider."

"Yes."

"I cannot make you any promises," he told her.

"I do not ask for any," she said. "Even apart from the one obstacle, there are others. There can be no promises, no future."

He was not at all sure he agreed with her, but there was no point in raising any arguments now, was there? The more he thought about it, the more likely it seemed to him that his father and Wilma between them would persuade Portia to resume her plans to marry him.

"No future," he said softly. "Only the present. At present I am free."

"Yes."

When he reached out a hand to her, she set her own in it, and he laced his fingers with hers, drew her closer to his side, and strolled onward, following the bank of the lake. Up ahead he could see a forest of trees stretching down almost to the water's edge.

They stopped when they were in the darkness of the shade provided by the trees. The grass was rather long and soft underfoot. He turned to face her, lacing the fingers of their other hands too and drawing them partway around his back so that she stood against him, touching him with her breasts, her abdomen, and her thighs. Her head was tipped back, though he could no longer see her face clearly.

"I intend more than kisses," he said, leaning over her.

"Yes," she said. "So do I."

He smiled in the darkness. She sounded fierce and prim, her voice at variance with her words and the yielding warmth of her body.

"Claudia," he murmured.

"Joseph."

He smiled again. He felt that he had already been caressed with intimacy. She had never spoken his name before.

And then he leaned closer and touched his lips to hers.

It had still not ceased to amaze him that of all the women he might have possessed or loved during the last fifteen years or so of his life, she should be the one his heart had chosen. Even Barbara faded into insignificance beside her. He yearned for this strong, intelligent, disciplined woman more than he had longed for anything or anyone else in his life.

They explored each other's mouths with lips and tongues and teeth, their hands clasped together behind his back. Her mouth was hot and wet and welcoming, and he stroked into it with his tongue, sliding over surfaces until she moaned and sucked it deeper. He drew his head back and smiled at her again. His eyes had grown accustomed to the darkness. She was smiling back, her expression dreamy and sensual.

He released her hands and shrugged out of his coat. He went down on one knee and spread it on the grass, then reached up for her hand.

She took his and then came down onto her knees too and lay down, her head and her back on his coat.

This, he was very aware, might be the only time ever. Tomorrow all might have changed again. She knew it too. She reached up her arms to him.

"I don't care about the past or the future," she said. "We allow them far too much power over our lives. I care for the present moment. I care for *now*."

He lowered his head and kissed her again and eased himself down until he was lying beside her.

It had been eighteen years for her, almost three for him. He could feel her hunger and tried to put some sort of brake on his own. But sometimes passion would obey no commands beyond its own fierce needs.

He kissed her mouth, ravished it with his tongue. He explored her with urgent hands, discovering a body that was shapely and alluring. He drew her skirt up and pushed her stockings down, caressing the firm smoothness of her legs until hands were not enough. He bent his head, feathered kisses from her ankles to her knees, kissed the backs of her knees and licked them until she gasped and her fingers tightened in his hair. He found the buttons at the back of her dress and unfastened them one by one until he could draw the garment off her shoulders with her chemise and expose her breasts.

"I am not beautiful," she said.

"Let me be the judge of that," he told her.

He caressed her breasts with his hands, ran his lips over them, licked her taut nipples with his tongue until she was panting again.

But she did not lie passive. She moved to his touch, and her hands roamed over him and beneath his waistcoat. They dragged his shirt free of his pantaloons and caressed their way upward over his bare back to his shoulders. And then one hand came free and moved down between them to cover his erection through his pantaloons.

He took her firmly by the wrist, moved the hand away, and laced her fingers with his.

"Mercy, woman," he said against her lips, "I have very little control remaining as it is."

"I have none," she said.

He chuckled, and his hand went beneath her skirt again and up along her warm inner thighs to the junction between them. She was hot and wet.

She moaned.

He fumbled with the buttons at his waist, moved over her, pressing her thighs wide with his own, slid his hands beneath her to cushion her against the hard ground, and pressed firmly into her until he was deep and felt her muscles clench about him.

She raised her knees and braced her feet on the grass. She tilted to him to take him deeper yet, and he drew a slow breath, his face against the side of hers.

"Claudia," he said into her ear.

It had been a long, long time—an eternity. And he knew he could not prolong what was about to happen. But he needed to remember that this was Claudia, that this was more than sex.

"Joseph," she said, her voice low and throaty.

He withdrew from her and thrust inward, and the rhythm of love caught them both in its urgent crescendo until everything burst into glory and he spilled into her.

Far too soon, he thought regretfully as his body relaxed into satiety.

"Like an overexcited schoolboy," he murmured to her.

She laughed softly and turned her head to kiss his lips briefly. "You do not *feel* like one," she said.

He rolled off her, bringing her with him until they were both lying on their sides.

She was quite right. Nothing had been wrong. On the contrary, everything had been right—perfect.

And for now it was enough. Now might be all they had. He hugged the moment to himself as he hugged her and willed the moment to become an endless eternity.

He saw the moonlight overhead, felt the cool breeze, felt the soft, relaxed warmth of the woman he held, and allowed himself to feel happiness.

Claudia knew she would not be sorry—just as she had never been sorry about that kiss at Vauxhall.

She knew too that there would be only tonight—or this evening. Tonight he must return to Alvesley.

She was as certain as she could be that Miss Hunt would not

readily give up such a matrimonial prize as the Marquess of Attingsborough. It would not take much effort on the part of the Duke of Anburey and the Countess of Sutton to make her see reason. And of course he—Joseph—would have no choice but to take her back since the betrothal had not been publicly ended. He was a gentleman, after all.

And so there was only this—only this evening.

But she would not be sorry. She would certainly suffer, but then she would have done that anyway.

She refused to doze off. She watched the moon and stars above the lake, heard the almost silent lapping of the water against the bank, felt the cool softness of the grass against her legs, smelled the trees and his cologne, tasted his kisses on her slightly swollen lips.

She was tired, even exhausted. And yet she had never felt more alive.

She could not see him clearly in the darkness, but she knew when he dozed, when he awoke again with a slight start. She felt a huge regret that just sometimes one could not hold time at a standstill.

This time next week she would be back at school preparing lessons and schedules for the coming year. It was always an exhilarating time. She would be exhilarated by it.

But not yet.

Please not yet. It was too soon for the future to encroach upon the present.

"Claudia," he said, "if there are consequences . . ."

"Oh, gracious," she said, "there will not be. I am thirty-five years old."

Which was a ridiculous thing to say, of course. She was *only* thirty-five. Her monthly cycle told her that she was still capable of bearing children. She had not thought of it. Or if she had, she had disregarded the thought. Foolish woman.

"*Only* thirty-five years old," he said, echoing her thought. But he did not complete what he had started to say. How could he? What would he say? That he would marry her? If Miss Hunt chose to hold him to his promise, he would not be free to do so. And even if she did not and he was free . . .

"I refuse to be sorry," she said, "or to think unpleasant thoughts at the moment."

Which was *exactly* the sort of brainlessness about which she lectured her older girls before they left school, especially the charity girls, who would face far more risks than those who had families to guard them.

"Do you?" he said. "Good."

And his hands moved caressingly up and over the flesh of her upper back, and his mouth nuzzled her ear and the side of her neck and she wrapped her arms more tightly about him and kissed his throat and his neck and jaw and finally his mouth. She felt the hardness of his erection press against her belly and knew that the evening was not quite over after all.

They stayed lying on their sides. He lifted her leg over his hip, nestled into position, and came inside her again.

There was less frenzy this time, less mindlessness. His movements were slower and firmer, her own more deliberate. She could feel his hardness against her wet heat, could hear the suck and pull of their loving. They kissed each other softly, open-mouthed.

And it seemed suddenly to Claudia that she really *was* beautiful. And feminine and passionate and all the things she had once believed about herself but lost faith in even before she was fully a woman. *He* was beautiful and he loved her and was making love to her.

Somehow he was setting her free—free of the insecurities that had dogged her for eighteen years, free to be the complete person she really was. Teacher and woman. Businesswoman and lover. Successful and vulnerable. Disciplined and passionate.

She was who she was—without labels, without apology, without limit.

She was perfect.

So was he.

And so was *this*.

Simply perfect.

He set his hand behind her hips and held her steady as he deepened his thrusts, though even then there was more sense of purpose than urgency. He kissed her lips and murmured words that her heart understood even if her ears could not decipher them. And then he was still in her, and she was pressing against him, and something opened at her core and let him through—and he came and came until there was no she and no he but only they.

They remained pressed wordlessly together for a long time before he released her and she knew with deep regret that now they were two again—and would remain so for the rest of their lives.

But she would not be sorry.

"I must take you back to the house," he said, sitting up and adjusting his clothes while she pushed her skirt down and then bent to pull up her stockings and the bodice of her dress. "And I must get back to Alvesley."

"Yes," she said, rearranging some of her hairpins.

He got to his feet and reached down a hand to her. She set her own in it and he drew her up until they were standing facing each other, not quite touching.

"Claudia," he said, "I do not know—"

She set a finger over his lips, just as she remembered doing at Vauxhall.

"Not tonight," she said. "I want tonight to remain perfect. I want to be able to remember it just as it is. All the rest of my life."

His hand closed about her wrist and he kissed her finger.

"Perhaps tomorrow night will be just as perfect," he said. "Perhaps all our tomorrows will."

She merely smiled. She did not believe it for a moment—but she would think about that tomorrow and the next day . . .

"You will come to the ball?" he asked her.

"Oh, I will," she said. "I would much rather not, but I believe the countess and Lady Ravensberg will be offended, even hurt, if I stay away."

And how could she stay away even without that incentive? Tomorrow night might be the last time she saw him. Ever.

He kissed her wrist and then released her hand.

"I am glad," he said.

21

The Duke of Anburey requested the presence of the Marquess of Attingsborough in the library, the butler informed Joseph as soon as he set foot inside Alvesley again. He did not go there immediately. He went up to his room, where he found Anne and Sydnam Butler sitting with Lizzie. She had not woken up since he left for Lindsey Hall, they informed him.

"My father wants to talk with me," he said.

Sydnam threw him a sympathetic look.

"Go," his wife said, smiling at Joseph. "We relieved Susanna and Peter only half an hour or so ago. We will stay awhile longer."

"Thank you," he said, standing beside the bed and touching the backs of his fingers to Lizzie's cheek. She had a corner of the pillow clutched in one hand, and held it against her nose. He was *so glad* that all the secrecy had gone from their relationship. He leaned over to kiss her. She mumbled something unintelligible and was still again.

There was a terrible row in the library after he went down there. His father stormed at him. He had apparently talked reason into Portia and persuaded her that his son would behave properly and she would never have to see or hear about the child ever again. She was prepared to continue with the engagement.

Joseph, however, was not prepared to be dictated to. He informed his father that he was unwilling to hide Lizzie away any longer. He hoped to move her to Willowgreen, to spend much of his time there with her. And since Portia had released him during the afternoon, she must now accept this new fact if the betrothal was to resume.

He held firm even when his father threatened to turn him out of Willowgreen—it was still officially his. Then he would live with his daughter somewhere else, Joseph told him. He was not, after all, financially dependent upon his father. He would set up another home in the country.

They argued for a long time—or rather, Joseph remained quietly obstinate and his father blustered. His mother, who was present throughout, endured it all in silence.

And then his father and mother left the library together and sent Portia to him.

She came, looking composed and beautiful in a gown of pale ice blue. He stood before the empty fireplace, his hands clasped at his back while she crossed the room toward him, took a seat, and arranged her skirts about her. She looked up at him, her lovely face empty of any discernible emotion.

"I am truly sorry about all this, Portia," he said. "And I am entirely to blame. I have known since the death of Lizzie's mother that my daughter must be even more central to my life than she had been before. I have known that I must make a home for her and give her my time and my attention and my love. And yet somehow it did not quite occur to me until today that I could not do it properly while living the sort of double life that society demanded of me. If it *had* occurred to me in time, I would have been able to discuss the matter openly with my father and yours before exposing you to the sort of distress you have endured today."

"I came to this room, Lord Attingsborough," she said, "on the understanding that that dreadful blind child would never be mentioned to me again. I agreed to resume my engagement to you and prevent your utter disgrace in the eyes of the *ton* on the condition that all would be as it was before you spoke so ill advisedly at the picnic this afternoon. And *that* would not have happened if that incompetent schoolteacher had not set her sights on a *duke* for a husband and neglected her charges."

He drew a slow breath.

"I see it will not do," he said. "While I understand your reasoning, Portia, I cannot agree to your terms. I *must* have my child with me. I *must* be a father to her. Duty dictates it, and inclination makes it imperative. I *love* her. If you cannot accept that fact, then I am afraid any marriage between us would be unworkable."

She got to her feet.

"*You* are prepared to break our engagement?" she said. "To renege on all your promises and a duly drawn up marriage contract? Oh, I think not, Lord Attingsborough. I will not release you. *Papa* will not release you. The Duke of Anburey will disown you."

Ah, she had had time for reflection since late this afternoon, then, as he had rather expected. She was not a young woman as far as the marriage mart went. Although she was well born and wealthy and beautiful, it would be an uncomfortable thing for her to be single again, with two broken engagements behind her. She might never have another chance to make such an advantageous match. And he knew she had set her heart upon being a duchess at some time in the future.

But to be willing to hold him to a marriage that would clearly bring both of them active misery was incredible to him.

He closed his eyes briefly.

"I think what we need to do, Portia," he said, "is speak to your father. It is a shame he and your mother did not stay longer. It must be dreadful for you to be without them today. Shall we call a truce? Shall we put a polite face upon things tomorrow for the anniversary celebrations and then leave the day after tomorrow? I will take you home, and we will discuss the whole thing with your father."

"He will not release you," she told him. "Do not expect it. He will make you marry me, and he will make you give up that dreadful creature."

"The centrality of Lizzie to my life is no longer negotiable," he said quietly. "But let us leave it for now, shall we? Soon you will have your mother for moral support and your father to argue and negotiate for you. In the meanwhile, may I escort you to the drawing room?"

He offered his arm, and she set her hand on his sleeve and allowed him to lead her from the library.

And so officially he was engaged once more. And perhaps— who knew?—he would never be free again. He very much feared that Balderston might agree to his terms and that Portia might marry him and then not honor them.

All of which he would deal with when the time came because he would have no choice.

But for now he was not free and might never be.

Ah, Claudia!

He had not dared think of her since setting foot inside this house again.

Ah, my love.

Lizzie sat at a little table in Joseph's bedchamber the next morning, dressed neatly in her picnic dress, which a maid had brought to the room earlier, neatly cleaned and ironed, and with her hair freshly brushed and caught up in her white hair ribbon, also newly ironed. She was eating breakfast and holding court.

She was to return to Lindsey Hall after breakfast, but in the meanwhile she had a string of visitors. Kit and Lauren came with Sydnam and Anne Butler and her son, and then Gwen came with Aunt Clara and Lily and Neville, and they were closely followed by Susanna and Whitleaf. All wanted to bid Lizzie a good morning and hug her and ask if she had slept well.

All had smiles for Joseph himself.

Perhaps they were only smiles of rueful sympathy, of course, because they all understood the ordeal he had been through yesterday, though most of it had been kept behind closed doors. But even so, he wondered why he had kept the secret for so long.

Society had its rules and expectations, it was true, but he had always belonged to a family that had love to spare.

And then his mother came. She hugged him wordlessly and then went to sit on a chair at the table while Lizzie lifted her face, knowing that yet again there was someone in the room besides just her and her father.

"Lizzie." His mother took one of her hands in both her own. "Is that short for Elizabeth? I like both names. You dear child. You look quite like your papa. I am his mother. I am your grandmother."

"My grandmother?" Lizzie said. "I heard your voice yesterday."

"Yes, dear," his mother said, patting her hand.

"It was after I went walking with Horace and got lost," Lizzie said. "But Papa and Miss Martin found me. Papa is going to train Horace so that he does not get lost with me again."

"But how adventurous you were," his mother said. "Just like your father when he was a boy. He was forever climbing forbidden trees and swimming in forbidden lakes and disappearing for hours on end on voyages of discovery without a word to anyone. It is a wonder I did not have a heart seizure any number of times."

Lizzie smiled and then laughed with glee.

His mother patted her hand again, and Joseph could see tears in her eyes. She was not without courage herself, coming here like this in defiance of his father. She hugged and kissed both him and Lizzie, and then it was time to leave for Lindsey Hall. She and Lady Redfield came outside onto the terrace to see them on their way.

Joseph rode over there with McLeith, Lizzie up on his horse before him and the dog running alongside until he tired and had to be taken up with them too, much to Lizzie's delight. McLeith was, of course, going to call upon Claudia, as he did almost every day. Joseph wondered if the man would ever persuade her to marry him, though he very much doubted it.

When they arrived at Lindsey Hall, Joseph sent the note he had written last night up to Miss Martin with a footman but then went back outside, where the Duchess of Bewcastle and Lord and Lady Hallmere were talking to Lizzie. McLeith went inside to see Claudia. Joseph strolled down to the lake with Lizzie and the dog.

"Papa," she said, clinging to his hand as they walked, "I do not want to go to school."

"You will not be going," he assured her. "You will remain with me until you grow up and fall in love and marry and leave me."

"Silly," she said, laughing. "That will never happen. But if I do not go to school, I will lose Miss Martin."

"You like her, then?" he asked.

"I *love* her," she assured him. "Is it wrong, Papa? I loved Mother too. When she died I thought my heart would break. And I thought no one but you could ever make me smile again or make me feel safe again."

"But Miss Martin can?"

"Yes," she said.

"It is not wrong," he said, squeezing her hand. "Your mother will always be your mother. There will always be a corner of your heart where she lives on. But love lives and grows, Lizzie. The more you love, the more you *can* love. You need not feel guilty about loving Miss Martin."

Unlike him.

"Perhaps," she said, "Miss Martin can come and visit us, Papa."

"Perhaps," he agreed.

"I will miss her," she said with a sigh as they stood on the bank of the lake and he looked along to where the trees grew down almost to the water. Just there . . . "And Molly and Agnes and Miss Thompson."

"Soon," he said, "I will take you home."

"Home," she said with a sigh, resting the side of her head against his arm. "But, Papa, will Miss Martin take Horace?"

"I think," he said, "she will be happy if he stays with you."

Claudia Martin was walking with McLeith some distance away, he could see. They must have come over the hill behind the house and down through the trees.

He determinedly turned his attention to his daughter again. And how blessed he was to be able to be with her openly like this after so long.

"We never did have our boat ride yesterday afternoon, did we, sweetheart?" he said. "Shall we find a boat and do it now?"

"Oh, ye-e-es!" she cried, her face lighting up with pleasure and excitement.

"I would not have been surprised," Charlie said, "to have found you ready to leave this morning, Claudia, as soon as the child returned and could go with you. I would have been annoyed on your behalf. It is Attingsborough's job to take her away, and it should be done as soon as possible. He ought not to have had her brought here in the first place. It has put Bewcastle in an awkward position and is a dreadful insult to Miss Hunt—and Anburey."

"It was not his idea to bring Lizzie here," Claudia told him. "It was mine."

"He ought not even to have brought the child to your attention," he said. "You are a *lady*."

"And Lizzie," she said, "is a person."

"Miss Hunt," he said, "has been dreadfully upset even though she has too much dignity to show it openly. She was humiliated before a houseful of guests from both Alvesley and Lindsey Hall, not to mention the local gentry who were at the picnic. I half expected that she would refuse to continue with her plans to marry Attingsborough, but it seems she has forgiven him."

Yes. She had not needed to be told. She had read the stark message Joseph had sent up after she had watched his approach from the schoolroom window. She had only half noticed that Charlie was with him and Lizzie. She had waited without hope—but had realized after reading his note that in fact she had been deceiving herself. She *had* hoped. But suddenly all hope, all possibility of joy, was snatched away.

As they emerged from the trees to walk toward the far end of the lake, she looked back to where she had lain last night with Joseph—and she could see him farther off, standing at the water's edge with Lizzie. By a great effort of will, she brought her mind back to what they had been talking about.

"Charlie," she said, "Lizzie was conceived more than twelve years ago, when the Marquess of Attingsborough was very young and long before he met Miss Hunt. Why would she feel threatened by Lizzie's existence?"

"But it is not her existence, Claudia," he said. "It is the fact that now Miss Hunt and a large number of other people—soon to be everyone of any significance—*know* of her. It is just not the thing. A gentleman keeps these things to himself. I know the expectations of society—I had to learn them when I was eighteen. You cannot be expected to know. You have lived a far more sheltered life."

"Charlie," she said, suddenly arrested by a thought, "do *you* have children other than Charles?"

"*Claudia!*" He was obviously embarrassed. "That is *not* a question a lady asks a gentleman."

"You *do*," she said. "You do have others. Don't you?"

"I will not answer that," he said. "Really, Claudia, you always spoke your mind far more freely than you ought. It is one thing I always admired about you—and still do. But there are bounds—"

"You have *children*!" she said. "Do you love them and care for them?"

He laughed suddenly and shook his head ruefully.

"You are impossible!" he told her. "I am a gentleman, Claudia. I do what a gentleman must do."

The poor dead duchess, Claudia thought. For, unlike Lizzie, Charlie's illegitimate children must have been begotten when he was already married. How many were there? she wondered. And what sort of lives did they lead? But she could not ask. It was something some sort of gentleman's code of honor forbade him to speak of with a lady.

"This has all rather spoiled the atmosphere I hoped to create this morning," he said with a sigh. "The anniversary is today, Claudia. Tomorrow or the next day at the latest I must leave. I am well aware that I am the only guest at Alvesley who does not have some claim to be family. I do not know when I will see you again."

"We must write to each other," she said.

"You know that is not good enough for me," he told her.

She turned her head to look more fully at him. They were friends again, were they not? She had determinedly let go of the hurt of the past and allowed herself to like him again, even though there were things about him she did not particularly approve of. Surely he was not still—

"Claudia," he said, "I want you to marry me. I love you, and I think you are fonder of me than you will admit. Tell me now that you will marry me, and tonight's ball will seem like heaven. I will not have an announcement made there, I suppose, since it is in honor of the Redfields and besides, neither of us has any close bond with the family. But we will be able to let it be known informally. I will be the happiest of men. That is a horrible cliché, I know, but it would be true nonetheless. What do you say?"

She had nothing to say for several moments. She had been taken completely by surprise—again. What had obviously been a deepening romance to him had been merely a growing friendship to her. And today of all days she was not ready to cope with this.

"Charlie," she said eventually, "I do not love you."

There was a lengthy, uncomfortable silence. They had almost stopped walking. There was a boat pushing out from the bank some distance away, she saw—the Marquess of Attingsborough with Lizzie. She was smitten with a memory of his rowing her on the River Thames during Mrs. Corbette-Hythe's garden party. But she must not let her thoughts wander. She looked back at Charlie.

"You have said the one thing," he told her, "against which I have no argument. You loved me once, Claudia. You *made* love with me. Do you not remember?"

She closed her eyes briefly. Actually she could not remember much apart from the inexpert fumblings and the pain and the happy conviction afterward that now they belonged together for all time.

"It was a long time ago," she said gently. "We are different people now, Charlie. I am fond of you, but—"

"Damn your fondness," he said, and smiled ruefully at her. "And damn you. And now accept my humblest apologies for using such atrocious language in your hearing."

"But not for the atrocious sentiments?"

"No," he said, "not for those. My punishment is to be lifelong, then, is it?"

"Oh, Charlie," she said, "this is not punishment. I forgave you when you asked. But—"

"Marry me anyway," he said, "and to the devil with love. You *do* love me anyway. I am sure of it."

"As a friend," she said.

"Ouch!" He frowned. "Think about it. Think long and hard. And I'll ask again this evening. After that I will not pester you. Promise me you will think and try to change your mind?"

She sighed and shook her head.

"I will not change my mind between now and tonight," she said. "It is too late for us, Charlie."

"Think hard about it anyway," he said. "I will ask again tonight. Dance the opening set with me."

"Very well," she said.

A silence fell between them.

"I wish," he said, "I had known at eighteen what I know now—that there are some things on which one does not compromise. We had better walk back to the house, I suppose. I have made an idiot of myself, have I not? You cannot see anything more than a friend in me. It is not enough. Maybe by tonight you will have changed your mind. Though it will not happen just because I want it, I daresay."

And yet, she thought as she walked beside him, if they had not met in London this year, he quite probably would not have spared her another thought all the rest of his life.

She could see that Lizzie was trailing her hand in the water—as *she* had done in the Thames not long ago. And then she heard the sound of distant laughter—his and Lizzie's mingled.

She felt more lonely than she had felt for a long, long time. There seemed to be a dark and bottomless pit right inside her.

Portia Hunt had no relatives at Alvesley Park. She did not have any particular friends there, either, apart from Wilma. And now Joseph had gone off to Lindsey Hall for the morning.

Joseph's relatives were not unkind. Although all except his immediate family disapproved of her as a choice for his bride, they felt genuine sympathy for her. She had had an unpleasant shock during the picnic, even if she *had* largely brought it upon herself. It was understandable that she had felt somewhat humiliated. And clearly there had been some great upset later in the afternoon and again late in the evening after Joseph returned from escorting Miss Martin home. Somehow the betrothal had survived, though—Wilma had informed them all of that.

Susanna and Anne had informed Lauren and Gwen and Lily that it was a great shame because Claudia Martin was in love with Joseph—and he with her, they dared say. It was with *her* he had gone searching for Lizzie, was it not? And it was *she* he had asked to come to the house to watch Lizzie while he spoke with his father and Miss Hunt. And it was he who had taken her back to Lindsey Hall though Kit had offered to escort her. He had not come back immediately, either.

But they were kind ladies. Although there were all sorts of things they might have been doing in preparation for the grand anniversary ball in the evening, they invited Miss Hunt to go walking with them—and Wilma too. They strolled along the wilderness walk beyond the formal garden and the little bridge. Lily asked Miss Hunt about her wedding plans, and she launched into a discussion of a subject that was obviously dear to her heart.

"How lovely," Susanna said with a sigh as they passed the turnoff to the steep path that would have taken them to the top of the hill, and kept on along level ground instead, "to be so in love and planning a wedding."

"Oh," Portia said, "I would not dream of being so vulgar, Lady Whitleaf, as to imagine myself *in love*. A lady chooses her husband with far more good sense and judgment."

"Indeed," Wilma said, "one would not wish to find oneself married to a miller or a banker or a schoolmaster merely because one *loved* him, would one?"

Susanna looked at Anne, and Lauren looked at Gwen, and Lily smiled.

"I think what is best," she said, "is to marry a man with a title and wealth and property and good looks and charm and character—and to be head over ears in love with him too. Provided he felt the same way, of course."

They all laughed except Portia. Even Wilma tittered. Tiresome and stuffy as the family all found the Earl of Sutton, it was also no secret among them that he and Wilma were partial to each other.

"What is *best*," Portia said, "is to be in control of one's emotions at all times."

They turned back in the direction of the house rather sooner than they might have done. Although the sky was still blue and cloudless and the tree branches overhead not so thick that they blocked out all the sunlight, a chill seemed to have settled on the air.

The Duke of McLeith was standing on the small bridge, his arms draped over the wooden rail on one side, gazing down into the water. He straightened up and smiled when he saw the ladies come toward him.

"You are back from Lindsey Hall already?" Susanna asked redundantly. "Did you see Claudia?"

"I did." He looked mournful. "She is, it seems, a dedicated teacher and a confirmed spinster."

Susanna exchanged a glance with Anne.

"I think," Wilma said, "she ought to be grateful for your condescension in taking notice of her, your grace."

"Ah," he said, "but we grew up together, Lady Sutton. She always had a mind of her own. If she had been a man, she would have succeeded at whatever she set her hand to. Even as a woman, she has been remarkably successful. I am proud of her. But I am a little—"

"A little—?" Gwen prompted.

"Melancholy," he said.

"Did Joseph return with you?" Lauren asked.

"He did not," the duke said. "He took his d— He went boating with someone. I chose not to wait for him."

"He is incorrigible!" Wilma said crossly. "He was fortunate indeed yesterday that Miss Hunt was generous enough to forgive him for saying what was really quite unforgivable in my estimation, even if he *is* my brother. But he is tempting fate today. He ought to have returned *immediately*."

"Well," Lauren said briskly, "I really must return to the house. There must be a thousand and one things to be done before this evening. Gwen, you and Lily were going to help me with the floral arrangements."

"Harry will be needing to be fed soon," Susanna said.

"And I promised to go and watch Sydnam and David paint," Anne said. "Megan will be waiting to go with me."

"Wilma," Lauren said, "your parties are always in the very best of good taste. Do come with us and give your opinion on the decorations in the ballroom and the arrangement of the tables in the supper room, will you?"

She paused and looked at Portia.

"Miss Hunt," she said, "perhaps you will keep his grace company for a while? He will think we are deserting him so soon after coming upon him."

"Not at all, Lady Ravensberg," he assured her. "But I have been told, Miss Hunt, that the view from the top of the hill over there is well worth the rather steep climb. Would you care to come with me to see?"

"I would be delighted," she told him.

"Joseph will be *very* fortunate," Wilma said after they had moved out of earshot, "if the Duke of McLeith does not steal Miss Hunt from right beneath his nose. And who could blame him? Or her? I never thought to be ashamed of my own brother, but *really*..."

"I have been more than a little annoyed with him myself," Gwen said, linking her arm through Wilma's. "Keeping such a secret from us, indeed, just as if we were all stern judges instead of *family*. *And* I am annoyed with Neville. He knew all along, did he not, Lily?"

"He did," Lily said, "but he did not tell even me. One must admire his loyalty, Gwen. But I wish we had known sooner. Lizzie is a very sweet child, is she not?"

"She looks like Joseph," Lauren said. "She is going to be a beauty."

"She is *blind*," Wilma protested.

"I have a feeling," Anne said, "that she is not going to allow that fact to be an affliction to her. Now that everyone knows about her, it is going to be very interesting to watch her development."

Wilma held her peace.

They all went about their various tasks when they reached the house and left the comforting of Miss Hunt to the Duke of McLeith.

22

"*What on earth did I do to deserve such a tumultuous summer?*" Claudia asked.

It was a rhetorical question, but Eleanor attempted an answer anyway.

"You decided to go to London," she said, "and I encouraged you. I even urged you to stay for longer than you had originally planned."

"Mr. Hatchard was evasive about Edna's and Flora's employers," Claudia said. "Susanna persuaded Frances to sing and invited me to stay for the concert. She sent the Marquess of Attingsborough to escort me to London because he was in Bath at the time—and he happened to have a daughter he wished to place at the school. Charlie chose this particular spring to leave Scotland for the first time in years. And you just happen to be the sister of the Duchess of Bewcastle and accepted an invitation to bring the charity girls here and so I have been tripping over Bedwyns at every turn since I left Bath. And . . . and . . . and so the list goes on. How do we ever discover the root cause of any effect, Eleanor? Do we trace it back to Adam and Eve? *They* were a pair to cause any imaginable catastrophe."

"No, no, Claudia." Eleanor came to stand behind her at the dressing table in her bedchamber. "You will pull your hair out by the roots if you drag it back so severely. Here." She took the brush from Claudia's hand and loosened the knot at her neck so that her hair fell more softly over her head. She fussed a little over the knot itself. "That is better. Now you look far more as if you are going to a ball. I do like that green muslin. It is very elegant. You showed it to me in Bath, but I have not seen it on you until tonight."

"*Why* am I going to the ball?" Claudia asked. "Why are you not the one going and I the one staying?"

"Because," Eleanor said, her eyes twinkling as they met Claudia's in the mirror, "you are the one those women insulted yesterday, and it is important to Lady Redfield and her daughter-in-law that you make an appearance. And because you have never hidden from a challenge. Because you have promised to dance the opening set with the Duke of McLeith even if you *did* make it clear to him this morning that you will not marry him, poor man. Because someone has to stay with the girls, and it is generally known and accepted that I *never* attend balls or other lavish entertainments."

"You have made your point," Claudia said dryly, getting to her feet. "And also I attend such entertainments because I sometimes consider them *obligations*—unlike some persons who will remain nameless."

"And you will go," Eleanor said, "because it may be the last time you see him."

Claudia looked sharply at her. *"Him?"*

Eleanor picked up Claudia's paisley shawl from the bed and held it out to her.

"I have misunderstood all summer," she said. "I thought it was the Duke of McLeith, but I was wrong. I am sorry. I really am. Everyone is."

"Everyone?"

"Christine," Eleanor said. "Eve, Morgan, Freyja ..."

"Lady Hallmere?"

Was it really possible that all these people *knew*? But as she took the shawl from Eleanor, Claudia knew that indeed they must. They had all guessed. How absolutely *appalling*.

"I cannot go," she said. "I will send down some excuse. Eleanor, go and tell—"

"Of course you will go," Eleanor said. "You are Claudia Martin."

Yes, she was. And Claudia Martin was not the sort to hide in a dark corner, her head buried beneath a cushion, just because she was embarrassed and humiliated and brokenhearted and any number of other ugly, negative things if she only stopped to think what they were.

She straightened her spine, squared her shoulders, lifted her chin, pressed her lips together, and regarded her friend with a martial gleam in her eye.

"Heaven help anyone who gets in your way tonight," Eleanor said, laughing and stepping forward to hug her. "Go and show those two shrews that a headmistress from Bath is not to be cowed by genteel spite."

"Tomorrow I return to Bath," Claudia said. "Tomorrow I return to sanity and my own familiar world. Tomorrow I take up the rest of my life where I left it off when I stepped into the Marquess of Attingsborough's carriage one morning a thousand or so years ago. But tonight, Eleanor . . . Well, *tonight.*"

She laughed despite herself.

She led the way from the room with firm strides. All she needed, she thought ruefully, was a shield in one hand and a spear in the other—and a horned helmet on her head.

There had been a grand dinner to precede the ball. It had been a joyful, festive occasion for the family and houseguests. Speeches had been delivered and toasts drunk. The Earl and Countess of Redfield had looked both pleased and happy.

Joseph would have led Portia straight into the ballroom afterward since that was where most of the houseguests were gathering, and the outside guests were beginning to arrive. But she needed to return to her room to have her maid make some adjustments to her hair and to fetch her fan, and so Joseph wandered into the ballroom alone.

He mingled with the other guests. It was not really difficult to be sociable and genial, to look as if he were enjoying himself—it all came as naturally to him as breathing.

The Earl and Countess of Redfield, to everyone's delight, danced the opening set with their guests, a slow and stately and old-fashioned quadrille.

Portia was punishing him, Joseph thought when the set began, by being late and stranding him on the sidelines. He had, of course, elicited the opening set with her. He went and talked with his mother and Aunt Clara and a couple of Kit's aunts. He soon had them laughing.

Claudia was not dancing either. He had tried to stay far away from her since her arrival with the party from Lindsey Hall. He had not, though, been able to keep his mind off her. And now that he was standing in one place, talking and listening, he could not keep his eyes from her either.

She looked very severe even though she was wearing the prettier of her evening gowns. She was standing alone, watching the dancing. It amazed him that he had not seen through her disguise the moment he first set eyes on her in Bath. For that very upright, disciplined body was warm and supple and passion-filled, and that face with its regular, stern features and intelligent gray eyes was beautiful. *She* was beautiful.

Just last night, about this time . . .

He deliberately shifted position so that he stood with his back to her. And he looked toward the ballroom doors. There was still no sign of Portia.

He danced the next set with Gwen, who liked to dance despite her limp, and was pleased to see that Claudia was dancing with Rosthorn. When the set was over, he took Gwen to join a group that included Lauren and the Whitleafs. He commended Lauren on the festive appearance of the ballroom and on the early success of the evening. Should he have a maid sent up to Portia's room, he wondered, to make sure she had not eaten something that disagreed with her or met with some accident? It was strange indeed that she would miss a whole hour of the ball.

But before he could make up his mind to take action, he felt a light touch on his shoulder and turned to find one of the footmen bowing to him and holding out a folded piece of paper.

"I was asked to deliver this to you, my lord," he said, "after the second set."

"Thank you," Joseph said, taking it.

A reply to his note to Claudia, was it?

He excused himself, turned away from the group, broke the seal, and opened the single sheet. It was from Portia—his eyes moved down to her signature first. He sincerely hoped she was *not* ill. His mind was already moving ahead to the summoning of a physician—without disrupting the ball, it was to be hoped.

"Lord Attingsborough," he read, "it is with regret that I must inform you that upon mature reflection I find I cannot and will not endure the insult of a bastard daughter flaunted before me by my own affianced husband. I also have no wish to remain longer in a home in which only the Duke of Anburey and Lord and Lady Sutton were properly shocked by your vulgarity and prepared to take you to task for it. I will therefore be leaving before the ball begins. I am going with the Duke of McLeith, who has obliged me by offering to take me to Scotland to marry me. I will not flatter you by declaring myself to be your obedient servant."

And then her signature.

He folded the paper.

Claudia, he noticed at a glance, was doing exactly the same thing some distance away.

"Anything wrong, Joseph?" Lauren asked, setting a hand on his arm.

"No, nothing," he said, turning his head to smile at her. "Portia has gone, that is all. She has eloped with McLeith."

Which was an odd way of answering her question, he realized even as he spoke. But his head was buzzing.

"Excuse me?" he said even as her eyes widened and her mouth formed into an O.

He hurried from the ballroom and took the stairs two at a time up to the next floor. He knocked on Portia's door and, when there was no answer, opened it cautiously. It was in darkness, but even in just the dim light of the moon from outside it was clear to him that she really was gone. Nothing adorned the top of either the dressing table or the table beside the bed. The wardrobe was empty.

Foolish woman, he thought. Foolish woman! Elopement was not the way to go. In the eyes of the world she would have broken off her engagement to him in order to run off to Scotland with another man. She would be beyond the social pale. She would be ostracized. Portia of all people—so very proper and correct in all her dealings with society.

And McLeith!

Should he go after them? But they had at least an hour's head start, probably longer. And what was the point, even if he caught up with them? They were both mature adults. Perhaps she would find some measure of happiness with McLeith. She would, after all, be married to a duke immediately instead of having to wait for the death of his father. And she would presumably live in Scotland, where perhaps the social stigma of having eloped would not attach so strongly to her.

But foolish Portia, he thought, standing at the window looking out onto a darkened lawn. She might have broken off her engagement and returned to her parents and then announced her forthcoming marriage to McLeith. It was unlike her to be rashly impulsive.

He liked her the better for it.

Claudia's letter, he assumed, had been from McLeith.

He allowed his thoughts to dwell on her unchecked for the first time since his return to Alvesley last night.

He hardly dared believe in his freedom. Even now he might go back down to the ballroom to find Portia there, come to her senses and come back to Alvesley and him.

There was only one way of finding out, he supposed.

At first Claudia had been rather relieved when Charlie did not appear to claim the opening set she had promised him. She really did not want this morning's question renewed. But then, after the set had begun, she felt somewhat annoyed. A gentleman she had met at the picnic yesterday had solicited her hand, and she had rejected him with the explanation that she had already promised the set.

It felt a little humiliating to be forced to stand alone watching everyone else below the age of fifty dancing. And perhaps that gentleman would think she had lied and simply did not wish to dance with him.

Charlie really ought not to have put her in such an awkward position. It was not courteous, and she would tell him so when he finally came. Of course, the thought did cross her mind that perhaps he was punishing her for her rejection of his proposal this morning. But he had asked her for the set *after* she had said a very firm no.

She danced the next set—a vigorous country dance—with the Earl of Rosthorn and had just joined Anne and Sydnam afterward when someone tapped her lightly on the shoulder. It was a footman, who had brought her a note. From Charlie? From *Joseph*? Charlie had still not put in an appearance.

"Excuse me," she said, turning away slightly for some privacy and then breaking the seal and unfolding the letter.

It was from Charlie. She ignored a very slight feeling of disappointment.

"My dearest Claudia," he had written, "it seems rather just to me that I should suffer now as perhaps you suffered eighteen years ago. For while I suffered then too, I was essentially the rejecter, as you are now. And it feels wretched to love yet be rejected. I will not wait for your answer this evening. You have already given it and I would not distress you by forcing you to repeat it. Miss Hunt is unhappy too. She feels, quite rightly, that she has been badly used here. We have been able to offer each other some comfort today. And perhaps we will be able to continue to do so for a lifetime. By the time you read this, we ought to be well on our way to Scotland, where we will marry without delay. She will, I believe, be a conscientious wife and duchess, and

I will be a dutiful husband. I wish you well, Claudia. You will always be to me the sister I never had, the friend who made my growing years happy ones, and the lover who might have been had fate not intervened. Forgive me if you will for failing to keep my promise to dance with you this evening. Your humble, obedient servant, McLeith (Charlie)."

Oh, goodness.

She folded the letter into its original folds.

Oh, goodness gracious.

"Is anything wrong, Claudia?" Anne placed a hand on her arm.

"Nothing." She smiled. "Charlie is gone. He has eloped with Miss Hunt."

She was waving the letter before her rather like a fan. She did not know what to do with it.

"I expect," Sydnam said, taking it from her and sliding it into his pocket, "tea is being served in the refreshment room. Come with Anne and me, Claudia, and I will fetch you a cup."

"Oh, goodness," she said. "Thank you. Yes. That would be just the thing. Thank you."

He offered his arm and she took it before remembering that he did not have another arm to offer Anne. She looked around the ballroom. Charlie was definitely not here. Neither was Miss Hunt.

Joseph had disappeared too.

Did he *know* yet?

Portia was *not* in the ballroom. Neither was McLeith.

Or Claudia.

Sets were forming for the next dance, and the elder of the vicar's two daughters had no partner, though she smiled brightly at her mother's side as if being a wallflower was the happiest fate she could possibly imagine. Joseph went and bowed to the mother and asked if he might have the honor of leading her daughter out.

Claudia returned to the ballroom with Anne and Sydnam Butler while he was dancing and coaxing laughter as well as smiles from the vicar's daughter. By the time he had returned the girl to her mother and made himself agreeable to them for a while, Susanna and Whitleaf, Gwen, and Lily and Neville were also part of Claudia's group. And from the way they all turned to watch him as he approached, Joseph understood that Lauren must have found her voice after he left her earlier.

"Well, Joe," Neville said, slapping a hand on his shoulder.

"Well, Nev." Joseph inclined his head to Claudia, who curtsied slightly in return. "I can see the word is out."

"Only among a few of us," Gwen assured him. "Lauren and Kit do not want the earl and countess to be told yet. This is their evening and it must not be spoiled in any way."

"I am not about to step up onto the orchestra dais," Joseph said, "and make a public announcement."

"This is a lovely ball," Susanna said. "And the next set is to be a waltz."

Whitleaf took her hand, set it on his sleeve, and patted it.

"We had better take our places, then," he said.

No one moved—including the Whitleafs.

"Miss Martin." Joseph bowed. "Would you do me the honor of waltzing with me?"

Despite the noise of conversation and laughter with which they were surrounded, it seemed to Joseph that every member of the group fell still and breathless, hanging upon the question and the answer that was yet to come.

"Yes," she said. "Thank you, Lord Attingsborough."

Under other circumstances he might have laughed aloud. She spoke in her schoolmistress voice. He smiled instead and offered his arm. She set her hand on it. And the whole group moved. One of Kit's cousins came to claim Gwen, and Whitleaf headed off for the dance floor with Susanna, Neville with Lily, and Sydnam Butler with his wife—they were going to waltz, apparently, despite his lack of one arm and one eye. Joseph and Claudia followed them.

He faced her while all the other dancers were gathering around them. Their eyes met and held.

"Are you upset?" he asked her.

Typically, she gave her answer some consideration before speaking.

"I am," she said then. "I loved him dearly when I was a girl, and unexpectedly I have come to like him again in the last few weeks. I thought we might enjoy something of a lifelong friendship. Now I suppose it will not happen. He is not perfect, as I thought him to be when I was a girl. He has character flaws, including a certain moral weakness and an inability to stand his ground in the face of change or disappointment. But we all have weaknesses. It is the human condition. I am upset at him and even *for* him. He will not, I believe, be happy."

She spoke gravely, her brow creased in thought.

"Are *you* upset?" she asked.

"I behaved badly," he said. "I ought to have told her about Lizzie before asking her to marry me. It ought to have been done privately. Instead I kept quiet and then humiliated her with a public announcement. And then I would not agree to her demands, which seemed quite reasonable to her—and probably would to most of polite society. She was without her parents or any of her family here and could not turn to them for advice or support or comfort. And so she has done something which is uncharacteristically rash for her. Yes, I am upset. I have, perhaps, been the cause of her permanent ruin."

It was a strange time and place for such a serious exchange. Color and perfumes and voices and laughter surrounded them, all the festive accoutrements of a grand celebration. And then the music began, and he set his arm about her waist, took her hand in his as her other came to rest on his shoulder, and swung her into the waltz.

For several minutes he had the peculiar sensation that he and Claudia were the focus of much attention. Almost everyone was dancing. When he glanced away from her, he could see Bewcastle dancing with the duchess and Hallmere with the marchioness. None of the four of them was looking his way. Neither were Lauren and Kit or the Rosthorns or Aidan Bedwyn and his wife. They were all, apparently, wrapped up in their enjoyment of one another and the waltz—as were the couples with whom he had recently been conversing.

And yet . . .

And yet he had the strange feeling that they were all very aware of him. Not just of him. And not just of Claudia. But of him and Claudia. As if they were not just wondering how he would react to the fact that his betrothed had eloped with another man or how Claudia would react to her friend absconding with another woman. As if they were all wondering what would now happen to the two of them—to Joseph and Claudia.

As if they all *knew*.

"I feel very self-conscious," Claudia said. She was looking prim and rather tight-lipped.

"Because of the waltz?" he asked her.

"Because I feel as if everyone is looking at us," she said, "which is absurd. No one is. And why *should* they?"

"Because they know," he suggested, "that we have both just been set free?"

Her eyes met his again and she drew breath to speak. But she said only one word.

"Oh," she said.

He smiled at her. "Claudia," he said, "let's enjoy the waltz, shall we? And to hell with anyone who may be watching us."

"Yes," she said primly. "To hell with them all."

His smile broadened to a grin, and she threw back her head and laughed—drawing several direct glances their way.

After that they enjoyed the sheer exhilaration of the dance, twirling together, scarcely looking away from each other, only partially aware of the kaleidoscope of color and candlelight swirling about them. They did not stop smiling.

"Oh," she said when the music came to an end, and she

sounded half regretful, half surprised to find herself brought back from the world they had inhabited together for almost half an hour.

"Let's get out of here," he said.

Her eyes widened.

"There is still half an hour to suppertime," he said, "and there is to be more dancing afterward. No one will be returning to Lindsey Hall for at least two hours."

"It is not a mere stroll on the terrace you are suggesting, then?" she asked.

"No." He released his hold on her and clasped his hands at his back. Around them there was a swell of conversation, the dance at an end. "The alternative is to spend the rest of the evening dancing with other partners and being sociable with other people."

She looked back at him, some of the severity returning to her face.

"I will go and fetch my shawl," she said.

He watched her go. This was not going to be a comfortable thing, was it? For either of them. Being in love when one knew it could lead nowhere was one thing. Being free to do something about it was another. But freedom could be deceptive. Even with Portia out of the picture, there were obstacles a mile high and two miles wide.

Was love enough to surmount them all?

But all obstacles, he had learned from thirty-five years' experience of living, however large or small, could be overcome only one at a time with patience and dogged determination.

If they could be overcome at all.

He strolled toward the ballroom door, deliberately ignoring the beckoning hand of Wilma, who was, fortunately, far away from the doorway. He went to wait for Claudia.

Claudia had been very strongly of the opinion earlier, while she waltzed with Joseph, that they were being watched with interest as a possible couple. But while she was fetching her shawl it occurred to her that perhaps the looks—if there had *been* any—had been simply ones of incredulity that she should so presume. Or possibly even looks of *pity.*

But when had she started to think of herself as unworthy of any man, no matter who he was?

She was no one's inferior.

By the time she had made her way back to the ballroom and found Joseph waiting for her outside its doors, there was purposefulness in her stride and a martial gleam in her eye.

And *when* had she started to think of him all the time as *Joseph?*

"Perhaps," she said, "we ought to go for just a short stroll."

He grinned at her. There was definitely a difference between a smile and a grin, and he *grinned.* She bristled with indignation. She was making a cake of herself in front of a large number of the aristocracy of England, and he was *amused.*

He took her by the elbow and guided her toward the outdoors.

"I have a theory," he said, "that your girls all obey you without question, not because they fear you, but because they love you."

"A goodly number of them," she said dryly, "would be *very* interested to hear that, Lord Attingsborough. They might not stop laughing this side of Christmas."

They stepped out onto the terrace. It was deserted but by no means silent. There was the sound of music from the ballroom above. There was also the sound of merrymaking and music of a different sort coming from the direction of the stables and carriage house, where grooms and coachmen and perhaps some off-duty servants were enjoying revelries of their own while they waited to convey their employers home.

"I am Lord Attingsborough again, am I, Miss Martin?" he said, turning to walk in the direction of the stables. "Is it not a little ludicrous in light of last evening?"

That irresponsibility had seemed somewhat excusable then because it was never to be repeated—she had *known* that Miss Hunt would not break off her engagement permanently. Last night had been a once-in-a-lifetime thing, something she would remember for the rest of her life, a private tragedy she would hug to herself and not allow to embitter her.

The fact that Miss Hunt had ended the betrothal again tonight—and permanently this time—ought to have simplified her life, raised hope in her, made her happy, especially since he had immediately asked her to waltz with him and then asked her to walk out here with him.

But her life seemed more complicated than ever.

"If you could go back," he asked, somehow picking up her thoughts where he had interrupted them, "and refuse my offer to escort you and your two charges to London, would you do it?"

Would she? Part of her said an unqualified yes. Her life would be as it had been if she had said no to him—quiet, ordered, familiar. Or perhaps not. Perhaps she would have met Charlie anyway at Susanna and Peter's concert—and perhaps she would have reacted slightly differently toward him. Without the existence of Joseph in her life, perhaps she would have fallen in love with Charlie again. Perhaps she would now be making a decision regarding him. Perhaps...

No, it was impossible. It never would have happened. Though perhaps...

"It is pointless to wish to change one detail from the past," she said. "It cannot be done. But even if it could, it would be foolish to do it. My life would have progressed differently if I had said no, even though it was only a few weeks ago. I do not know *how* it would have progressed."

He chuckled before striding away from her into the revelries about the carriages and returning a few moments later with a lit lantern.

"Would *you* do things differently?" she asked.

"No." He offered his free arm and she took it.

He was tall and solid and warm. He smelled good. He was handsome and charming and wealthy and aristocratic—he would be a *duke* one day. And he was very, very masculine. If she had ever dreamed, even at her age, of love and romance—and of course, she *had* dreamed—it would have been of a man altogether different in almost every way.

"What are you thinking?" he asked.

They were walking down the main driveway, she realized, in the direction of the Palladian bridge. It was rather a dark night with high clouds hiding the moon and stars. The air was far cooler than it had been last evening.

"Of the man of my dreams," she said.

He turned his head toward her and lifted the lantern so that he could see her face—and she his. His eyes looked dark and unfathomable.

"And?" he prompted.

"A very ordinary, unassuming gentleman," she said, "with no title and no great wealth. But with an abundance of intelligence and good conversation."

"He sounds dull," he said.

"Yes, and that too," she said. "Dullness is an underrated quality."

"I am not the man of your dreams, then?" he asked her.

"No," she said. "Not at all."

They stepped onto the bridge and stopped by the stone parapet on one side to watch the water flow dark beneath on its way to the lake. He set down the lantern.

"But then," she said, "I cannot possibly be the woman of your dreams."

"Can you not?" he said.

She could not see his face, the lantern being behind his head. It was impossible to know from his tone alone whether he was amused or wistful.

"I am not beautiful," she said.

"You are not *pretty*," he conceded. "You very definitely are beautiful."

What a bouncer. He would carry gallantry to the end, would he?

"I am not young," she said.

"It is a matter of perspective," he said. "To the girls in your school you are doubtless a fossil. To an octogenarian you would appear to be a sweet young thing. But we are almost exactly the same age, and since I do not think of myself as old—far from it— I must insist that indeed you *are* young."

"I am not elegant or lively or . . ." She ran out of ideas.

"What you are," he said, "is a woman who lost confidence in her beauty and charm and sexual attractiveness heartbreakingly early in life. You are a woman who sublimated her sexual energies into making a successful career. You are a woman of firm character and will and intelligence and knowledge. You are a woman bursting with compassion and love for your fellow creatures. And you are a woman with so much sexual love to give that it would take far more than your quiet, dull scholar to satisfy you—unless he too has hidden depths, of course. For the sake of argument let us suppose that he does not, that he is simply ordinary and dull with conversation to offer you and nothing much else. No *passion*. He is not a dream man at all, Claudia. He is verging upon nightmare."

She smiled despite herself.

"That is better," he said, and she realized that he *could* see *her* face. "I have a marked partiality for Miss Martin, school-teacher, but it is possible that she might choose to be a cold bed-fellow. Claudia Martin, the woman, would not be. Indeed, I have already had proof of it."

"Lord Attingsborough—" she began.

"Claudia." He spoke over her. "We have had our fairly brief stroll. We can return to the house and ballroom now if you wish. It is altogether possible that not above half of the guests here have noticed we are gone. We can enjoy the rest of the ball— separately so as not to arouse gossip among that smaller half. And tomorrow I can come and take Lizzie, and you can return to Bath, and we can both deal with receding memories over the coming weeks and months. Or we can extend our stroll."

She stared at him in the darkness.

"This is one of those moments of decision," he said, "that can forever change the course of a life."

"No, it is not," she protested. "Or at least, it is not more important than any other moment. *Every* moment is a moment of decision, and *every* moment turns us inexorably in the direction of the rest of our lives."

"Have it your way if you must," he said. "But this moment's decision awaits us both. What is it to be? A desperate attempt to return to the way things used to be before I presented myself at Miss Martin's School for Girls, a letter from Susanna in my coat pocket? Or a leap in the dark—almost literally—and a chance for something new and very possibly quite wonderful? Even perfect."

"Nothing in life is perfect," she said.

"I beg to disagree with you," he said. "Nothing is *permanently* perfect. But there are perfect moments and the will to choose what will bring about more such moments. Last evening was perfect. It was, Claudia. I will not allow you to deny it. It was simply perfect."

She sighed. "There are so many complications," she said.

"There always are," he told her. "This is life. You ought to understand that by now. One possible complication is that the little lodge in the woods might be locked tonight as it was not yesterday afternoon."

She was speechless—except that she had understood the moment he asked her to come walking with him where they would go. There was no point in trying to deny it to herself, was there?

"Perhaps," she said, "they keep the key over the lintel or beside the step or somewhere else easy to find."

She still could not see his face. But for a moment she caught the gleam of his teeth.

"We had better go and see," she said, drawing her shawl more closely about her.

"Are you sure?" His voice was low.

"Yes," she said.

This time when they walked on, instead of offering his arm he took her hand in his and laced their fingers. He held the lantern aloft. It was needed at the other side of the bridge, where the trees obscured even what little light was provided from the sky. They found the faint path by which they had returned yesterday and followed it through the woods until they arrived at the hut.

The door was unlocked.

Inside—she had only half noticed yesterday—there was a fireplace with a fire set in the hearth and logs piled beside it. There was a table with a few books on it and a tinderbox and lamp. There was a rocking chair with a blanket draped over it. And against one wall there was the narrow bed upon which they had found Lizzie.

It all looked prettier, cozier tonight. Joseph set the lantern down on the table, took up the tinderbox, and knelt at the hearth to light the fire. Claudia sat in the chair, rocking slowly, holding the corners of her shawl, watching him. There was the pleasurable anticipation of what was to come. All day her breasts had been tender and her inner thighs and inner passage slightly aching from last night's lovemaking.

It was to happen again.

How absolutely lovely marriage must be . . .

She rested her head against the chair back.

The fire caught and he got to his feet and turned to her. His eyes looked very blue in the lantern light, his hair very dark, his features chiseled and handsome. He set one foot on a runner of the chair to stop it rocking, set his hands on the arms, and leaned over her to kiss her openmouthed.

"Claudia," he said, lifting his head a few inches from hers, "I want you to know that you are beautiful. You think you must be unlovely because circumstances once forced an essentially weak man to leave you and because you are now in your middle thirties and unmarried and a schoolteacher. You think it impossible that any man could find you sexually appealing any longer. You probably even tell yourself that last evening happened only because I guessed I would not be free today to pursue our relationship further. You are wrong on every count. I want you to know that you are incredibly beautiful—because you are the product of who you have been and become in over thirty years of living. You would not be as beautiful to me if you were younger, you see. And I want you to know that you are endlessly appealing sexually."

She gazed up at him.

"*This* appealing." He took one of her hands in his and spread it, palm in, against the bulge of his erection.

"Oh," she said.

"*Endlessly* appealing," he said.

Her hand slid to her lap, and he reached up both hands to remove all the pins from her hair. She was going to have to repair it later, she thought, without benefit of a brush or a mirror. But she would think of that later.

"It is a crime," he said as her hair fell in heavy waves over her shoulders, "to dress this hair as ruthlessly as you do, Claudia." He took her hands in his and drew her to her feet. "You are *not* my dream woman. You are right about that. I could never have dreamed you, Claudia. You are unique. I am in awe. I am humbled."

She gazed into his eyes to detect irony, or at least humor,

there, but she could see neither. And then she could see nothing very clearly at all. She blinked away tears. And then he leaned closer and licked them away with his tongue before drawing her closer and kissing her deeply.

She was beautiful, she told herself as they undressed each other slowly, pausing frequently to caress or embrace each other. She was *beautiful*. She ran her palms over the muscles and light hairs of his chest after removing his evening coat and waistcoat, his elaborately tied neckcloth, and his shirt. And he moved his hands all over her before cupping her breasts, rubbing her nipples with his thumbs, and then bending his head to take them, one at a time, into his mouth and suckling her so that raw desire stabbed downward into her womb and along her inner thighs.

She would not feel self-conscious or inadequate. She was beautiful.

And desirable.

There was no doubt of that once she had removed his silk evening breeches and his stockings.

She was desirable.

And she was not the only one who was beautiful.

She twined her arms about his neck, pressed her full naked length against his, and found his mouth with her own. When his tongue pressed into her mouth she sighed. He was right, there *were* perfect moments even though they were both pulsing with need.

"I think," he said, drawing back his head to smile at her, "we had better make use of that bed. It will be more comfortable than the ground was last night."

"But narrower," she said.

"If we were planning to sleep, perhaps," he agreed, smiling at her in such a way that she felt her bare toes curl on the hard floor. "But we are not, are we? It is quite wide enough for our purpose."

He drew back the blankets, and she lay down on the sheet and lifted her arms to him.

"Come," she said.

He came down on top of her and she spread her legs and twined them about his. They were both ready. He kissed her and murmured low endearments against her ear. She kissed him back and twined her fingers in his thick hair. And then he slid his hands beneath her, she tilted herself to him, and he came inside her.

His size still shocked her. She inhaled slowly as she adjusted her position to allow him full access, and closed her inner muscles about him. There could surely be no lovelier feeling in the world.

Though perhaps there could. He withdrew from her and pressed deep again and repeated the action until she could feel his rhythm and match her own to it and revel in the sheer carnality of their coupling. There could be no lovelier feeling than *this*— both during the first few minutes of controlled pleasure and during the final minute of deeper, more urgent lovemaking as the climax neared.

And then it came—for both of them at exactly the same moment, and she opened to the outpouring of love and gave back in equal measure, and *that* was the loveliest feeling of all, though it was almost beyond feeling and well beyond rational thought or words.

She was beautiful.

She was desirable.

And finally . . .

Ah.

Finally she was simply woman.

Simply perfect.

No, she thought as she gradually began to return to herself, she would not go back and change a single detail of her life even if she could. There were all sorts of complexities, complications, impossibilities to face when she had been restored entirely to herself and sanity, but that time was not yet. There was this moment to live.

He inhaled deeply and audibly, and then let the breath go on a sigh.

"Ah, Claudia," he murmured. "My love."

Two words that she would treasure for a lifetime. Even the costliest jewel could not tempt her if it were offered in exchange for them.

My love.

Spoken to *her*, Claudia Martin. She was one man's love. Just a few weeks ago all this would have been quite beyond the bounds of credibility. But no longer. She was beautiful, she was desirable, and . . . She smiled.

He had lifted his head and was looking down at her with heavy-lidded eyes, one hand smoothing back her hair from her face.

"Share the thought," he said.

She opened her eyes.

"I am woman," she said.

"Hard as this may be to believe," he said with laughter in his eyes, "I *had* noticed."

She laughed. His kissed her eyelids one at a time before kissing her lips again.

"It only astonishes me," he said, "that it seems like a novel idea to you."

She laughed again.

"You have no idea," she said, "how a woman's femininity becomes identified with an early marriage and the production of a number of children and the running of an orderly home."

"You surely might have had those things if you had wished," he said. "McLeith cannot have been the only man who showed an interest in you when you were a girl."

"I had other chances," she admitted.

"Why did you not take any of them?" he asked her. "Because you loved him so dearly?"

"Partly that," she said, "and partly an unwillingness to settle for comfort over . . . over integrity. I wanted to be a person as well as a woman. I know that may seem strange. I know it is hard for almost anyone else to comprehend. It is what I wanted, though— to be a *person*. But it seemed that I could not be both—a person *and* a woman. I had to sacrifice my femininity."

"Are you sorry?" he asked her. "Though you did not do it with any great success, I might add."

She shook her head. "I would do it all again if I could go back," she said. "But it *was* a sacrifice."

"I am glad you did it," he said, feathering light kisses along her jaw line to her chin and then lifting his head again.

She raised her eyebrows.

"If you had not," he said, "you would not have been there to call upon when I was in Bath. And if I had met you elsewhere, you would not have been free. And I might not have recognized you anyway."

"Recognized me?"

"As the very beat of my heart," he said.

Her eyes filled with tears again, and she bit her upper lip. She heard the echo of what he had said in the carriage on the way to London when Flora and Edna had asked him to share his dream.

I dream of love, of a family—wife and children—which is as close and as dear to me as the beating of my own heart.

She had judged him quite insincere at that time.

"Don't say things like that," she said.

"What has this been about, then?" he asked, somehow turning them so that he lay on the inside of the bed, pressed against the wall, and she lay facing him, held firmly by his arms lest she fall off the bed. "Sex?"

She thought for a moment.

"*Good* sex," she said.

"Granted," he agreed. "I did not bring you here for good sex, though, Claudia. Or not *just* or even primarily for that."

She would not ask him why, then. But he answered the unspoken question anyway.

"I brought you out here," he said, "because I love you and because I believe you love me. Because I am free and you are. Because—"

She set her fingertips over his lips. He kissed them and smiled.

"I am *not* free," she said. "I have a school to run. I have children and teachers dependent on me."

"And are you dependent upon them?" he asked.

She frowned.

"It is a valid question," he said. "Are you dependent upon them? Does your happiness, your sense of self, depend upon continuing your school? If it does, you have a genuine point. You have as much right to pursue your happiness as I have to pursue mine. Fortunately, Willowgreen can be run from a distance as it has been for the past number of years. Lizzie and I will take up residence in Bath. We will live there with you."

"Don't be silly," she said.

"I will be as silly as I need to be," he said, "to make things work between us, Claudia. I was in a basically arid relationship for twelve years even though I was fond of poor Sonia—she did, after all, give me Lizzie. I came within a whisker this year of entering into a marriage that would surely have brought me active unhappiness for the rest of my life. Now suddenly, just this evening, I am free. And at last I want to choose happiness. And love."

"Joseph," she said, "you are an aristocrat. You will be a *duke* one day. My father was a country gentleman. I have been a governess or teacher for eighteen years. You cannot just give up all you are to live at the school with me."

"I would not have to give up anything," he said. "Nor *could* I if I wanted to. But one of us does not have to sacrifice our life for the sake of the other. We can both live, Claudia—and love."

"Your father would have an apoplexy," she said.

"Probably not," he said. "But the matter would admittedly have to be broached carefully with him—yet firmly. I am his son, but I am also a person in my own right."

"Your mother—"

". . . would adore anyone who could make me happy," he said.

"The Countess of Sutton—"

"Wilma can think or say or do what she likes," he said. "My sister is certainly not going to rule my life, Claudia. Or yours. You are stronger than she is."

"The *ton*—"

"...can go hang for all I care," he said. "But there are precedents galore. Bewcastle married a country schoolteacher and got away with it. Why cannot I marry the owner and headmistress of a respected school for girls?"

"*Will* you let me complete a sentence?" she asked him.

"I am listening," he said.

"I could not *possibly* live the life of a marchioness or a duchess," she said. "I could not *possibly* mingle with the *ton* on a regular basis. And I could not possibly be your wife. You need heirs. I am thirty-five years old."

"So am I," he said. "And one heir will do. Or none. I would rather marry you and be childless apart from Lizzie than marry someone else and have twelve sons with her."

"That sounds all very fine," she said. "But it is not practical."

"Good Lord, no," he agreed. "With all those boys I would never know a moment's peace in my own home."

"Jo-seph!"

"Clau-dia." He set one finger along the length of her nose and smiled at her.

A log crackled in the hearth and settled lower. The blaze began to die down. The little hut was as warm as toast inside, she realized.

"There are some problems, admittedly," he said. "We *are* from somewhat different worlds, and it seems that they would make an awkward fit. But not an impossible one—I refuse to believe it. The idea that love conquers all may seem to be a foolishly idealistic one, but I believe in it nonetheless. How can I believe otherwise? If love cannot conquer all, what can? Hatred? Violence? Despair?"

"Joseph." She sighed. "What about Lizzie?"

"She loves you dearly," he said. "And if you marry me and come to live with us, she does not have to fear that you will take the dog away from her."

"It is all quite impossible, you know," she said.

"But there is no conviction whatsoever left in your voice," he told her. "I am winning here. Admit it."

"Joseph." Once more her eyes filled with tears. "This is no contest. It *is* impossible."

"Let's talk about it tomorrow," he said. "I'll come over to Lindsey Hall to see Lizzie, and you and I will talk. But perhaps you should have a word with my cousins before you leave here— Neville, Lauren, Gwen. Perhaps you had better *not* talk to Wilma, though she would be able to tell you the same thing. They will all tell you that I never played fair as a lad, that I always had to have my own way. I was quite detestable. I still do not play fair when I want something badly enough."

He had snuggled closer—if that were possible—while he talked, and was now nuzzling her ear and the side of her neck while smoothing his hand over her hip and buttock and along her spine until her toes curled again.

"We had better dress and go back to the house," she said. "It would be too shameful if everyone were ready to return to Lindsey Hall and I was nowhere to be found."

"Mmm," he said into her ear. "In a moment. Or several moments might be better."

And he moved them again so that this time he was lying on his back and she was lying on top of him.

"Love me," he said. "Never mind practicalities or impossibilities. Love me, Claudia. My love."

She spread her legs to set her knees on either side of his hips and raised herself onto her arms to look down at him. Her hair fell forward to form a sort of curtain about them.

"Once upon a time," she said, sighing one more time, "I thought I was a woman of firm will."

"Am I a bad influence on you?" he asked.

"You certainly are," she said severely.

"Good," he said and grinned. "Love me."

She did.

24

It was a blustery day. White clouds scudded across a blue sky,
bathing the ground in sunshine one moment, darkening it with
shade the next. Trees waved their branches and flowers tossed
their heads. But it was warm. And it was potentially the loveliest
day of his life, Joseph thought as he arrived at Lindsey Hall late
in the morning.

Potentially.

It had not been an easy day so far.

His father had quivered with fury even just with the news
that Portia had run off with McLeith. He had not excused her ac-
tions for a moment—far from it. But neither had he excused
Joseph for driving her to take such drastic measures.

"Her disgrace will be on your conscience for the rest of your
life," he had told his son. "If you *have* a conscience, that is."

And then Joseph had broached the topic of Claudia Martin.
At first his father had been simply incredulous.

"That spinster schoolteacher?" he had asked.

Then, when he had understood fully that it was indeed she,
he had exploded in a storm of wrath that had had both Joseph
and his mother seriously worried for his health.

Joseph had held firm. And he had shamelessly played his
trump card.

"Mr. Martin, her father," he had explained, "was guardian to the Duke of McLeith. The duke grew up in their home from the age of five. He thinks of Claudia almost as a sister."

McLeith was not much in his father's favor this morning, of course, but nevertheless the man was of a rank to match his own, even if it *was* only a Scottish title.

Joseph's mother had asked the only question that really mattered to her.

"Do you *love* Miss Martin, Joseph?" she had asked.

"I do, Mama," he had told her. "With all my heart."

"I never did really like Miss Hunt," she had admitted. "There is something cold about her. One can only hope she loves the Duke of McLeith."

"Sadie!"

"No, Webster," she had said. "I will not be quiet when the happiness of my own children is at stake. I am surprised, I must confess. Miss Martin seems too old and plain and stern for Joseph, but if he loves her and if she loves him, then I am content. And she will welcome dear Lizzie into your family, I daresay, Joseph. I would invite them both to tea if I were in my own home."

"Sadie—"

"But I am not," she had said. "Are you going to Lindsey Hall this morning, Joseph? Tell Miss Martin if you will that I will call on her this afternoon. I daresay Clara will go with me or Gwen or Lauren if your father will not."

"Thank you, Mama." He had raised her hand to his lips.

There had still been Wilma to face, of course, before he left for Lindsey Hall. She was not to be avoided. She had been waiting for him outside the library and had forced him into the small visitors' salon next to it. Surprisingly—perhaps—she had had nothing but recriminations to call down upon the head of the unfortunate Portia. But she had been deeply shocked by the rumors she had heard last night—rumors none of her cousins would either confirm or deny. Not that rumors had been necessary.

"You *waltzed* with that teacher, Joseph," she had said, "as if no one else existed in the world but her."

"No one did," he had told her.

"It was quite indecorous," she had said. "You made an utter cake of yourself."

He had smiled.

"And then you *disappeared* with her," she had said. "Everyone must have noticed. It was quite scandalous. You had better be very careful or you are going to find yourself trapped into marrying her. You do not know what women like her are capable of, Joseph. She—"

"It is I," he had told her, "who am trying to trap *her* into marriage, Wilma. Or to persuade her to marry me, anyway. It is not going to be easy. She does not like dukes or even dukes in waiting, and she has no desire whatsoever to be a duchess—even if such a fate is comfortably far in the future provided we can keep Papa healthy. But she *does* like her pupils—especially, I suspect, her charity girls. She feels an obligation to them and to the school she began and has run successfully for almost fifteen years."

She had stared at him, almost speechless for once.

"You are going to *marry* her?" she had asked him.

"If she will have me," he had said.

"*Of course* she will have you," she had told him.

"Lord, Wil," he had said, "I hope you are right."

"Wil." She had looked arrested. "You have not called me that for *years*."

He had caught her by the shoulders suddenly and pulled her into an impulsive hug.

"Wish me luck," he had said.

"Does she really mean that much to you?" she had asked him. "I cannot see the attraction, Joseph."

"You do not have to," he had said. "Wish me luck."

"I doubt you will need it," she had said. But she had tightened her arms about him. "Go and get her then if you must. I daresay I will tolerate her if she makes you happy."

"Thank you, Wil." He had grinned at her as he released her.

Neville had clapped a hand on his shoulder when they met on the stairs after he escaped from the salon.

"Still on your feet, are you, Joe?" he had said. "Do you need a sympathetic ear? A companion with whom to ride neck or nothing across the roughest terrain we can find? Someone with whom to get thoroughly foxed even this early in the day? I am your man if you need me."

"I am on my way to Lindsey Hall," Joseph had said with a grin. "Once my relatives have stopped delaying me, that is."

"Quite so." Neville had removed his hand. "I left Lily and Lauren and Gwen all huddled together in our room, all close to tears because Uncle Webster's voice was carrying from the library and it did not sound pleased with life. And all agreeing that *finally*, despite Uncle Webster, dearest Joseph was going to be *happy*. I think they must have been referring to the possibility of your marrying Miss Martin."

He had grinned back at Joseph before slapping a hand on his shoulder again and then continuing on his way downstairs.

And so now at last Joseph was arriving at Lindsey Hall, buoyed by hope despite the fact that he knew nothing was yet decided. Claudia herself was the remaining hurdle—and the greatest. She had loved him last night with passionate abandon, especially the second time when she had been on top and had taken the initiative in a manner that could make his temperature soar even in memory. She also *loved* him. He felt no real doubt about that. But making love to him, even loving him, was not the same thing as marrying him.

Marriage would be a huge step for her—far more so than for almost any other woman. For most women marriage was a step up to greater freedom and independence, to a more active and interesting life, to greater personal fulfillment. Claudia already had all those things.

He asked for her when he arrived at the house, and she sent down Lizzie. She came alone, with the dog leading her, and stepped inside the salon when a footman opened the door for her, her face lit up with smiles.

"Papa?" she said.

He strode toward her, wrapped his arms about her, and twirled her about.

"How is my best girl this morning?" he asked her.

"I am well," she said. "Is it *true*, Papa? Edna and Flora heard it from one of the maids, who heard it from another maid, who heard it from one of the ladies—it might have been the duchess, though I am not sure. But they all say it is true. *Has* Miss Hunt gone away?"

Ah.

"It is true," he said.

"Never to return?"

"Never," he told her.

"Oh, Papa." She clasped her hands to her bosom and turned her face up to his. "I am *so* glad."

"So am I," he said.

"And is it *true*," she asked him, "that you are going to marry Miss Martin instead?"

Good Lord!

"Is that what Flora and Edna and all the maids say too?" he asked her.

"Yes," she said.

"And what does Miss Martin have to say about it?" he asked her.

"Nothing," she said. "She was cross when I asked her. She told me I ought not to listen to the gossip of servants. And when the other girls asked her too, she got *very* cross and told them she would make them all do mathematics problems for the rest of the morning if they did not stop even if this *is* a holiday. Then Miss Thompson took them all outside except for Julia Jones, who was playing the spinet."

"And except for you," he said.

"Yes," she agreed. "I knew you would come, Papa. I waited for you. I wanted Miss Martin to come down with me, but she would not. She said she had things to do."

"She did not say *better* things, by any chance, did she?" he asked.

"Yes, she did," Lizzie told him.

It sounded as if Claudia Martin was as prickly as a hedgehog this morning. She had had a night—well, a few hours anyway—to sleep upon her memories of last evening.

"I am thinking of selling the house in London," he told Lizzie. "I am planning to take you to Willowgreen to live. It is a large house in the country with a park all about it. There will be space there for you and fresh air and flowers and birds and musical instruments and—"

"And you, Papa?" she asked him.

"And me," he said. "We will be able to live in the same house together all the time, Lizzie. You will no longer have to wait for my visits—and I will no longer have to wait until there are no other obligations and I can visit you at last. We will be together every day. I will be home, and it will be your home too."

"And Miss Martin's?" she asked.

"Would you like that?" he asked her.

"I would like it of *all things,* Papa," she said. "She teaches me things, and it is fun. And I like her voice. I feel safe with her. I think she likes me. No, I think she *loves* me."

"Even when she is cross?" he asked.

"I think she was cross this morning," she said, "because she wants to marry you, Papa."

Which, he supposed, was perfect feminine logic.

"You would not mind, then," he asked her, "if I married her?"

"Silly," she said, clucking her tongue. "If you marry her, she will be my sort-of mama, will she not? I loved Mother, Papa. I really did. I miss her dreadfully. But I would like to have a new mama—if she is Miss Martin."

"Not sort-of mama," he said. "She would be your step-mother."

"My sort-of stepmother," she said. "I am a bas— I am your *love* child. I am not your proper daughter. Mother taught me that."

He clucked his tongue, took her firmly by the hand, opened the door, and marched her in the direction of the stairs. The dog trotted after them.

Claudia was still in the schoolroom. Julia Jones was not. She had finished playing the spinet and had gone about some other business.

"I need your opinion on something," Joseph said, shutting the door firmly behind them as Claudia rose to her feet and clasped her hands at her waist, her spine ramrod straight, her lips pressed into a thin line. "Lizzie informs me that if you were to marry me, you would be her sort-of stepmother. Not her full stepmother because she is not my full daughter. She is only my *love* child, which she understands to be a kindly euphemism for bastard offspring. Is she right? Or is she wrong?"

Lizzie, who had removed her hand from his grasp, looked from one to the other of them almost as if she could actually see them.

"Oh, Lizzie," Claudia said, sighing and relaxing and transforming herself all in one second from stern, starchy school-teacher to warm woman, "I would not be your *sort-of* stepmother or even your stepmother except in strictly legal terms. I would not even be your sort-of mother. I would be your *mama*. I would love you as dearly as any mother ever loved her child. You *are* a love child in all the best meanings of the term."

"And what if," Lizzie asked while Joseph gazed unblinkingly at Claudia and she gazed unblinkingly anywhere but at him. No, that was unfair—she was looking steadily at his daughter. "What if you and Papa were to have children? *Legitimate* children."

"Then I would love them too," Claudia said, her cheeks an interesting shade of pink. "Just as dearly. Not more so, not less. Love does not have to be portioned out, Lizzie. It is the one thing that never diminishes when one gives it away. Indeed, it only grows. In the eyes of the world, it is true, you would always be different from any children your father and . . . and I might have if we were married. But in *my* eyes there would be no difference whatsoever."

"Or in mine," Joseph said firmly.

"We are going to live at Willowgreen, the three of us," Lizzie said, walking toward Claudia with her hands outstretched until

Claudia took them in hers. "And Horace. It is Papa's home in the country. And you will teach me things, and Papa too, and I will have all my stories written down and make a book of them, and perhaps some of my friends can come and visit us sometimes, and when there is a baby I will hold it and rock it every day and..."

The pink in Claudia's cheeks had turned to flame.

"Lizzie," she said, squeezing the girl's hands, "I have a school to run in Bath. I have girls waiting for me there and teachers. I have a *life* waiting for me there."

Lizzie's face was upturned. Her eyelids were fluttering, her lips moving even before she spoke.

"Are those girls more important than me, then?" she asked. "Are those teachers more important than Papa? Is that school nicer than Willowgreen?"

Joseph spoke at last.

"Lizzie," he said, "that is unfair. Miss Martin has her own life to live. We cannot expect her to marry me and come to Willowgreen with us just because we want her to—because we love her and do not know quite how we will live without her."

He was looking at Claudia, who was obviously in deep distress—until his final words. Then she looked indignant. He risked a grin.

Lizzie drew her hands free.

"Do you not love Papa?" she asked.

Claudia sighed. "Oh, I do," she said. "But life is not that simple, Lizzie."

"Why not?" Lizzie asked. "People always say that. *Why* is life not simple? If you love me and you love Papa and we love you, what could be simpler?"

"I think," Joseph said, "we had better go out for a walk. This triangular discussion is definitely not fair to Miss Martin, Lizzie. It is two against one. I will raise the matter with her again when we are alone together. Here, take the dog's leash and show us how you can find your way out of the house and around to the lake without any other help."

"Oh, I can," she said, taking the leash. "Watch me."

"I intend to," he assured her.

But as the three of them stepped outside a couple of minutes later, Lizzie stopped and cocked her head. Even above the sound of the water gushing from the great fountain she could hear something else, it seemed. Miss Thompson and the other girls were approaching. She held up a hand in greeting and called to them.

"Molly?" she cried. "Doris? Agnes?"

The whole group approached and bobbed curtsies.

"I am going to come with you," Lizzie announced. "My papa wants to be alone with Miss Martin. He says it is unfair to her for there to be two against one."

Miss Thompson regarded her employer with pursed lips and eyes that danced with merriment.

"You will not be leaving today after all, then, Claudia?" she said. "I shall let Wulfric know. Go and enjoy your walk."

And she shepherded the girls—Lizzie included—back into the house.

"Right," Joseph said, offering his arm. "It is one on one, fair odds, a fair fight. If you *wish* to fight, that is. I would far prefer to plan a wedding."

She clasped her hands firmly at her waist and turned in the direction of the lake. The brim of her straw hat—the same one as usual—waved in the wind.

Eleanor had been waiting up for her last night—or rather early this morning. Claudia had poured out much of the evening's proceedings, and Eleanor had quite possibly guessed the rest.

She had repeated her offer to take over the running of the school, even to purchase it. She had urged Claudia to think carefully, not to choose impulsively, and not to think in terms of what she *ought* to do rather than what she *wished* to do.

"I suppose," she had said, "it is a cliché and an oversimplification to advise you to follow your heart, Claudia, and I am not at all qualified to offer such advice, am I? But... Well, this is really not my business, and it certainly is *long* past my bedtime. Good night."

But she had poked her head back about the door seconds after leaving the room.

"I am going to say it anyway," she had said. "Follow your heart, for goodness' sake, Claudia, you silly thing."

By this morning it seemed that everyone *knew*.

It was all excruciatingly embarrassing, to say the least.

"I feel," she said as she strode in the direction of the lake, Joseph beside her, "as if I were on the stage of a theater with a vast audience gathered all about me."

"Waiting with bated breath for your final lines?" he said. "I cannot decide if I am part of the audience, Claudia, or a fellow actor. But if I am the latter, I cannot have rehearsed with you or I would know what those final lines are."

They walked in silence until they came to the bank of the lake.

"It is impossible," she said, noticing that the wind was creating white-topped waves on the water.

"No," he said, "not that. Not even improbable. I would call it probable, but by no means certain. It is that small amount of uncertainty that has my heart knocking against my ribs and my knees feeling inadequate to the task of holding me upright and my stomach attempting to turn somersaults inside me."

"Your family would never accept me," she said.

"My mother and my sister already have," he told her, "and my father has not disinherited me."

"*Could* he?" she asked.

"No." He smiled. "But he could make my life dashed uncomfortable. He will not do so. He is far fonder of his children than he will ever admit. And he is far more firmly under my mother's thumb than he knows."

"I cannot give you children," she said.

"Do you know that for certain?" he asked her.

"No," she admitted.

"Any girl fresh from the schoolroom might not be able to if I married her," he said. "Many women cannot, you know. And perhaps you can. I *hope* you can, I must confess. There is all that dreary business of securing the succession, of course, but more important than that, I would *like* to have children with you, Claudia. But all I *really* want is to spend the rest of my life with you. And we would not be childless. We would have Lizzie."

"I cannot be a marchioness," she said, "or a duchess. I know nothing about what would be expected of me, and I am far too old to learn. I am not sure I would want to learn anyway. I like myself as I am. That is a conceited thing to say, perhaps, and suggests an unwillingness ever to change and grow. I *am* willing to do both, but I would rather choose ways in which to grow."

"Choose to change sufficiently to allow me into your life, then," he said. "Please, Claudia. It is all I ask. If you are not willing to have Lizzie and me live in Bath with you, then come to live at Willowgreen with us. Make it your home. Make it your life. Make it anything you want. But come. Please come."

She felt all the unreality of the situation suddenly. It was as if she took a step back from herself and saw him as a stranger again—as he had first appeared to her in the visitors' parlor at school. She saw how very handsome and elegant and aristocratic and self-assured he was. Could he possibly now be begging her to marry him? Could he possibly love her? But she knew he did. And she knew she could hold this image of him in her mind for no longer than a few seconds. Looking at him again, she saw only her beloved Joseph.

"I think we should make Willowgreen like my school," she said. "Only different. The challenge of educating Lizzie, when I thought she might be a pupil, has excited me, for of course I have seen that it is altogether possible to fill her with the joy of learning. I do not know why I have never thought of including children with handicaps among my pupils. There could be some at Willowgreen. We could take some in, even adopt some—other blind children, children with other handicaps, both physical and mental. Anne was once governess to the Marquess of Hallmere's cousin, who was thought of as simpleminded. She is the sweetest young woman imaginable. She married a fisherman and bore him sturdy sons and runs his home and is as happy as it is possible to be."

"We will adopt a dozen such children," he said quietly, "and Willowgreen will be their school and their home. We will love them, Claudia."

She looked at him and sighed.

"It would not work," she said. "It is altogether too ambitious a dream."

"But that is what life is all about," he said. "It is about dreaming and making those dreams come true with effort and determination—and love."

She stared mutely at him.

That was when they were interrupted.

The Marquess and Marchioness of Hallmere with their two elder children and the Earl and Countess of Rosthorn with their boys appeared from among the trees, returning, it seemed, from a walk. They all waved cheerfully from some distance away and would soon have been out of sight if the marchioness had not stopped suddenly to stare intently at them. Then she detached herself from the group and came striding toward them. The marquess came after her more slowly while the others continued on their way to the house.

Claudia had made the grudging admission to herself during the past week that the former Lady Freyja Bedwyn really was not the monster she had been as a girl. Even so, she deeply resented this intrusion upon what was obviously a private tête-à-tête.

"Miss Martin," she said after favoring Joseph with a mere nod, "I hear you are thinking of giving up your school to Eleanor."

Claudia raised her eyebrows.

"I am glad you presume to know what I am thinking," she said.

She half noticed the two men exchange a poker-faced glance.

"It seems an odd sort of thing to do just at the time when you have achieved full independence," Lady Hallmere said. "But I must say I approve. I always admired you—after you had the courage to walk out on me—but I never liked you until this past week. You deserve your chance at happiness."

"Freyja," the marquess said, taking her by the elbow, "I think we are interrupting something here. And your words are only going to cause embarrassment."

But Claudia scarcely heard him. She was looking intently at Lady Hallmere.

"How do you know," she asked, "that I have just achieved independence? How do you *know* about my benefactor?"

Lady Hallmere opened her mouth as if she were about to speak, and then closed it again and shrugged.

"Is it not common knowledge?" she asked carelessly.

Perhaps Eleanor had said something. Or Susanna. Or Anne. Or even Joseph.

But Claudia felt somehow as if someone had just taken a large mallet and hit her over the head with it. Except that such violence might have clouded her thoughts, whereas she felt now as if her mind had never been more crystal clear. She was able to think of several things all at once.

She thought of Anne by some very strange coincidence applying to Mr. Hatchard for a teaching position at her school when she lived a mere stone's throw from the Marquess of Hallmere's home in Cornwall.

She thought of Susanna being sent to the school as a charity girl at the age of twelve just shortly after the coincidence of having applied for a position as Lady Freyja's maid.

She thought about Lady Freyja Bedwyn paying a call at the school one morning several years ago. *But how had she known about the school or where to find it?*

She thought about Edna's telling her just a few weeks ago that Lady Freyja knew about the murder of her parents in their shop years ago—just before Edna was sent to the school in Bath.

She thought about Anne and Susanna trying to tell her down the years that perhaps Lady Freyja, Marchioness of Hallmere, was not quite as bad as Claudia remembered her.

She thought about the fact that when Lady Hallmere and her sister-in-law had needed new governesses for their children, they had looked for them in her school.

She thought...

If the truth were a large mallet, she thought, it surely would have flattened her head to her shoulders years ago.

"It was you," she said. The words came out as little more than a whisper. *"It was you!"*

Lady Hallmere raised haughty eyebrows.

"It was you," Claudia said again. *"You* were the school's benefactor."

"Oh, the devil!" Joseph said.

"Now you have done it," the Marquess of Hallmere said, sounding amused. "The proverbial cat is out of the proverbial bag, Free."

"It *was* you." Claudia stared at her former pupil, horrified.

Lady Hallmere shrugged. "I am very wealthy," she said.

"You were a *girl* when I opened the school."

"Wulf was a Gothic guardian in many ways," Lady Hallmere said. "But he was remarkably enlightened when it came to money. We all had access to our fortunes when we were very young."

"Why?"

Lady Hallmere tapped her hand against her side, and Claudia sensed that she would have been more comfortable if she had been holding a riding crop. She shrugged again.

"Nobody but you ever stood up to me," she said, "until I met Joshua. Wulfric did, of course, but that was different. He was my brother. I resented the fact that my father and mother had died and left us, I suppose. I wanted to be noticed. I wanted someone other than Wulfric to force me to behave myself. You did it by walking out on me. But you were not dead, Miss Martin. I could wreak revenge on you as I could not with my mother. You cannot know what satisfaction it has given me over the years to know that you depended upon me even while you despised me."

"I did not—"

"Oh, yes, you did."

"Yes, I did."

Joseph cleared his throat and the Marquess of Hallmere scratched his head.

"It was magnificent revenge," Claudia said.

"I have always thought so," Lady Hallmere admitted.

They stared at each other, Claudia tight-lipped, Lady Hallmere feigning a haughty nonchalance that did not look quite convincing.

"What can I say?" Claudia asked at last. She was horribly embarrassed. She owed a great deal to this woman. So did many of her charity girls, both past and present. Susanna might have been lost without this woman. Anne might have continued to live a miserable existence with David in Cornwall. The school would not have succeeded at all.

Oh, goodness, she could not possibly owe everything to *Lady Hallmere* of all people!

But she did.

"I believe, Miss Martin," Lady Hallmere told her, "you said it all in the letter you left with Mr. Hatchard a few weeks ago. I appreciate your thanks though I do not need them. I am sorry I spoke rashly a few minutes ago. I would have far preferred it if you had never known. You must certainly not feel beholden to me. That would be absurd. Come along, Joshua. Our presence is de trop here, I believe."

"Which I tried to tell you a few minutes ago, sweetheart," he said.

Claudia held out her right hand. Lady Hallmere looked at it, her expression at its haughtiest again, and then placed her own in it.

They shook hands.

"Well," Joseph said as the other two walked away, "this stage play is full of unexpected twists and turns. But I believe the closing lines are about to be spoken, love, and they are yours. What *are* they?"

She turned to look fully at him.

"How foolish a notion *independence* is," she said. "There is no such thing, is there? None of us is ever independent of others. We all need one another." She stared at him, exasperated. "Do you need me?"

"Yes," he said.

"And I need you," she told him. "Oh, Joseph, *how* I need you! Changing my life into a wholly new course is going to be just as terrifying this time as it was when I was seventeen, I am sure, but if I could do it then when I had lost a love, I can certainly do it now when I have found one. I am going to do it. I am going to marry you."

He smiled slowly at her.

"And so we come to the epilogue," he said.

And he went down on one knee and arranged himself in picturesque and deliberately theatrical fashion on the grass, the lake behind him. He possessed himself of one of her hands.

"Claudia, my dearest love," he said, "will you do me the great honor of becoming my wife?"

She laughed—though actually it came out sounding remarkably like a watery gurgle.

"You look quite absurd," she said, "and really rather romantic. And impossibly handsome. Oh, of course I will. I have just said so, have I not? Do get up, Joseph. You are going to have grass stains on the knee of your pantaloons."

"It might as well be both knees, then," he said. "They will match."

And he drew her down until they were kneeling face-to-face, their arms about each other.

"Ah, Claudia," he said, his mouth against hers, "do we dare believe in such happiness?"

"Oh, yes," she assured him, "we certainly do. I am not giving up a whole career for anything less."

"No, ma'am," he agreed, and kissed her.

Bath had probably never known such a grand day as that on which Miss Claudia Martin, owner and headmistress of Miss Martin's School for Girls, married the Marquess of Attingsborough at Bath Abbey.

There were so many titled people among the guests that one wag was heard to wonder as he waited with a large crowd of other interested persons in the cobbled yard outside the Pump Room for the bride to arrive if the rest of England was empty of titles for the present.

"And nobody would ever miss 'em," he added, causing a large woman with an even larger basket over one arm to wonder why he had come to watch, then.

All who had any claim to be related to the marquess were on the guest list, of course. So were large numbers of his friends and acquaintances, including all the Bedwyns except Lord and Lady Rannulf, who were in imminent expectation of adding to their family. The Duke of Bewcastle had permitted his duchess to attend with him since Bath was not very far from home and she had been enjoying vigorous good health despite her delicate condition.

Claudia did not fail to see the irony of it all.

Indeed, while Frances's personal maid, brought to the school for the express purpose of dressing her hair, was in the middle of creating a style that was elegant but not too fussy, she started to laugh and could not stop. The poor maid was forced to pause in her task of forming a cluster of smooth curls to replace the usual simple knot at Claudia's neck.

Susanna, Frances, and Anne were all crowded into the bedchamber, watching. Eleanor and Lila Walton had already left for the abbey with a neat crocodile of boarders and charity girls, all in their best dresses and on their best behavior. The day pupils would attend with their parents. The nonresident teachers would be there too.

"This is going to be the most absurd marriage ever," Claudia said between laughs. "I could not have imagined anything more bizarre in my oddest dreams."

"*Absurd,*" Susanna said, looking from Anne to Frances. "I suppose it *is* an apt description. Claudia is going to be married in the presence of a good half of the *ton.*"

"She is going to have a *duke* for a father-in-law," Frances said.

"And a duke's heir for a husband," Anne added.

They all looked at one another poker-faced before they too collapsed into laughter.

"It *is* the funniest thing," Frances agreed. "Our Claudia to be a *duchess* one day."

"It is a just punishment for all my sins," Claudia said, sobering as her attention returned to her image in the glass and she saw all the splendor of her new apricot-colored dress with the frivolous new straw hat that Frances's maid was just pinning to her hair above the luscious curls at her neck. A straw hat in early October!

Goodness! Did she really look ten years younger than she had just a few months ago? Surely it was just her imagination. But her eyes looked larger than she remembered them and her lips fuller. There was surely more color in her cheeks.

"But who," Susanna said, "could resist Joseph's charms? I have always been exceedingly fond of him since Lauren first introduced me to him, but he has risen immeasurably in my estimation since he had the good sense to fall in love with you, Claudia."

"And who," Anne said, "could possibly resist a man who dotes so much on his child? Especially his blind, illegitimate child."

"It is a very good thing that we have Lucius and Sydnam and Peter," Frances said. "We might be mortally jealous of you, Claudia."

Claudia swiveled on the stool. The maid tidied the top of the dressing table and left the room.

"Is it natural," Claudia asked, "for a wedding day to evoke such opposite emotions? I am so happy that I could fairly burst. And I am so sad that I could weep."

"Don't do it," Susanna said. "You will make your eyes red and puffy."

As they had been last evening. It had started with the final, farewell dinner in the school dining hall, to which the day pupils had stayed—and the surprise concert and speeches that had followed it. It had continued with the exchange of hugs and final words with every pupil and teacher. And it had concluded with a couple of hours in Claudia's private sitting room—soon to be Eleanor's—talking and reminiscing with these three friends and Lila and Eleanor.

"I was happy teaching here," Anne said now, "and I was not at all sure I would be happy with Sydnam when I married him. But I am, and you will be with Joseph, Claudia. You already know it."

"It is perfectly natural to be sad," Frances assured her. "I had Lucius and the promise of a singing career to go to when I married, but I had been happy here. It was home, and my dearest friends were here."

Susanna got to her feet and hugged Claudia carefully so as not to disturb either her hair or her hat.

"This school was home and family to me," she said. "I was taken in here at the age of twelve when I had nowhere else to go, and I was educated and loved. I would *never* have left if I had not met Peter. But I am very glad I did—for the obvious reason and because I could not bear now to be the last one of us to be left here. I am that selfish, you see. But I cannot *tell* you how happy I am for you, Claudia."

"We had better go," Anne said. "The bride must not be late, and we must be at the Abbey before her. And what a very lovely bride. That color is perfect on you, Claudia."

"I love the hat," Susanna said.

Claudia held back her tears as each of them hugged her and went down to the carriage that was awaiting them.

After they were gone, she drew on her gloves and looked one last time around her bedchamber. Already it looked empty—her trunk and bags had already been removed earlier in the morning. She went into her sitting room and looked around it. All her books were gone. It was hers no longer.

For the past week the school had officially been Eleanor's. After today it would be Miss Thompson's School for Girls.

It was a terrible thing to leave one's life behind. She had done it once before, and now she was doing it again. It was like being born again, leaving the safe comfort of the womb to brave the vast unknown.

It was a terrible thing even though she ached with longing for the new life, for the home that awaited her, for the brave, intelligent blind child who would be her daughter, for the other child who would be born in a little more than six months—she had told no one yet except Joseph yesterday when he had arrived from Willowgreen—and for the man who had stepped into her school almost four months ago and into her heart not long after.

Joseph!

And then she went downstairs, where the servants were lined up to say good-bye to her. She held her poise and had a final word with each, most of whom were in tears. Mr. Keeble was not. He stood woodenly by the outer door, waiting to open it for her.

And somehow saying good-bye to him, her elderly, crotchety, loyal porter, became the hardest thing of all. He bowed to her, somehow setting his boots to creaking. But she would have none of such formality. She hugged him and kissed his cheek and then nodded briskly for him to open the door and hurried outside, where Joseph's coachman was waiting to hand her into his carriage.

She would not weep, she thought as the door closed and the carriage rocked into motion and she left behind the school and fifteen years of her life for the last time. She blinked her eyes several times.

She *would* not weep.

Joseph was awaiting her at the Abbey.

So was Lizzie.

So was a churchful of aristocrats.

It was that thought that rescued her. She first smiled and then laughed to herself as the carriage turned onto the long length of Great Pulteney Street.

Absurd indeed.

One of God's little jokes, perhaps? If so, she liked his sense of humor.

Not so long ago, it seemed, Joseph had stood beside Neville at the front of a church, awaiting the arrival of a bride. He had been the best man then, Nev the bridegroom. Now the situation was reversed, and Joseph understood why his cousin had been quite unable to sit or stand still on that occasion and why he had complained about the tightness of his neckcloth.

It was absurd to imagine that Claudia simply would not show up. She had agreed to marry him and she had written to him every day—as he had to her—since July, except during the ten days late in August when he had brought Lizzie to Bath. She had also burned her bridges by selling the school to Miss Thompson. She had instructed Hatchard, her man of business in London, to keep an eye out for young children with handicaps and no home.

And if all those things were not enough to reassure him, there was the dizzying new fact that she had confided to him only yesterday. She was increasing! They were going to have a child of their own. He still had not quite absorbed this new knowledge to the full—though he had raged at her for all of thirty seconds after she told him before grabbing her and half squeezing the life out of her. She ought to have told him sooner. Good Lord, if he had only known, he would have rushed her into a marriage by special license, and to the devil with this grand wedding that his army of female relatives, headed by Wilma, had concocted without his by-your-leave.

There had been another marriage by special license a couple of months ago. Either McLeith or Portia or both of them together had seen sense after leaving Alvesley on the night of the anniversary ball. They had gone to London instead of Scotland, announced their betrothal to the Balderstons, and had a small but quite respectable wedding a few days later.

Joseph's stomach was feeling decidedly queasy and Neville threw him a sympathetic glance.

And then Claudia arrived, and he turned to watch her approach alone down the wide center aisle, between pews filled with guests.

She was beautiful. She was... How had she described herself once after they had made love? Ah, yes. She was woman. Schoolteacher, businesswoman, friend, lover—all the things she was and had ever been were overlaid by that one central fact.

She was simply woman.

Typically, she was simply, neatly, elegantly dressed—with the exception of the absurdly pretty straw hat that sat atop her head, tilted slightly forward. He smiled—at the hat, at her.

She smiled back and he forgot about the hat.

Ah, Claudia!

They turned together to face the clergyman.

"Dearly beloved," he began in sonorous tones that filled the large church.

And in no time at all the nuptial service was ending and they were married, he and Claudia Martin, now Claudia Fawcitt, Marchioness of Attingsborough. For the rest of their lives. Until death them did part. Through good times and bad, sickness and health.

Her eyes gazed into his. Her lips were pressed into a thin line.

He smiled at her.

She smiled back and the summer sun, gradually receding into autumn beyond the Abbey doors, shone warm and bright through her eyes.

They signed the register and then began the long walk up the nave of the Abbey past smiling guests, who would soon crowd into the Upper Assembly Rooms for the wedding breakfast.

It was Claudia who stopped at the second pew, where Lizzie was sitting between Anne Butler and David Jewell, gorgeously clad in a froth of pink lace with a matching satin bow in her hair. Claudia leaned past her friend, whispered something to his daughter, and drew her to her feet.

And so, with half the beau monde watching, they walked up the nave, the three of them, Lizzie in the middle, her arms linked through theirs, looking radiantly happy.

There were those who would be scandalized at the sight. They could go hang for all Joseph cared. He had seen his mother smiling at them and Wilma wiping a tear from her eye. He had seen his father gazing sternly at them, a look of fierce affection in his eyes.

He smiled at Claudia over the top of Lizzie's head.

She smiled back, and they stepped out of the church into the Pump Room yard, which was surely as crowded as the Abbey behind them. Someone cheered and almost everyone else joined in. The Abbey bells were ringing. The sun was breaking clear of the cloud cover.

"I love you," he mouthed to Claudia, and her eyes told him that she had heard and understood.

Lizzie tipped back her head and looked from one to the other of them as if she could see them. She laughed.

"Papa," she said. "And Mama."

"Yes, sweetheart." He bent to kiss her cheek.

And then, to the noisy delight of the spectators and the few guests who had already spilled out of the Abbey behind them, he leaned across her and kissed Claudia on the lips.

"*Both* my sweethearts," he said.

Claudia's eyes were bright with unshed tears.

"I am *not* going to be a watering pot now of all times," she said in her schoolmistress voice. "Take us to the carriage, Joseph."

Lizzie nestled her head against her shoulder.

"This instant," Claudia said in a tone that must have had fifteen years' worth of pupils jumping to attention.

"Yes, ma'am," he said, grinning. "No. Make that, *yes, my lady.*"

They were all laughing as he hurried them across the yard, past crowds of well-wishers, and finally through the stone arches and a tunnel of assorted cousins and Bedwyns, all of whom had sneaked out early and armed themselves with flower petals.

By the time they reached the street and the carriage, Claudia had an excuse for the tears that trickled down her cheeks. They were tears of laughter, she would have said if he had asked.

He did not.

He set Lizzie on one seat, took his place beside Claudia on the other, set one arm about her shoulders, and kissed her thoroughly.

"What are you doing, Papa?" Lizzie asked.

"I am kissing your mama," he told her. "She is also my bride, remember."

"Oh, good," she said, and laughed.

So did Claudia. "Everyone will *see,*" she said.

"Do you mind?" He leaned back from her to note again how vibrantly beautiful she looked.

"Not at all," she said, lifting her hand to his shoulder and drawing him back toward her as the carriage moved forward on its way to the Upper Rooms. "This is the happiest day of my life and I do not care if the whole world knows it."

And she leaned forward, took Lizzie's hand in hers and squeezed it, and then kissed him.

He spread his hand over her abdomen, which surely was slightly rounded already. All his family was here. His present and his future. His happiness.

Love. I dream of love, of a family—wife and children—which is as close and as dear to me as the beating of my own heart.

Had he spoken those words once upon a time?

If he had not, he certainly ought to have.

Except that he no longer had to dream that particular dream.

It had just become reality.